2—

TOKYO SEVEN ROSES

VOLUME II

Anthem Press
An imprint of Wimbledon Publishing Company
www.anthempress.com

This edition first published in UK and USA 2013
by ANTHEM PRESS
75–76 Blackfriars Road, London SE1 8HA, UK
or PO Box 9779, London SW19 7ZG, UK
and
244 Madison Ave. #116, New York, NY 10016, USA

Original title: Tokyo sebun rozu
Copyright © Hisashi Inoue 2002
Originally published in Japan by Bungei Shunju Ltd., Tokyo
English translation copyright © Jeffrey Hunter 2013

A CIP record for this book is available from the British Library.

ISBN-13: 978 0 85728 045 9 (Hbk)
ISBN-10: 0 85728 045 7 (Hbk)

This title is also available as an eBook.

This book has been selected by the Japanese Literature Publishing Project (JLPP),
an initiative of the Agency for Cultural Affairs of Japan.

TOKYO SEVEN ROSES

VOLUME II

Hisashi Inoue

Translated by Jeffrey Hunter

ANTHEM PRESS
LONDON · NEW YORK · DELHI

1945

December 24

At a little past 1 P.M., Lieutenant James Honda from the 441st CIC (Counter-Intelligence Corps) Detachment of CIS (Counter Intelligence Section) entered my solitary cell carrying two cans of beer.

"Merry Christmas," he said.

Popping two holes into a drab olive-colored can—the color indicating that it was U.S. military supply—he thrust it out to me.

"I have a Christmas present for you."

He opened the other one and vigorously clinked my can with it.

"Congratulations. Really," he said.

I had a hunch that I might soon be set free.

On the morning of October 19th, I was cutting stencils for mimeographs in the Tokyo Metropolitan Police Department Documentation Section Annex when I was arrested by five CIC officers. Since that day, I was locked up in a solitary cell—though in fact there were others there when I first arrived—that was originally a storage room in the basement of the main building. I underwent harsh interrogation from October through November, but in December there were many days I wasn't questioned at all. Our group may have seemed threatening because of its name— Association to Demand Compensation from the United States for their Sadistic and Indiscriminate Bombing, including the Use of Atomic Weapons—but actually it was only rather pathetic, and the GHQ must've finally figured out that it was really nothing more than ten middle-aged men who had lost family members in the air raids and had gathered together on a single occasion at a small shrine in Joto Ward in feeble protest.

I quipped to James: "By 'Christmas present,' do you mean to say that you'll be loading me onto a B-29 to Guam or Saipan?"

When I was taken to the CIC interrogation room on the fifth floor of the Radio Tokyo Building (Japan Broadcasting Corporation Tokyo Broadcasting Hall) for the first time, this second-generation Japanese-American pounded on the desk and roared in fluent Japanese: "If you lie, you'll be sent to Guam or Saipan! You'll be forced to do hard labor for the rest of your life, do you understand?" That was what I meant by my "Christmas present."

James just said, "You're as free as a bird. You can go home."

My hunch had turned out to be right. I felt the beer being absorbed in the very pit of my stomach.

"I'd like to have General MacArthur's answer as a souvenir to bring back to the outside world. I wonder how the mighty general responded to my demands?"

"Oh, not that again," muttered James with a look of disgust as he wiped beer foam from his mouth with the back of his hand. "There's no reason to expect SCAP to give you an answer."

From the beginning of my interrogation, I had been absolutely determined. The U.S. carpet bombings of Tokyo had taken the lives of my eldest daughter, her husband, and my elder brother. And it was the U.S. that has made my two younger daughters and five other women in my life into prostitutes. I'd made up my mind that, before I died, I would speak my mind to the U.S. And so every time I was summoned for questioning, I'd blurt out: "The U.S. is guilty of gross violations of international law! It's deplorable that the U.S. would cover up its responsibility simply because it's the victor. It's completely unfair!"

Actually, I was just mimicking the words of a Japanese literature professor at Hiroshima Teacher's College, but after saying them two or three times, they became my own words, too.

Meanwhile, at each session the CIC interrogator would ask me the same questions (later I discovered that this interrogator ranked third among 880 officers of the CIC). He'd demand: "Are you a rightist? Or a Communist? Who's the big shot backing you?"

I would later come to learn that the mission of the CIC 441st Detachment was to investigate the movements of ultra-nationalists and rightists as well as to check up on Communists and union leaders,

Koreans living in Japan and university professors. By force of habit, the CIC officers assumed that our association was being backed by some right-wing boss or left-wing kingpin. None of that had anything to do with me, so I just kept insisting: "A major principle of international law maintains that air raids are to be directed at military targets only and that noncombatants are not to be killed. But this principle has been violated, and I can't forgive the taking of my relatives' lives. And since the atomic bomb is an inhumane weapon, it violates the fundamental principle of international law proscribing the infliction of unnecessary pain and suffering during wartime. I want to hear the opinion of the honorable General MacArthur on these points. If possible, I'd like to bring a case before an appropriate court to address these illegal actions."

Come to think of it now, I was making some pretty dangerous charges, but that was the night that I flew into a rage because I had found out that seven women in my household were sleeping with American military officers. Kiyoshi had screamed at me while holding me down: "Talk big starting the war, then kiss up to MacArthur now that you lose the war. What the hell do you grown-ups think you're doing? You're all ridiculous. You're all a bunch of cheap cowards!"

Maybe it was those words that had roused in me the recklessness to demand answers from General MacArthur.

James said: "No reply from SCAP, but I heard an opinion from LS Chief Carpenter."

"LS?"

"That's the Legal Section at GHQ. They specialize in the investigation of war crimes. They're the ones who identified Hideki Tojo and Fumimaro Konoe as suspected war criminals."

James removed a piece of tightly folded paper from the breast pocket of his uniform. That paper, which made such a delightful sound as it was unfolded, and appeared to me to be so white that it must have been steeped in white paint, made me wonder how good it would feel to write my diary on it.

"There are some difficult Japanese words on the paper," James explained. "I'm not sure I can pronounce them correctly. So please pay attention. Firstly," and he held up one finger, "apart from cases specifically addressed by treaty, rights under international law are limited to nation-states. These rights do not apply to individuals.

"Secondly, Mr. Yamanaka, the only thing you can do is to petition the Japanese government to redress your rights based on domestic law.

"Thirdly, what if, just suppose, the Japanese government agreed to try a case within the Japanese court system on behalf of the victims of the atomic bombings and people like you who lost family members due to the American air raids? Would it be possible to pass judgment against the U.S.? The answer is no. And Japanese sovereignty, even if such a thing were to exist right now, would not apply to the U.S., so a Japanese court decision would be meaningless.

"Fourthly, what if you and your fellow plaintiffs were to file a lawsuit in U.S. court seeking reparations and damages…"

"Is it possible?" I asked.

"In theory, yes," replied James. "But the result would be predictable. There are two possible outcomes. One, the Japanese government wouldn't let you do it. And two, provided that the Japanese government turned a blind eye, and your case reached an American court, and you were lucky enough to get it to trial, in the end you'd lose anyway."

"Why?"

"Because under U.S. law, it is a basic tenet that the U.S. Government cannot be held liable for whatever illegal acts government personnel might commit while executing their official duties."

"So, are you saying that there is nothing to do but accept things as they are?"

"The LS commander isn't saying that. He advises that you continue to patiently seek redress of your rights from your own government."

Well, that's very kind of him, I thought to myself. I started to get ready to leave. James was sitting on the desk, whistling. When it came to getting ready, though, I didn't have much to pack. One pair of American-made underwear, called a union suit, that Fumiko had given me, one pair of military-supply pure wool drab olive socks, and a toothbrush and tooth powder, also from Fumiko. That's about it. For a long time, I refused to wear something that my daughter had obtained by selling her body, and so I left the clothing in the corner of my solitary cell. But in early December

I started to wear them, on the night following a visit I received from the former proprietor of the Hongo Bar, who told me: "In November, the average number of the people who collapsed at Ueno Station and died due to the cold was 2.5 per day. On one really cold day, six people died. I guess the biggest enemy to human beings is cold, not hunger." That union suit was extremely warm, as if I were holding five or six pocket warmers. I realized that foolish stubbornness would get me nowhere.

I had a hard time removing the paper with the words to the funeral march "Deep Mourning" that I'd hidden in the gap in the wainscoting and putting it into my pants pocket without being noticed by James.

When I was thrown into the storage room in the basement of the main building, four people were already in the cell. Three of them had closely cropped heads that had grown out a bit, but not enough to hold a part yet. They looked like the kind of petty government officials who, up until noon of August 15th, cropped their hair short like soldiers and bravely declaimed, "The final battle on the mainland is near when each of us will strike down ten of the enemy!" Then, as soon as the war was over they let their hair grow out again to flutter in the wind of peace. And just as I'd suspected, all three turned out to work in the Adachi Ward Office. But they weren't just any ward clerks: the guy with the toothbrush moustache bossing everyone around was the mayor; the guy with the horse face who devoted his spare time to massaging the mayor's shoulders was the general affairs section chief; and the guy with the bulging forehead who took care of the other two by laying out their futons, bringing their meals and removing their dirty dishes, was the general affairs section vice-chief. These three were arrested for embezzling huge amounts of cotton clothing fabric from military supply, which was supposed to be provided to war victims living in Adachi Ward.

Every night, the three of them conducted a fascinating ritual before going to sleep. Hitler Moustache would complain to Horse Face, "Are we the only ones who cooked the books a little with ration supplies? In Edogawa Ward and Mukojima Ward, they're all doing the same." Horse Face would then reply, "It's a farce, Mayor!

We're being scapegoated, that's all." Then he'd glare at Fat Head, who'd turn to his superiors, get down on his hands and knees and bow his head to the floor, gushing with apologies, "I'm the one who messed up, I know. Please, forgive me!" Both the mayor and the section chief would look at him and nod, then the mayor would lie down, and then the section chief would follow suit. The vice-chief would maintain his supine pose for several minutes before slinking off to lie down himself. They repeated this ritual every single night. I was amused to notice, however, that it was always the section vice-chief who was the first among the three to gently drift off to sleep.

My fourth cellmate had stolen ceramic coins. Due to the lack of metal, from July of this year, the Japanese government directed kilns all over the country to fire ceramic 5-sen coins. I believe the coin, which was described in all the newspapers, bore the design of chrysanthemum flowers on the front and a peach on the back. My cellmate traveled to Arita, and at a kiln there filled his rucksack with about 5,000 ceramic coins and brought them back to his home (which was actually an air raid shelter) in Kanda Sarugaku-cho. He stashed them there, waiting for the day they'd become legal tender. Five thousand 5 sen coins comes to 250 yen. No matter how long he waited, however, the ceramic coins never went into circulation. When he went to the post office and, with an innocent look, made inquiries, he was informed by the postmaster, who knew what was going on, "Since we lost the war, it looks like they won't be used. Though fifteen million coins were made, every last one of them was destroyed in the middle of August." That night my cellmate binged on methyl alcohol that he got from a pushcart vendor at a black market in Suidobashi. He returned to his air raid shelter and started digging up the coins. Ranting "How the hell did Japan lose the war!" and "Win or lose, why don't we just go ahead and use the coins anyway?" he took the useless five-sen coins and hurled them on the ground, handful after handful. Then he got into a fight with a cop from the Sarugaku-cho 2-chome police station who happened to pass by…

The ceramic coin thief told me this story by way of introduction. At the end, he showed me the top of his shaved head. Flashing a bitter smile, he said, "Even though those coins have never been used as actual currency, they're still coins. Look. I'm being punished for throwing them away." And sure enough, the top of his head was covered by the coin-shaped circles caused by ringworm.

In deference to my senior fellow incarcerees, I spread my thin futon next to a pile of junk at the very back of the storage room. I was surprised upon waking the following morning to find that what I had considered to be junk the night before was actually a mountain of music scores, tied in bundles one *sun* thick and piled in the thousands. There were music scores of old military-type songs like "The Meeting at Shusuiying" and "The Drawn Sword Corps." There were also "Patriot's March," "Pacify the Country," and "The Camp Moustache Contest." Most of the scores had been stamped "Toyama Army Academy Military Band." Some were marked "Imperial Guard Military Band," which was written in ink instead of stamped. Once the war ended, all of the military bands had been broken up, and it seemed that the music scores were acquired by the Metropolitan Police Department. Trying to avoid detection by my four cellmates, I silently tore off half of the music score at the top of the bundle closest to me. I absolutely needed that paper for jotting down reminders of my experience. If I don't write in my diary each day, as has long been my habit, I can't keep track of whether or not that day has actually taken place.

For 120 days, from July 8th to September 27th of this year, I was locked up in Yokaichiba Prison in Kujukurihama Beach. It was hard work digging trenches in preparation for the anticipated final battle of the mainland. The trenches we dug in the sand would collapse by the next day. We'd dig them again, and again they'd collapse. It was idiotic. It was also tough eating sardines all the time. Sardine meatballs, sardine jelly, sardine crackers and sardine cakes—sardines were the main dish of every meal. After a while, just the word "sardine" would give me diarrhea. It was also tough not knowing what had happened to my family. But the worst thing of all was that I wasn't allowed paper and pencil. If I spend one day without recording anything about it, even if it's only a single line, I feel as if I were dead that day. One hundred and twenty days like that nearly drove me crazy. That's why I tore off a piece of that music score.

At the top of the torn-off piece the words "Deep Mourning" were written horizontally, with what I figure to be a copy pen, because the vertical strokes of the characters were much thicker than the horizontal ones. Below that were the words "Meiji Era 30th Year January, composed by F. Eckert." written horizontally in a smaller script. I kept my diary by writing one line per day on the back of this paper with the short pencil given me by Kobayashi at the Documentation Section Annex. If James had found out about this and confiscated it, it would have been worse than being sent to Saipan or Guam.

After discretely touching my pocket to make sure "Deep Mourning" was inside, I left my solitary cell carrying my small package wrapped in cloth under my arm. For an instant my thoughts went to the three Adachi Ward officials and the ceramic coin thief. Since the storage room had later been divided into three sections and we were isolated from one another, we didn't see each other after the first few days. It makes me wonder if they're still performing that same ritual before going to sleep, and whether the ceramic coin thief's coin-shaped ringworm scars have healed.

"What about the others?" I inquired.

"Others?"

"I mean the other nine who signed the oath before the altar at Atago Shrine in Joto Ward. I suppose they've all been released?"

"Mr. Yamanaka, you're the only one who's been pardoned," said James as we walked up the stairs leading to the service entrance. "The other nine will spend the rest of the year here. They won't get out until the end of February or the beginning of March. Not while it's still cold outside, anyway."

"So there are still things you need to find out from them?"

"No. Our investigations of your group are all completed. It's like—you know that fancy expression, something about mountains and a mouse?"

"The mountains quake and a mouse escapes."

"Yeah, that's it. We know full well that you ten are just ten little mice, not dragons or tigers. It was more like a boys' secret club than anything else. But it's not a good idea to release them right away. If we go easy on them this time, the same thing is likely to happen a second or third time. It's been decided to make them suffer a little by spending the winter in a cold cell. You know what I mean? A little moxa, moxi… what's the word?"

"Moxibustion."

"Yeah, that's it."

"Then why am I?"

"Connections."

"Huh?"

"This is hard to explain, too. You have some connections. You know what I'm talking about?"

"No, I don't."

Placing his right index finger over his lips, James climbed the stairs to the top. He seemed to be whispering to himself, searching for the right word. Then he glanced outside the entrance and shouted: "It's him! He's your connection!" Following James's gaze, my eyes landed on a black Datsun. A foreigner wearing a coat with a fur collar was leaning against it, talking to a woman in the passenger seat. The woman was Fumiko.

"He lit a fire under LS Colonel Carpenter. He persuaded him to let you out early."

I retreated five or six steps backwards down the stairway. I was more embarrassed than angry. My face had gone scarlet.

"Navy Lieutenant Commander Robert King Hall. Your daughter's lover."

"Now I understand," I said to James, who had turned back toward me. "But he's a lot younger than I imagined." Since I knew he was a section chief at the GHQ Civil Information and Education Section, I assumed he must be around forty years old. And when I had heard that he had punched Army First Lieutenant Whatshisname, the new American manager of the Imperial Hotel, I imagined him being as big and burly as a polar bear. But in fact he is about thirty, and as thin as a reed.

"We were both instructors together at the CASA in California," added James, giving a short, appreciative whistle. "He's a brilliant guy." He shrugged. "CASA is the military's Civil Affairs Staging Area. He was the Education Section Chief of CASA's Occupation Planning Staff there. I was a Japanese instructor. Bob—'Bob' is his nickname—Bob has an academic record that is absolutely the best. First he graduated from Harvard, then went to the University of Chicago, then Columbia University, then got his PhD at the University of Michigan. But he has a very hard head. He's smart, but with a head like a rock. Do you know what that means?"

I shook my head.

"Bob has always believed that if we occupied Japan we should outlaw the use of the Chinese *kanji* that make up the Japanese written language. No matter what anyone else says, Bob stubbornly rejects all other opinions. He just absolutely insists that we should force the Japanese to use the *katakana* syllabary and refuses to budge."

"So he's obstinate."

"Yes, obstinate, that's the word."

"But why *katakana*?"

"*Katakana* is an excellent invention, according to Bob. That's where Bob's theory of outlawing *kanji* starts. The Japanese hardly use this wonderful invention, restricting it to things like telegrams and a few other special applications. Children spend almost all their time in school learning those nasty caterpillar-like scrawls of *kanji*. That's a terrible waste of time, says Bob."

There was something of interest here, I thought.

"Then, in the past all important documents in Japan were written in *kanji*. Of course all militaristic writings are in *kanji*. If *kanji* were outlawed and the use of *katakana* required, eventually Japanese wouldn't be able to read characters and their connections to militaristic thinking would naturally be cut off."

Pretty naïve.

"And if the Japanese could only use *katakana*, censorship would be much easier. There are very few American censors with adequate ability to read *kanji* at present, but things would be different if the newspapers, magazines and books were all written in *katakana*. The Japanese language itself is very easy. *Katakana* is even easier. If *kanji* were outlawed and the use of *katakana* required, any American could become a censor very quickly."

What an idea.

"Up to that point, I can agree, at least to a degree. But from there on, we always argued. Bob says that we should get the Japanese used to doing everything in *katakana*, and then switch them over to *romaji*."

At this, I didn't think anything. I couldn't. I was flabbergasted by the reasoning.

"There are many words with the same sound but different meanings in Japanese. For example, the word *shosetsu* can be either a musical bar or a novel, and you'd never know which one was meant without seeing the *kanji*. Eliminating *kanji* is bad enough, but changing everything into *romaji* is absurd. That was always my rebuttal. But Bob would say, 'James, you have Japanese blood running through your veins, so when you hear the proposal that *kanji* be outlawed, you can't help but react emotionally. In other words, you're just not able to discuss reforming the Japanese language objectively.'"

James's former colleague was leaning on the door of the security guard's room across a two-meter wide corridor, just opposite the opening to the stairway where we were, smoking a cigarette.

"Hi, Bob," James said, extending his right hand. "I'm not criticizing you, I'm criticizing your theories."

"But you left out something very important," said Hall, shaking James's hand perfunctorily. He was speaking in perfect Japanese. "Once the Japanese are used to writing in *katakana*, they'll catch on to *romaji* without a hitch. They're very clever. That's an important point."

"And once they're accustomed to *romaji* letters, they can use typewriters, is what you're going to say next, right?"

"Yes. And once they can use typewriters, Japan will make rapid progress on many fronts."

"Yes, but… Oh, never mind. We can continue with this later. I'll wait until then. Bob, this is Mr. Yamanaka." James took one step aside, leaving me face to face with Hall.

"Pleased to meet you. I'm Hall. Robert King Hall. I've been looking forward to making your acquaintance," and this time it was Hall who extended his right hand, as he approached me. I hesitated for a moment, but in the end I took his hand. It was limp and soft, and as white as a glove. "Would you like to have a steak at the Hibiya Sanshin Building over there? The steaks in the American Red Cross Service Room are the best in Japan right now, or at least I think so."

11

When I thought what he had done to my unmarried Fumiko, I began to tremble.

"There's also a café, where they serve cake and ice cream."

"Say something," said Fumiko, standing next to the MP officer. She wore a neckerchief in green checks over a red background on her head and a heavy brown coat, high heels and lipstick of such a bright shade of red that the color of her neckerchief seemed pale next to it. She looked like she was eating a strawberry. "Bob went through a lot of trouble for you. That's why you were released so quickly."

I walked past Hall and stood in front of Fumiko. "You should be ashamed of yourself," I said, and slapped her across the face. Then I walked quickly out the service entrance, around the back and out to the front of the First Cavalry Division Military Police Quarters. A phonograph record was playing on the second floor. A velvety woman's voice was singing, in the most dulcet tones, that song that James had been whistling. The only words I could make out were "something-something white Christmas." Four or five men were singing along with the record, and another two or three were laughing throughout the song. It seemed like a very cheery gathering.

I felt like a coward for having slapped Fumiko instead of Mr. Romaji Hall, and I wondered what had happened to my determination to kill ten Americans before going to my death, which I'd resolved when I was stashed away in that hole in Kujukurihama Beach; but in spite of myself, the ebullience of the military police upstairs lifted my spirits a bit and I felt better. I would save my slap for my next meeting with Hall, should there ever be one.

"Welcome back." The outer door to the kitchen next door to my office opened and the former proprietor of the Hongo Bar stuck his head out. "Kobayashi left a copy of the key to the annex with me."

"Thank you for coming to visit me."

"It's no big deal. It was inside the same police headquarters, after all. It's just like going to the toilet. I have some coffee on. Come on in." I sat down on a stool in front of his counter, and as I was savoring my first cup of coffee in sixty-eight days passing down my throat like a soft caress, the MPs upstairs exploded in laughter.

"They're very jolly up there."

"They're excited. This is their first cold Christmas in a long time."

"I see. They've been fighting in the tropics, so all their Christmases were warm."

"That's it. Apparently it doesn't feel like Christmas to them unless it's cold."

"By the way, who cut the mimeograph stencils while I was away?"

"Kobayashi. He's slow and his writing is messy, and he kept saying to himself, 'This is no good,' all the time he was doing it."

"I wonder if he already finished today's work."

"He gave up before noon. He said you were getting out around noon today and he left the key with me." He placed it on the cooking counter.

"How did he know I'd be getting out today? That's strange."

"Set a thief to catch a thief, they say. He used to be a Special Higher Police detective. He has a nose for these things."

A sound like thunder erupted overhead. Someone was stomping on the floorboards. A large group ran down the stairs. The cook and I looked at each other, puzzled. In the yard, men were singing that "something-something white Christmas" song off key. Drawn outside by the music, the cook and I saw ten young MPs, their shirts off, singing and stretching their arms to the heavens, trying to catch the paltry flakes of snow falling from the gray sky.

December 25

I haven't been fired from my job cutting stencils even though I had been arrested on suspicion of activities contravening the aims of the Occupation and kept in a solitary cell in the basement of the Tokyo Metropolitan Police Department for sixty-seven days because, much as I hate to admit it, of the intervention of Fumiko's patron, or her lover, or boyfriend, or whatever the hell I'm supposed to call him—anyway, that Mr. Romaji Navy Lieutenant Commander Hall. When I got home yesterday after my long absence, my wife told me in so many words.

"I heard you hit Fumiko," she first said, looking at me with a deep wrinkle of distaste between her eyebrows, the same expression she had when she saw a garden slug, which she absolutely hated.

"How long are you going to act like a child? As a matter of fact, you should actually get down on your knees to Fumiko and thank her. No, even that wouldn't be enough," she said, turning and walking into the kitchen to light the portable clay cooking stove. Then: "The fact that they let you out and that you're able to keep working at the police headquarters is due to Fumiko's efforts on your behalf. Fumiko is the one who persuaded Mr. Hall to take some action."

This isn't the way you talk to your husband who has just come home after months in jail—at least not in my book. No matter what the circumstances, before she started nagging me she could at least give me a smile or a kind word, something like "I know how hard it must have been for you." A husband and wife can be angry enough to kill each other, glaring at each other, ready to leap at each other's throat, but if at that instant one of them cracks even the smallest bit of a smile, it immediately becomes a bridge between the trenches that they've dug themselves into and offers the chance of restoring marital harmony. That's what being married is all about, after all.

"Who asked her to? Certainly not me."

"There you go again." She fanned the cooking stove exaggeratedly. "Just admit that you treated Fumiko badly. If you can do that, even I'd be able to say that I understand your feelings. You must be hungry."

"Don't be stupid. Is there anyone who isn't hungry these days?"

"Then go to the house down the street and apologize to Fumiko. I'll braise some meat in butter while you're there. Both the meat and the butter were given to us by Mr. Hall. If you don't thank Fumiko, you'll pay for it in the end."

"I don't want any," I said. If my aching stomach could have heard my words, it would have flipped over inside me. "I don't want to eat if I have to be beholden to someone for it. And why are you making such a display with that fan?"

"Suit yourself, then," she said, moving the charcoal from the portable cooking stove into the portable foot warmer. "Go get yourself some of saltwater broth with two or three wheat dumplings the size of rabbit droppings that you'll get at a cafeteria somewhere, or some stew made from leftovers of the Occupation soldiers with an empty cigarette pack floating in it."

After placing the charcoal in the clay fire container inside the kotatsu, she slid the lower half of her body underneath the expensive looking, cream-colored wool kotatsu blanket and snuggled under it. When I looked closely at the blanket, I saw that it was very heavy wool. It almost seemed like it should smell of milk. It must have been another of that Hall's gifts to Fumiko.

"The girls are doing what they're doing because they can't bear to see the elderly Furusawas, Kiyoshi and even myself reduced to that kind of fare. A parent doesn't know his own child's heart. Something's wrong with you, anyway, getting dragged away by the police twice in one year."

"Both times were for thought crimes. It's not as if I killed someone or stole something."

"What thought crimes? Don't talk as if you did something noble. You're not some scholar or Communist. You're a fan maker. You're the father of three children, the foster father of two young women, and the protector of two old people. Don't make me laugh, this big talk about prosecuting the Americans. You're all hot air. If you're serious, why don't you go out and stab MacArthur?"

"Shut up!"

"You can't make fans with thoughts and words. While your competitors are about to leave you in the dust, you just sit there, doing nothing, as if you lost your mind."

"I don't have to take that kind of thing from you." I threw my air-raid bag onto the earthen floor of the entryway. "In case I need to remind you, I didn't ask to be arrested for thought crimes. I was just doing my best to get along, minding my own business, when they took me away." I picked up my air-raid bag and dashed outside into the snow, which was whirling about like white flies.

It's true; I had lived my life without any connection to "seditious thoughts." When I was an apprentice copyist at Daiichi Tokosha in Suzuran-dori, Kanda, I accompanied my boss once when he was giving a special presentation at the local Consumers' Union. Someone at the presentation mentioned that since all the printer's type had been confiscated to melt down for war use, they were being forced to produce their own type for printing their bills and reports, so he wanted to learn mimeographing. "Could the basics be mastered in three days?" the man asked. My boss replied, "One day is plenty." He was a tough old bird who had served as a mimeograph soldier during the First Sino-Japanese War. He carried his mimeograph backboard, ink, wood frame, roller and special gampi paper in his backpack and, wielding a stylus instead of a gun, followed the troops, printing the reports from inferiors to their superiors, the orders from superiors to their inferiors and the daily troop communications. Mimeographing was cheap, simple, light and didn't require electricity. Military secrecy could be protected simply by burning the original after it was copied. This portable print shop, an indispensable part of the war effort, was highly valued.

At the start my boss had been displeased to be appointed to the odd position of "mimeograph soldier," but eventually he became fascinated by this new printing technology. When he was decommissioned, he founded a mimeograph printer in Kanda. He'd had a stylus in hand in the nearly fifty years since then. His Gothic font writing against the "X"-grating backboard was perfect, but his square Gothic and block script writing were magnificent, and he was an expert at stencil printing as well. He was also an accomplished instructor, and his assurance that he could teach mimeographing in a day was no empty exaggeration. Ten days after his presentation, my boss and I were summoned to appear before the police and severely reprimanded. Apparently the Consumers' Union was actually a gathering of anti-government activists. They were also devotees of mimeograph printing for the same reasons as the army: it was cheap, simple, didn't require power and could preserve secrecy. That single day I attended my boss's lecture presentation was—though unbeknownst to me at the time—the closest I'd ever come to the world of "seditious thoughts." There's no way I could be accused of being a thought criminal. The very fact that I could be elevated to that lofty rank was proof that the world was hopelessly upside down.

"Shinsuke," someone called out to me just as I got to Shinobazu Pond. "Where are you going to sleep tonight?" Old Mr. Furusawa, who was staying at our house, was stamping his wooden sandals on the earth, trying to knock the snow out from between the raised treads.

"Could you hear up what was happening from the second floor?"

"I came halfway down the stairs and was eavesdropping."

"Shame on you."

"Since we've come to live with you, you and your wife argue a lot. Am I wrong?"

"You're not the reason."

"Well, I'm glad to hear that."

"It's her attitude, if you ask me. She's become a completely different person. She used to be so gentle and reserved in her speech. Now all she does is snap at me."

"She doesn't trust men. We men have been talking big for eighty years, running the country and dominating everything. 'The nation has to be this way, which means women have to do such-and-such'—we've been ordering them around like that for decades. But the nation has been destroyed. 'So what was all that stuff that you men were saying? What were all those orders and commands? They were all just silly nonsense.' That's what women are thinking."

"I see."

"'If men had been able to make us happy and give us good lives, there might be some reason for letting them order us about, but even though it was the men who had made this awful mess we're in now, they still want to be the boss...' Well, that's what I think women are thinking. In fact, I know for a fact that's what *my* wife is thinking. So, how about it? Feeling any better?"

"A lot better, actually."

"Go home, then."

"No, I think I'll leave things as they are for a few days. If I see my girls, I'm going to feel like yelling at them again, and I need time to think. Don't worry about me. I'll sleep at the office."

"Then promise to come back by New Year's Eve. Otherwise, you really will have run away from home."

"I know."

"We men just have to accept this reality. And if we accept it we can come to like it. But it's going to be tough." And saying this, he pressed two Lucky Strikes into my hand and disappeared in the falling snow.

It was the time when the evening shift was to begin. The former proprietor of the Hongo Bar had warned me about the trains—avoid them as much as possible because at least one person is crushed to death in them every day. So I walked back to the Documentation Division Annex Office of the Tokyo Metropolitan Police Department. The clothes I'd been wearing for the past ten years had holes here and there, and the snow blew through them. Another warning of the former proprietor of the Hongo Bar came back to me: "When the poor catch cold, they've reached the end of the line. There's no medicine, and doctors won't even look at you unless you bring them rice. And since no one's eating anything of any nutritional value, they have no residual strength. With these three conditions in place, a normal cold immediately turns into pneumonia. Diseases that we used to be able to cure are fatal now."

So I walked toward the office at the speed of an athlete in competition, breaking into nearly a run halfway there, because I remembered that the former proprietor of the Hongo Bar had also said: "When night falls, Tokyo becomes a mugger's paradise. There are one 116 stick-ups a day. It's gotten past being scary to the point where you can only be impressed by the number of robberies. And there's about one murder a week." My legs stopped of their own accord just before Nijubashi. When I realized where I was, I found myself bent over like a pocketknife. The force of habit is a powerful thing, I thought.

"You look like a boiled octopus," said the former proprietor of the Hongo Bar, ushering me into the kitchen, his eyes as wide as saucers. "I've never seen anyone with so much steam rising from him." He took several towels and a blanket from the MP storage for me. He slept in a four-and-a-half-tatami-mat room next to the kitchen where a little pot-bellied stove was burning. Heating up some soup made from leftovers, he said: "You can stay here as long as you like while I'm the cook here." I passed Christmas Eve thus saved from catching a cold by the cook.

This morning I got up with the cook. He made bread, dissolved some dried egg powder in water, prepared omelets for twenty and ground coffee beans. I tried to stay out of his way as he rushed about the kitchen like a madman, doing as he told me—drawing water, bringing in charcoal and carrying dishes up to the second floor.

The dining hall is very spacious. Before it became the First Cavalry Division Military Police Headquarters Military Police Liaison Office Quarters, it was used for police officers' wedding receptions and joint investigation conferences. It seemed about the size of two elementary school classrooms. In the middle of the room was the Victrola 4-R made by the Nihon Victor Company in 1929, especially for Western-style rooms. I remember when it first came out, the advertising slogan was tantalizing: "Ten minutes of music with one full turn of the crank." The price was astounding, too: 375 yen. You could have ten Western suits, jackets and pants, made for that amount of money. It was five months' worth of a bank teller's salary, or 20,000 sticks of sugar candy. It was, in other words, a model that everyone wanted. I stared at the amber-colored Victrola for some time, nodding in admiration, but I realized that I shouldn't be particularly surprised to see it there. With a PD—procurement demand—you could get just about anything you might want for free.

The internal police department memos I printed every day recorded the contents of the PDs sent to the Japanese government by the Occupation Forces. I could understand requests for houses, furniture and cars, but I could only shake my head about demands for goldfish or teddy bears. Once, I remember, I came across a request for a cock ring and a dildo, and I dropped my stylus. For the life of me, I can't see why sex toys are needed to carry out the policies of the Occupation. Another PD asked that marble toilets be installed in the Ginza Matsuya Department Store, which had been requisitioned by the Occupation. Where do they think we're going to find marble in this country, a scorched wasteland as far as the eye can see?

Three of the dining room walls were made of plaster. They were covered with dozens of posters of American movies stars. I recognized a few: Rita Hayworth beckoning to the viewer with her forefinger, Hedy Lamarr with one eye closed seductively, Ginger Rogers in fishnet stockings and Lana Turner reclining with one knee raised. I had never seen most of the actresses in films, though. Also posted on the wall, next to the posters of movie stars, was a sheet of parchment paper (so rare these days) about the size of an open newspaper, with twenty names on it. The strange thing about it was that next to the names were lipstick marks—for example, five after "Schmidt," seven after "Crane," and nine after "Poole."

After breakfast, I asked the cook what the lipstick marks meant. "That's the trouble with going to war," he replied. "That's a record of their booty." Seeing my dubious expression, he explained cautiously, "It may not be what you want to hear, but, well, to put it simply, each lipstick mark represents a Japanese girl."

So their war booty was Japanese women.

"I think it was before the attack on Iwojima, a marine commander roused the spirits of his men by telling them that if they just got through this battle, they'd be in Tokyo, and in Tokyo all the beautiful girls of Tokyo would fall at their feet. Every single one of them would be theirs for the taking, so they should fight this battle for the girls of Tokyo. And not just at Iwojima. I'm sure officers everywhere said something of the sort to motivate their men. The soldiers took them at their word."

"But these are the military police. Isn't it their job to stop soldiers from doing just this?

"MPs are human, too," said the cook, breaking the match he'd been using as a toothpick between his teeth with a snap. "There are more lipstick marks every day. Each time I see a new one, I think what a stupid thing war is."

I had just swept the floor of my office and sharpened my pen on the unglazed bottom of a teacup when Kobayashi arrived at work. I told him that I was staying away from home for a while and asked if I could sleep here for four or five days.

"Just don't burn the place down," he said. Then he let out a sigh. "What on earth has happened to Japanese women?" He tossed a bunch of letters onto the table. "These are all love letters."

"Love letters?"

"There's been an outpouring of love letters to General Belly Button. I never suspected this from our sweet Japanese girls." He stretched out on the couch with its springs protruding and blew his tobacco smoke upward. I read the first letter on the stack:

Ah, great and eminent general.
Gloriously donning the crown of the all-powerful commander,
boldly leading the tens of thousands
of loyal and brave American soldiers
under your masterful baton,
manfully occupying
defeated Japan.

"This reads like a poem," I said.

"I guess that's her idea," said Kobayashi, "but that's one of the tamer love letters to General Belly Button."

"Why do you keep calling him General Belly Button?"

"Because he's above the divine prick. The Emperor? Get it? It's a big joke these days."

It made me cringe. It didn't seem right to turn someone who, up to now, had been worshiped as a god, as a supernatural being, into the butt of a crude joke overnight. The only ones who might have the right to do that are the people who, even back in the old days, had insisted the Emperor wasn't a god. People who had believed he was divine, and who had forced others to think of him the same way, shouldn't just change their loyalty from the Emperor to MacArthur as casually as they might order a bowl noodles at a roadside stand—not to mention using their former god as the butt of a cheap joke. Maybe Japanese were incapable of really believing in anything. Maybe all they could do is bow and scrape to whoever is in power at the time, lick their boots and pay lip service to their new masters. I shook my head, wanting to rid myself of these unpleasant thoughts.

The letter continued like this:

The courteous demeanor of the American soldiers and officers of all ranks, free of the slightest arrogance or high-handedness, and their modest reserve are admirable beyond compare, and can only be a reflection of your own indisputably elevated character, General. I am a woman of the defeated nation of Japan. My husband perished like dew on the battlefield and my parents were, sadly, killed by your nation's bombs, but I do not bear you any hard feelings. A hundred times more than any resentment is my desire to see your visage, which is why I put these words to paper, conveying to you my true feelings.

The name and address of the sender were heavily blacked-out with ink. No doubt the GHQ did this to prevent the Japanese police from searching the woman out and giving her a good talking to.

The next letter was written in beautiful calligraphy.

Here I record my dream that you, Your Excellency, might embrace me.

That you would take my lips on yours, that you would warmly caress my hair with your soft cheek, your spirit and mine united as one, our hearts embracing, our passion shared, and in ecstasy, like a dream, I would become pregnant and raise our progeny to be as tall and strong as you. This is my dream; make it come true. If you do, I will be overcome with joy. I humbly await your instructions.

As I sat there, overcome by this effrontery, Kobayashi got up from the sofa. "This one is a masterpiece," he said, pulling out a pink envelope. The envelope was handmade from two pieces of patterned paper pasted together. The stationery was also patterned paper. It contained the following message:

I want to have your child. K. K. K.

"'K' stands for 'kiss,'" Kobayashi said.
Near the Ks there was a lipstick mark.
"You want me to print these?" I asked.
"Just think of it as your job and do your best."
"It's a waste of stencils. A waste of the ink and paper they're printed on."
"We need to preserve them as part of the record."
"But why did the GHQ send these over to us?"
"You can be sure that General Belly Button is getting a kick out of them. If they were irritating, upsetting or angering him, he

wouldn't have the names and addresses of the senders blacked out. He's enjoying them, which is why he protects the writers. That's got to be it."

"In other words, he wants to rub our noses in it…"

"I think so."

It took me until the afternoon to finish the stencils, perhaps because there were so many, but more likely because they were all so disgusting that I could hardly bring myself to even look at them.

December 26

While I was drinking coffee in the kitchen this afternoon, I had a sudden urge to see a film, and I invited the cook to come with me to see *The Ware Case*, with Clive Brook, which is playing in Hibiya. Brook is an elegant, handsome actor, and I came to like him after seeing him in *Shanghai Express*. "At the start of the film they find a hand floating in the pond at a mansion. I'm sure Brook will be playing a famous detective. After all, he made a name for himself playing Sherlock Holmes. If we went now," I said, "you'd be back in plenty of time to prepare dinner."

He seemed ready to accept my invitation, but then he shook his head, "No, I think I'll pass. When I went to see *Call of the Yukon* the other day, I got into trouble. I got slapped on the face by a girl who called herself Rakucho Otoki."

"Who is that?"

"She's the boss of a gang of ticket scalpers in the Marunouchi movie district."

The cook explained that starting a couple months back all the movie theaters have been as packed as rush-hour train cars. The theaters even stopped selling tickets at a certain point, afraid that someone was going to get hurt in the crowds. Long lines would form in front of the theaters, and girls with red lipstick and scarlet fingernails, large bags slung over their shoulders, walk up and down the line whispering, "I've got tickets, get your tickets here."

"I was worried about getting back to the kitchen in time, so it seemed like a good idea. I told the girl I'd take one, and asked her how much. Eight yen, she tells me. Now, I couldn't see how a 3 yen ticket could sell for 8 yen, more than twice the real cost, so I shouted, without thinking, 'Eight yen! That's robbery!' And then the girl…"

"Was that Otoki?"

"No. She suddenly bursts out crying."

"What?"

"That's their game. Immediately four or five girls rushed up, and one said in a threatening voice 'How dare you make our friend cry? You come with us.' She was plump, with a pale complexion and an oval face, about nineteen or twenty. That was Rakucho Otoki."

"And then what happened?"

"They dragged me off to an open space behind the Nichigeki Theater and she slapped me hard on the face. Before moving her operations to Ginza, she used to belong to a band of kids that sold novelties in Asakusa, so she was a tough street fighter. My face hurt like I'd been stung with a lash."

"That's terrible."

"Then she tells me to give the girl I made cry 50 yen as an apology. I threw five 10 yen bills at them and ran as fast as I could. I don't think I want to go to any movie theater for a while."

Since last night, my life has been filled with stories of formerly pliant Japanese women rebelling against their menfolk. The world has clearly undergone some kind of seismic shift.

When I left the kitchen, I could hear someone above talking.

"Konnichi wa!"

"Hey, Ojo-*san*, drive!"

"You are very ustukushii!"

By the door to my office, there was a young woman with a fresh-looking face. She was wearing a shabby but well-cared-for short navy-blue coat with bamboo buttons.

"I was told that I could find Clerk Kobayashi here," she began.

"Well, he's not."

"But the receptionist at the Documentation Section said he had come here."

"Maybe he's on his way. He might have stopped to talk to someone." The MPs upstairs were getting more boisterous, so I invited her inside, explaining that I was in charge of printing the interoffice communications of the Documentation Section.

"My name is Kikue Kimura," she said, with a bow of her head. Her hair was pulled tightly into a knot at the back. "I'm a typist at the Foreign Ministry, but at present I'm on loan to the War-End Central Liaison Bureau."

"That must be hard work," I said. The bureau is in charge of all communications between the Occupation Forces and the Japanese government, which is a very difficult position to be in. They're the ones the Occupation Forces turn to first for their PDs and anything else they wanted. I asked her to wait while I went to tried to find Kobayashi.

I first went to the kitchen and brought her a cup of coffee and a roll, then searched every inch of the headquarters for Kobayashi, without success. When I returned to tell the young woman this, she said, "I have to get back now. If I'm away too long, they'll get suspicious."

"Suspicious?"

"Yes."

"Who? About what?"

"I can't tell you that. Excuse me." And with that she turned her back to me and loosened the belt to her skirt. I had no idea what she was doing, but I decided it was best if I left the room. She stopped me, saying, "No, I'm finished. Please give this to Mr. Kobayashi." She was holding a thin envelope in both hands. It was made of heavy, water-repellant paper.

"This must be very important."

"That's why I kept it under my clothes. Will you do the same thing, please, Mr. Yamanaka?" I loosened my belt and slipped the envelope against my skin. The envelope was still warm. It gave me a strange feeling—a combination of being ill at ease, bashful and embarrassed.

"If this got into the wrong hands, the heads of one or two top ministers will roll. Please promise to give it to Mr. Kobayashi," she said, giving me a stern look.

"I promise," I reassured her.

It's 9 P.M., and Kobayashi still hasn't come back.

December 27
This is day four since I had the squabble with my wife and walked out of the house. I'm staying at my place of work, so mornings are

a snap. The second and third floors of the building are the First Cavalry Division Military Police Headquarters and the Military Police Liaison Office Quarters, the living quarters of the military police. Since the end of the war, at night Tokyo has been plagued by an outbreak of robberies and muggings. Even places like Ginza and Yurakucho suddenly become deserted by nine at night, but I'm inside the Tokyo Metropolitan Police Department, and on top of that, the quarters of the MPs, who strike terror in the hearts of all. It's the safest place in Japan these days. Roughly once a day the cook, the former proprietor of the Hongo Bar, tries to persuade me to go home, saying something like, "I'm sure your wife is sorry that she talked to you that way." Or "I sneaked a cup of powdered eggs for you. Why don't you take it to your wife?" Or "Your house is in Nezu, one of the few places in the city that wasn't destroyed in the bombings. It's a prime target for burglars. I think being back at home would be much more useful than having a bar on the door." But I just pretend not to get his hints, because frankly, I can't think of another place I'd rather be than here.

My daily routine is completely predictable. I help the cook with his duties, doing exactly as he asks, and then I wash the dishes. After that I get to work at my actual job, cutting stencils and printing mimeograph copies of documents for the Police Department's interoffice communications, and then I sit down and record the day's events in this diary. I enjoy sleeping here, too. I spread my mattress next to the cook's in a little room next to the kitchen, pull the blanket smelling of milk that he got for me from the MP's supply cabinet over myself, and I'm out like a light. In these days of turmoil and confusion, it's very rare for anyone to be living such a peaceful life. I'm very satisfied with it. From seven o'clock this evening, the cook and I sat by the pot-bellied stove in his room and played Japanese chess. We're both bad players who care more about their rooks than their kings. In three hours we managed fifteen games, nine wins and six losses for me. Chess is the reason today's diary entry is so brief.

December 28
Kobayashi wasn't here this morning, either. In his place, another clerk, named Umetani, brought the documents for me to print.

"Is Mr. Kobayashi sick?" I asked.

Umetani is a typical clerk type, about my age, who wears rayon covers over his cuffs to keep them from getting soiled with ink. "You don't like having me in charge?" he asked.

"Today is the last day of business for the year. The office will be closed from tomorrow."

"Yes, naturally."

"I wanted to ask Mr. Kobayashi if I could stay here in the period over the holiday, that's all."

"You live in a dugout shelter? Cramped, cold and damp. I also plan to come to work over the holidays. So I don't see any problem with your staying here. Your family will have more room in the shelter with you away, anyway. I suppose it can't be helped. You can spend your time here crushing fleas," and he left, having decided on his own that I live in a dugout shelter. Umetani has a sharp tongue, but a good heart.

My day's work was more love letters from Japanese women to General MacArthur. There were eight today, one of which was particularly intense:

My menstruation has stopped, I'm nauseous, my stomach aches, my head feels heavy, and I can't sleep. Your child is causing me considerable suffering. Yes, Your Excellency, I'm three months pregnant. It was at ten in the morning of Monday, September 17, when a large crowd gathered at the entrance of Daiichi Seimei Building, having heard that you would be entering it for the first time. I was among them, and while I was waiting for your arrival, I felt an indescribable thrill, my heart raced, and I began to tremble. I heard my father and my brother, who had been killed in the war, saying "Congratulations." I also heard the voice of my mother, killed in the air raids. "You're going to become a bride today. I'm so glad that you found such a fine partner," she said.

When I returned to my senses, the crowd parted and a long, black limousine had pulled to a stop. The door opened, and there you were, Your Excellency, wearing your sunglasses. For a brief moment, Your Excellency, perhaps only a second, you looked at the waiting crowd. Your gaze, Your Excellency, came to rest finally on me, and you smiled the slightest bit. I felt a pleasant shock run through me and I fainted. While I was unconscious, I clearly sensed a globe of the sun wearing sunglasses sharply penetrate my body from below, reaching inside me. The globe of the sun stopped moving when it reached my womb. This is how I was impregnated with Your Excellency's child.

I'm not asking that you acknowledge this child. I will raise it myself into a fine adult. We are, however, suffering from a lack of food. I'd like to ask for help just this one time. When you receive this letter, please send one hundred pounds of butter to the address above.

This story of a phantom pregnancy brought about by an intense love for General Mac was, in its own strange way, beautiful. The only drawback, the flaw in the gem, so to speak, was that last line, when she suddenly lapsed into a businesslike request out of desperation.

After delivering the printed documents to the Documentation Section Annex within the Police Department, I had some free time. Whenever I have free time, that thin envelope that I have put away in the drawer of the desk in my office occupies my thoughts. The image of the shiny, smooth face of Kikue Kimura, the Foreign Ministry typist on loan to the War-End Central Liaison Bureau, flashes in my mind. "If this got into the wrong hands, the heads of one or two ministers will roll," she had said. What can be wrapped inside that thick, water-repellent paper? Does this package have any connection to the sudden disappearance of Mr. Kobayashi?

"Mr. Kobayashi," I said to myself, looking around the empty office, "I'm just going to take a little peek for you. I'm sure you won't mind." I opened the water-repellent paper as carefully as if I were removing a scab.

It contained ten documents fastened together with a paper string through a hole punched in the upper right corner. The document on top was five pages in length, the first written in English. The paper had been torn from a notebook and the writing was rough and hastily dashed off. It had been written with neither a pencil nor a fountain pen, but, it seemed, with that interesting new invention that the MPs living on the second and third floors are carrying in their pockets—a ballpoint pen.

I've only seen a ballpoint pen two or three times, from a distance, so I don't really know much about them, but I've been told that the tip is pointed and a small ball is set in the point. When the ball rolls across the paper, the thick ink inside the pen is drawn out. They're not expensive, like a fountain pen, and you don't have to use a siphon to fill them with ink, or regularly dip the point in the inkbottle, as you do with a quill or a glass pen. They write smoothly on any type of paper. As I looked closely at the words written on the paper in cheery blue ink, the English words I'd studied in junior high began to come back to me, tumbling out one after another. It seemed to be some kind of a receipt.

One car, Buick model 1930.

To be used by U.S. Government for purpose of transporting high ranking officers on official business. After all, who won The War? You or me? I hereby certify that this car is to be used to pick up any girl who fucks, and furthermore who cares what the hell is it to you.

—The winning army, U.S.A.
GI Joe
on this date 19, Dec. 1945

The second page was an ordinary piece of paper with a translation of the English written with a glass-tipped pen. The fibers in the paper make the ink splash, so you can immediately tell it's a glass pen. From the third page, it was in the format of a report:

The War-End Central Liaison Bureau, cooperating with the Yokohama Police Headquarters, is investigating crimes committed by U.S. military personnel. The crimes reported for the months of September and October can be broken down as follows:

Murders by U.S. military personnel	4
Rapes	29
Theft of Money	235
Theft of Goods	552
Theft of Automobiles	32
Other Acts of Violence	105
Total	957

In other words, U.S. military personnel commit an average of fifteen to sixteen crimes a day in Yokohama. Since it is widely recognized that only a third of rapes are ever reported, the actual number of incidents can be assumed to be considerably higher.

Thefts of automobiles are effected by a relatively uniform method, so care should be taken. A theft that occurred on December 29 is considered typical and therefore it will be useful to record it in detail here. The victim, a Mr. S, is a private physician. He has owned an automobile, which he used to visit patients, since before the war. Because of shortages of gasoline during the war, he kept the automobile in the mountains of Kamakura, but after the war, when gasoline was again available on the black market, he once again began to use the automobile to make his rounds.

At 4 P.M. on the day of the incident, Dr. S was washing his car when four U.S. soldiers approached him and asked if he understood English. When he replied, "A little," they soldiers said that they had an urgent need for his automobile and would return it to him when they were finished, hopping into the car. Dr. S insisted that he wanted a written pledge that they would return the vehicle, and one of the soldiers wrote a receipt in the notebook that Dr. S used as his medical notebook. This is the attached memo.

In similar cases of car theft, the thieves commonly leave an official-looking receipt.

I looked through the other documents, and they were all similar in content. Each reported in detail on murders and rapes committed by U.S. soldiers. What on earth were the MPs doing? They were lying about upstairs on their Christmas break right now, but weren't they taking it a bit too easy? As I glared up at the ceiling, the lunch bell rang.

The cook, ringing the bell like an elementary school lunchroom monitor, peeked in my doorway and said: "Shinsuke, I'm going on a little excursion. I want to go get my hair cut at Keisei Takasago. A friend of mine runs a barbershop there. I'll be back by three."

"Enjoy your haircut. And take your time. You usually don't have to start cooking for dinner until four anyway."

"Mealtimes have been pushed up an hour. The guys upstairs are going to spend the night patrolling Tokyo in their Jeeps."

"They're giving up their holiday?"

"It looks like it. On Christmas Eve there were thirty robberies in Tokyo. As the end of the year approaches they're afraid more incidents will occur, so the police need to call on the MPs to keep things from getting out of hand. You know, Shinsuke, not a single police station in Tokyo has a car anymore. They receive a phone call reporting a crime, they should rush to the scene, but all they have is a bicycle, the train, or in some cases, their legs. There's no way they can be expected to catch the criminals. So that's why Major General Andrew W. Gullion, U.S. Army Military Police Acting Provost Marshal General, has gotten involved. Your dinner, Shinsuke, is on the kitchen counter. Please wash the dishes."

There are two advantages to going to Keisei Takasago to get your hair cut. The Keisei Line employees are on strike right now. It's a very strange kind of strike, in which they are still keeping the trains running, but allowing passengers to ride free of charge. The cook will be able to make the round trip from Ueno to Keisei Takasago and back for free. The second advantage is that most of the barbers in the city, including the one right here in the Metropolitan Police Department, require that you bring your own towel and soap, or they won't take you. Some places are even worse, declaring that they can't wash your hair because they don't have any fuel to heat the water. They return your soap to you, but it's always smaller than it was when you handed it over to them, because when you weren't looking, they've shaved some of it off. And the authorities have set the cost of a haircut at 3 yen 9 sen whether the barber washes your hair or not. Nothing is more depressing than to have to leave the barbershop after a cut and a shave without having a rinse, not to mention having your soap pinched on top of that. Keisei Takasago is still part of the city, but they're probably not such skinflints out there. Plus, of course, this barber is a friend of the cook, so it should be fine.

Worse than the barbers are the public baths. Because of the fuel shortage, the baths only operate every other day, and a crowd is always gathered in front an hour before the place opens. When the doors open, you rush in and toss your 20 sen to the clerk. The glass in the front door is often smashed by the rushing crowds, and when you bend down to remove your wood sandals, people just walk right over you. When you're taking off your clothes, you can see the fleas dancing and the lice crawling on the wood floor of the dressing room. By the time you finally get your clothes and your underwear wrapped up in the cloth you brought for that purpose, you have to wait in line naked just to put one foot in the bath. If you're lucky, the wait's five minutes; if you're not, it can more than twice that. Soap is precious, so everyone has a string passing through their bar that they grip as if their life depended on it, and when they're sitting in the tub, they hold the soap up over their head, because they don't want it to get wet and dissolve in the water, shrinking away to nothing. Some people, when they get out of the tub, walk through this forest of "soap trees" brushing against the bars of soap with their hands— and then they use the soap they pinched from others to wash their face. The water is always lukewarm, and you have to wash yourself standing up, always keeping your eye on your clothing in the dressing room. It's more a battleground than a bathhouse, to be honest. The only one who's relaxed and enjoying herself is the old woman at the entrance who collects the money. No matter how crowded it gets, she manages to collect her 20 sen from every customer.

After I finished washing the dishes and was taking a little break, I had a visitor. The girl with the fresh-looking face who had come to see Kobayashi the other day, Kikue Kimura, stopped by again. I told her that Kobayashi hadn't returned and I myself was a little worried about him.

"Please return the envelope that I gave you the other day, then," she said, boldly entering the office.

I brought her some coffee from the kitchen. "I have to say, I don't understand," I told her.

"What don't you understand?"

"Your envelope." I took it out of my desk drawer and placed it next to the enamel coffee cup. "You said that if it fell into the wrong hands, the heads of several ministers would roll. Of course it's filled with deplorable crimes committed by the U.S. forces, but making them public wouldn't change anything."

"You opened the package, didn't you?" said Kikue Kimura, glaring at me. Her eyes were like blazing torches. "You read the documents."

"Yes, I read them."

"I shouldn't have left them with you," she said as she pressed the envelope to her breast. "I misjudged you."

"We're suffering from a drastic coal shortage. From what I know, Tokyo Imperial University Hospital is no longer serving food to its patients because they don't have enough fuel for cooking. More people die there from starvation than illness, which makes you wonder why they even bother to call themselves a hospital—"

"I'm going."

"Now, just listen. Without coal, they can't sterilize the surgical equipment. So at Tokyo Imperial University Hospital, twice a week they tear down a wooden classroom on the campus and burn it in the boiler. We're living in a hell of electricity outages. We have electricity one day, then none the next. There's no food. During the war, you could always go out to the countryside to try to buy food, but what about now? You can't get on a train, so you can't get to the countryside. You have to stand in line for four or five days to buy a ticket. Just try standing out in the winter cold for four or five days and see if you don't freeze to death. In fact, every morning there are reports of several people doing just that. Say you're lucky and you somehow manage to get your hands on a ticket. It only gets worse from there. The locomotives are using low-grade coal, which has only half the power of the real thing. They can't get up speed. They have to stop frequently, for twenty or thirty minutes, to clean the accumulated coal dust out of the firebox. Trains are late by three or four hours, and no one knows when they'll arrive at their destination. These are the quarters of the U.S. military police, so they get all the coal and food they need from the Allied Forces Supply and Procurement Division. This is a different country. But just take one step outside, and you're in hell."

"And?"

"And I don't think anything will happen if you make these documents known in that hell. The events described in them are hellish, but our world is a hell of hungry ghosts. They'll cancel each other out, and people will just shrug it off."

Kikue Kimura sat silently drinking her coffee.

"Do you know about the farmer-soldiers incident?"

She did not answer.

"There were about ten lines about it in the newspaper, and it wasn't a big deal. Given the way things are in Japan today, it was just another ordinary happening, the kind of thing that goes on every day without attracting any special attention. But it involved army officers, so the Occupation Forces authorities in Ibaraki Prefecture investigated it, and I don't really know why, but an investigative team from the Military Police here went out there to look into it, too. Now, I only heard this indirectly, but a troop of farmer-soldiers, the Utsunomiya Division, were stationed at the airport in Mito, at the very end of the war, actually…" and I went on to relate, as accurately as possible, what I had been told by the former proprietor of the Hongo Bar, who had heard it from the military police who actually investigated the incident. In any case, this division of farmer-soldiers was supposed to be ready to defend the airport when called upon, but they spent their days tilling fields in the area, half-farmers and half-soldiers. After the defeat, the farmer-soldiers division was disbanded. But a certain Eikichi Kanda, age 33, who had been the supply officer for the troop and was an army major, was a very smart fellow, and his attention was drawn to the military supplies held by the troop. Major Kanda sent each of the farmer-soldiers in the troop home and started a farm in Ibaraki with just the division's officers. "I wanted to contribute to the postwar food shortage, so I joined together with my former comrades to continue our farming activities," he explained.

He and the other officers then confiscated the military supplies that had belonged to the division, sold them on the black market, using their earnings to wine and dine themselves on a nightly basis, hire prostitutes, build new houses, buy up land in the area and construct movie theaters. They threw the money around with such abandon that they eventually attracted the attention of the authorities, who, when they finally stepped in to put a halt to it, found that the 600 bales of rice originally in the division's inventory had been reduced to forty. Only 560 of 2,000 blankets were left, 1,000 barrels of cement had been reduced to 300, 2,000 pairs of military boots whittled away to 250, 500 barrels of nails to twenty-five… The only things intact were four carriages.

"Kikue, things like this are happening every day. A doctor in Yokohama having his car stolen is nothing."

"Do you really think so?" she said, sitting forward in the chair and looking intently at me. "A crime is a crime. Doesn't every crime deserve to be denounced?"

"Yes, that's true, in principle," I said. "And it's especially hard to overlook the attitude that the victors, who pride themselves on being our superiors, should be allowed to get away with whatever they please. That's just picking on the underdog. In fact, just a while ago, when I looked at these documents, I found myself getting angry and asking what on earth those MPs upstairs were doing. But… but… " and at that point I decided to change the direction of our conversation. "You're not thinking of taking these papers and showing them to someone, are you?"

"I want to give them to a newspaper."

"You're wasting your time," I said, taking a bundle of copies of the *Asahi Shimbun* that I'd received from the Documentation Section for test printing and dropped them on the desk. "Any day will do, but just look—for example, the front page of the December 15th edition. A whole section, twenty lines, blank. Why do you think that is?

"The censors, I suppose."

"Yes, precisely. The article that was supposed to appear here must have caught the eye of the Civil Censorship Department. That's why *Asahi* had to print the paper with this blank space. If you take those documents to the press, they'll meet the same fate. Even if you managed to find a courageous reporter, his article would end up a blank space on the page. And what would happen then, Kikue, is that the reporter and his editor-in-chief would get a harsh reprimand from the GHQ, but I can't imagine that any ministers' heads would roll."

Kikue remained frowning for some time, then suddenly her face relaxed. "Not to a Japanese newspaper. I was planning to give them to an American newspaper," she said triumphantly, like a female warrior who had just landed a punishing blow. "But my boss seems to have guessed what I'm up to, and he's been digging through my desk. That's why I decided to leave the papers with Mr. Kobayashi… You saw the documents. That's why I've told you all this. Please don't tell anyone else."

"What's Kobayashi's role in this?"

"To make a full report of the crimes committed by the U.S. servicemen based on the records of the Metropolitan Police Department."

"So you're in this together?"

"Yes, we're comrades."

"But what do you expect will happen if an American newspaper publishes these?

"I think the reason that the GHQ won't publish the crimes committed by U.S. military personnel is that they don't want it to get back to America. Everyone back there is convinced that their husbands, their sweethearts, their sons, are bringing justice and democracy to the uncivilized Japanese. But that's not what's really happening. Instead, they're running around stealing things at gunpoint and raping Japanese women. If the American public knew that, there'd be an uproar. That's the kind of country America is. So the best way to stop the criminal behavior of the U.S. forces is to appeal to public opinion back in the States. That's what Mr. Galbraith told me."

"Galbraith?"

"An economist who's here to study the effects of the bombings. He's promised to introduce me to an American newspaper."

A few moments after the brave young woman left, I remember that I may have actually seen this economist Galbraith at the Imperial Hotel.

December 29
While I was washing the dishes in the kitchen this morning like I always do, the janitor came to tell me that Clerk Umetani of the Documentation Section wanted to see me.

"I'll be there in five minutes, once I finish up," I said.

As I scrubbed off a piece of egg stuck to a plate, the janitor stared with eyes as wide as saucers. "Is that egg?" he exclaimed. "A fried egg? At least someone is eating real food." He let out a sigh.

"At lunch they're having hamburgers. I'll put one aside for you. Come by later," said the cook, who was chopping onions. "But you mustn't tell anyone else."

"Thank you for the wonderful New Year's present," said the janitor, beaming and bowing repeatedly, then suddenly turning serious. "I hope you don't think I'm being too bold, but I'd be really grateful for a handful of salt. Of course, in that case, I'll pass on the hamburger."

"I think I can manage it. But just this once."

"Thank you," said the janitor, bowing again. "It's so hard to find salt. I really appreciate it. Recently the government said that they'd found a way to make salt from urine, so we just had to hang on a little longer. I was counting on that, but it seems it was a lie."

"Did the government really say that?"

"Yes, they did," he replied, nodding so vigorously that it seemed his head might pop off. "First they were going to use sawdust to absorb the urine, then dry it in the sun, and then burn the sawdust in a big kettle."

"Well, that seems pretty simple."

"There's more to it. After they burn it, they get ashes, and then they have to add water to the ash, and simmer it. That results in salt.

They were saying that you could make 1 *kan* 500 *momme* of salt from a year's worth of one person's urine."

"That's amazing."

"But we don't have the fuel needed to simmer the mixture."

"I see."

"It's like all their plans. They also say that the salt you get from Japanese urine will be yellow."

"Ah, because we're one of the yellow races."

"No, because we're all exhausted. When you're exhausted, liver fluids are mixed with your urine, and they make the salt yellow."

I left the annex with the janitor. It was cold, sharp enough to sting the tip of my nose. In the space of fifty paces between the annex and the main building stood a persimmon tree. Two or three leaves clung to the tips of its branches, trembling in the cold December wind, ready to fall at any moment.

It was almost the end of the year and the beginning of the New Year holidays, but everyone looked as busy as usual.

"It's no use going home, so they stay here even during the holidays," said the janitor, reading my thoughts. "At home it's cold, cramped, and they have no fuel, so they can't even make hot water to drink. The office, on the other hand, is warm, and they can drink all the tea they want, even if it's weak, so it's better than being at home."

"I see. And where do you live?"

"Shinjuku."

"That must be nice and convenient."

"Yes, it's nice because I can walk to work."

"Did your house survive the bombings?"

"No, it was burned to the ground on May 25th. All of Shinjuku except Isetan was destroyed. I live in a triangle hut on some burned-out land." The janitor drew a triangle in the air and hunched a little to illustrate. I've seen the huts around town, dug about a foot into the earth without any corner posts, the roof reaching all the way down to the ground, but I hadn't known what they were called.

"The dampness is a problem. It makes a lot of people sick. The only reason that I've still got my health is that I can spend so much time at the office."

The world had become a very strange place—unhealthy to be at home, staying well by going to work.

"But Shinjuku has changed. It's become terrifying. Children are abandoned every night. There's a public phone that has become a favorite spot to leave kids."

I parted with the janitor at the service entrance and entered the Documentation Section, where I found Umetani seated with his legs curled around a hibachi, writing something.

"You have a son named Kiyoshi, don't you Mr. Yamanaka?" he asked, directing me to a chair and pushing the hibachi toward me.

"Yes, he attends the Fifth Municipal Middle School. Did he do something?"

"I have a report from the police at Ueno Station that Kiyoshi was beaten up there."

My mouth fell open, and Umetani quickly waved his hand to reassure me. "No need to worry. He's all right. But he got worked over by some very tough customers, so you should warn him to be careful."

"And who were they?"

"The Ueno Blood Cherry Gang."

"What's that?"

"Their pimp is an ex-Special Forces soldier. They're a dangerous group. They know Kiyoshi's face now. They may try to attack him again."

"Oh. But how did police headquarters and you come to know about Kiyoshi?"

"The report from Ueno came in just when I was at the Security Office talking to someone, and when I heard the victim's name and address, I thought it might be your son. Another boy, Shoichi Takahashi, got beat up, too. Do you know who he is?"

"Yes, he's Kiyoshi's best friend, from our neighborhood. He goes to Azabu Middle School."

"He was hurt pretty badly and had to be taken to Juntendo Hospital."

"I wonder why they were hanging around Ueno Station in the morning?"

"They weren't hanging around. They were attacked when your son and four other boys arrived from Akita Prefecture with a load of rice."

"From Akita? Rice?"

"Yes, apparently they're using their vacation to start up a business as rice mules."

"It may not be a lot, but I give Kiyoshi an allowance. There's no reason why he has to do that."

"I think the more pressing question is where he got money to begin with," said Umetani, taking the half cigarette stuck behind his ear and putting it in his mouth. "Together the five of them brought back a full bale of rice, which must have cost them 900 yen." He wrote the numeral "9" in the air with a piece of coal he'd picked up from the hibachi with the metal chopsticks. "When you add in transportation and other expenses, that's another 800 yen. So where did those five young men come up with 1,700 yen?"

"What can they get for a bale of rice in Tokyo?"

"At least 2,300 yen, with no arguments. Which means they earn a profit of about 500 yen." He took a deep draw on his cigarette and stuck a toothpick into the butt, which was what everyone did to smoke the cigarette to the very end. "And another thing. Why were the Blood Cherry Gang after them?"

"Why indeed?"

"This is no laughing matter. They say a girl can go to hell in three days, a boy in five. You should keep close tabs on your son. That's what I wanted to tell you."

I thanked him for this, then thought to ask about Kobayashi, who was still missing.

"He's had a bit of bad luck, I'm afraid. His vacation was canceled and he was sent to Yamaguchi Prefecture."

"How come?"

"There are a lot of illegal ships plying the Genkai Sea. Fisherman take their boats to Korea and offer Japanese waiting for repatriation a ride back home. They take them for everything they can. At the same time, a lot of Japanese in Korea are renting fisherman's ships and turning them into illegal ferries. In both cases, they charge about 50,000 yen for passage back to Japan."

"That's very expensive, no matter how desperate they are to come home."

"Anyway, every day several fishermen's boats are carrying repatriates to the shores of Yamaguchi and Fukuoka. This causes a lot of problems, including quarantine. So Kobayashi was sent there to investigate."

"Where are the fishermen from? Korea?"

"Some are. But the ones that sail from Japan to Korea are the worst. If they were bringing these people back free of charge, or for the actual cost of the journey, it would be one thing, but it's very ugly the way they're preying on the sufferings of their fellow countrymen."

Umetani put out the stump of his cigarette, now about the size of a die, and carefully placed it in his desk drawer. If you had ten of these butts and took them apart, you'd be able to roll then into a "new" cigarette.

After hearing this news of home, I thought I'd best to go back to Nezu Miyanaga-cho to check on things. I walked. The area from Manseibashi—in other words, Suda-cho, Awaji-cho, Surugadai, Jimbo-cho, Hitotsubashi, Ogawamachi and Ta-cho along the Kanda River—had survived the bombings, and going from burned Yurakucho and Marunouchi into these areas was like going from a desert into a deep forest. It was calming and put me at ease.

My wife was away, and there was no any sign of Kiyoshi. The fire was in the hibachi in the living room was still lit, so I stirred it up with the tongs and heated some water over it. The bag of charcoal in the entryway was printed with the words "Top-Quality Sakura Charcoal."

"How wasteful," I clucked my tongue disapprovingly. "Shameless." The tea in the tea cupboard was Uji Kanbayashi; the black market price must have been 100 yen for 100 *momme*, at least. "Unbelievable," I said to myself, clucking my tongue again. I began to examine the house and found three cans of dried eggs in the olive-drab color of U.S. military supplies on the Shinto altar and a pyramid of ten cans of peanuts stacked in the corner of the kitchen. What I was most astonished by, however, was the large white box sitting in the middle of the kitchen with the letters "GM" imprinted below the door handle. A refrigerator.

"Who does my wife think she is?" We have at least ten electrical outages each day. What good are electrical appliances under these conditions? "The fool!" All of these shiny new things had been purchased with the flesh of seven Japanese women, two of whom were her own daughters, the fruit of her loins. I simply couldn't understand the feelings of a woman who could enjoy a cup of Uji Kanbayashi tea when what she was really drinking was the lifeblood of her daughters. I noticed that the bottom drawer of the tea cupboard was packed full of Lucky Strikes, but I only took one. That's how mad I was.

"Welcome home," said old Mr. Furusawa, coughing to announce his presence as he descended from the second floor. "Your wife went to Juntendo Hospital. Kiyoshi's fine, but they were worried about Shoichi."

"Why on earth, I want to know, did Kiyoshi decide to become a rice mule? Do you know anything about it?

"For an English dictionary," said Mr. Furusawa, savoring the tea I poured for him. "He wanted to buy the *Concise English-Japanese Dictionary.*"

"Mr. Furusawa, you can't buy the *Concise English-Japanese Dictionary* anywhere these days. The printing plates were destroyed in the fires, and even if they'd survived, there's no paper to print them on."

"They're available in the used book stores in Kanda. Since August 15th, the number of people who want to study English has exploded. And as you know, the paper of that dictionary is perfect for rolling cigarettes, so everyone is looking for it. The price '3 yen' is printed on the colophon page, but you can't get one for anything less than 50 yen now. And your son is so eager to study English that he became a rice mule so that he could buy the dictionary."

"Well, at least he had an admirable motive."

"It's an inspiring story, the kind you don't often hear nowadays. He doesn't mind riding in a packed train for more than forty-eight hours if it means he can buy his dictionary. I think he deserves our admiration. I hope you'll commend him for his initiative."

"I still don't understand."

"What don't you understand?"

"All he'd have to do is take a can or two of dried egg powder or peanuts to the black market in Shinbashi or Shinjuku, and he's have 50 or 100 yen in a flash. Why does he have to go all the way to Akita?"

"He knows what was exchanged to get those cans." Mr. Furusawa raised his face, wrinkled as a dried apple, and looked steadily at me. "As a brother, he doesn't want to buy his dictionary with anything that his sisters earned with their bodies. I'm only too well aware that I'm living off the lifeblood of Fumiko and my granddaughter Tokiko, so I know how Kiyoshi feels. That's why I lent him the money he needed for the trip to Akita."

As a gesture of thanks, I took out a package of Toraya sweet bean jelly from the back of the tea cupboard and broke it in two, giving half to Mr. Furusawa.

"This is your wife's treasure. There'll be trouble if we eat it."

"You leave that to me. Let's make this our lunch." We ate the sweet bean jelly with our tea. There was another package of the bean jelly, which I slipped inside my jacket as a present for the cook at my office.

"You're not coming home, Shinsuke?" asked Mr. Furusawa, his expression suddenly darkening. "Isn't the office closed for the holidays?"

"Yes, but I'm still pretty busy." If I told him how I really felt, it would only depress him. "Last month, U.S. military personnel committed 554 crimes. Assaults on women are the most common. Rape, followed by theft, extortion and shakedowns. The Documentation Section Annex of the police station where I'm working is the Liaison Office for the First Cavalry Division Military Police Headquarters, so there's a lot of work," I said, stepping down into the entryway. "Oh, by the way, Mr. Furusawa, have you heard of the Blood Cherry Gang?"

"Blood Cherry Gang?"

"They're the ones who beat Kiyoshi up."

"It's the first I've ever heard of them."

"When Kiyoshi comes home, can you try to ask him about them without making it seem like a big deal?"

"I'll do my best. In exchange, please come back here by New Year's Eve to see the New Year in with your wife. It's just the day after tomorrow, you know."

As I left with his voice at my back, a light snow began to fall like grains of salt from the heavens. Looking to the right, I saw Ueno Hill blanketed in white.

The midnight tolling of the bell at Kaneiji Temple has always been a part of the New Year celebration in this area. Would it ring this year? I'd heard that the bell was no longer there, having been requisitioned by the military and melted down.

December 30

"When you walk from where we are at the Tokyo Metropolitan Police Department toward Yurakucho, there's the train tracks overhead, right? If you turn right at the lane just before the tracks, there's the Tokyo Bathhouse. You know, it's backed up against the Hibiya Movie Theater. I've heard that it's not so crowded. Do you want to go?"

And so the former proprietor of the Hongo Bar and I went to the public bath this afternoon. On the way, I told the cook about Kiyoshi's trip to Akita, and he was extremely impressed. "I'm amazed he could get his hands on a ticket," he said, slowly shaking his head back and forth. Whenever he was impressed by anything, he rocked his head back like a bobble-head toy. "You usually have to stand in line for a week to get a ticket. And if you're lucky enough to get one, you still have to wait at least a half-day at the wicket to get inside the station. When you get to platform, it's still not over, because the platform is as packed as a public bath. Two or three trains will go by before you're close enough to get on one, and after you get on, you can't go to the toilet until you get off. When you reach your destination, you got to through the same thing to return. Riding a train these days is like a journey through hell."

"Now that you mention it, last night on the radio, the announcer asked the head of the Passenger Department of the Transport Ministry what he thought about the uncontrolled aggression of passengers these days. The department head answered that travel conditions were impossibly bad and he didn't dare ask anything of passengers, that he simply felt sorry for them."

"That's why I say that it's really something that your son went all the way to Akita and back. And on top of that, he's a middle school student, and he was carrying a load of rice. That's impressive. Shinsuke, your son has a bright future ahead of him."

When we arrived at the Tokyo Bathhouse, it was as crowded as Ueno Station. There was a clerk at the entrance shouting instructions: "After you've paid your entrance fee, use this rope to tie up your footwear and your clothing and hand them to the young assistants in the dressing room. They'll give you a number so you can redeem your belongings later."

It was a five minutes' wait in the dressing room—during which we listened to the clerk repeat his instructions to each batch of arriving customers—before we finally made our way into the washing area and got into the bath. The dream of people my age is to lay back and relax in the tub, resting our head on the edge as we look up at the ceiling and let our bodies float in the hot, clean water, unlocking the door to the mind and letting all our troubles drift away. But thirty other men were packed into this tub, and there wasn't even enough room to shift position, not to mention lay back and relax. Nor was any clear, clean water in sight, just a muddy, lukewarm brew that smelled of urine. Worrying about the clothes you'd checked with the attendant and keeping your right hand up in the air so your soap wasn't stolen, you not only didn't let your troubles drift away, they threatened to pull you under.

Still, even lukewarm water felt good, and by the time I returned to the dressing room, I felt all toasty, like I had a hot water bottle deep down inside me.

As we were leaving the bathhouse, there were screams coming from the women's bath, followed by a roar like that of a wild beast and then a piercing shriek. I leaned over to see what was going on: Three or four women with bright red lipstick and faces white as radishes were brandishing heavy sticks. One was yelling: "You Western sluts! Spreading your legs for those niggers and honkies!" "We should knock some sense into you with this," screamed another, with a face as red and plump as a sweet potato. "Next time, I'll knife you!" spat a woman with a long face shaped like a cucumber. Then, as if by a prearranged signal, they all shouted, "Go fuck yourselves!" and dashed out of the bathhouse with a stride as energetic as the spring in a horse's tail.

The clerk tapped the head of one of the men watching this ruckus and said: "The show's over. Those of you going out, out, those coming in, in."

When I got outside, the cook was nowhere to be found. Then a voice said: "If you're looking for the fellow you were with, he took after those women." The man, about fifty years old, had a crew cut and was carrying soap, washcloth, pumice stone, loofah and towel.

He said, "I see you're still alive, Mr. Yamanaka."

It was the owner of the Naito Paper Shop in Ginza 7-chome. I remembered his close-cropped haircut; he used to sell me paper to make fans, back in about 1938.

"You've made it through, too," I said.

"Ginza 7-chome and 8-chome weren't burned. Our store is still standing."

"That's good news."

"But our warehouse in Ginza 6-chome went up in flames. A 250 kilogram bomb hit it and all the parchment paper I had hidden there burned. The ashes rained down on Ginza for half a day."

"What about your son?"

"He gave his life for the Empire on Iwojima."

"Oh…"

"But recently I heard that the reports on the self-sacrificial deaths on Iwojima were a lie, and three thousand Japanese were taken prisoner and sent to the American South to pick cotton."

"Wouldn't it be great if your son were one of them."

"I spend every day praying for that. So, how about going somewhere for something to eat? It's freezing out here."

We went into a noodle stall at the end of the alley. Taking our time over the eight or nine paltry noodles floating limply in the broth of slightly salty liquid, we talked about old times. Eventually the conversation turned to the brawl in the women's bath we'd just witnessed.

"That bath is the headquarters of the Rakucho prostitutes."

"Headquarters?"

"The prostitutes in Yurakucho and Shinbashi almost exclusively serve American soldiers. Whenever they finish with a john, they go for a soak in the Tokyo Bathhouse and exchange information with the other girls."

"You seem to be up on this."

"Well, this is my neighborhood, so naturally I hear things. And the Rakucho prostitutes don't get along with the prostitutes in Ueno."

"Ueno?"

"Yes, the girls in Ueno go with Japanese men, so whenever the two groups meet, there's trouble. The Ueno women call the Yurakucho girls 'Western sluts,' and the Yurakucho girls call the ones from Ueno 'stray dogs.' They hate each other."

"Why are the girls from Ueno 'stray dogs'?"

"I guess it's because they have sex with their clients out in the open, on Ueno Hill. And those women were from the Ueno Blood Cherry Gang."

I choked, hearing this.

"It seems like some boys that the Rakucho Gang adopted as mascots were beaten up by the Blood Cherry Gang from Ueno. The Rakucho Gang retaliated, and what we just saw was the Blood Cherry Gang retaliating for the retaliation."

I felt as if ice were being pressed up against my spine. I began to tremble. "You said that the boys were 'mascots' of the prostitutes? What do you mean?"

"They give the boys chocolate and chewing gum they get from the soldiers. They take them to the movies. But still, it's odd."

"What is?"

"Chewing gum. In the beginning, Wrigley, the American company, opened a branch in the Ginza. Remember the advertising campaign? 'The World's Most Popular Candy.' They really spent a lot of money, but it never took off."

This was a digression, but holding off hearing the truth, I humored Naito. "I guess it was counter to the Japanese custom that it's bad manners to talk or walk with food in your mouth. But then, the Jintan Company put out its own gum."

"Yes, that's right. They all failed miserably, but now gum is so popular. You see female office workers chewing gum as they walk. The Japanese have really changed."

I couldn't disagree with that. Just look at the Yamanaka family. Of my three daughters, one was sent off to the other world by an American bomb, and the other two are giving their bodies to high-ranking U.S. officers. And now my son is the mascot of a prostitute gang. Since August 15th, my family is no longer recognizable. It was so upsetting that I began to weep.

"Mr. Yamanaka, are you all right?"

"I guess I've caught a cold. My voice sounds strange doesn't it?"

"You should take care," said Mr. Naito, as he paid for my noodles.

As we were parting, I asked casually: "The boys who are 'mascots' for the prostitutes, I wonder how they repay the women for being nice to them?"

"Well, in the language of the old days of Yoshiwara, I guess you could call them the prostitutes' 'fancy boys.' Anyway, my shop is in the same place, Mr. Yamanaka, so stop by and see me. I'd like to spend a night reminiscing with you."

I was now trembling so badly that my whole body was shaking. I felt like an icicle. My teeth chattering, I managed to make my way back to the Documentation Section Annex.

The cook isn't back yet...

December 31

Yesterday, in the middle of writing in my diary, I began to shake so violently that I had to throw down my glass-tipped pen and wrap myself up in a blanket. I faintly remember the cook making me drink some saké with an egg in it, but everything after that is a blank. I've made it my sacred duty to compose an entry in my diary every day, and now, when the year is about to end in just a few moments, I've managed to grip my pen as I lie here on my stomach, but my thoughts are in a haze and I can't write anything. The midnight temple bells are ringing somewhere. It's the broadcast of temple bells from all around the country that they do at the end of the "Red and White Song Contest" that's been on up to now. The announcer just said: "Here is the bell from Kaneiji Temple in Ueno," so I guess the Kaneiji bell wasn't requisitioned and melted down. But it's been an awful year. So terrible, indescribably terrible...

1946

January 1

As if my brain was being eaten alive by my high fever, I spent the entire day plagued by nightmares.

A woman in her forties was running barefoot from Shinobazu Pond toward Nezu Miyanaga-cho, her head on fire. "Shinobazu Pond has no water. I can't put out this fire on my head!" she screamed as she ran past me. It was her wooden fire helmet that was on fire.

"Wait! I have water!" I shouted to her. "Take off your helmet!"

"I can't!" she screamed back. "It's burned on to my head. I'm burning! I'm burning to death!" And she ran, in erratic leaps and hops, toward Nezu Shrine.

I ran after her with a bucket of water. "Here's water, here's water…"

The next thing I remember is the former proprietor of the Hongo Bar holding a cup of water to my lips. I drank it and returned to my nightmares.

People with scarlet faces, burned and swollen to twice their size, were walking down Ginza Dori, where countless severed high-voltage cables from the streetcars were sending off sparks. "Can I do something for you?" I asked, not knowing whether it was a man or woman. "Where are you going? Your eyes are covered with napalm—shall I take your hand?" He or she didn't answer. The only sound was the crackling of the wires overhead. "Are you all right?" I heard a voice say clearly. I opened my eyes and saw my wife. Next to her was Tomoe. I don't remember clearly, but I think I nodded.

A dozen or more scorched legs are standing upside down, jammed into the emergency water trough at Ueno Kuromon-cho, like black lacquer chopsticks in a chopstick holder. Their heads were on fire, so they had to douse the fire. How horrible, I thought, as I passed by. I opened my eyes to find an icepack on my forehead. I saw the cook reading the newspaper beside my bed. It was four pages, a rarity these days. It must be the New Year's edition. Normally it's only two pages, I thought, drifting back into my nightmares.

January 2

Gaining strength from a stew made by the cook—potatoes, cabbage, carrots and corned beef in a beef-bullion stock—by afternoon I was able to sit up in bed.

"I don't think a 10 yen stew of army leftovers would've saved me," I said to him by way of thanks. (Maybe the cook didn't know what I was talking about: Right after I was released from the prison in Yokaichiba someone told me that 107 100-watt light bulbs had been affixed to the roof of the Ozu Market in Shinjuku, and the sky lit up so brightly you could see glow from Okubo, the next station. So I made a point of getting off the train at Okubo Station and looking in the direction of Shinjuku, and exactly as promised, the sky over Shinjuku glowed as bright as if a dozen incendiary bombs had been exploded there simultaneously. Like a moth drawn to a flame, I made my way to Shinjuku, and that was the first time I caught a glimpse of army-leftovers stew. A thick, gray mixture the consistency of laundry paste was boiling away in a big kettle. "I hope you don't think you can stand there sniffing this fine-smelling stew for free," said the man behind the pot. He had a scar across his cheek, and he ladled a serving of the gluey mess into a bowl and shoved it into my face. I handed him the 10 yen, but the foul odor kept me from finishing even half of it. Word was there are often empty packs of Lucky Strikes floating in it or, if you're chewing on something you think is tough ham, check that it isn't a used condom.)

"I'm amazed you were able to get a hold of potatoes and carrots at this time of year," I said to the cook.

"The farmers in Katsushika Shibamata are supplying the MPs' quarters with produce, and they've all been able to harvest their crops successfully." The former proprietor of the Hongo Bar was still reading yesterday's newspaper, not tired of it yet.

"I can't believe that." Everyone knew that last year all the vegetable plots in the vicinity of Tokyo had been hit by a plague of thievery. The culprits, of course, were the residents of Tokyo.

"You may not believe it, but the vegetable plots of Shibamata escaped." He tapped his salt and pepper crew cut with one finger. "The farmers there were smart. In the potato field, they put up a sign: 'One of these Potatoes Has Been Injected with Cyanide.' Not a single potato in the field was touched."

"I see."

"In the carrot patch they put a sign: 'Take as Many as You Want.' That patch was safe, too. But in Ichikawa, across the Edo River, the fields were wiped out."

"Why?"

"Because the farmers there put up signs saying, 'Put Yourself in the Growers' Place.' The Ichikawa Agriculture Cooperative had the signs printed up, but most of them ended up with the graffiti, 'Put Yourself in the Thief's Place.'"

"People don't like to be told what to do."

"That must be it. This is the result of people being bossed around for the last ten years by officials. The Shibamata farmers were very smart to use threats and cajoling instead of telling people what to do. But you know, the MPs aren't very fond of Japanese vegetables," said the cook, lowering his voice. "They never eat the salad."

"Why?"

"Because we use night soil as fertilizer. Why should the victors have to eat the shit of the vanquished is the way they see it, I guess."

I borrowed the New Year's Day newspaper from the cook. How many years had it been since the newspaper had four pages? The New Year's editions the last two years were just two pages. I can't remember what it was the New Year's Day before that. It seemed so long ago. But I do remember well last New Year's Day: An air raid warning sounded at five in the morning. When it was called off fifteen minutes later, I took my four children to Meiji Shrine for our New Year's morning shrine visit. There was almost no one there, and I learned later that only 2,900 people visited the shrine that day.

I remember Kiyoshi angrily protesting, "I know that the city's population has shrunk, between the bombs and people evacuating, from six and a half million to two and a half million, but this is tragic. Has everyone forgotten that Japan is the land of the gods?"

On the way home, we took a look at Misujimachi and Ueno Kuromon-cho near Asakusabashi Station, which had been destroyed in the air raids. Our relatives in both places were safe. My cousin in Misujimachi said, "Five or six incendiary bombs fell in the area, but it was no big deal. We scooped up the ones that didn't detonate and threw them in the Sumida River." He pointed proudly to his bamboo dustpan hanging in the house. He'd attached a long handle to it so that he could pick up undetonated bombs without getting too close. Three months later, he was dead—killed in the air raids in the old downtown area. When tens of thousands of incendiary bombs are raining down on you at once, there's no time to pick them up and toss them.

On January 2nd of last year there was, surprisingly, no air-raid warning. I took the whole family to the Hogakuza Theater to see *Child of Japan* performed by the Soganoya Goro Theater Company. I don't remember the story, because the theater was packed to overflowing and I could hardly see the stage. What I do remember is that the tickets cost 3 yen 80 sen. When it was over, we ate red rice at a cafeteria. While it was the red color of beans, it was actually red sorghum. To lift our spirits, we watched a newsreel at a theater in the Ginza.

We spent the holiday from January 3rd to January 6th in a dugout shelter. Air-raid sirens sounded about twice daily. The biggest drawback to the shelters is their dampness, but the shelter in Miyanaga-cho is always nice and dry. It's also quite roomy. It's 150 *tsubo* in area, and it has two toilets. The best thing about it is that it's warm in winter—in fact, in winter it might be fifteen degrees warmer than the ground outside—and cool in summer. If you spread straw mats over boards or lattice on the floor and lay out your bedding there, you could sleep your way soundly through an air raid. A city official who came to inspect it once declared that the Nishimachikai shelter in Denenchofu 2-chome, Omori Ward, and the Nezu Miyanaga-cho shelter in Ueno were the two most luxurious shelters in the city.

Nevertheless, a dreaded enemy, rivaling the B-29s, lurked in the shelter: fleas. If you checked your underwear after a short nap there, you could easily find them, groggy with their feast and so puffed up with your blood so that they looked like frogs' eggs. Kiyoshi used to make playthings of them, catching them and putting them on a smooth lacquer tray where, without any traction, they could no longer make use of their mighty jumping powers, and simply slipped and slid. After enjoying their antics for a time, he'd drop them in the hibachi, where they'd pop like tiny firecrackers. I remember observing Kiyoshi and his flea circus out of the corner of my eye while playing cards with my daughters.

That family is gone forever. What transpired in the air-raid shelters as we waited for the all-clear no longer existed now that the war was over and peace had come. Whenever I think that, my first reaction isn't so much sadness as bewilderment at the incredible strangeness of it all. Something monumental has taken place in the last year. Something like "the spirit of the times" has passed through us and disappeared into the void.

January 3

Today I left the annex for the first time in three days, walking the fifty meters to the main building to get the newspaper. The wind blowing across the courtyard didn't make me shiver, so I seem to have been restored to health. When I returned to the office, Kiyoshi was waiting for me. He was wearing a navy blue sailor's jacket, and he looked very grown up.

"This is from Mother," he said, taking a layered food container out of a cloth wrapping. His voice was surprisingly cheerful. "She said to tell you to stop sulking like a child and come home."

"I'm not sulking. The Yamanaka family has fallen apart. I just want some time alone to think about how I can put it back together again."

"You don't have to worry yourself about that. You and your generation started this war. And you lost it. It's our turn now."

"I didn't start the war."

"No, but you didn't do anything to try to stop it, did you?"

"Don't be ridiculous. How could I, as a single individual, have stopped the war?

"At the very least, you didn't oppose it. Even as a single individual, you could have spoken out and expressed your opposition."

"Life isn't that simple."

"Maybe, but not opposing the war is the same as endorsing it."

His manner was different than that of the Kiyoshi of the past. He had always reacted to things emotionally, but now he was very rational. He was like a different person.

"So you've become a mule for black-market rice," I said, counterattacking as I picked up a nori seaweed-wrapped roll from the container. "I heard that you're hanging out with prostitutes under the tracks at Yurakucho. Don't you think you're acting a little too big for your britches?"

"I suppose Mother told you."

"No, I have my own sources of information. That's what I'm thinking about right now—how I can put back together a family that includes a juvenile delinquent."

"Don't worry about me," he said calmly. "The girls from Yurakucho just supply me with cigarettes and chocolate from the U.S. soldiers. Bringing that rice down to Tokyo is our real work."

The former proprietor of the Hongo Bar, who had been concentrating on reading the newspaper up to now, raised his eyes and looked at Kiyoshi. "Are you saying being a mule is a job?"

"Yes. In fact, that's why I'm here today." Kiyoshi stood up straight and, fixing his gaze intently on me, said, "I'm moving out of the house tomorrow." Smiling at my astonished silence, he continued: "I'm making it on my own, Dad. I don't want to be supported by you or my sisters any longer."

"Are you quitting school? You mustn't."

"I'll stay in school. I'll even go on to university. The only difference is I'll pay my own way, working."

"No, that's impossible. You're still just a kid, son."

"I won't be alone. I have friends."

"Friends?"

"Sho will be with me, and the older guys."

"Who are these older guys?"

"Some university students we met." Kiyoshi told the story how when he was in a barracks-style used book shop in Kanda one day, coveting the *Concise English-Japanese Dictionary* in his hands, a student wearing an air force jacket with a Tokyo Imperial University pin on the collar came up to him and said, "You want that dictionary that bad, huh?"

"I really do," he'd responded.

"Then why don't you think about coming to Akita with us and bringing back some rice to Tokyo." Kiyoshi was interested, so the student explained further: "First, you need a stake. You need to come up with about 350 yen. Maybe you can borrow it from someone. You'll be paid 500 yen each trip, so that's a profit of 150 yen each time. You can buy three copies of the *Concise English-Japanese Dictionary* with that. How about it?"

Kiyoshi and Sho decided to trust the Tokyo Imperial University student and at 6 P.M. on the appointed day, they went to the underground entrance to Ueno Station with their 350 yen. Seven university students were there—including some from the Tokyo University of Foreign Studies, Sangyo University and Waseda University—singing a parody they'd composed to the tune of "Eight Leagues over Hakone Pass."

The Tohoku Line is fraught with danger—
More terrifying than an entrance exam.
A hundred cops and a thousand conductors
Searching top to bottom, front and behind.
Three *to* of rice on your back
One *to* of rice in your hands
In the crowded cars, a pencil behind your ear
Fluently reading a Western book
And singing "*Dekansho*" to keep the police off your track.
We bravely travel through Ou,
Cradling our sacks under our arms, wearing high boots,
Stomping merrily in time on the floor—
This is the life of the student mules.

All of the students had been inducted to fight in the war; they'd survived and been decommissioned and returned to their universities, but soon found themselves at a loss how to support themselves. The boy in the air force uniform had come up with a plan. One of the group would enter the railway training school so that he could get them tickets. If you had a source for train tickets, no business was more profitable than being a rice mule. From that point on, once a week the students made a trip on the Tohoku, Ou or Joetsu Line to the north country, procure some rice and bring it back to Tokyo. They called themselves the Tokyo Students Rice Relief Club and the song was their club anthem.

"The officials come through searching for rice several times along the way, but it's no big deal. Our pal in the railroad training school is on the train in his uniform, and we have acreage survey maps and plans of the bridges and tunnels."

"Which he got from the school."

"Right. So when they come through searching for rice, we just open the maps and act like we're studying them."

"No officials, no parents to worry about, just MacArthur, Emperor Moatside. It must be nice being on your own," said the cook, sliding the newspaper toward me. "But still, as your father, he's naturally concerned where you're living and with whom. Just let him know that, and put his mind at ease."

"Near Asakusabashi. The area north of the station wasn't destroyed. The ex–air force guy has a house there."

"I see. So you're all living there together?"

"Yes. The older guys are helping us with our studies. Aside from one trip a week to get rice, me and Sho are the cooks." Kiyoshi wrote the address on a scrap of paper and placed it on the tatami. "The ex–air force guy's entire family was killed during the air raids. And then he, who everyone assumed would never return alive, came back to his house, which is still standing. Whenever he drinks, he laughs in a very loud voice and says, 'Life sure is funny.'"

I put the address that Kiyoshi had written into my shirt pocket. "Visit your mother once a week so she knows you're okay. That's my condition."

"All right."

The aroma of cocoa that the cook was heating up for Kiyoshi was slowly filling the room. "The Emperor's human, they're saying now," said the cook. "And he's declared that the claim that the Japanese are a superior race destined to rule the world, which was our credo during the war, is false."

This is the Imperial proclamation: "The ties between us and our people have always stood upon mutual trust and affection. They do not depend upon mere legends and myths. They are not predicated on the false conception that the Emperor is divine and that the Japanese people are superior to other races and fated to rule the world."

"It's a little late for that" was my honest reaction. "Anyway, we've always known that the Emperor isn't a god."

"Of course," said the cook, placing the cocoa near Kiyoshi's knees. "The Crown Prince couldn't be born unless the Emperor and the Empress slept together; the Emperor eats, he uses the privy. Everyone knows that."

"How about when they used to call Japan a divine nation. Did you believe that?" asked Kiyoshi.

"Not really. I mean, we used to sing this spoof of 'The Camp Song':

Having left our country, vowing
courageously to return defeated,
Determined to come back alive, without glory
Whenever I hear the bugle sounding 'Retreat!'
I flee, as fast as my legs can carry.

"Which was a little different from the original, which went like this:

Having left our country, vowing
courageously to return victorious
determined not to come back alive, without glory,
Whenever I hear the bugle sounding 'Charge!'
I see a wave of flags in my mind.

"This spoof first became popular around the time of the funeral of Marshal Isoroku Yamamoto. It was about then that I realized we weren't going to be saved by any divine wind."

"Me, too," said the cook, who had harmonized with me in the second half of the song.

"That's what's wrong with you Dad," said Kiyoshi, sipping from his cup of cocoa, then slapping the cup down and spilling it. "If you knew the Emperor wasn't a god, all you had to do was come out and say so. If you didn't believe that Japan was a divine nation, why not speak up and say it? You didn't believe it, but you pretended to. You lied to yourself. You lived a dishonest life. You were an imposter. That's the worst kind of fraud there is."

Once again, I have to admit, Kiyoshi argued his case rationally.

"And that rescript in the paper today is complete nonsense," he went on. "I can still recite the Imperial Rescript Declaring War by heart. On War Commemoration Day on the eighth of each month from January 1942 to last August, the school principal always read it aloud to us, and the teachers all taught us the meaning, too. Last year an official from the government's textbook supervision department came to school: 'By the grace of Heaven, Emperor of Japan, seated on the throne occupied by the same dynasty from time immemorial, enjoin upon ye, Our loyal and brave subjects...' It says 'subjects,' Dad. It says 'enjoin you,' old man. And the declaration you just read reflects exactly the same attitude. The Emperor says 'Our people,' like we belong to him; we're still his subjects. You grown-ups are absolutely hopeless," Kiyoshi declared angrily, picking up his jacket. "You can't stop lying to yourselves, so you'll never change, even if you want to." He slammed the door and left.

January 4

I was shining my shoes, thinking I'd go to see how things were going back at the house in Nezu Miyanaga-cho, when Fumiko stopped by. As before, her lips were painted as red as chili peppers.

"Hi," she greeted me, American style, chewing gum. In four short months, her American officer boyfriend had managed to undo all the careful training that my wife and I had achieved over twenty years. I didn't reply, but just kept wiping my shoes with the rag.

"You need new shoes," she said, sitting down on my desk. "Shall I get a pair for you?"

"No thanks."

"There's a hole in the sole. You really need a new pair. I'll ask Robert for you."

"I said no thanks. When it warms up a little, I'll wear wooden sandals."

"But Robert won't let you walk around in shoes like that. He'll find some somewhere, I know."

"I have no intention or plan to ever meet this 'Robert' or whatever his name is."

"He says he wants to meet you."

"What does he want with me?"

"Ask him in person. It seems to be something very important."

"If he wants to talk to me, he should come and tell me. That's the proper way to do things."

"He says he'd like to have dinner with you."

"Where does he want me to go?"

"The Imperial Hotel.

"If that's the case, you should go," said the cook, who had brought us coffee. "Where's the only place in Japan today that you can get a decent meal? The Imperial Hotel. You know that, Mr. Yamanaka. You can get a steak there.

"If I want a steak, thanks to you I can have one right here."

"The quality of the meat there is entirely different. The best meat from all the butcher shops of Japan goes to the American Embassy, the Imperial Hotel and the Daiichi Hotel."

"The Daiichi Hotel?"

"American officers are quartered there, too. The meat that finds its way here is third or fourth rate."

Listening to him talk, I found myself gradually thinking of going to dinner with this Robert. I was ashamed of myself.

"When they ask you what you want, say Chaliapin Steak." Tetsuzo Inumaru, the former manager of the Imperial Hotel used to say that it was the gateway to the Empire of Japan, and for many years people had believed that, me included. I had heard that under the manager was a person with the position of housekeeper, in charge of the guest rooms, and under him was an individual responsible for each floor, called a captain. The most important job of the captain was to check the beds after they were made up by the maids. He would drop a coin on the bed, and if it didn't bounce, the maid got a scolding and had to remake the bed. I wouldn't actually like to sleep on a bed with such tightly tucked bedding, and anyway, the hotel is a place for the wealthy and important, and

I'll never been there as an actual guest. Ordinary citizens like me have no prospect of experiencing the Imperial Hotel, but still we all know what Chaliapin Steak is.

"It must be delicious."

"Fukuo Tsutsui made a wonderful contribution to the meat cuisine of the world with that dish."

"Who's he?"

"He apprenticed as a cook with me at the Toyoken Restaurant underneath Murai Bank in Nihonbashi in the early 1910s."

I had heard of Toyoken since I was a boy. One of our neighbors knew a lot about fine dining, and he used to tell me that in the Meiji Period, most Western restaurants served English-style meals— Fugestudo, which was French style, being an exception. The menu started with a consommé, then steak, roast beef or cold beef served with vegetables, and finally pudding and coffee. Seiyoken Restaurant was the top-ranking restaurant of this type. Then, in the 1910s, French cuisine, with its complex sauces, became popular, and Toyoken was the leading example. There was always a long line in front of Toyoken, he said.

"He was a brilliant chef," continued the cook, "and very quickly snatched up by the Imperial Hotel, where he was appointed the chief chef of the New Grill in 1935. It was a great achievement, like an ordinary foot soldier rising to the rank of major or general. And then the following year the Russian opera star Chaliapin came to sing at Hibiya Public Hall. You know who Chaliapin is, don't you?"

"Yes, I do. When I was apprenticing at Daiichi Tokosha, I used to pass by the Meikyokudo Record Shop every day, and I remember one day seeing a banner hanging from the shop saying something like "Self-taught bass singer becomes a star at the Metropolitan Opera; Miracle of the 20th century, Chaliapin sings *Boris Gudonov*. On Sale Now." It was a giant banner, reaching from the third floor of the building to the ground.

"Chaliapin loved steak, but unfortunately when he was in Japan he was suffering from a gum infection. His teeth hurt and he couldn't chew his beloved steak. Fukuo Tsutsui came up with the idea, inspired by sukiyaki, of scoring a thin strip of beef with a knife, marinating it in grated onion, and then cooking it."

"That sounds very good."

"Chaliapin thought so too, and he ordered it every day he was in Japan. Learning of this, Manager Inumaru—a real businessman—approached the singer and said they would like to name the steak after him and preserve it for eternity in the Imperial Hotel menu. Chaliapin gave his approval. You really should have it at least once in your lifetime."

I accompanied Fumiko to the Imperial Hotel, but not because of the Chaliapin Steak. I had a feeling that Navy Lieutenant Commander Robert King Hall was going to ask me for the hand of my daughter Fumiko in marriage.

"Did you just say something?" asked Fumiko, knocking at a door that had the number 301 in brass.

"I think that Mr. Robert might be thinking of asking for your hand in marriage. If he does, I'll have to give my approval, just like Chaliapin did, won't I?"

Fumiko laughed loudly, leaving me somewhat astonished as the door opened before me. There were six steps to climb, and once at the top I could see a living room to the right and a bedroom to the left, without any dividing wall. Both rooms were piled high with books.

"Please make yourself at home," said the navy lieutenant commander, who was dressed in a suit. He continued to hold my hand after shaking it and thereby led me to a sofa, before turning to Fumiko and saying, "A steak sandwich and coffee, please," and then sitting directly opposite me. A table was between us.

His attitude was entirely different than the first time I saw him. He was much more energized. I was a bit overwhelmed, and, unable to say that I wanted a Chaliapin Steak, I sat silently, looking at the spines of the books piled around us: *A Study of Chinese Words in the Japanese Language*; *A History of the Study of Chinese Characters in Japan*; *History of Japanese: Writing Systems*; *Study of the Origin of Chinese Characters*; *Principles of the Forms, Pronunciations and Meanings of Chinese Characters*; *History of Chinese Literature*… Most of them were published in Japan. A variety of Japanese dictionaries and *kanji* dictionaries were on the floor.

"We still haven't been properly introduced," he said in his amazingly fluent Japanese. "Let me begin. My name is Robert King Hall. Please call me Bob."

"Bob?"

"It's a nickname for Robert. I was born in 1912. In the Japanese way, that's the 1st year of Taisho, the Year of the Rat."

"I see."

"In April I'll be thirty-four."

"Do you have a wife back in the United States?"

"I'm single."

I smiled. "That's nice."

"Not really. I feel that not having a family is the burden I must bear."

"But you're healthy." After all, he was using Fumiko as his common-law wife. He couldn't very well say that he wasn't able to get married. "Maybe it's time to settle down."

"I'd like to have a family, but I can't spare the time that would take away from my research. That's my dilemma, my burden. I want to make a name for myself as a scholar."

"What's your area of specialization?"

"I don't have one."

"You don't have one?"

"At Harvard I studied physics. Then at the University of Chicago I took my master's and doctorate in mathematics. At Columbia I earned degrees in political science and Asian studies."

"You're too ambitious."

"There's more. I earned a PhD in philosophy at the University of Michigan. In other words, my area of specialization is human knowledge. That's why I have no time to spare for a family."

Human knowledge his specialty, four universities, two doctorates... He was some kind of freak of nature. Looking more closely at the navy lieutenant commander, I noticed that his forehead protruded conspicuously.

"Right now I'm involved with the Japanese language. After I leave the military, I sometimes think I'd like to enter the Japanese language and literature department of Tokyo Imperial University."

"So, you intend to continue studying as long as you live."

"I've also worked. Before the war, I was the vice-director of an institute at Harvard that taught English to foreigners, and after the war began I composed a *Dictionary of Military Terminology* for the publisher that produces Webster's dictionary."

"Where did you learn your disturbingly excellent Japanese?"

"I was sent by the State Department to reeducate the Japanese incarcerated in the detention camps in democracy. I visited all the camps in California. That's when I got interested in the Japanese language. You could say, actually, that all of the Japanese immigrants to the United States are my Japanese instructors. I was especially fascinated by your demonic *kanji*."

"*Kanji* are demonic?"

"Oh, yes, terribly demonic. After that I entered the School of Military Government at Princeton University."

"What's a School of Military Government?"

"Several of them were set up around the country when we entered the war. One is at Columbia. To put it simply, they are institutions focusing on how to administer Japan once we occupied it, and to foster officials to carry out that administration."

"Wait a moment. From the time America entered the war it was already thinking about how to administer its occupation of Japan?"

"Of course. When a war starts, there are three possible outcomes: win, lose or draw. When a government enters a war, it has to start preparing for all three."

"I see." So this was the rational thinking that the Americans were always talking about. The newspapers these days are constantly repeating that from now on we have to base ourselves not on spiritual values but rational thinking, but I had no idea what "spiritual values" and "rational thinking" actually referred to. Now, for the first time, I felt as if I could distinguish between them.

"By day three, I had left the other students at the School of Military Government in the dust."

Is there any subject that was beyond the capacity of this prodigy? I cocked my head in disbelief.

"From day four, I was appointed an instructor. In other words, the school realized that my talents would be wasted as a student."

His impeccable mastery of Japanese made it clear that he is some kind of genius, but what an unpleasant person he is.

"Right before I came to Japan, I was the Education Section Chief of CASA's Occupation Planning Staff. CASA stands for Civil Affairs Staging Area. And presently I'm the chief of the Language Section of the GHQ's Civil Information and Education section and the director of the Language Simplification Unit."

The navy lieutenant commander loosened his necktie and picked up a folder from the table. "Now allow me to ask about your personal history. Your name is Shinsuke Yamanaka."

"Yes…"

"You were born in 25th year of Meiji, in other words 1892."

"Yes, the same year as the novelist Eiji Yoshikawa. I'm fifty-four years old."

"You graduated from a professional school."

"Yes, the professional department of Meiji University."

"You've received what would be considered a high level of education in Japan, then."

"I suppose you could say that. Fumiko graduated from girl's higher school, you know. She earned very good grades. She was always competing with two or three other girls to be the top of her class. For a Japanese woman, she's well-educated."

"How about knowledge of Japanese?"

"Well, she can speak it as well as anyone else. And she's a good singer. I'm sure you know already, but she's very bright and cheerful."

"I'm asking about you."

"Me?"

"Yes. How is your mastery of *kanji*?"

"I suppose I know more than the average Japanese. After all, I cut mimeograph stencils. Writing *kanji* is my trade. You understand what a mimeograph is?"

The wunderkind nodded vigorously and mimed the use of a roller. "All right. We'll categorize you as someone who has a greater mastery of *kanji* than most Japanese." He lifted a piece of paper from the table and held it out to me. At first I thought it might be some kind of certification saying how impressed he was that I knew a lot of *kanji*, but when I looked at it I saw it was a copy of the Imperial rescript that had appeared in the newspaper. "Do you know what this is?" he asked.

"Yes, I read it in yesterday's paper."

"What does it say?"

"The Emperor says, he declares, that he's not a living deity, and upon consideration he's an ordinary human being."

"All right, please read the rescript."

"Huh?"

"Read it aloud. This is your first test."

"Test?"

"I intend to demonstrate that the Japanese people have too many *kanji* to master. I've asked you here to represent a typical Japanese adult. I'm studying the degree of knowledge Japanese have of their *kanji*."

My hopes for both Fumiko and Chaliapin Steak were frustrated, and I was in low spirits, but I read the first half of the rescript aloud without hesitation. In the middle I ran into a few problems.

惟フニ長キニ亘レル戦争ノ敗北ニ終リタル結果、我国
民ハ動モスレバ焦躁ニ流レ、失意ノ淵ニ沈淪セントス
ルノ傾キアリ。詭激ノ風漸ク長ジテ道義ノ念頗ル衰
ヘ、為ニ思想混乱ノ兆アルハ洵ニ深憂ニ堪ヘズ。

然レドモ朕ハ爾等国民ト共ニ在リ、常ニ利害ヲ同ジウ
シ休戚ヲ分タント欲ス。朕ト爾等国民トノ間ノ紐帯
ハ、終始相互ノ信頼ト敬愛トニ依リテ結バレ、単ナル
神話ト伝説トニ依リテ生ゼルモノニ非ズ。天皇ヲ以テ
現御神トシ、且日本国民ヲ以テ他ノ民族ニ優越セル民
族ニシテ、延テ世界ヲ支配スベキ運命ヲ有ストノ架空
ナル観念ニ基クモノニモ非ズ。

We feel deeply concerned to note that consequent to the protracted war ending in our defeat, our people are liable to grow restless and to fall into the Slough of Despond. Radical tendencies in excess are gradually spreading and the sense of morality tends to lose its hold on the people, with the result that there are signs of confusion. We stand by the people and We wish always to share with them in their moments of joys and sorrows. The ties between Us and Our people have always stood upon mutual trust and affection. They do not depend upon mere legends and myths. They are not predicated on the false conception that the Emperor is divine, and that the Japanese people are superior to other races and fated to rule the world.

Unfortunately, I found myself stumped by five phrases:

動モスレバ
沈淪セントスル
詭激ノ風
現御神トシ
延テ世界ヲ支配スベキ運命

Whenever I stumbled, the Navy Lieutenant Commander jumped in to tell me the correct pronunciation:

yaya mo sureba
chinrin sen to suru
kigeki no kaze
akitsumikami to shi
hiite sekai wo shihai subeki unmei

It was as if he were the Japanese and I were the foreigner. No, and I don't say this because he bested me—I don't think many Japanese could have read that rescript without a hitch. The naval lieutenant commander was a linguistic wizard.

Next he asked me what the *kanji* meant. I was able to answer correctly in most cases; the only word I didn't understand was *kigeki*. He explained that it meant words and actions that are extreme or radical.

"This declaration is of historic importance," said the navy lieutenant commander with a happy expression. "For the first time in history, the emperor himself is saying that he is not a god but a human being just like the rest of the Japanese people. General MacArthur is certain that democracy and freedom for Japan will be revived because of this declaration."

The comments of Emperor Moatside were published alongside the declaration, so I had already read them. I nodded, and the navy lieutenant commander said triumphantly: "Even you, who has a solid knowledge of *kanji*, weren't able to read or understand the declaration perfectly. Why?"

Now I saw where he was going. I understood why he had books about *kanji* piled up against the walls.

"So you're saying that *kanji* are the problem."

"Precisely. *Kanji* are the problem and should be banished from the Japanese language."

"That's a bit extreme."

"Not really. The emperor has made a clear separation from the period before and during the war, calling for Japan to make a fresh start. Japan has laid down its arms. It should toss out *kanji* in the same way."

"We can't do that."

"It's easy. Shinsuke, imagine that all writing had disappeared from Japan."

As I sat there astonished that he should call me by my first name, Fumiko returned carrying a plate with a sandwich on it and a tray with a thermos.

"Why don't you have something to eat?"

I made a gesture stopping her from putting the food down on the table and said to the navy lieutenant commander: "So what if all writing disappeared from Japan? Would the Japanese language disappear?"

"No, it wouldn't. The spoken language would remain. And that spoken language could be written in *romaji*."

"*Romaji?*"

"Yes, *romaji*. Is that impossible?"

"No, I suppose it isn't impossible."

"All right, so people would read those *romaji*. The spoken language would be reproduced, wouldn't it? What's the problem?"

"But…"

"This is for the benefit of the Japanese people. In Japan before and during the war, almost all of elementary education was devoted to mastering reading and writing *kanji*. By switching to *romaji*, a huge block of school time would be freed up. That time could be applied to the study of other subjects. Children could study democracy."

"Now hold on a minute."

"Be quiet. And when you drive out the demonic *kanji*, the efficiency of Japanese business would improve, too." His voice had risen and his face was red. He was excited. I looked to Fumiko for assistance, and she just shook her head.

"When he goes red in the face, there's no stopping him. You just have to let him have his say."

"Fumiko, you mustn't talk like that," said the navy lieutenant commander, shaking his pointer finger vehemently in her face. "As the chief of the CIE Language Section, I'm only thinking of the Japanese people. Put the heavy burden of these *kanji* down. Convert to *romaji* as quickly as possible. Then you'll be able to use typewriters, like we do. You have no idea how useful typewriters are when it comes to business."

Fumiko fled to the bedroom, sat down on the edge of the bed, and began flipping through a large English magazine. I was angry. There was no reason for this arrogant know-it-all to act that way to Fumiko.

"We laid down our weapons before you. But we can't lay down our language. You have no right to order us to give up using *kanji*."

"I think we do. You surrendered unconditionally. That means just what it says—no conditions. Japan has given up its old system of weights and measures for meters in order to modernize, hasn't it? Shinsuke, it's the same thing."

"Those are two different things. And Dr. Hall, can you please not call me by my first name? This is Japan. Please stop trying to force your customs on others," I said as I stood up and made my way down to the door.

"Wait!" His voice followed me. "I'm going to conduct another test of your *kanji* skills tomorrow. Please come here again at the same time."

"Don't be silly. I have a job. I came here for my daughter's sake today, but I don't have time to listen to your strange ideas over and over again."

"From tomorrow, your job is to be my research subject. The CIE Language Section will employ you."

I stood with my hand on the doorknob in horror.

"I'll make all the necessary arrangements with the Metropolitan Police Department Documentation Section. From today you are a full-time employee of the Language Section. Understand?"

January 5
My temporary job at the Metropolitan Police Documentation Section is, in truth, as a part-time temporary employee mimeographing internal memos for the police department. It's not exactly a secure position, and I can be let go at any time. Yesterday I was told that I am now an employee of the Occupation Forces GHQ—the fearsome and omnipotent presence whose very mention can make birds fall from the sky, a crying baby grow quiet, hair grow on a bald head and flowers bloom on telephone poles.

"It's a big promotion. You should accept it gladly," the former proprietor of the Hongo Bar urged me. "The pay will be much better, too. And the best thing is that you'll be working at the Imperial Hotel. The manager there, I think his name is Morris or something like that, is an army first lieutenant. And an even better thing would be if you could put a good word in for me with that army first lieutenant and get me hired in the kitchen of the Imperial Hotel."

"I don't like the fact that my boss is my daughter's lover."

"You're going to be around him all the time, so you'll be able to keep after him, telling him you don't want to see your daughter in this position, that he needs to marry her, that you'll commit hara-kiri if he doesn't do right by her, that that's what Japanese fathers do."

"His Japanese is better than mine. And he knows a lot about Japan. Those kind of threats will have no effect on him. Anyway, the real problem is that he's the chief of the Language Section of the GHQ's Civil Information and Education section and the director of the Language Simplification Unit, which is aiming to reform the Japanese language. He wants to use me as a guinea pig to see how well the typical Japanese has mastered his native language. If I can show him that my Japanese is good enough, he might give up his plans to reform the language. If it's not, he plans to eliminate *kanji* and the *kana* syllabary from the Japanese language. I'm a son of Nezu, born and bred in Old Edo, baptized in the waters of Aisomegawa River, which flows past Nezu Gongen Shrine, around Shinobazu

Pond, and from Shamisenbori into the Sumidagawa River, so I'm not the type to exaggerate, but…"

"You're already two stops past exaggeration."

"Well, I don't mean to exaggerate, but the entire future of the Japanese language is resting on my Japanese language ability, to a lesser or greater extent. That sends shivers down my spine."

"This is right up your alley. You read every single word of the newspaper, and you spend at least two hours a night writing in your diary. Thomas upstairs seems to think you're some kind of scholar."

Thomas is the chief of the Military Police Liaison Office of the First Cavalry Military Police, who are quartered in the second and third floors of the Metropolitan Police Documentation Section annex. Whenever we pass each other he greets me with excessive courtesy, and recently he gave me a couple Lucky Strikes and said something to me, which made me a little uncomfortable. Now I understood what was behind it.

"I happened to catch a glimpse of you writing in your diary, where you write such small and difficult *kanji*. As a mimeograph stencil cutter, you know a lot of *kanji*. I think this is a very suitable job for you."

"And yet I couldn't read the entire Emperor's rescript. It seems to me that I need the permission of Kobayashi, who gave me this job, anyway. And Kobayashi hasn't been here since the end of the year."

"As far as the Police Department is concerned, the orders of the Occupation are absolute. You don't need to worry about that."

Still, I didn't feel it right to change jobs without permission. And if possible, I'd actually like to have had the Metropolitan Police tell the GHQ that they couldn't have me, so I went to the Documentation Section to see if anything could be done.

The atmosphere was completely different than usual, which is incredibly quiet, the only sounds the clacking of abacus beads, pens scratching on paper, or the occasional stifled cough of someone with a cold. Today everyone was gathered around the charcoal heater talking animatedly. It was as bustling as the festival days on the 6th and the 22nd of every month at Nezu Gongen Shrine in the old days. I pulled Mr. Umetani, who was sputtering excitedly about something along with the others, away from the circle by his sleeve and explained my situation.

"We haven't received anything from CIE, but if they want you, you have to go."

"I'm not qualified. Can't you recommend someone here who has a better mastery of the Japanese language?"

"Don't be ridiculous," Umetani replied without a moment's hesitation. "We can't make any kind of suggestion from our side."

"But it's for the sake of our mother tongue."

"Haven't you noticed what's going on here?" With his chin, Umetani indicated the people sitting around the heater. "The other day Emperor Moatside finally dropped the bombshell on the Japanese government that all militarists must be dismissed from public service. The Ray-Ban Emperor seems intent on actually expelling anyone who supported the war from public office and excluding them from government service. One of the sentences in the directive reads: 'There must be eliminated for all time the authority and influence of those individuals and organizations, including their active supporters, who deceived and misled the people of Japan into embarking on world conquest.' And it goes on to specifically cite: 'Commissioned or non-commissioned officer, enlisted man or civilian employee who served in or with the Military Police (Kempei-Tai) or Naval Police, or other special or secret intelligence or military or naval police organizations.'"

"And the Special Higher Police are included in 'other special or secret intelligence or military or naval police organizations'?"

"Most seem to think so."

"That means that several people could be expelled from the Police Department."

"That's what all the hubbub is. Those who are expelled will not only lose their salaries but be stripped of their right to their pensions as well. That's the same as a death sentence. No one is able to get any work done. Making a suggestion right now to the GHQ is out of the question."

"But the Japanese language is at risk."

"Do you think we care what happens to the Japanese language?" he barked, then returned to the group of people, gesturing excitedly.

January 6

Yesterday, I returned to my home in Nezu and immediately went up to Kiyoshi's room on the second floor to straighten it up. While I was doing so, I remembered that my three daughters' old school textbooks were packed away in a room at the end of the upstairs hall, and I went to retrieve them. There were seven books on grammar. I spent most of the night reading through them, but of course I didn't find the passage I was looking for that would say something like, "The Japanese language could not exist without *kanji* and *kana*, the native syllabary, for the obvious reason that…" They were all written based on the assumption that Japan's written language consists of the combination of *kanji* and *kana*, and I realized that my quest for some kind of justification in these textbooks was a foolhardy one.

"What are you looking for? I can't sleep with all that page turning," complained my wife.

I just ignored her. The only possible reply would have been, "I'm looking for something that will save the Japanese language." I knew she wouldn't believe me, so my only option was silence.

Staying up late took its toll, and when I opened my eyes the radio was playing the usual noontime light music, with an accordion trio so jolly that it couldn't help but wake you up. I ate a quick breakfast of black-market rice cakes in sweet-potato miso soup and went outside.

The sky on the first Sunday of 1946 was clear and blue. The strong north wind had scoured the clouds away.

I strolled down the main street toward Sendagi, turning left near the Yama Bathhouse and walking toward S. Hill. Just before the hill I turned right, arriving at Nezu Gongen Shrine. Raising my coat collar, I wondered what had brought me to the shrine. I soon had my answer. Today was the 6th, and the 6th and the 22nd are special days for the god Gongen-*sama*, the birth god of the sixth Tokugawa Shogun Ienobu, so they're festival days for the people of Nezu. Before the war, the shrine precincts would be filled to overflowing with outdoor stalls on these days, and a variety of popular entertainments and sideshows—trained monkeys, plate-spinners, sword masters, lion dancers, and so forth—would compete for the coins of the locals. It was livelier than any other shrine festival. A lot of high school and university students who claimed to be mathematical wizards also competed for the crowd's attention. They'd do multiplication and division tricks with numbers in the seven or eight figures, with a spiel that went something like this: "If our children aren't good at arithmetic, Japan will fall behind the rest of the world in scientific advancement, and its dreams of world domination will be for naught, so today, since we're friends and neighbors, I'd like to teach our youngest citizens the secret, all-powerful speed arithmetic method devised by that great genius Albert Einstein…" At the end they tried to sell you a pamphlet for improving your mental powers, so you realized they were fake students. If I concentrate, I can almost hear their gravelly voices.

Stepping under the torii gateway to the right just before S. Hill, I walked along the granite-paved pathway leading up to the shrine. My wooden sandals made a pleasantly sharp clack against the stone; the sound seemed just right for the New Year. As I entered the gate in which statues of guardian deities were installed, their paint peeling off, I came upon my neighbor Mr. Takahashi.

"I heard from Kiyoshi that Sho moved out also."

"Yes. He was all excited about being a rice mule with Kiyoshi while attending middle school. He says he can't stand his parents' irresponsible attitude. First they lose a war that they say they're absolutely sure they'll win, and then the parents who used to insist that the emperor was a god and tell their children to throw away their lives for him now call that emperor 'Ten-*chan*.' He left saying he didn't want to be supported by such a dishonest, spineless father. I guess becoming independent isn't a bad thing, but…"

Accompanying me, Mr. Takahashi returned to the worship hall. Mr. Takahashi was now one of his newspaper's editorial writers. Because of the shortage of film and photographic equipment, the photography staff of the newspaper had been reduced, and Takahashi was placed in charge of it and give the additional task of being an editorial writer, which meant he had to know a lot about many different subjects. I decided to ask him what he thought about the problem of our national language. I couldn't just ask without explaining the circumstances and my involvement, which I did. Given how complex and involved the situation is, by the time I'd filled him in we had walked around the perimeter of the 6,800 *tsubo* shrine precinct one and a half times.

"That really is a complicated issue," he said.

On the western edge of the shrine precincts there's a red torii gate leading up toward the Otome Inari and Komagome Inari shines on the grounds. Sitting down on a round stone near the torii gate, Takahashi removed a Sumoka Tooth Powder can, which they used to sell before the war, from his coat pocket. He pulled a cigarette butt out of it and tried to stuff it into the bowl of a Japanese pipe. I took out a Lucky Strike and offered it to him, and he broke into a beaming smile. It was nice to see; when he smiled he looked like a happy little boy. The north wind had stopped, and the sun poured down. It was like being in a steam-heated room, and it felt very good. Since there was no wind, we were able to light two cigarettes with a single match.

"What's complicated about it?"

"I'm a newspaper man, so let me start from the standpoint of the newspapers. The fewer the *kanji* the better it is for the newspapers. For starters, they can save on type."

"That's reasonable."

"Next, newspapers want to have as many readers as possible, so they try to reduce the number of *kanji* they use to make the paper easier to read. Because of these things, the newspapers always support limiting the number of *kanji* in use. For example, back in 1923, twenty newspaper companies in Tokyo and Osaka released a joint declaration of a campaign to reduce the number of *kanji*. The Great Kanto Earthquake slowed them down a bit, but by 1925, most newspapers, following their announced policy, had succeeded in reducing the number of *kanji* they used.

"Now, the actions of the Ministry of Education and the military are also important." Picking up a stick, Mr. Takahashi wrote on the ground: "Ministry of Education, Military, Newspapers."

"The Ministry of Education has been supporting a restriction on the number of *kanji* since the Meiji period."

"Why?"

"In order to make education as widespread as possible."

"I see."

"The same for the military. If there are too many *kanji*, it's hard to train and educate soldiers. The military gained a lot of points for its argument during the first Sino-Japanese War."

"What do you mean by that?"

"Japan beat the Qing dynasty. Why should Japan, the victor, uncritically continue to make use of the writing of the nation it defeated? That was the public opinion at the time. The military used this groundswell against *kanji* to put pressure on the Ministry of Education. Of course, the Ministry of Education wanted to restrict the number of *kanji*, too. So in textbooks that went into use from the thirty-fourth year of Meiji, they established a clear policy that elementary school textbooks would be limited to about 1,200 *kanji*. To the best of my knowledge, this was the first official action to limit the number of *kanji*."

I sensed that what Takahashi was telling me would come in useful. From time to time the sound of the bell at the worship hall being rung by shrine visitors rose lightly into the peaceful January sky. As I listened, it occurred to me that perhaps meeting Mr. Takahashi here was a blessing conferred on me by Nezu Gongen-*sama*.

"The newspapers enthusiastically supported these efforts by the Ministry of Education and the military. With the Ministry of Education, the military and the newspapers all working together, resistance was futile. Of course, public opinion was moving in the same direction, so limiting the number of *kanji* became a kind of national policy. That joint declaration of newspapers said that they would be limiting to 3,000 the number of *kanji* that required *furigana*, the *kana* notation that indicates pronunciation. Up to that time the number was 6,800, so it was a reduction of more than half. This national policy is still having an effect."

I groaned. So this wasn't something that had just changed since August 15th.

"However, a backlash to this groundswell for decreasing the number of *kanji* began to appear in early Showa. In 1930 we invaded Manchuria, starting a war with the country where *kanji* originated, and suddenly the number of place and personal names in the news increased. The government, military and newspapers were forced to backpedal on the policy they had initiated. Another factor was that around this time the military started using very difficult *kanji* and Chinese compounds for their announcements and proclamations."

"A 180 degree reversal of what happened after the first Sino-Japanese War."

"By using a lot of *kanji*, the military were able to sound solemn and important."

"A simple tactic."

"Yes, we can see that now. Right-wing organizations adopted the same rhetoric. Some of them even stampeded into our newspaper offices shouting that restricting the number of *kanji* besmirched the dignity of the national polity. And for all those reasons, the pages of newspapers came to be filled with a lot more *kanji* than *kana*. Since the pressure from the military and the right-wing was lifted as of August 15th, the earlier policy of limiting the number of *kanji* has begun to come to the forefront again. This time it's being backed by the Allied Forces, so it's become a much more powerful tide, and a good number of intellectuals have gone beyond the idea of limiting the number of *kanji* to abolishing them altogether."

Mr. Takahashi fell silent for a while, and then wrote with the branch in the dirt again:

Arai Hakuseki
Scholars of Western learning

"Are you saying that maybe these scholars also advocated the abolishment of *kanji*?" I said, surprised that the story had suddenly leaped back in time to feudal days.

"They'd studied Western languages. They'd seen the Roman alphabet. When they saw how few letters Western languages had, they were astonished. How had Westerners created such an advanced civilization with so few letters? That's what most of them probably thought. One of them, though he came along a little later, was Yukichi Fukuzawa. Have you read any of his books?"

"At one point he was one of my favorite authors. I've read *An Encouragement of Learning, Autobiography* and..."

"Did you ever read *Elementary Reader for Children*?"

76

"I've never heard of it."

"In the preface, Fukuzawa says that the Japanese created *kana* from *kanji*, and in that respect alone, *kanji* are a marvelous invention, but their day is past, and from now on the Japanese need to use their own invention, *kana*, and *kanji* should gradually be phased out. Of course, he adds, if they were suddenly abolished, there'd be chaos, so we should start by trying to avoid using the more complex and difficult ones and gradually move in the direction of abolishing *kanji*. Another great figure in the argument to abolish *kanji* is, of course, Hisoka Maejima, but enough of this background. The fact is, since the middle of the Edo period, the tide has been moving in the direction of the abolishing *kanji* or the restricting their number. The combined effort of the Ministry of Education, the military and the newspapers is part of the trend."

"Are you saying that we don't really need *kanji*, Mr. Takahashi?" Had my intuition been mistaken? Japan having lost the war, had the powers of the god Gongen had been diminished, too?

"Well, given the nature of the problem, I don't think you can rush to that conclusion. I would be very indebted to you if I could have another Lucky Strike."

"Do we need *kanji* in Japanese or not? If you can tell me clearly what you think about that, I'll give you the whole pack." I took two cigarettes for myself and placed the pack on top of the stone.

"We need *kanji*," he said, lighting up and expelling the words and the smoke at the same time. "We have a thousand years of tradition writing in a mixture of *kanji* and *kana*, and you can't undo that in fifty or a hundred years."

"I understand that, but that's not a very convincing defense of *kanji*," I said skeptically, as if I were the director of the Language Simplification Unit of the CIE.

"When there's that much history and tradition, the language will have adopted many ingenious things. For example," Mr. Takahashi said, as he squatted and, using his branch as a chisel, wrote on the earth as if he were carving:

春が来た春が来たどこに来た
山に来た里に来た野にも来た

Spring has come spring has come where has it come
To the mountains to the villages and to the fields

"How about it? That's wonderful, isn't it?"

"Well, it's certainly a nice song."

"No, that's not it. The ingenious system of orthography is what I'm talking about. 'Spring,' 'mountain,' 'village,' and 'field' are all nouns. And 'come' is a verb. Nouns and verbs are concepts that point to an object or an activity. They are substantive. Over many centuries, we Japanese have come up with the system of using *kanji* to express concepts that have substance. And we've tried to write words that express relationships with *kana*. It's impossible to say how much this has helped us Japanese think in an organized way. And when we write with this system, the breaks between the two are clear at a glance. It's a brilliant system."

Next Takahashi wrote several famous poems by Buson:

菜の花や月は東に日は西に

Mustard flowers and the moon in the east, the sun in the west.

五月雨や大河を前に家二軒

Two homes before the swelling river in the May rains.

御手打ちの夫婦なりしを衣替え

Man and wife, once sentenced to death, change into their summer clothes.

"In these cases, too," he went on, "the rule in Japanese writing is that words referring to substantial entities are written in *kanji* and words expressing relationships are written in *kana* is perfectly observed. That creates a clear break between phrases that makes the meaning transparent. And this principle also makes the writing beautiful to look at, so that just viewing it is a pleasure. And because the breaks between phrases are so clear, no additional punctuation marks are needed. If you had to put punctuation marks in short poems like haiku, they'd lose their poetic intensity and become rambling and unfocused. I think that the ideas of restricting or outlawing *kanji* overlook this point. Restricting or eliminating *kanji* is foolhardy, equivalent to tossing out this important rule."

"That's the sort of argument that would please those of artistic temperament, certainly," I said, playing the devil's advocate in my role as stand-in for the chief of the CIE Language Section. "But most Japanese are not artists. For ordinary Japanese, *kanji* actually are a considerable burden."

"More than half of Japanese words are actually Japanese pronunciations of Chinese words," said Mr. Takahashi, tossing his Lucky Strike on the ground. "If you restrict the number of *kanji* in use or abolish them altogether, half of Japanese vocabulary will simply go missing in one fell swoop. All Japanese words that originated from Chinese will simply vanish."

"Vanish?"

"Yes. If that sounds like an exaggeration, we could say they'd become unrecognizable, but the point is they could no longer function as words." Lifting his Lucky Strike and tapping the sand off the end, Mr. Takahashi then inhaled deeply on it. The tip glowed brighter than a firefly's behind. Come to think of it, when I was a boy, there were lots of fireflies in Nezu. The fireflies from the pond on the shrine precincts, Aisome River and Goninbori illuminated the whole area like a river of light. There were also swarms of mosquitoes, of course.

When I awoke from my brief reverie, Mr. Takahashi was once again writing on the ground, in *kana*:

Shonin wa sono shonin no tame ni shonin ni tatsu koto wo shonin shita.

しょうにんはそのしょうにんのためにしょうにんにた
つことをしょうにんした。

As I peered down at the ground struggling to read, Mr. Takahashi said: "You could stare at the sentence for days and not know what it meant, because all the *shonin* have gotten lost." And he erased the *kana* and wrote the sentence again in a mixture of *kanji* and *kana*, revealing the meaning as if by magic:

上人はその商人のための證人に立つことを承認した。

"Without *kanji*, the meaning can't be communicated. Any number of similar examples could be offered."

"I see." This I could use in my argument with Navy Lieutenant Commander Hall.

"And if *kanji* were eliminated, their generative capacities would be lost. Each character has the capacity to create an infinite number of others. The fertility of *kanji* should not be overlooked." He wrote a single character on the ground quite largely:

員

"This *kanji*, *in*, is more prolific than a rabbit. If you put it together with *sha*, as in company, you get *sha-in*, company employee. If it decides to have an affair with *gaiko*, meaning diplomacy, you get *gaiko-in*, or salesman. When it shacks up with *gi*, for parliament, it becomes parliament representative, *gi-in*. When it moves in with *do*, for action, it becomes *do-in*, or mobilization. When it sidles up beside *sho*, for station, it becomes *sho-in*, station member, and when it elopes with court, *saiban*, it become judge, or *saiban-in*. When it pulls *za*, or troupe, over to its side, it becomes *za-in*, or troupe member. When it drapes itself on the arms of troop, or *tai*, it becomes *tai-in*, troop member; when it cozies up to *yaku*, or official position, it becomes *yaku-in*, or official. *Kanji* are very productive. They can produce any number of new words to respond to the needs of the times. *Kana* don't have this generative power. If we restricted ourselves solely to our native words, Japanese would have a very limited vocabulary. That's for certain."

"So you could say, for example, that by mastering a thousand *kanji*, I could produce thirty or forty thousand words, just by combining that original thousand in different ways?"

"That's right, Shinsuke. There are plenty of other reasons why the Japanese language needs *kanji*, but to really cover them all in a thorough fashion, I'd need some time to organize my thoughts."

"I hope you'll share them with me on another occasion. It's not a fair exchange, but I promise to supply you with Lucky Strikes if you do."

"That would be excellent," Mr. Takahashi said as he erased the writing on the ground with his foot. "If you use *kanji* well, you can communicate very concisely. That saves paper, which means you can print more articles in the same space. That's why it's very important for journalists to study *kanji*, I think. For my own benefit, I'd be happy to get together with you and continue this discussion."

"Thank you. It would be an enormous help."

"The only way in which *kanji* need to be restricted is to restrict people from using them carelessly, self-importantly or to obscure the truth. You're a graduate of the Meiji University professional school, aren't you, Shinsuke?"

"I spent most of my time skipping classes, but technically, yes."

"You must have had to study a lot of English. How many English words do you think you know?"

"Well, I remember that I studied Professor Hidesaburo Saito's *Idiomological English-Japanese Dictionary*. But I probably only remember less than six thousand words."

"About the same as me. But after spending elementary, middle, high school and university studying with great effort to learn six thousand English words, don't you think it's unfair to say that two or three thousand *kanji* are too many to learn? It's your native language, after all. It's the language you use in the correspondence of daily life, the language of the love letters you write to woo your wife and start a family, the language of the letters you write to friends to form the enduring bonds of amity, the language in which you write your last will and testament to entrust your affairs to your children after your death. It's the language you use all your life. Nothing good can come out of complaining about the fact that *kanji* are part of that language."

"I agree with you."

"Without *kanji*, we'd be cut off from more than a thousand years of our history. That would be a terrible loss." Slowly rising to his feet, Mr. Takahashi gently caressed the stone that we had been sitting on. "Do you know what this is?"

"No."

"It's the Writers' Stone. Scholars have discovered that Mori Ogai and Natsume Soseki sat on this stone and conceived the plots of their novels. It appeared in the newspapers, I think, but that was when the B-29s were bombing the hell out of the city, so perhaps you weren't reading the papers."

Or it might have been when I was sitting in the prison in Yokaichiba.

"Anyway, they say Soseki liked this stone particularly. Right after he came back from England, the first place he lived was Sendagi 57, just two hundred meters from here. Nezu Gongen became part of his regular strolling course, and this stone became the seat where he thought about things. No doubt he was sitting here when he came up with *I Am a Cat* and *Botchan*."

Feeling humbled by this information, I stepped back.

"I come here from time to time, sit down on this stone, and say, 'Thank you, Mr. Soseki, for writing those wonderful novels for us.' It gives me a sense of calm. If *kanji* were abolished, we'd be cut off from *I Am a Cat* and *Botchan*, wouldn't we? We can't allow that to happen."

I stood there for a while gazing at the stone. The bell at the worship hall rang. I felt deeply glad that I'd come to pay my respects to Gongen-*sama*.

January 7

When I arrived at the Tokyo Metropolitan Police Department Documentation Section early this morning, I came upon a man using the stove poker as a lever to ply off the wainscoting in the hallway. He was wearing a headscarf, like the Kabuki character Yosaburo in his thief's attire. I ran up to him, thinking he was stealing the wood for fuel, only to find that the "thief" was actually Mr. Umetani.

"Did you hear the BCJ weather report this morning? It's not going to get any higher than 10 degrees centigrade today. So I'm gathering fuel for the Documentation Section."

It took me a few minutes before I remembered what BCJ stood for, and then I recalled that it was the abbreviation for the Broadcasting Corporation of Japan.

"Eight employees of the Documentation Section have colds, but the janitor only brings by a half-box of charcoal. That doesn't even last to noon. They say that they're going to replace the wainscoting within the month anyway, so we may as well burn it before that," said Umetani as he removed his scarf. "Did you want something, Mr. Yamanaka?"

"I wanted to talk to you about my new job at the CIES. I don't want to quit the Documentation Section and go there. They say they're going to hire me full-time, but the job consists of using me as an example of a typical Japanese and testing my knowledge of *kanji*, and when they're done with me, they're certain to toss me aside. In times like these, I can't afford to be unemployed, so do you think I could continue to mimeograph the interoffice communications for the police department in the mornings?"

"That's up to them," said Mr. Umetani, carrying an armload of wainscoting boards toward the Documentation Section office. I picked up the remaining boards and followed after him. Just as we were entering the office, three men from the personnel office passed us and began to ply off wainscoting the same way, using pokers. It was as if the Tokyo Metropolitan Police Department was paying its employees to be firewood thieves.

"I'm not saying this to flatter you, but you are a very accomplished stencil cutter, you know how to keep your mouth shut and I have no complaints about your work attitude. You really are an indispensable part of our interoffice communications. Some have even suggested we employ you full-time, but if they say they need you there the entire day, we can't oppose that. Why don't you talk to Navy Lieutenant Commander Hall, the head of the Language Section?" Then lowering his voice, he added, "Word has it that he and your daughter are an item. The Americans can't say no to a woman; if your daughter asks him, I'm sure he'll agree."

"I'll think about it," I said, picking up the "Interoffice Communications" from the candy box being used as a document tray.

"By the way, we did receive the official notice from the War-End Central Liaison Bureau about you," Mr. Umetani said, handing me a sheet of red-lined paper with the words "Foreign Ministry" printed on it. I'd forgotten that the War-End Central Liaison Bureau was the external affairs arm of the Foreign Ministry.

From January 8, it is requested that temporary employee Shinsuke Yamanaka of the Documentation Section of the Tokyo Metropolitan Police Department be transferred to the

Language Section of the Civil Information and Education
Section of Allied General Headquarters.

—Language Section Chief Navy Lieutenant Commander
Robert K. Hall

"Now, when you're at your new workplace," Mr. Umetani went
on, "there's something I'd like you to find out for me. GHQ has
issued an order changing the name of the Broadcasting Corporation
of Japan to BCJ, but there seems to be a movement to change it to
yet another name. If you find out what the new name is, could you
let me know what it is?"

"How would I be able to find out something like that?"

"The CIE occupies more than half of the Tokyo Broadcasting
Hall in Tokyo. In other words, your new office will be the Tokyo
Broadcasting Hall in Uchisaiwai-cho, and information about
broadcasting is certain to be floating around there. If you hear
anything, just let me know."

I went back to the annex and sat in front of the mimeograph frame
with my stylus. There was only one interoffice communication today:

From the evening into the night of January 5, Saturday, armed
gangs perpetrated thirty-five robberies in the western suburbs
of Tokyo. All of the assailants were U.S. military personnel, in
groups ranging from two to ten, all sharing the same modus
operandi. They wore masks and threatened their victims with
firearms, pistol-whipping their victims, robbing them and
fleeing the scene. According to the Occupation Forces U.S.
First Cavalry Division Military Police Liaison Office located in
the annex to the Tokyo Metropolitan Police Department, the
practice of attacking Japanese households to acquire weekend
spending money is becoming widespread. The Military Police
Liaison Office has issued strict orders to all U.S. military personnel
regarding this matter in order to bring it under control, which
should eventually have an effect. For the time being, members
of the Japanese police force confronting situations of this sort
should refrain from rigorous law enforcement. Whenever such

an incident is reported, instead of responding directly to the scene, first report it to Military Police Liaison Office at Tokyo Metropolitan Police Department. We remind you that according to orders from the Staff Section of the Supreme Commander of Allied Forces, none of these incidents may be reported in the newspapers, so it's useless to release this information to either the newspapers or the radio stations.

I ended up making three holes in the stencil. The paper was of poor quality, but the memo also made me so angry that I'm afraid I applied more force than necessary.

January 8

In the morning, dark clouds that seemed a harbinger of snow hung low across the sky, creating a uniform gray atmosphere, but a little before ten, as I left police headquarters and cut across Hibiya Park on my way toward Shinbashi, blue patches began to break through the clouds and the sky became a bit brighter. It was colder than yesterday, however. Crossing the street from alongside Hibiya Public Hall, I came to Fukoku Seimei Headquarters. Beyond it was the six-story Tokyo Broadcasting Hall of the Japan Broadcasting Corporation, a solid, blue-gray edifice. In this area, these three large buildings— Fukoku Seimei Headquarters, Tokyo Broadcasting Hall and Mitsui Bussan next to it—had survived the bombings, preserving a small portion of the appearance of Tokyo from before the war.

Climbing the four massive stairs to the building entrance, each large enough to support a small boat set sideways, I pushed open the heavy doors, the size of two tatami mats each, and suddenly my vision was blocked by a wall of white. I was temporarily confused, but I soon realized that it was condensation from the heated building clouding my glasses. These days very few buildings are heated, and I'd actually forgotten that glasses fog up.

I walked timidly past the MPs with their helmets pushed down low over their faces and made my way to the reception desk, where I showed the sheet of paper with the red lines to the girl seated there; her hair was arranged neatly in a bun. Looking at me for perhaps five seconds, she said: "Take the elevator to the fifth floor. Walk down the hall, and diagonally to the right you'll see a sign with the words, 'Language Section.'" Her diction was perfect standard Japanese, and I almost felt as if I were listening to the news on the radio. She was just the kind of receptionist you'd expect at the Japan Broadcasting Corporation.

To get from the reception desk to the elevator, I had to pass through one more heavy door, and once again my glasses fogged up. It was even warmer there, enough to make a person perspire. It also had the same odor as the Imperial Hotel. It seemed that coffee was being brewed throughout the Tokyo Broadcasting Hall.

On the fifth floor, I cautiously opened the door of the Language Section, with its panel of smoked glass. A woman with a permanent wave and red lipstick looked up from her typewriter and asked in a husky voice, "Yes?" I handed her the sheet of paper, and she made an unintelligible response before disappearing behind a large partition. The room was narrow but deep, like three eight-tatami-mat rooms lined up front to back. There were six desks.

With her sandals making a slapping sound against the floor, she reappeared. "Please come this way," she said. "By the way, my name is Miss Kurita, and I'm in charge of the office here at the Language Section. If you have any questions, just ask me." She snapped her chewing gum vigorously.

I followed her past the partition where, wearing a navy blue hanten jacket, Language Section Chief Navy Lieutenant Commander Hall was concentrating intensely on calligraphy. He had the expression of a surgeon. I decided to take a seat and wait.

A chart of *kanji* hung on the wall to the right, before which was Language Section Chief Hall's desk, opposite a window facing Hibiya Street. A long banner of paper was attached to the wall above the window. Even the title was long: "September 22, 1945, Memorandum for Japanese Imperial Government from the Supreme Allied Command of Japan, Radio Code for Japan." I started to read it, and eventually I found myself standing to see the words at the top:

1. Newscasts must adhere strictly to the truth.
2. Nothing shall be broadcast which might, directly or indirectly, disturb public tranquility.

3. There shall be no false or destructive criticism of the Allied Powers.

4. There shall be no destructive criticism of the Allied Forces of Occupation and nothing which might invite mistrust or resentment off the troops.

5. No announcement shall be made concerning movement of Allied troops unless such movements have been officially released.

6. Broadcasts of entertainment programs, including dramas, satires, adaptations, poetry, comedic routines or comedies; lectures or discussions on the subjects of agriculture, forestry, mining or banking; lectures or discussions on the subjects such as history or geography; announcements from government institutions or agencies, including informational or educational programs or any other type of programs, shall not include any materials that can be interpreted as compromising or harming the relations among the Allied Powers or defaming any one of the Allied Powers.

—Signed for the Supreme Commander of the Allied Forces,
Harold Fair, Lieutenant Colonel,
Adjutant General's Department

The same anger I felt yesterday when I was cutting the interoffice communications stencil rose up in my chest. In yesterday's *Asahi Shimbun*, Yu Maki, a female leader of the Japan Communist Party, said that she agreed completely with all of the orders issued by General MacArthur. Ridiculous! How is the ban by the Allied Powers preventing the newspapers or radio from saying anything bad about them any different from the Japanese government's control of the press up to August 15th? If you say, "What do you expect, all governments are the same," I suppose that's the end of it—but it doesn't make it any less despicable. As I continued to glare at the writing on the wall, Lieutenant Commander Hall turned around in his chair, wiping the ink from his fingers with a tissue, and said, pointing to the banner: "I think that's my masterpiece. It took me an entire day, but it's well-done, don't you agree?"

"Is the Japan Broadcasting Corporation abiding by these restrictions?"

"Of course."

"And the newspapers and publishers?"

"Naturally. The print media has specific regulations applying to it, but the general content is pretty much the same."

"Is this supposed to be American truth and justice?"

The Lieutenant Commander looked at me closely, narrowing his eyes, which glinted with a sharp light.

"When you do something wrong, you should apologize for it honestly, not cover it up," I said. "That's truth and justice. But you refuse to allow any reporting on incidents that would inconvenience you. You ban any negative information. That's what numbers 5 and 6 are about, aren't they?"

"We can talk about that at length later. The important thing now is how perversely complicated the Japanese language is." Nimbly sidestepping my question, this thirty-four-year-old man who had studied at four universities and earned two doctorates energetically shrugged off his Japanese coat with the word "Isehan" printed in bright white on the collar. "Japanese is the devil's language. It's the invention of Satan himself. Now, that isn't just my opinion. As a matter of fact, Francis Xavier, who came to Japan in the mid-sixteenth century, said the same thing. He was the first Christian missionary to arrive in Japan. And the Jesuits of the early seventeenth century, who compiled the first Japanese-Portuguese dictionary, said that 'Japanese and its writing system are, without question, devised by Satan. By making Japanese such a difficult language, Satan is attempting to block the spread of Christ's gospel in this country.'"

"And according to you, Satan's first-line defense is *kanji*. But Mr. Hall, that idea, if you'll excuse me saying so, reflects a lack of erudition." This was just the opportunity I had been waiting for. I pulled my chair closer and sat up straight and unfolded all at once the information that I had garnered from my neighbor Mr. Takahashi at Nezu Shrine—in other words, that the Japanese language created a unique system of expression using *kanji* to represent substantial concepts and *kana* to express relationships; that more than half of Japanese vocabulary derives from *kanji*, and that abolishing characters would deal a fatal blow to the language; and that the generative power of characters makes Japanese a rich and convenient language. "So, as you can see, Japanese couldn't exist without *kanji*. You may be a linguistic savant, but in the end you're a foreigner, and you've only scratched the surface of the Japanese language; the essence, the core of the language is beyond your understanding. If you think you fully understand the Japanese language, that's just arrogance, pure and simple. You may be a mental giant, but you've overestimated yourself."

The former member of the Webster's Dictionary editorial staff didn't flinch in the face of my logic and outspokenness; in fact, a faint smile danced on his lips.

"You seem to be under the wrong impression," he replied.

I felt the wind go out of my sails, like a baseball player who had hit a home run but forgot to touch home plate.

Adopting the tone of a coach scolding a clumsy player, Hall went on: "Here in the Language Section, we're not debating the merits of *kanji*. We've already reached our conclusion on that subject. Likewise with *kana*. We're investigating converting Japanese writing into *romaji*."

"That's ridiculous."

"And when the Japanese people have grown accustomed to using *romaji* and the alphabet, the next step will be adopting a foreign language."

"There's not a single Japanese person who wants that."

"No doubt they'll object. But the other people of the world want this."

"I can't believe that. And what language are we Japanese supposed to use? English?"

"It doesn't have to be English; French would be fine. Or Spanish or Portuguese, which entered Japan during the Warring States Period. Dutch, which many Japanese intellectuals studied at the end of the Edo Period, wouldn't be a bad idea, either. Or, in order not to waste the knowledge of *kanji* that you already have, you could adopt Chinese. We'd rather you didn't select Russian, but other than that, it would be completely up to the Japanese people. In my personal opinion, I think Indonesian is a very easy language to learn. It's just been systematized very recently. As a result, it has few grammatical idiosyncrasies and it's relatively consistent. That makes it easy to master. The phonetic system is quite similar to Japanese as well. Yes, Indonesian is a very good choice. What do you think, Mr. Yamanaka?"

"It's ridiculous," I replied again. Actually, I didn't just reply—I shouted angrily: "The idea of robbing the Japanese people of their language is cruel. *You're* the devil. *You're* Satan."

"There is a precedent," he replied coolly. "You forced the Korean people to abandon their language and adopt Japanese instead. You made Japanese a required elementary school subject in India, China, Thailand, Burma and Indonesia. You tried to make Japanese the lingua franca of the Greater East Asian Prosperity Sphere. Now you conveniently overlook what you did to others and become outraged when someone else tries to do the same to you. Isn't that odd?"

I wasn't expecting an attack from that direction, and I had no response.

"I think that this failure of logic can also be traced back to the Japanese language."

The woman with the permed hairdo, Miss Kurita, came in with coffee. I think it would be more accurate to say that she came in to observe us, having heard our voices rising in anger. She wiped the table very slowly, picked up bits of trash from the floor and seemed hesitant to leave the room. Language Section Chief Hall raised his coffee cup to his long nose and savored its odor, continuing without concern for our observer.

"How do you refer to yourself when you're at police headquarters, Mr. Yamanaka? What first person pronoun do you use?" he asked.

"I say *watashi*. What does that have anything to do with?

"What if you were speaking in front of the chief of police?"

"*Watakushi*, I guess."

"And back at home?"

"*Ore*."

"How about when you go to a café with an old university friend?"

"Probably *boku*."

"And when you write in your diary?"

"*Jibun*."

"What about you, Miss Kurita?"

"At the office, *atashi*," replied our observer, popping a fresh stick of gum in her mouth. "At an arranged marriage meeting, *watakushi*, at home, *atai*. I know that it's childish to still call myself *atai* at the age of twenty-five, but where I grew up in Yanagibashi, even eighty-year-old women call themselves *atai*." Carrying the tray against her swaying hips, Miss Kurita retreated to the other side of the partition.

"Do you see what I mean, Mr. Yamanaka? The first person singular pronoun is one of the most important things for an individual. Human beings establish their identity through the use of the first-person singular pronoun. Americans and British create their individual identity through the first-person singular pronoun 'I.' In the same way, the French do it with *je*, the Spanish with *yo*, the Portuguese with *eu*, the Dutch with *ik*, the Chinese with *wǒ* and Indonesians with *saya*. But in Japanese you have all these different first-person singular pronouns. And you change them at the drop of a hat, depending upon the social context. You also do it very naturally. As a result, the Japanese never build a true identity as an individual."

How many languages did this thirty-four-year-old American know? I was so taken aback by this display of erudition that I couldn't find words.

"So you see, in our world, where the consistent use of one first-person singular pronoun is part of the normal process of building an identity as an individual, the Japanese are the exception. The Japanese expediently change their first-person singular pronoun from social context to social context. To put it another way, the Japanese use the first-person singular pronoun as a tool to blend into their social context. If the social context is militarism, then everyone becomes an exemplary militarist. If the social context is democracy, then everyone becomes a model democrat. You can take this farther to say that by manipulating the first-person singular pronoun like a contortionist, the Japanese maintain a constant smokescreen that prevents outsiders from ever understanding who they are. In other words, you may not think so yourselves, but from the outside, you're devilishly hard to understand. As long as that's the case, you can't be reintegrated into international society. That's why I want the Japanese to pick a language, *any* language, that has a real first-person singular pronoun as their new national language. And I want the Japanese to master that foreign language with a genuine first-person singular pronoun, establish strong individual identities and rebuild themselves as a nation that is comprehensible to outsiders."

As I sat sipping my coffee in a state of complete perplexity, my preachy friend removed his uniform from a hanger and slipped it on.

"There is another way," he said. "The constitution is also important. The language and the constitution—until both of those are transparent, so that foreigners can understand the Japanese, I don't think Japan has any future."

"So your plan is to first restrict the use of *kanji*, then outlaw *kanji* entirely and require all writing to be done in *kana*, then in *romaji*, and then replace Japanese with a foreign language, in that order?"

"Yes, and that entire process has to be carried out in as brief a period as possible. I think five years should be enough. But the Japanese are a very clever people, so they might well accomplish it in three."

"This is an absolutely outlandish plan," I said, after silently urging myself to remain calm. "If I were a more courageous man, I'd break this coffee cup and cut your throat with it."

"You wouldn't succeed. At the School of Military Government at Columbia University, I studied judo and karate. I'm a third rank in both."

"Just who do you think you are?"

"God, I suppose. I can't defeat the devil of Japanese unless I'm God." Putting on his sunglasses and glancing in the small mirror hanging on the wall, the judo and karate expert whistled and left the room.

"You did pretty well up to the halfway mark," said Miss Kurita, who'd come to clear away the coffee cups. "You were winning up to the point where you were talking about how *kanji* are absolutely indispensable for Japanese."

"When he said that Japanese should choose some other language as our new national language, I lost track of things. He took me by surprise."

"If it comes to that, I hope it's English. I can speak a little English, and that would make it easier." Miss Kurita paid no attention to my frown, jerking her pointed chin in the direction of the entrance. "Let me show you to your desk."

I don't know when it was brought in, but a small desk was now sitting next to Miss Kurita's. It was so small that a single sheet of Western paper would have filled the surface. The seat was just a wood stool. Miss Kurita then proceeded to question me in considerable detail about my home address, educational background and work history. It was necessary, she said, for making arrangements for my salary and an identification card. "As far as your job goes, your main responsibility is to talk about the Japanese language with the boss, like you were doing earlier."

"If that's it, I'll probably end up murdering him. I can't bear to hear my language criticized like that."

"The second part of your job is to put together a schedule for the visiting United States Education Mission coming to Japan. This will keep you very busy. I don't think you'll have time to murder the boss."

"United States Education Mission?"

"A group of education scholars and officials from educational institutions are going to be visiting Japan. Officially, the U.S. Department of State, responding to a request from General MacArthur, is sending the mission to observe the state of education in Japan, but in fact our boss pressured the chief of the CIE, Brigadier General Dyke, to arrange it. Our boss selected almost all the participants as well. They'll be arriving in early March."

"That's only two months away."

"Yes. There's a great deal to be done: negotiations with the Ministry of Education, arrangements with scholars on the Japanese side, and advance parlaying with the War-End Liaison Committee. We're going to be so busy our heads will be spinning."

"I quit," I said emphatically, standing up. "This is ridiculous. How do you expect a complete amateur like me to conduct something as complex and difficult as negotiations and parlays and whatever."

"You're not expected to do it all, Mr. Yamanaka," said Miss Kurita, pulling me back down by my sleeve. "The American staff will be taking care of most of it, and we're just assisting them." Miss Kurita lifted a binder of papers about the size of a weekly magazine and as thick as an English-Japanese dictionary down from the shelves at the side of the room. On the front cover was written, with a writing brush, "Materials Related to the Visit of a Mission of American Authorities to Assist and Advise the Supreme Allied Command Special Staff and Civilian Information and Education Section." It was stamped TOP SECRET. The handwriting was the same as the "Radio Code for Japan" hanging on the wall. I opened the binder, and saw the first page written in the same dark characters:

Proposal

In order to advise the CIE and the Ministry of Education concerning the re-establishment of the Japanese educational system, a mission of eminent American educators will be invited to Japan for approximately thirty days.

From the second page was a long list of names—the president of Harvard University, the president of the University of California, the president of the University of Chicago, the chancellor of the University of Minnesota, the president of the University of North Carolina, president of Vanderbilt University, the dean of the School of Education of the University of California, the director of the Institute of Advanced Studies at Princeton University, the dean of Columbia Teachers College, the director of the Guggenheim Foundation, the director of the Division of Humanities of the Rockefeller Foundation, senators, the Commissioner of Education of the state of Connecticut, Commissioner of Education of the state of Alabama, the superintendent of schools of the city of Atlanta, the superintendent of schools of the city of Philadelphia, the vice-president of the American Federation of Teachers, the executive secretary of the National Education Association, an official of the State Department... About the only people who weren't on the list were the security guard at the school entrance and the janitor.

What's the point of having such a large group of eminent people visit Japan?"

"They're going to bring the American educational system here."

"How kind of them."

"And another purpose is to transform the Japanese writing system into *romaji*. That's the real aim of our boss."

I felt as if I were suffocating.

January 9

"Mr. Yamanaka, can you do something about your hair?" said Miss Kurita, as she chewed her gum. "You need to go to the barber."

I had just dashed into the Language Section on the fifth floor of the Tokyo Broadcasting Hall, having cut through Hibiya Park, just three minutes after finishing my stencil cutting of interoffice communications at the Documentation Section annex of the Metropolitan Police Headquarters. Miss Kurita is right: I haven't had the chance to sit down in a real barber's chair for a while. Not since having my head shaved early in September of last year at the prison in Yokaichiba, in fact. The former proprietor of the Hongo Bar had once taken me out into the yard behind the Documentation Section Annex and played barber with me, but he was an amateur, and my hair looked presentable for only a few days after that. Now it was like an unkempt garden, which I was all too well aware of.

"Finding a barber in Tokyo is harder than finding a needle in a haystack," I answered, walking to the front of the bookshelf behind Miss Kurita's desk. The shelf was packed with American military portable rations. The ones wrapped in green were breakfast, the blue ones, lunch, and the brown ones, supper. I'd heard that a fancier "dinner" portable ration also existed, but Language Section Chief Navy Lieutenant Commander Hall was not that generous with his Japanese staff.

Sitting across from Miss Kurita, I spread the contents of the blue lunch mess kit out on the table. First there was a little can. Next, ten biscuits tightly wrapped in wax paper. Next, packs of powdered soup and a pack of instant coffee, four cigarettes, chewing gum and chocolate. There were even a machine-punched fork and spoon. And a thick paper napkin.

"How fancy, a napkin on the battlefield," I said, impressed, as I opened the can to find flavored dried beef. I emptied the powdered soup into a teacup, added hot water from the kettle sitting on the 1 kilowatt electric heater next to Miss Kurita. As the steam clouded my eyeglasses, I deeply inhaled the soup's aroma. I felt like I was in the Grill at the Imperial Hotel.

"The boss doesn't like it when his staff isn't neat and clean," said Miss Kurita. "Lieutenant Commander Hall is especially particular about neat hair."

"It seems that working for the Occupation Forces, you lose touch with the realities of daily life of the people," I said, dipping the biscuits in the soup and cramming them into my mouth. "Tokyo is a scorched wasteland. Where are you supposed to find a barber in the ashes? Any barbershop that survived the bombings is sure to have a fifty-meter-long line of people waiting. That's how it is in Nezu. You have to have an awful lot of free time to go to the barber. And it's even worse at the public baths, which are murderously crowded. Did you know that there was a riot at the Shippo Bathhouse in Meguro last night?"

"Really? How do you know about this?"

"From interoffice communications at the Police Department. In order to alleviate crowding, public baths have an every-other day policy for men and women. The Shippo Bathhouse is open for women on odd-numbered days and for men on even-numbered days. But about nine last night, a crowd of about a hundred women showed up at the bathhouse and demanded to be allowed in, breaking into the changing room. The reason they were crashing the men's night at the bath was they'd gotten all covered with mud after they caught some former naval officers trying to remove sacks of soy beans hidden in the storehouse of the Naval Technical Institute. They mobbed the officers' car, determined not to let them escape with their booty, and got dirty in the struggle."

"Who won—the naval officers or the women?"

"The men with the car had the advantage, obviously. After they jostled each other for a while, the officers just kicked the women away and drove off. I'm sure that contributed to the women's anger when they went to the bathhouse. When the proprietor told them it wasn't their day, they just yanked him out of his chair and stormed in. The Meguro police had to send a dozen officers to bring the situation under control... There're not enough barbershops, and there're not enough public baths, and the proof of that is the stench in the trains. I know I'm one of the contributors to the smell, but you almost gag every time you step into a train… Anyway, as much as I'd like to go to a barber, I don't see how it's possible."

"You really do go on, don't you, Mr. Yamanaka?"

"I'm enjoying this lunch, and when I'm enjoying myself, I feel like talking." I wiped my mouth with the napkin.

"You're hair's a mess, but your clothes are worse," said Miss Kurita as she stood up and walked slowly around me.

"Well, my national civilian uniform is more than five years old," I said, drinking my instant coffee.

It was at the end of 1938, eight years ago, I think, that khaki was established as the national defense color. Two years later, in January 1940, the national civilian uniform regulation was issued. An official from the ward office dropped by our block group meeting to explain it all in detail. The reason the national civilian uniform was the same khaki color and had the same upright collar as military uniforms is that "in case of an emergency, they can be converted immediately into military uniforms. And if you add a decoration made out of purple braid to the national civilian uniform, it can be formal wear, too." At the time I'd been pressured to act as the vice-chairman of the Tokyo Fan Makers Association, and one of my duties was to see off at the train station members of the association who'd been drafted. I had a national civilian uniform made for that purpose at Takashimaya Department Store in Nihonbashi in the January 1941. It was made of wool and cost 50 yen. Later they were made of rayon, which tore easily and quickly wore out. Whenever I heard someone complain that rayon lasted less than half a year, I used to think how fortunate I was to purchase my national civilian uniform at just the right moment. My single uniform had become my daily wear from about three years ago. I was still wearing it, even though it's pretty threadbare.

"And your shoes are simply a tragedy," Miss Kurita said.

It was true that both my soles were coming off and I'd tied them on with string. "The strings act as treads to keep me from slipping in the snow," I said, showing them to her. "The first snow is late this year. The New Year Week is over, and it still hasn't snowed. I'm afraid my treads are feeling unwanted."

"There's no need for sarcasm."

"It's even harder to come by clothing and shoes than a barber or a bath. What choice do I have but to be sarcastic? Everybody's in the same boat, which at least makes it easier to accept."

"At any rate, the boss has told me to do something about your appearance. Captain Donovan, a female officer in the Language Section, is very particular about cleanliness. To an extreme degree. She's away for a week, touring schools in the Tohoku region, but if we don't get you cleaned up before she gets back she'll have a fit. The boss is more concerned about her tantrums than he is about the dirt, fleas and lice you probably have. I'm going to make an appointment."

"For what?"

"For the barber."

"The barber?"

"Yes, the barber. He may not be able to take you today, but I'm sure he can squeeze you in tomorrow." Miss Kurita lifted up the phone and said to the Japan Broadcasting Corporation operator, "It's Kurita at the Language Section. Please connect me to the BBC."

January 10

This past year has been a series of momentous events, not only for Japan but for Shinsuke Yamanaka personally. Looking back at this record, I see that my eldest daughter Kinuko was married at the beginning of May, and then killed by the direct hit of an incendiary bomb and dispatched to the other world at the end of the same month. My older brother was killed in the same air raid, and I just barely escaped with my life after being chased by a P-51 Mustang strafing me in an open field between Matsudo and Ichikawa. In June I was arrested for violating the National Security Law and sent away to a prison in Yokaichiba, Chiba Prefecture. An entire lifetime worth of incidents is crowded into those two short months. Then in September, after being released from prison and returning to Nezu Miyanaga-cho, I found that my second and third daughters, Fumiko and Takeko, had become the bedmates of high-ranking U.S. military officers. I landed a part-time job working mornings at the quite unexpected location of the Metropolitan Police Department, but after just a brief time there, I was arrested on suspicion of obstructing the aims and purposes of the Occupation and held in solitary confinement from October through December in a cell in the basement of the very same Tokyo Metropolitan Police Department. I was cleared of the charges and returned to my job, and after only a few brief days of seemingly normal life, drafted to work in the afternoons at the Language Section of the Civilian Information and Education section of the GHQ.

They talk about a cat having nine lives, but I doubt that anyone who had nine lives would ever have experienced so many events. Another way of putting it, I suppose, is that the war has certainly made a mess of my life. Given all that's happened to me, I suppose I should be immune to surprises by now, but today's chance encounter still astonished me. After thirty years, I found myself reunited with Icchan from Gongendoko. This is how it came about:

I made my appearance at noon at the Language Section on the fifth floor of the Tokyo Broadcasting Hall, and while I was standing in front of the shelf trying to decide on a green, blue or brown mess kit for my lunch, Miss Kurita came in and announced: "You have an appointment at the BBC at 1:30."

"BBC?"

"Barber... Beauty... Club," she said, pronouncing the words very slowly and carefully.

"What's that?"

"The barbershop and beauty salon for the Occupation Forces. You know the Daiichi Seimei Building at Horibata?"

"Yes, the building housing the GHQ, the Allied Forces General Headquarters, where General MacArthur is ensconced."

"The PX, the Post Exchange, there—the U.S. military base store— has a barber shop. The manager of the PX barbershop, upon the direct order of the general, has formed the BBC. A lot of the buildings in Tokyo are now occupied by the Allied Forces. Half of the Tokyo Broadcasting Hall has been requisitioned, along with the Imperial Hotel, the Yurakucho Hotel, the Daiichi Hotel, the Sanno Hotel, the Marunouchi Hotel, Taisho Building, Hibiya Imperial Seimei Building, Sanshin Building... Basically all the surviving Western-style buildings have been taken over by the Occupation. Most of the buildings have a barbershop and a beauty shop inside them. General MacArthur ordered that they all be organized into a club, for the purpose of promoting hygiene awareness and improved service. That's the BBC." As she explained, Miss Kurita directed me out into the hallway, after which she carefully locked the door. At least once a day, Miss Kurita said, Lieutenant Commander Hall reminded her, "It's possible that an employee of the Japan Broadcasting Corporation might find their way into Language Section and get a glimpse of the documents related to language policy, so never leave the office empty for more than five minutes. And don't forgot to lock the door when you leave." After testing the door handle several times to confirm it was locked, she murmured, "That should do it," and walked toward the stairs. "Let's not take the elevator this time. If we have to share it with some Americans, they may not appreciate your odor right now."

"Don't worry about me. I always use the stairs."

"Don't take it wrong. You can use the elevator on the way back. While I'm at it, let me show you around the building."

The Tokyo Broadcasting Hall is a six-story ferroconcrete structure with a basement. The CIE is mainly on the fifth and sixth floors. According to Miss Kurita, there are thirteen recording studios, located on the north and west sides of the building. The east and south sides of the building face streets, and the studios are located on the north and west sides to avoid street noise. Offices and workrooms occupy the sides of the building facing the street.

Walking down the marble steps about two *ken* wide to the fourth floor, we came to a room next to the stairway with the sign "Sound Effects Center." The door was open, and we could hear the conversation taking place inside.

"Someone stole the beans?" A middle-aged man with a mustache and wearing a beret was angrily scolding a younger man. "That's why I told you to lock the door whenever you leave the room"

"I'm sorry."

"The sound of waves plays a major part in tonight's broadcast. How are we going to make the sound of waves without beans?

"I'm sorry."

"If 'I'm sorry' was enough, we wouldn't need the Occupation or the police. Somewhere our bean thief is having a snack of roasted beans."

"What can we do?"

"You're going to have to go to the market in Shinbashi and look for some beans. Go tell your sob story to the Drama Department Office and wrangle some money out of them."

The young man ran out in front of us, starting to take the stairs, as the man in the beret shouted, "Don't run! If you fall and hurt yourself, you're not going to be able to enjoy your roasted beans after the show!"

There was a big door in front of the stairway on the third floor with a placard that said "Studio 1." So this was the famous studio from where *Farm Village Hour* and *Battlefront Hour* were broadcast. We went down to the second floor. "Studio 1 is very large," said Miss Kurita. "Someday you should get the guard's permission and go in and see it. The entrance is on the third floor, but the ceiling goes all the way up to the top of the fifth floor." There were a number of small studios on the second floor. When we descended to the first floor, the stairs led right to the building's side door.

Miss Kurita pointed toward a long corridor where there was a glass door with a curtain. "BBC" was printed on the glass. Next to it was a sheet of paper with the words "No Japanese" in large letters.

"You'll have to get cleaned up before you go in there. Follow me, Mr. Yamanaka," said Miss Kurita, walking down the stairs into the basement.

My glasses fogged up again. It was warm, steam coming from somewhere, and my glasses fogged up again. I removed my glasses, and before me saw an opening one *ken* in height and width from which the steam was pouring forth. A guard emerged from the steam, saw Miss Kurita, and said: "Thanks for the portable rations. The kids are crazy about them." He bowed very low, shut the door, and left.

"This is the bathing room. It's big enough for six or seven to enter at once."

"In these times, they have the bath heating from noon? How extravagant! Just what you'd expect from the Japan Broadcasting Corporation."

"The Americans here love Japanese-style baths. They don't have the bath going in the morning and at noon for the Japanese staff, you can be sure." Indeed, at the entrance there was a sign on the post saying "Japanese may not use the bath before 5 P.M."

"But the Americans are all eating lunch now, so I think you can take your time. And I also received permission from the CIE Office and the security office."

"I'm going to take a bath?"

"I need to give you a complete makeover today. That's my job. But there's some place we need to go before that."

"A place we need to go?"

"Yes. Everyone calls it the Magic Storeroom," she said, continuing on into the depths of the dimly lit corridor. We turned a corner and faced a door marked with the words "CIE Storeroom."

"I'll come back for you in ten minutes," said Miss Kurita, after speaking to someone inside. "You're allowed to take two union suits, two white shirts, two suit jackets and two pairs of pants. Nothing more."

An odor I remembered from before the war seeped out through the crack of the open door—the odor of the clothing department of a department store in 1936 and 1937, the smell of warm milk and cloth.

"In ten minutes, then," Miss Kurita said, turning and disappearing down the hall.

Someone was already there. I stepped in gingerly, then stood near the doorway for a bit. The space was about as large as an elementary school classroom, and because the walls were concrete, it had the appearance of a giant box. It was filled by huge mountains of clothing. Four naked light bulbs illuminated them. The second mountain was a mountain of suit jackets. At the very top of the mountain I found an indescribably elegant and sturdy-looking black jacket. I reached out for it with a shout of delight.

"Thief!" a voice called out from the other side of the mountain. It was a loud voice, like that of a famous old woman who sold rice balls at Shinbashi market. "I saw it first. It's mine. Let go!" When I didn't let go, a face appeared from the other side. It was flat and broad, with a large mole to the right of the small nose. The single hair growing out of the mole twitched as the face emerged. It was a face I could never forget.

"Icchan from Gongendoko!"

"Huh?"

"I've pulled the hair out of your mole at least three times."

"Wait, that square face like a rook in chess—ah! Shin-*chan* the fan maker!"

"Yes, it's me, Shin-*chan*. And you, Icchan, you haven't changed a bit!"

"You neither."

"I'm sorry, but I need this three-button suit."

"All right," said Icchan, reluctantly letting go.

I used to play with Icchan before we entered elementary school. I'm a year older, and Icchan always used to follow me around. In short, I was the boss and he was my follower, and I used to enjoy taking anything he had from him, candy, toys, whatever. I guess old habits die hard.

"What are you doing here, Shin-*chan*?"

"I'm working in the Language Section of the CIE, and the boss is very fussy about our appearance, so I'm here looking for some clothes."

"If that's the case, we were bound to meet some time in this building. I come here once a week."

"So you're working in broadcasting?"

"No. I come to check up on the barber here. There's this organization called the BBC, and I'm the director."

"The director of the BBC?"

"It sounds important, but all it really is, is keeping an eye on the barbers serving the Occupation Forces."

"That's still pretty important. So my old pal Icchan is the director! You've really come up in the world."

Icchan disappeared from Nezu in the early Taisho Period. After graduating from elementary school, he learned the barber's trade, to follow in his father's footsteps, but he fell in love with the Mitsukoshi Youth Band, stole his mother's pin money and bought himself a saxophone. His father was furious with him. In those days, a saxophone was very expensive. You could buy one and a half barber chairs for the price of a saxophone. Icchan's father gave him two or three good whacks across the face and kicked him out of the house.

The saxophone went back to the store the same day. And the next morning, Icchan was gone.

Several rumors about his whereabouts spread through Nezu. The woman who ran the candy store came back from a funeral in Osaka and said that Icchan was playing big metal plates—cymbals, no doubt—in the Osaka Mitsukoshi Youth Band. The man who ran the dried good stores said, after coming back from a trip to Jogashima, that he saw Icchan playing a shiny flute—a piccolo, probably—in the Yokosuka Naval Band. Whenever a new story surfaced, Icchan's mother would dash off to find out whether it was true, but she always came home disappointed. Eventually Icchan's younger sister got married and her husband took over the Gongendoko Barbershop; from that time on the people of Nezu stopped talking about Icchan.

"Where did you go when you left home?" I asked, holding a union suit up to check its fit.

"I caught a ship for San Francisco," said Icchan, briskly packing wool socks into a cloth bag. "The ship had a band, so I begged them to let me join as their assistant. But they never even let me touch an instrument."

"Why not?"

"I had no talent."

"Really?"

"I realized it myself. After that the ship's barber approached me and I became his assistant."

"So there was no reason to leave home in the first place."

"That's not true. The basic English I learned on the ship came in handy, and both the ship's barber and I found a job at a hotel in San Francisco, cutting hair. I stayed and worked in the U.S. for many years. I came back to Japan in 1941. I was living in Kobe."

"You should have come back to Nezu. Think about your parents." Halfway through saying those words, I checked myself. Icchan's father got drunk during the celebrations for the fall of Nanjing, fell into Aisomegawa River and drowned, and his mother died a year later.

"The year before last, I got a job at the Imperial Hotel Barbershop, and I learned what had happened to my parents and that my sister and her husband had closed the shop and evacuated to Asamushi in Aomori, her husband's home town. I plan to go see them sometime, but for now I'm too busy. By the way, do you know how often the GIs go to the barber to keep their regulation haircuts looking the way they're supposed to?"

"To be honest, I've never thought about it."

"They get them cut once every ten days. That's per army regulations. And one more question: How many U.S. soldiers are stationed in Tokyo?"

"Thirty-three thousand, I think."

"Right. That means that thirty-three thousand soldiers have to get their hair cut every ten days. A single barber can do about twenty haircuts in a day. So here's another question: How many barbers are needed to give thirty-three thousand soldiers a regulation GI haircut every ten days?"

Seeing that I was having a hard time figuring that out, Icchan said impatiently, "One hundred sixty-five. It's no easy matter to supply that many barbers on a daily basis. The only way to assemble that many is to offer them special bonuses, overtime pay, and wool socks and union suits as inducements. The director of the BBC sounds important, but I'm really just a labor recruiter."

I'd finished selecting my allotment of clothing, but now Icchan was busily putting together a package of union suits. I looked at him, noticing the dried-apple wrinkles on his flat face, and felt the weight of time's passing.

"I'm afraid I've done a terrible thing to the 2.4 million residents of Tokyo," Icchan remarked mysteriously as he sat on one of his bundles in an effort to compress its contents. "If I'd had more courage, the Occupying army might never have come to Tokyo at all."

To sum up: The day that General MacArthur moved into the New Grand Hotel in Yokohama after landing at Atsugi Air Force Base, a finely dressed high-ranking military officer entered the barbershop of the Imperial Hotel. "I'd like a shave," he said, sitting in the chair. It was the first time a member of the Occupation Forces had entered the barbershop. The staff was nervous. As Icchan, the head barber, approached with a razor, the officer tensed up almost imperceptibly.

"I experienced very cruel racial discrimination in the States," Icchan told me. "When I returned to Japan, the U.S. government confiscated everything I owned. And on top of everything, they dropped two atomic bombs on my country, as if it were nothing. I shouldn't let this officer live. That's what I thought at that moment." But he couldn't bring himself to slit the throat of a person who sat down in a barber chair defenseless, trusting his life to the barber. He couldn't betray a client that way. Icchan calmed himself and carefully shaved the officer. When he finished, he said, both he and the officer were drenched in sweat.

"Later I learned that that officer was Lieutenant General Robert Eichelberger, commander of the Eighth Army. He'd come to Tokyo to check on the security situation. He sat down in my chair knowing well that he might be killed. If a barber in Tokyo was willing to do his work as a professional, it was safe for General MacArthur to come to Tokyo. If the barber tried to slit his throat, Tokyo was too dangerous. The general would have to remain in Yokohama. That was Eichelberger's plan when he entered the barbershop. In other words, he was an advance scout. He returned to Yokohama and reported that it was safe to go to Tokyo. When I learned that, I felt as if I had let the Japanese people down. But as a professional, I think I did the right thing, but there was a moment there... At any rate, I suppose that led to me being called to the barbershop at the GHQ PX, and then eventually being appointed the director of the BBC..."

Naturally, Icchan joined me in the bath. While we were soaking, he said to me, "Will you let me cut your hair?" At that moment, I heard a distant echo of the happy voice of the little boy who used to catch dragonflies with me in Aisomegawa River so many years ago.

January 11

It's the first time I had breakfast at home in four days. The soup is always the foul-smelling sweet-potato miso, but today's was made of something better. Tiny pieces of bacon floated together with the grease in the soup. The nasty odor of the sweet-potato miso and the greasiness of the bacon cancelled each other out, creating an unexpectedly pleasant flavor. Strangely impressed by my discovery, I was examining a piece of bacon in my chopsticks when old Mr. and Mrs. Furusawa came down from the second story and looked at me in surprise.

"What a nice haircut."

"And your suit is real wool, isn't it? With creases in your slacks! I thought some fine gentleman had dropped by."

"They're hand-me-downs from the Occupation," said my wife, coming out of the kitchen with a freshly made omelet on a large platter. It was as big and thick as something an Olympic discus thrower might heave. "This is from the army, too, as always." She'd blended a large portion of corned beef into the omelet. Bread was toasting on the hibachi, and a big tin of butter sat nearby. These were all probably brought home by my daughters; when you surveyed the scene it was clear that we were living on the largesse of America.

"There used to be a barbershop in the neighborhood called Gongendoko, and when I was a young I played with their little boy, Icchan, and got into all sorts of trouble with him. I just happened to run into him the other day at the Tokyo Broadcasting Hall—the first time we'd seen each other in thirty-three years. The expression 'the times have been kind to him' couldn't suit him better. He's become the head of all the barbers working for the U.S. military. He's got an office in the basement of the Imperial Hotel and is in charge of more than two hundred Japanese barbers. It's really something. He cut my hair himself. He says that two out of three times, he cuts MacArthur's hair."

"Well, I guess your head has moved up in the world then."

"It's Icchan who's moved up in the world. My head is still the same as always."

"But he used the same clippers that touched the head of Emperor Moatside on you, didn't he?"

"He uses special clippers for MacArthur. And he's not permitted to use the same clippers he uses for American officers on any Japanese. That's been regulated by the 'Special Hygiene Regulations for Barbers and Beauticians' set by the Japanese government."

"I see. It's true that our heads are dirty. Most Japanese have lice, and a lot also have ringworm."

As he sucked toothlessly on a piece of bread, Mrs. Furusawa interjected, "That's enough of that kind of talk. We're eating."

Mr. Furusawa rubbed his shaved head in chagrin and slumped a little, slurping his soup. He hadn't shaved his head to prevent lice.

He shaved it because he had lost both his son and daughter-in-law, his grandson, and his granddaughter-in-law in air raids, and his sole surviving granddaughter was the kept woman of an American military officer living in the Imperial Hotel. He may have been thinking of himself as a kind of lay priest. Perhaps because such memories had been stirred up, we ate the rest of our breakfast in silence.

My wife served real roasted green tea. She has found a place that exchanges a canister of dried egg powder for a canister of tea—another example of the magic powers of Occupation goods.

"Those hygiene regulations are pretty strict, they say," I said, inviting Mr. Furusawa out onto the sunny veranda to continue our conversation. "Of course the Japanese government issued those regulations based on the wishes of the GHQ. Icchan was complaining about how restrictive they are, and how much they slow things down. When you cut a GI's hair, you have to take the clippers apart in front of him, wash them with soap and water, and disinfect them in cresol. Towels can't be washed at the barbershop, but have to be sent out to the cleaners after each use. Shaving brushes are banned as unsanitary. His job is to see to it that three thousand three hundred soldiers get their standard GI cut every ten days, with only two hundred barbers. I can understand his position."

"Does the Occupation supply the towels, soap, cresol and the cleaners?"

"Of course."

"Well, then, that's okay, isn't it? Your friend Icchan is just sulking. After all, upon the orders of the Occupation, which no one would dare disobey, towels, soap and cresol all pour into the general controller's office. You could make a lot of money if you managed to strategically reroute some of those goods."

"Come to think of it, Icchan was wearing a gold Omega watch and a ring with some kind of gem."

"Of course. That's how the world works."

"But the Americans really value cleanliness."

"I've heard that they're having a lot of trouble with roundworms."

"Roundworms?"

"My granddaughter's lover said that almost all the GIs are suffering from roundworms. The GHQ has done a quick investigation, and the culprit is Japanese produce. We use night soil to fertilize our crops. That seems to be the cause…"

"I see."

"So the GHQ has made plans for hydroponic cultivation in Yokohama."

"What's that?"

"Using water instead of soil to grow plants."

"Can you do that?"

"It's not impossible. We were researching it here in Japan, too. I read about it in *Asahi Science* several years ago." Mr. Furusawa had built Furusawa Enterprises into the leading supplier of agriculture tools and fertilizer in all of eastern Tokyo in a single generation, and he knows a lot about farming. "They also say that venereal disease is spreading like wildfire among the GIs, and on top of that they're getting roundworms. That must have led the GHQ to conclude that we Japanese are really a filthy, unhygienic people. And so they look at our barbershops in the same way."

Duly impressed by Mr. Furusawa's keen analysis, I left for work with Ueno Hill clearly visible against the backdrop of a bright blue winter sky. Trying to argue with Language Section Chief Hall, who is behind the plot to replace the Japanese written language with *romaji*, is like digging a well to save a burning house, but nevertheless, I feel I have to persevere. I decided to drop in on Mr. Takahashi for another lesson about my native tongue. And by asking how his son Shoichi, who has left home to live on his own, is doing, I might find out about my own son, Kiyoshi, who is living with Shoichi.

I was heading for Mr. Takahashi's back door when I suddenly heard the sound of hammering behind me. I looked back in surprise to see three carpenters working on my brother's house on the corner. The roof had been completely removed and ten white pillars had been raised.

A second story? I stood and watched the carpenters work. There are no building materials or carpenters to be found anywhere, and even if you could somehow get your hands on them, they'd be incredibly expensive. It would take mountains of yen just to put up a little tool shed these days. The only way to get wood or workers is to barter daily necessities for them. Adding a second story to a house in times like these is an extraordinary extravagance. Sen-*chan* must have gotten the lumber from the Americans, I thought.

The house originally belonged to my brother. After he was killed in the air raid in May, Sen-*chan* from the Mimatsuya had been living there. She'd been my brother's lover, so I didn't object to it, but gradually I began avoiding passing the house whenever possible. My daughters Fumiko and Takeko are now living there, too. When she was younger, Sen-*chan* had been a Kisakata geisha, and I feel certain that she had something to do with my daughters becoming the mistresses of high-ranking American officers at the Imperial Hotel. That makes me want to say my piece to Sen-*chan* whenever I pass the house—which is why I avoid doing so whenever possible.

"I was just making some coffee," said Tomoe in a clear voice, sliding open the glass doors. "If you're not in a hurry, can I offer you a cup?"

"Where are Fumiko and Takeko?

"These last three days they've been… at work."

Tomoe muffled her voice when she said the word "work." I knew what Fumiko's "work" was, at least. She was Lieutenant Hall's bedmate. Takeko was probably doing something similar.

"Tokiko, Kayoko and Kumiko all left for the Imperial Hotel early this morning. It's just me and Sen-*chan* here today."

When I first met Tomoe in May of last year, she was the young wife of a large saké brewer in Toride. When her husband was killed, she was left to care for her father-in-law, who had gone of his rocker, and her two children, but she always kept her sufferings to herself. You would never know from her modestly arranged hair and her gentle eyes with their long lashes that she also made her living by prostituting herself to an American officer.

"We have peanuts, too, Shinsuke," said Sen-*chan*, sticking her head out from the house. She was wearing a red padded jacket, and a cigarette dangled from her scarlet lips. "Peanuts from the Americans. They're good." You could tell at a glance that she was a former geisha.

If I refused, I'd offend them. I followed Tomoe into the house. My brother had kept a desk and a large chair in his spacious, earthen-floor entryway, where he used to ply the trades of moneylender, employment agent, and other roles thankfully still mysterious to me. Now the entryway had wood flooring and the left wall was lined with a fine glass-doored bookcase filled with difficult-looking books.

"I didn't know my brother was such a reader."

"The only thing he read was the stock market quotes," said Sen-*chan*, passing a can of peanuts my way.

"Well, you're certainly not reading these... Could these be yours, Tomoe?"

"I used to teach Japanese literature at a girls school in Mito," said Tomoe, bringing me a cup of coffee. "These books are from the house in Toride."

"Tomoe is a graduate of Tokyo Women's Higher Normal School. With a major in Japanese literature. Impressive, no?" said Sen-*chan* with pride, as if she were describing her own accomplishments. She beckoned to the carpenters and offered them coffee.

"I had a feeling you were educated," I said, expressing my appreciation for both the coffee and her academic background.

"I wanted to review my studies. And in the future, perhaps my children will read them. I simply wasn't able to let them go."

"That's right. How are your children? As I recall, they're staying with your brother in Fukushima."

"The boys will be here in less than a week. That's why we're adding the second story," said Sen-*chan*.

"You were lucky to get permission for them to come here," said one of the carpenters squatting behind us. "The population of Tokyo last September was 3.4 million, but by the end of last year it was over 4 million. That's an increase of two hundred thousand a month. There's nothing to eat, nowhere to live, and the city can't accommodate this growth, so M has issued an order to keep people out."

"M" was the new nickname for MacArthur.

"Even M can't stop people from coming here if they want to," said another carpenter.

"There are more than a hundred thousand kids who were evacuated en masse and can't get back. Families who left the city for the countryside are in the same boat. And there's no room in the countryside, either. Then on top of that, another seven or eight million will be repatriating from overseas. The only places those people can settle are Tokyo and Osaka. I think the city's going to keep right on growing."

"If they try to come in, the MPs will pound them."

"They'll come anyway."

"You don't have to worry about these boys here, though. These people have a connection that trumps anything. Anyway, let's get back to work. If we finish this job in a week, I'll give you a bonus. How about five packs of Lucky Strikes, ten to a pack?" The carpenters quickly returned to work.

Drinking my coffee, I recalled a memorandum I had cut a stencil for the other day. It was a report about how the Yoyogi Police Station had had to place some twenty officers on guard in Yoyogihara after Tokyo residents started cutting down large pine, oak and zelkova trees. Residents of Kanda and Asakusa were the first to do this, and it sparked a run in the area, with people coming from all over the city at night with two-wheeled carts. The Yoyogi Fukamachi Neighborhood Association took note of this, and on the night of January 8th, they rallied the entire neighborhood association and cut down five hundred large trees. An MP happened to be passing by and reported it to the Yoyogi Police Station, "I know that Japan had outlawed Shinto as the state religion, but I can't believe that people should be permitted to transform Yoyogihara, connected to Meiji Shrine, into a razed field." In response, the police station sent out guards. Given this kind of incident, I could understand why the GHQ would want to outlaw more people from coming into Tokyo.

"I know your connection must be someone important in the GHQ, but are you sure this is a good idea?"

"What?"

"Won't having your children here cause problems?"

"You're worried that my children will become juvenile delinquents if they find out what kind of work I do, is that it?"

"Not exactly. After all, these are the very hard times, and it's a struggle to survive. People need to do what they need to do, and I think that anything short of thievery or murder is perfectly justifiable. Your children will understand that. No one has the right to criticize you."

"Then what kind of problems are you talking about?"

"Well, they lost their father in an American air raid. Now the Americans have taken their mother from them. The Americans are the enemies of both their parents. That's what I'd be worried about. That seems to be a possible reason for your children going astray."

And then something completely unexpected happened: Tomoe laughed. "I chose this work precisely because it has to do with America."

"Chose it?"

"We're living with runaway inflation, prices doubling every month. You can have all the money in the world and it won't pay for much of anything. I do, however, have my own small savings, from selling the Toride house and our belongings, and I think I could have supported myself as a smuggler or a shopkeeper in the black market." Tomoe was no longer laughing. She was filled with self-assurance. "I didn't become a smuggler because I had something else in mind."

"In mind?"

"Yes. I share my pillow with an American military officer every night because I need to."

"What need?" I stammered, taken aback by her reference to "sharing her pillow."

Sen-*chan* slid toward us on the tatami. Underneath her heavy makeup, I could see the same self-assurance brimming up in her eyes. "Think about it. Your daughters Fumiko and Takeko looked up to their sister Kinuko like a goddess. She was a genius at the abacus. She worked in the Metals Department of the head office of Mitsubishi Corporation. She was such a beauty that except for nights when there was an air-raid alert, she received a love letter every day, so the Yamanaka family always had something to light the bath with at night. She married the heir to the largest fertilizer wholesaler in Tokyo. Her life seemed perfect. You must know how proud Fumiko and Takeko were of their sister, Shinsuke."

"You always pack so much into what you say, Sen-*chan*, I have no idea where you're going with it. What are you trying to tell me?"

"What I'm trying to tell you is, who was it that took Kinuko from Fumiko and Takeko?"

"A bomb dropped by the Americans."

"And that's why Fumiko and Takeko are sleeping with Americans now."

"That's the part I don't understand."

"You are dense, Shinsuke. Think about it. Who took Tokiko Furusawa's parents, her brother, and her sweet sister-in-law from her?"

"The American bombs."

"Kayoko Makiguchi was the daughter of an oil wholesaler in Yotsuya. Kumiko Kurokawa's family were caretakers for the Iwasaki family in Takanawa. Now both of them are orphans. Who's to blame?"

"Again, the American bombs."

"And what about me? My nineteen-year-old son, whom I struggled to raise all on my own, a single mother, was killed by the Americans on Leyte. My place of work in Asakusa was burned down by American bombs. I even had to lose the life of my precious lover..."

"I get it. All seven of the women here hate the Americans and are bent on taking their revenge against them. Is that the idea?"

"Right."

"But I don't get the next part. Why are you... giving your bodies to the Americans?

"As part of our revenge. We intend to make the Americans pay for having cast us down into the depths of despair. To do that, we have to get close to them. We can't take our revenge unless we're sleeping with them. Please remember that."

A chill ran down my spine as a thought pierced my heart like a spear.

"Revenge?"

"Yes, I think you could say that."

"You're going to infect them with syphilis." They both looked at me as if someone had just pointed out to them that their underwear was showing.

"You're going to sacrifice your bodies, catch syphilis from someone, and then, what's the name of that germ?

"*Treponema pallidum.*"

"Yes, and spread that *Treponema* to the Americans. That's just the kind of plan you'd think of, Sen-*chan*. And you've persuaded my Fumiko and Takeko to do the same. I know you won't agree with what I'm about to say, but you've got to give up this foolish idea. 'Life is the seed of all things.'"

"And as we used to say when I was a geisha, 'What's good's a seed if you've nowhere to plant it!'" Sen-*chan* laughed, and Tomoe joined her.

"This is no laughing matter. What good is revenge if you harm yourselves?"

"He's so old-fashioned."

"I think he's read too many potboilers." They both laughed heartily.

Tomoe was the first to regain control of herself. "We're thinking of something much bigger than that."

"Bigger? Like what?"

"Overturning the policies of the Occupation."

This time I looked at them as astonished as if someone had pointed out that my fly was open. It seemed strange that a statement of such grand proportions could come out of Tomoe's small, well-formed mouth. I took some time to quiet my emotions and ask: "What Occupation policy are you planning to overthrow?

"We will destroy a policy that would make Japan into something other than Japan."

"And what might that be, for example?"

"Not now. We've promised among ourselves not to talk about this with anyone else."

"Are you serious? Are you really serious about this?"

"Yes."

"And Shinsuke, I'll put a curse on you if you mention this to anyone. Do you understand? Keep quiet."

"Who could I tell it to, something as crazy as this? But no matter how I look at it, I can't see how just the seven of you can have any effect on the GHQ."

"We won't know unless we try."

Silence fell over the three of us, the only sound coming from the hammering on the second floor.

After a while, Sen-*chan* tapped her lap. "That's right, there was something else I wanted to say to you. I just wanted you to know, Shinsuke, it wasn't me who suggested the girls do this. It was Takeko who first started talking about revenge. I want you to get that straight."

"But you must be the strategist."

"No, that's Tomoe. I'm just the… instructor. Of course, when I'm needed, I also do my part."

"Instructor?"

"Aside from Tomoe, they're all very young. They're still children, really. They have no battlefield experience. Without my help, they'd just lie there like beached tuna and men get bored with that right away. I teach them how to make the right sounds, how to use tissues…"

"That's enough."

"But they're all very quick learners."

"I don't want to hear about it." I got up and went to look at the bookshelf. What incredible determination Takeko showed for a girl less than twenty years old. She had the palest skin of my three daughters, and seemed so delicate. Just the word November and would give her frostbite, and her hands and feet would swell up like balloons. When it got really cold after New Year's, the swollen areas would start to get infected and raw. At the end of March, when the first cherries started to bloom in Kyushu, she would recover as if nothing had happened, but up to that time she had to have Vaseline applied to the chafing and keep it covered with gauze and cloth bandaging. Kinuko always did this for Takeko. She also washed the gauze and the bandages. Chapped hands are painful, but chapped feet are worse. The damaged skin hurts when it comes into contact with your shoes, and just walking is an ordeal. Kinuko knew this and she used to let Takeko lean on her shoulder as she walked her to school every morning. The American's carpetbombing took the life of the sister who had been so kind to her; I could understand why she had been the one to first suggest revenge. But even still…

As I stood thinking about these things, I gazed absentmindedly at the spines of the books in the bookcase. Gradually something began to materialize, leaving me so startled that I forgot for a moment what the two women had been telling me. *Principles of the Forms, Pronunciations, and Meanings of Chinese Characters*; *Study of the Origins of Chinese Characters*; *A Study of Chinese Words in the Japanese Language*… a great many of the books on Tomoe's bookshelf were also in the piles of books in the Imperial Hotel room of Language Section Chief Hall.

"Have you been lending your books to anyone recently?"

"No," said Tomoe, looking at me suspiciously. "I haven't lent them to anyone. These are our textbooks, so I need them here."

"Textbooks?"

"We're studying Japanese," Sen-*chan* piped up. "Because of her training and experience, Tomoe is teaching us, and she's a good teacher." She walked to the blackboard hanging from the lintel in the back of the room and wrote three rather complicated characters: 櫻 獸 壽. She then recited three little chants:

Nikai no onna wa ki ga hen da.
Ro ro ta ichi-ro no inu.
Samurai no fue wa ichi inchi.

[*Nikai no onna wa ki ga hen da*: "The *woman* (*onna* 女) on the *second floor* (*nikai*, a homophone for two shells 貝貝) is *off her head* (*ki ga hen*, a homophone for the side element is 'tree' 木)" equals 櫻, meaning "tower."]

[*Ro ro ta ichi-ro no inu*: "*Ruff!* (*ro*, reading the character for 'mouth' as *ro* in *katakana*, which is written with the same symbol, but used here as onomatopoeia for a barking sound) *Ruff!* (*ro*), in the *field* (*ta* 田) there's one (*ichi ro no* 一口の, literally *one mouth*, with 'mouth' serving as a counter for dog here) dog (*inu* 犬)" equals 獸, or "beast").]

[*Samurai no fue wa ichi inchi*: "The samurai's (士) flute (*fue*, or the *katakana* symbols *fu* フ and *e* エ) is one (一) inch (or *sun*, 寸)" equals 壽, or "felicitations," "long life."]

Her strange chanting was obviously a key to remembering how to write them.

"See how easy that makes it? Because of my profession, I often have to write the character *kotobuki*, 'felicitations,' but I always forget how and have to check a dictionary, which is a bother. But now that I know the secret is 'the samurai's flute is one inch,' I never forget how to write it. Tomoe has taught us a lot of these tricks for remembering characters."

"It's called mnemonics," said Tomoe. "*Kanji* are complicated and hard to learn. Many find studying *kanji* onerous, but it doesn't have to be. There are a lot of ways to make it fun."

As she spoke, I wondered if Tomoe could overcome Chief Hall's arguments. "What do you think of the idea that we could eliminate our writing system?" I asked her. "That we'd suffer no inconvenience, because the spoken language would remain?"

"That's just foolishness."

"Why?"

"The spoken language is always changing. That's its inherent nature. But the written language expresses various concepts directly, visually, and in a concrete form on a level that transcends the changes in the spoken language. That's a rather complicated way of saying it. Let me try again. The spoken language is always changing, and it's supposed to change. It's vague and freewheeling— that's the spoken language. The written language stays the same. The spoken language could be compared to a boat, and the written language to an anchor. The anchor keeps the boat from being washed away."

"I see."

"So, because of the written language, temporally, the culture can be transmitted without interruption for centuries and even millennia, and spatially, we can communicate with ten billion other users of the language. The written language also links us to the distant future. That's difficult for the spoken language. The idea that Japanese would survive without the written language is fanciful."

"But *romaji* are a written language. What about giving up *kana* and *kanji* and writing our language in *romaji*?"

"But that would cut us off on the vertical axis, the axis of time. The Japanese of the future would never be able to know anything about their past."

With the help of Tomoe and Mr. Takahashi from the newspaper office, I just might be able to beat Language Section Chief Hall.

January 12

At 8:30 A.M., as usual, I arrived at the Documentation Section and printed the interoffice communications. My official status right now—according to the orders of the War-End Central Liaison Bureau—is full-time employee of the Language Section of the SCAP Civilian Information and Education section (the menacing CIE), but I'm determined not to give up my job cutting and printing stencils of interoffice memos for the Metropolitan Police Department. I don't fully understand the reason myself, but somehow this is what my intuition tells me to do. In these tumultuous, confusing times, my intuition is all I have to guide myself.

Today's main interoffice memo was a letter of encouragement from the GHQ Public Relations Section to the Japanese police.

Recently Japanese newspapers are claiming that there has been a rise in crime, but the statistics show that there is no crime wave occurring in Japan now. According to the Police Department's official statistics, in the three months of September, October and November 1945, the number of crimes, even with changes in population factored in, are actually lower than they were in those three months in 1940. Newspapers are claiming that "the largest crime wave since the establishment of the modern police force" is underway, and writing of "the lamentable failures of the police to deal with rapidly rising rates of crime." Such claims are not only belied by reality, but are also extremely dangerous in the light of the present state of Japanese society during the tumult of the early postwar period. We call on the police not to be disturbed by the attitudes expressed in the Japanese newspapers and encourage them to continue in the course of their duties as they have up to now.

After I finished printing and delivering this to the Documentation Section Annex, I read a copy of the memo I'd kept for myself while sipping coffee brought to me by the former proprietor of the Hongo Bar. I wondered why the GHQ found it necessary to send this kind of letter of encouragement to the police department. "They're going to make that one public, aren't they?" asked the cook.

"Yes, it seems that they're going to hand out this memo to the journalists at the regular weekly press conference at noon today."

"That must be why Umetani wanted an extra fifty copies."

"Which means it's just a trick. The GHQ is indirectly putting pressure on the press. If they know that the GHQ is supporting the police, they'll go easy on the criticism of the police."

"I guess the GHQ takes good care of its friends."

"It's in their own interest. As the GHQ, they want the world to think that the Occupation is going smoothly, that they're preserving the peace, so they don't want the newspapers reporting the truth."

"I see."

Come to think of it, this morning's interoffice communications contained a joint report from the vice ministers of the First Ministry for the Demobilization (until last November, the Army Ministry) and the Second Ministry for the Demobilization (the former Navy Ministry) to the emperor.

It's well-known that many of the demobilized soldiers have become black marketers, and some of them, known as "Special Attack Corps officers gone bad," have taken up thievery as a livelihood. They were sent off to war by cheering crowds waving the banner of the Rising Sun, but they came back defeated, in tattered uniforms, and were greeted with cold glares. It's understandable, given the circumstances, that many of them took to the black market or became bandits and thieves. A large number also rushed into the welcoming arms of the Committees to Aid Demobilized Soldiers set up by the Communist Party in Yokohama and Maizuru. So the emperor summoned these two vice ministers and inquired, "Can't something be done about this?" The report included in the interoffice memo this morning was the reply of these two vice-ministers:

> The majority of demobilized soldiers, apart from a small group of farmers who have land to return to, find themselves facing the dramatic changes the nation is undergoing, a cold reception from the public and the impossibility of supporting themselves under the present economic circumstances. They have lost the will to live and are experiencing a state of profound despair, and some have turned to vice. The total number who have

become active in the black market or taken up thievery is small, however, and most are non-commissioned officers or enlisted men of relatively low levels of education. Nevertheless, if this trend is left unchecked, in the future there is a significant possibility that even those of the officer class will succumb to these tendencies, and, because they are superior to ordinary soldiers in both intellect and strength of character, that would indeed be a lamentable turn of events. Various assistance associations are striving admirably to respond to the needs of these unemployed demobilized military personnel by assisting them to find gainful employment, as they are for the general population, but demobilized soldiers are also experiencing a serious loss of morale, and these efforts have not met with the desired rate of success to date. It is thought that powerful material and spiritual support are needed immediately.

I had to shake my head in disgust several times as I cut this stencil. The officials whom the emperor had turned to for a solution had done little more than string together a series of half-baked comments, reflecting a complete lack of urgency or even concern. The generalissimo was simply being tactfully led in circles by his former faithful ministers. And how dare they say that ordinary soldiers are inferior to their officers in intelligence and strength of character? These former military leaders were making mockery of both the emperor and the soldiers.

"Ordinary citizens are involved in the black market and embezzling government property, decommissioned soldiers are black marketers and thieves, the U.S. military are muggers and rapists—the crime rate must be much higher than it was before or during the war. Everyone knows that. MacArthur just doesn't want to admit it," said the former proprietor of the Hongo Bar, heading back to the kitchen.

"Why doesn't Emperor Moatside want to admit it?" I asked.

"Because he thinks he's a brilliant leader. He must think that it's impossible for crimes to be committed in any place where he's in charge."

It's Saturday, so the Language Section of the CIE is closed. When I got back to Nezu I went immediately to Sen-*chan*'s house on the corner, where I read three books about the Japanese language and asked Tomoe various questions before Musei Tokugawa's program reading from *Gone with the Wind* came on the radio at seven. This Monday I have to engage in a debate with the chief of the CIE Language Section, the director of the Language Simplification Unit, a man with two doctorates by the age of thirty-four and the lover of Fumiko. That's why I'm studying so hard.

January 13

After breakfast I went to my neighbor Mr. Takahashi's house, hoping to persuade him to give me another lecture about the Japanese language. "Will you come to Nezu Gongen again and give me a little talk?" The sky above was almost frighteningly clear and blue. There was no wind.

"A new kind of cigarette is going on sale today. I'd like to try to buy a pack."

"What is it called?"

"Peace. A pack of ten unfiltered cigarettes is 7 yen."

"It has an English name? It's all so strange to me. Just a few months ago if you uttered an English word people would call you a traitor and throw stones at you. Now we're naming our cigarettes in English. By the way, I've brought you some Lucky Strikes as my tuition." I loosened my cloth bundle and showed him the pack of cigarettes. His features melted in happiness for a moment, but then, saying that he wanted to try to buy a pack of Peace anyway, just for the hell of it, we headed out to the main street. We tried three tobacco shops on the way to Nezu Gongen, but they were sold out. There had been lines in front of all of them from five in the morning, and they had sold out just fifteen minutes after opening at nine.

"They certainly are popular. I'll get up early tomorrow morning and get in line. I'll buy four or five packs and give them all to you," I said

Mr. Takahashi shook his head. "They're only on sale on Sundays and holidays, and there's a limit of one pack to a person. Peace is always hard to come by, I suppose."

We went to the western edge of the shrine precincts and, like last time, seated ourselves on the writer's stone. I gave Mr. Takahashi the entire cloth bundle, which contained a carton of Lucky Strikes. Just as he was haltingly starting on his lecture, Neighborhood Association Leader Kiichiro Aoyama came up to us, his Inverness cloak flapping in the breeze and his usual oily smile on his lips.

"I see you're having a little pleasure outing."

As I was privately fuming that no matter how bright the sun was shining or how still the wind was, we were sitting outdoors in the middle of January, where even the world's biggest fool wouldn't be engaging in a pleasure outing, Aoyama slipped in between us.

"I suppose Gongen-*sama* led me here. Shin, actually, I had a favor to ask, and I was just thinking of stopping by your house."

I don't know how where he got off calling me "Shin." I turned away.

"May I have a cigarette?" he asked, and before I could say no, he took two from the pack I was holding, stuck one behind his ear, and lit the other from the end of Mr. Takahashi's cigarette, all with the smooth grace of a skilled conjurer.

"Four families in one house is hard to bear. I try to get out and about like this whenever I can." Posing, he puffed on his cigarette, two creases neatly forming between his brows.

"Pretentious jerk," I muttered to myself as I exhaled smoke. "Everyone in Nezu is living four families to a house," I said out loud. "You're not the only one suffering." Nezu had survived the bombings, perhaps through the protection of Gongen-*sama*; as a result, hordes of people with only the most tenuous relations living here had converged on the area like an avalanche.

"Yes, that's true. These Western cigarettes sure are great."

"They say that an average of fifty windows are stolen from the trains every day, for the glass," I said, repeating one of the facts that I'd gleaned from an interoffice memo.

Mr. Takahashi nodded. "At any rate, this is no place to live. If it goes on like this, Tokyo's going to become one giant slum, a living hell. That's why the GHQ has issued the order limiting the population to three million. They want to keep the population down until they get the city up and running properly again. Since it's MacArthur's order, maybe people will listen. In other words, your problem may be resolved soon, Mr. Aoyama."

"Hmm." Aoyama neatly extinguished his cigarette and tucked it behind his empty ear. "There are exceptions to the order. They're allowing people who they believe are critical to rebuilding Tokyo to move here, so the population of Nezu just keeps growing with carpenters, plasterers and construction workers."

What a boor, I thought. Takahashi's gallant attempt at smoothing things over did not play for me. "What is it that you want, exactly?" I asked without ceremony. "We were in the middle of something important here."

"You seem to have gotten a job with the Occupation. Congratulations." As usual, he had all the latest information.

"And?"

"Three of the people living with me are out of work. I was hoping you could find something for them."

"I work in the Language Section. The Language Section of the CIE, not the Occupation employment office. You can understand that much, can't you? Try someone else if you're looking for jobs with the Occupation. For example, the employment office at Koishikawa, or the American Club."

"These people I'm thinking of can't speak English or type. They don't have a nurse's or driver's licenses. That's why I'm counting on you, Shin. I'd be happy if you could even get them jobs washing dishes at some base. The GI's leftovers go to the Japanese staff, I've heard. I also heard that the Japanese cooks prepare extra food, to make sure there are leftovers. They do it on purpose, and then share it with the Japanese employees later. Isn't that a beautiful example of brotherly love? And the GIs also cut off the crusts of their bread and throw them away, which the Japanese staff retrieves. That would solve the food shortage in my household. The workers at the Occupation bread factories are allotted one loaf a day for their own consumption, they say. I'd like to know if that's true. I'd be indebted to you for life if you got these three jobs at a bread factory."

"Can't help you."

"Is that so?" Aoyama rose. "I'd think having me in your debt would be very useful to you in the future."

"Let me make myself clear. First, as I said, I work at the Language Section of the CIE, not a place that recommends people for jobs with the Occupation. Second, last year I had my three-wheeled truck taken away, and on top of that I was thrown into prison—because *you* reported me to the authorities. You might think that's nothing, but my bitterness toward you will remain burned into my heart for as long as I live. Even if the Language Section were the personnel department, I wouldn't lift a finger for you. And let me just add, while we're at it: stop calling me Shin."

"Tokyo Seven Rose," said Aoyama, in an affected, stagey manner. "That's a nice name."

"Seven is plural, so shouldn't it be Tokyo Seven Roses?" asked Mr. Takahashi.

Aoyama just ignored him, and murmured again: "Tokyo Seven Rose."

"What's that supposed to be?"

"The name of a group of seven beautiful women, Shinsuke. A name that may well become known throughout Tokyo, depending on you."

Hearing the word "seven" came as a shock.

"The first rose is, they say, thirty-six or thirty-seven, a former Asakusa geisha. The refined technique she's acquired over her long professional career has earned her the popularity of high-ranking GHQ officials, they say... The second rose is said to be thirty-one or thirty-two, a widow, originally from north Kanto. She's as beautiful as an actress, well-educated for a woman, a graduate of a teachers college, and is the favorite of someone of the officer class... Rose number three. Eighteen or nineteen, they say. The daughter of a well-to-do tradesman. She lost her entire family in the air raids. Petite and cute, fresh as a maid, the object of the affections of another GHQ official..."

Sen-*chan*, Tomoe, now Kayoko Makiguchi. How had he unearthed the personal histories of the seven women living in my late brother's house? They were careful not to stand out, so how...

"Rose number four. Also reputed to be eighteen or nineteen. The eldest daughter of the caretaker of a certain very wealthy family. She lost everything in the air raids, and is now under the protection of a high-ranking GHQ official. She has the prominent features of an actress who plays male roles in Takarazuka, and is another first-rate beauty..."

Kumiko Kurokawa. No one outside our family is supposed to even know that the seven were "working" at the Imperial Hotel.

"Rose number five. Again, said to be about twenty. The youngest daughter of a wealthy family in Senju, a beauty with a somewhat exotic, foreign look. Energetic and lively. Excels at tennis, pleasing a GHQ official on the court during the day and in bed at night…"

Tokiko Furusawa.

"The sixth and seventh roses are sisters. The older is a very graceful beauty, and the special friend of a GHQ naval officer. The younger is lovelier than a flower—"

"You'd better stop with your nonsense right there."

"You know as well as me that it's not nonsense."

"Get out of here.

"I'll get out of here if that's what you want. But I'll be back to your house in four or five days. For those four or five days, no one will know anything about Tokyo Seven Rose. But depending on how our conversation goes then, everyone in Nezu may know the surprising truth about these beauties." Flapping his cape like a flag, he walked toward the shrine building.

Mr. Takahashi silently smoked two or three Lucky Strikes, then murmured, "During the war he lorded it over us with the threat of the authorities, and now he pretends to be one of the hoi polloi, but he's still only interested in pushing people around. Don't pay any attention to that bastard. Ignore him."

"But, to tell the truth, what he said… it may not be the whole truth, but he's not that far off."

"Gifu, Ehime, Tochigi, Ibaraki—all of them use complicated characters with a lot of strokes and seem to be hard-to-read place names, but for the people who live there, there's nothing the least bit difficult about them," Mr. Takahashi started right in. He picked up a branch, and wrote the character for *iwao* on the ground. "I've been able to write my name, Iwao Takahashi, since I was in first grade. Considering *kanji* difficult simply because they have a lot of strokes is a ridiculously shallow argument."

January 14

"The idea that *kanji* are difficult because they have a large number of strokes is a ridiculously shallow argument."

This was how I began my presentation to Navy Lieutenant

Commander Robert King Hall, when he appeared at the CIE Language Section office at 2 P.M. It was, of course, just a rehash of my lesson with Mr. Takahashi yesterday.

"Do you follow me, Lieutenant Commander? Even a Japanese first grader can read *kanji* like 鯱 (*shachi*), 湊 (*minato*), 錦 (*nishiki*) and 邱 (*kyu*)—and write them, too." I wrote the *kanji* on a sheet of the personal stationery sitting on his desk, using his beloved Parker fountain pen. "Why are first-graders so gifted? Because these *kanji* appear in the names of their favorite sumo wrestlers. On the radio and in the newspapers they're always hearing and reading names like *Shachi*nosato, *Dewaminato*, *Kusunishiki* and *Taikyuzan*. As a result, they don't find them at all difficult."

"That's interesting," said the thirty-four-year-old officer who is plotting to reform the Japanese language, nodding as he spooned sugar into the cup of coffee that Miss Kurita had brought him. "Please go on."

"They also can easily read such characters as 壇 (*dan*), 襷 (*tasuki*), 櫓 (*yagura*), 掬 (*sukui*), 蹴 (*keri*) and 裾 (*suso*), and some of them can even write them. I'm talking about first graders here. Amazing, isn't it?"

"The secret is in sumo again, right?"

"Right. They know the sumo throw called *butsudangaeshi*, so they can read and write the character *dan*. Similarly, those other complicated *kanji* I mentioned are in the names of sumo techniques. *Tasuki zori, uwate yagura, sukui nage, nimai keri, suso harai.* As a result, one can't necessarily conclude that a *kanji* is difficult just because it has many strokes."

"To the best of my knowledge, there are fifty thousand characters. I can't imagine that they're all used in sumo."

"I'm not finished," I said, pausing to sip some coffee that Miss Kurita had brought me, also to compose myself before continuing. "There are, on the other hand, *kanji* with ridiculously few strokes, but..." and here I wrote the kanji down that looks like this 丶, "very few Japanese can read it." Until Mr. Takahashi explained it to me, I had no idea what it meant, either. "This *kanji* is read..."

"*Chu*. It means flame or lamp."

"You're right." I had to admit I was impressed. It's a shame he's an American, I thought momentarily as I wrote the *kanji* 丨 . With his encyclopedic knowledge of characters, he should have been Chinese. "Now if you can read this, I'd say you're qualified to be a lecturer in Japanese at Tokyo Imperial University."

"It's read *kon*. It means to penetrate from top to bottom."

I was getting unnerved. Maybe his claim to have graduated from four universities and hold two doctorates was true after all. I remembered one more piece of ammunition that Mr. Takahashi had prepared me with. I wrote 乂 on the sheet of paper.

"*Gai*," he replied without a moment's hesitation. "It's a depiction of two blades crossing—a scythe. It means to cut, I believe." Fumiko's patron leaned back in his chair. "Any more questions?"

"That's enough."

"Is that all? You're no fun."

"Now on to the conclusion. As I just demonstrated, the difficulty of *kanji* has nothing to do with the number of strokes. A *kanji* you're familiar with is easy, even if it has many strokes. On the other hand, a character that you rarely see can be quite difficult, even if it only has very few strokes."

"And?"

"The idea that *kanji* need to be outlawed because they're difficult is short-sighted. Moreover, in Japan *kanji* have a strong ally—*furigana*, the reading of the character written alongside it in phonetic *kana*. If you think a *kanji* you're using might be difficult to read, you can just write *furigana* alongside it. So there's no need to convert the Japanese written language into *romaji*."

"I'm afraid your argument has a fatal flaw, Father."

"What?" The words "father" and "fatal flaw" had stopped me in my tracks.

"What you've said is one hundred percent correct as far as reading *kanji* is concerned, Father. But what about writing them? You may be able read the *kanji* for rose 薔薇, but it's pretty difficult to write them. If you write *kana* alongside 黴毒, which means syphilis, any elementary school student can read it, but unless they'd studied very hard, they probably couldn't write it."

"That's not so." The lesson I'd received from Tomoe the day

before came back to me. "You can remember how to write it by taking it apart."

"How do you take it apart?"

"For example, the *kanji* 戀, for love." Repeating the mnemonic "heart (心) that proclaims (言) 'Dearest, dearest' (糸 糸)," I proceeded to combine all of those elements into the *kanji* 戀. "The *kanji* for bear 熊," I went on, "combines the *katakana* for *mu* (ム) plus the *kanji* for month (月) plus the *katakana hi* (ヒ), and *don-don-don-don,* the sound for "lumbering like a bear," one stroke (丶) for each *don.* Fish (魚) is remembered by the phrase *kutta wa yonhiki* (I ate four), with the *katakana ku* (ク) and the *kanji* for field (田, *ta*) as a pun for *kutta* (I ate) and 'four' for the four strokes at the bottom (丶 丶 丶 丶). Stealing (盗) is remembered as 'the next (次) dish (皿).' And 'parent' (親) is watching (見) beside the standing (立) tree (木)."

"I understand what you're trying to tell me now," said Lieutenant Commander Hall, suddenly covering his face with both hands for some reason.

"What's the matter?"

"You're standing beside the tree watching worriedly over Fumiko. That's a very painful image for me, Father."

"Huh?"

"But please don't doubt my sincerity. I'm planning on marrying Fumiko."

All I intended to do was demonstrate the mnemonic device for remembering how to write the *kanji* for "parent," but Lieutenant Commander Hall seemed to have interpreted it as my attempt to express my concern to him as Fumiko's father. This was my chance. I couldn't let it slip away.

"I had three daughters. The eldest was killed by your firebombs. The next has become your plaything. To tell the truth, this has been heartbreaking as a parent."

"I know."

"I'm not insisting you do anything right now, but I hope you'll make her an honest woman soon."

"Trust me."

"That would be a mistake!" said a loud voice from behind us.

I turned around and saw a blonde woman in a military uniform walking toward us.

"This is Captain Donovan, Mr. Yamanaka," said Miss Kurita from the reception area, forming her hands into a megaphone. "She's the director of the Education Division. Her Japanese is excellent, too."

"Pleased to meet you," I said, rising and bowing hurriedly.

The towering woman stood defiantly in front of Lieutenant Commander Hall and began to berate him in English. She had a faint blonde moustache and freckled cheeks, but in spite of that she was a great beauty with a classic profile, resembling the queen in a new deck of cards. I couldn't figure out what they were saying to each other in English, but it was clear that Lieutenant Commander Hall was getting the worst of it. Eventually he stood up from his chair and, placing his arm around her shoulder, drew her out of the room.

"What were the lieutenant commander and the captain talking about?" I asked Miss Kurita, returning to my desk. "I'm sure it wasn't a strategy session."

"She overheard."

"What?"

"What you and the lieutenant commander were saying. She's jealous."

"Jealous?"

"She had sex with the lieutenant commander."

"You're joking…"

"I saw it with my own eyes. Last Monday evening, I came back to get something I'd forgotten and the lieutenant commander's desk was creaking. I peeked over the partition, and they were doing it."

"Ah…"

"She was really something. She had her right arm around the lieutenant commander's neck, but she was able to gesture with her left hand for me to go away. She's unflappable."

"Hmm…"

"I feel sorry for your daughter, too."

I was speechless.

"Our lieutenant commander has a reputation for being the biggest womanizer in the entire GHQ."

I stood up and went straight home.

Tomorrow I plan to slam my resignation down on that Bluebeard's desk.

January 15

From today, a cafeteria serving three meals a day for the staff of the Japan Broadcasting Corporation opened on the fifth floor of the Tokyo Broadcasting Hall: breakfast from six to eight in the morning, lunch from eleven to two, and dinner from five to eight. When I first heard about this from Miss Kurita, I thought that we'd be eating together with the Americans. The GHQ is occupying about half of the building. There are also offices of foreign news services—Reuters, UP, AP, INS—on the second floor. As a result, the building is overflowing with Americans, and at the appointed times they all ride the elevator up to the fifth floor and enter the dining hall with the tables all covered with white tablecloths. Every time the door opens, the delicious aromas of butter and coffee seep out into the hall. Whenever I smell those aromas or glimpse the white tablecloths, I'm envious, so if the rumor I'd heard was true, I'd be very happy.

To tell the truth, I'm terrified to sit down to dinner at my own house. The possibility that one of what Neighborhood Association Leader Kiichiro Aoyama calls the "Seven Roses" might be off from work that night or suddenly arrive home spoils my enjoyment of whatever we have to eat. Anticipating the anger and shame I'd feel if I actually had to sit down face to face with one of them, each morsel of food sticks in my throat like a piece of gravel. And I also know that I'd probably end up lashing out and saying something unpleasant to my wife, who's allowed the girls that we've been entrusted with to be deflowered by American military officers, and that I'd also find myself shouting at her and blaming her failure as a parent for my son Kiyoshi's leaving home. On top of all that, seeing the faces of old Mr. and Mrs. Furusawa, whose loss in the past year of their son and grandson, their home, and now their granddaughter has suddenly left them in a kind of daze, is so distressing that everything tastes like sand. If this cafeteria is nice, I could eat my dinner at the office, spend the next few hours until nine visiting the various studios in the building, and not have to return home until everyone was in bed.

"Do you want to go have a look?"

Miss Kurita shook her permanent-waved head vigorously, rejecting my invitation. "I've already scouted it out. The only thing on the menu is wheat dumplings. The mess kits here in the office are a better deal." She took a blue box off the shelf.

"But don't you think it would be fun to sit slurping dumpling soup next to the Americans?"

"I guess I didn't explain it clearly. The kitchen is the same, but the dining room is separate."

"Oh."

"They just put out some tables and wood stools in the north corridor. Here's your lunch," she said, sliding a blue mess kit to me. "I'll make some coffee."

"Thanks. I'll gratefully accept this, but I think I'll go take a look anyway. But why did the leaders of the Broadcasting Corporation suddenly decide to set up a cafeteria? Even if they only serve wheat dumplings, it can't be easy to get your hands on flour these days."

"It was Brigadier General Dyke's idea."

"You mean Dyke, the chief of CIE?" I could picture Chief Dyke, a tall American with a long, horse face who was always walking at a lightning speed down the corridors wearing a jacket with a peacock embroidered on the back. He appeared to be in his late forties, and his large eyes behind his wire-rimmed glasses always seemed to be glaring at something in an unfriendly way. When you rode the elevator with him, however, he was actually quite considerate, deferring to Japanese in a gentlemanly fashion. The peacock embroidery was the logo of the American broadcasting network NBC, where he had been in charge of public relations before the war. People said he wore the jacket because of his strong attachment to his former workplace. If this was true, I suppose you'd have to say that in spite of his important position, he still had an immature streak.

"The Japan Broadcasting Corporation employees were all cooking in their offices. The smell of Japanese food—rice, fish, *takuan* pickles—three times a day was driving the Americans crazy, so all food preparation within the building was outlawed, and instead the cafeteria was set up, supplied by the GHQ."

"That means the dumplings must be made out of one hundred percent genuine flour," I said. My mind was made up. I got up and made my way clockwise to the north hall.

It was a circuitous route. I first had to go toward the front of the Tokyo Broadcasting Hall that faces the main street from Hibiya to Shiba (now called A. Avenue by the Americans). There is a service entrance on the south side, which faces Mitsui Bussan across a narrow alley. Beyond the alley is the Tokyo Newspaper Building, which publishes the paper created in 1942 by combining the *Miyako Shimbun* and the *Kokumin Shimbun*. The *Miyako Shimbun* used to publish stories about the love affairs of geishas and entertainers, and was at one time the most popular paper in Nezu, which once had a geisha district. (I still remember articles from the paper, like "Radio—The Geisha's Foe," from the early twenties, soon after radio broadcasts began. "Geishas say that radio is their foe. The reasons are, first, there's been a drop in their clientele since radio broadcasts began, because now families sit and listen to the radio together. Second, listening to the radio gives you wrinkles, because it makes you laugh and laughing leaves lines in your face. Radio also makes your skin darker. This is due to the emission of ultraviolent light from its vacuum tubes..." Of course, most of it was nonsense, but at the time I seriously believed it.)

Anyway, the north side of the building is directly up against Fukoku Seimei Building, but it isn't visible from inside the Tokyo Broadcasting Hall. This north side of the building is where the Broadcasting Hall stores musical instruments, which is why there are no windows. This is where the cafeteria had been situated. It was an extended, narrow space lit by seven or eight light bulbs hanging from the ceiling. Under them several long tables were laid out, and on the wall were three rectangular signs: "Miso–flavor broth with dumplings and pork, 5 yen," "Salt-flavored broth with dumplings and bacon, 5 yen," and "Cafeteria Coupons Not Required; Employees Only."

I felt faint when I saw the words "pork" and "bacon." How many years had it been since such heartening words had graced the walls of a restaurant? And 5 yen was cheap. At the black market in front of Shinbashi Station, a five-minute walk away, one scrawny dumpling floating in a broth of mysterious origin was selling for 7 yen.

There was a large opening in the rear wall, where the kitchen was located. A cook sat there selling tickets. I handed him two 5 yen bills, and asked for a bowl of each. There was a limit of one bowl per customer, I was told, and the salt-flavored broth was sold out. The cook returned a 5 yen bill to me, then gave me a ticket for the miso-flavored broth. In the next moment, he took back the ticket and ladled a bowl of soup for me. It was so quick that the whole process of handing me my ticket and then collecting it again seemed a silly waste of time. I was about to say something about that, but when I saw five fat dumplings floating luxuriously in the bowl, I was hit by a wave of pleasant surprise and was too preoccupied with mouthwatering anticipation to spit out a word.

The cafeteria was nearly full. I went back toward the entrance and found a seat next to two men deep in conversation, seated across from each other. I began to slurp my soup, which unfortunately turned out to be sweet-potato miso, with its characteristic rancid odor. The pork I'd been so looking forward to turned out to be ham ends, which were probably the leftover bits of ham from the Americans' breakfasts. But the dumplings were the real thing, and they filled me up.

"So *all* of the instruments are gone?" the middle-aged man said to his companion, wiping the corners of his mouth with the back of his necktie.

"About eighty percent got pinched," the younger man in a jacket, replied, as he poured a cup of weak tea from a large earthen teapot. The tea was all-you-can-drink, just what you'd expect from a first-rate place like the Japan Broadcasting Corporation. "They even took the piano from Studio 6. They had uniforms and instrument cases when they came in. The staff at the security office let them right in, practically showed them the way. But it turns out those cases were empty. And when they left, they took our prized Stradivarius and Guanerius with them."

"They planned it very carefully."

"Yup. They must be pros."

"But how did they get a piano out of here?"

"They must have taken it apart. That's the only way I can think of."

"'Divide each difficulty into as many parts as is feasible and necessary to resolve it,' I guess."

"What's that?"

"A line from a script that was just finished. It's supposed to be something Descartes said."

"I see. Well, it fits perfectly here."

"How many of them were there?"

"About twenty. They claimed to be Kiyoshi Sakurai and his band."

Kiyoshi Sakurai and his band are very popular right now. They played at the Asakusa Taishokan this New Year, and drew a record crowd. If you announced yourself as Kiyoshi Sakurai and his band and walked past the security guards, they'd be likely to just assume you were performing on one of the popular music shows. And at the same time, unless you were a real hardcore fan, you wouldn't recognize the faces of any individual musicians, so you wouldn't be suspicious. Very clever, I thought to myself, chewing with satisfaction on my third dumpling, until the younger man said something that stopped me in my tracks.

"The security guard at the service entrance only remembers two band boys. They both seemed about the age of middle school students, and one had a big mole at the bridge of his nose. The kid with the mole said he'd be playing during the broadcast and walked past the security guards blowing on a harmonica. He was really cocky and bold—and was playing the "Toreador's March" from *Carmen*."

My son Kiyoshi's friend, Mr. Takahashi's son Shoichi, has a mole. Which just happens to be at the bridge of his nose. And on top of that, he's a whiz at the harmonica. And the "Toreador's March" from *Carmen* just happens to be one of his best numbers. Without thinking, I blurted out to the younger man: "The other boy, did he have any marks on his palms? Snow burns?"

"I just heard about this from a Juvenile Welfare Department officer, I didn't see them myself. But does this ring some kind of bell for you?

"No, not really, I guess…"

"Hold on a minute. Don't I see you visiting the studios a lot?" asked the middle-aged man, turning directly toward me. "Which department are you in?"

"I don't work at the Japan Broadcasting Corporation. I'm employed at the CIE Language Section. I heard you mention a kid with a mole at the bridge of his nose, and just said the first thing that popped into my head. But actually, the kid I know is a girl."

"But you were saying something about the other boy."

"Pay no attention to me. I just misspoke."

The two men kept looking at me, but eventually the middle-aged man just shook his head and stood up. The younger one stepped toward the rear of the room to return his bowl.

I know where Kiyoshi and Shoichi are living. I need to go and check up on them to put my mind at ease. The sooner the better.

January 16

When our fan-making business was at its peak, I used to go to Asakusabashi once a week to visit the shibugami paper wholesaler at Kuramae. The office of the Yanagibashi Geisha and Teahouse Association ordered four thousand fans for geishas to give to their best customers during the kawabiraki river festival. When times were good, I used to invite friends and colleagues to restaurants by the riverbank, too. The first-class restaurant Ryukotei, I'm embarrassed to say, was one of my regular haunts. Every third time I was there, the mistress of the place would take out a paulownia-wood box and say: "Do you know what this is? When the writer Toson Shimazaki went to France, his literary friends gave him a farewell party, and this is what he used on that occasion." After this preamble, she would ceremoniously remove from the box a red saké cup like it was a national treasure. She seemed to be exceptionally proud of it. "I don't know if you know, but for the last eight years before he went to France in 1906, he lived near here. His address was Asakusa Ward Shinkatamachi-1, just a three-minute walk from here. When his wife died, he got involved in a rather indelicate relationship with his niece, which was why he decided to go to France, but anyway, this neighborhood was a place of both happiness and sadness for him. He must still have many memories, because he often stops by to this day. And each time he does, I bring out this saké cup."

I looked over at the former site of the Ryukotei Restaurant on my right, and with the Kandagawa River at my back I walked under the girder bridge of the Sobu Line tracks and proceeded about one *cho* north to the area where Kiyoshi was living. Buildings here remained intact, but they were tinged with soot, perhaps from when the surrounding area had been incinerated in the fire bombings. Checking the address, I entered the garden of a house surrounded by a wooden fence—though all that was left of the fence was the frame, the boards having been pried off—for firewood, no doubt. I called out, "Is anyone home?" and an old woman wearing a padded cotton jacket and mompe trousers with the knees worn out, her back as curved as the shell of a turtle, appeared. She was missing two or three front teeth, along with any trace of feminine charm. I mentioned that I believed my son Kiyoshi was staying here, and she said: "Kiyoshi and Sho are still at school."

"I'd like to wait for him, if that's all right."

"Sure. But you have to remember, whatever you see here, you never saw." And mumbling that riddle-like phrase, she invited me into the six-mat room that opened directly from the entryway. An iron teakettle was buzzing over the heat of a rectangular hibachi of zelkova wood.

"You don't see many iron tea kettles these days."

"The boy brought it back from Iwate."

The cushions were new and fluffy. "These seem to be new. I hesitate to even sit on them."

"Yes, the boy had them made. Have some tea."

I was surprised to see that it was top-quality green tea. "This is a rare treat, too."

"The boy bought it in Saitama."

There was a dried persimmon as a sweet to accompany the tea. "Everything here is such an unexpected gift. I took off from my job this afternoon, but I'm certainly glad I came. I didn't think I'd ever see this fine a dried persimmon again. As long as we still have these, Japan's all right. This is really a treat."

"The boy brought it back from Yamagata."

"This is from the boy, too? He certainly gets around for just being one boy. He must be running about like crazy. I'm quite impressed."

"There's more than one boy. Six are living upstairs, and four downstairs. That's ten altogether."

"What's your relationship to the boys?"

"I was in the toilet so I was late getting to the air-raid shelter. Then the shelter took a direct hit."

"You were fortunate."

"Not so fortunate. My entire family was in that shelter. I'd have rather have gone to the other world with my daughter-in-law and my grandchild."

"And how do you know the ten boys here?"

"They found me."

"Ah…"

"Up to November of last year I was homeless, living in a sewer in Ueno. The boys came by and asked me if I wanted to come live with them. If I cooked, cleaned and did laundry for them, they said, I could stay here as long as I liked."

Ten days ago, when Kiyoshi visited me at the Documentation Section Annex, he said that when the older boy in the air force uniform returned to Tokyo he learned that his entire family had been killed in the air raids. He went back to university to resume his studies, but seeing how there were food shortages everywhere, he and his friends decided to form the Tokyo Students Rice Relief Club and live together in the boy's family house. In short, they'd formed a group to smuggle rice from the countryside into the city, and he and Sho would be joining the group. This had to be that older boy's house and the headquarters of the Tokyo Students Rice Relief Club.

"How's Kiyoshi doing?"

"Oh, he helps me in the kitchen. He's a bright boy."

"And Shoichi?"

"He's good at laundry."

"Do you know if they were home on the evening of the day before yesterday?"

"The evening of the day before yesterday?" She glared up at the ceiling as if thinking and seemed to be mumbling. Finally she rose to her feet slowly with an "Ooof!" and walked over to a blackboard hanging in the hall. The blackboard was filled with a mix of numbers and symbols like $f \approx \approx = \neq \neq \neq \infty \infty < $ and $\in$. It seemed to be the schedule of the Tokyo Students Rice Relief Club. In the brief time I've been employed at the Metropolitan Police Department, I must have acquired the skills of a detective by osmosis, just as children living next door to a temple learn to recite the sutras.

I'd been working at the Documentation Section Annex of the Metropolitan Police Department until noon today, and the "Kiyoshi Sakurai and his Band Incident" had already been officially reported. It was only natural that there would be a report, but the official details were somewhat different from the rumors I'd heard at the Japan Broadcasting Corporation employee cafeteria. According to the official report, the incident took place on January 14th, at 4:30 P.M. A dozen or so musicians carrying instrument cases came in through the employees' service entrance. The security guard confirmed the time on the big clock in the employees' entrance hall, so that was certain.

An individual who seemed to be the manager approached the security guard and said, "This is Kiyoshi Sakurai and his band, who'll be appearing on *Audience Request Concert—Light Music Evening—The Music of Masao Koga* from seven thirty tonight. The program's going to be broadcast live from Hikokan Hall, but the people there are busy setting up, and we need to rehearse. Tonight Mr. Koga himself is going to be in the audience, and Noboru Kirishima, the big star, will be performing. We want to give our very best performance, so we conferred with the person in charge, and he arranged for us to rehearse in Studio 1. An hour will be plenty of time."

Checking the studio schedule, the security guard saw that Studio 1 was broadcasting *Farmers Hour* from 8 P.M. The program was going to consist of the pianist Hajime Wada performing a collection of popular songs and Wakae Kimura reading from the dramatic narrative *Shiobara Tasuke's Edo Diary*. There wouldn't be that much set-up involved. (Short digression: CIE Chief Dyke, the former NBC bigwig, had issued a statement to the effect that "radio belongs to the people," and programs with audience participation are desirable.) *Farmers Hour* and *Light Music Evening* have become the leading shows with audience participation. The thirty-second interval between their broadcast times wasn't sufficient for bringing in a new studio audience, so *Light Music Evening* was to be broadcast live from Hikokan Hall.

The security guard calculated setting up the studio for *Farmers Hour*, including bringing in chairs for the studio audience, so he'd written "In use from 6" on the schedule. "Make sure you're out of there by half five," he said to the "band manager," who then led his "musicians" into the studio.

Later the security guard was sharply criticized by his boss for not following proper procedures. But the Shinbashi detective investigating the incident took exception. "This is all very well in hindsight, but it's too much to ask," he stated. No one had ever attempted this sort of heist before, and in addition, on this occasion, an American officer in uniform was standing by the side of the "band manager." He seemed to be imitating MacArthur, right down to the aviator Ray-Ban sunglasses and a corncob pipe pressed tightly between his lips. As the security guard explained, "Female Japanese popular singers and famous bands often have American military personnel following them around as fans or patrons, and I thought he was one of them. I was afraid if I held the band up, he'd yell at me."

Most Japanese would take the side of the security guard because most Japanese are afraid of getting yelled at by an American.

"Accordingly, this seems to represent a new style of crime in which Japanese and Americans are working in tandem. As this incident demonstrates, the criminal acts of the U.S. military personnel are becoming more ingenious, and are often accomplished with assistance from Japanese. It will be necessary in the future to exercise even greater vigilance and attention," concluded the report that I printed.

The report also mentioned two young men: one stayed near the entrance playing the harmonica, while the other seemed engrossed in reading a book that appeared to be a dictionary.

"The night before last—that was Monday, right?" said the old woman, having returned to the hibachi. "The boys came home in the morning."

"Were Kiyoshi and Shoichi with them?"

"Yes. You don't need to worry about them. It's not like they're out visiting the geisha districts. They came back on the first Ou Line train, carrying a big load of rice, dried persimmons and other things."

"And after that?"

"After they ate the breakfast I made for them, they went to school, rubbing their eyes. They're good boys."

"What time did Kiyoshi get back from school?"

"He was pretty late."

I was asking her if she remembered what time it was when the lattice door opened with a rattle and a young man entered the house. He was unshaven and had a crew cut, allowing me to see the white ringworm circles on his scalp.

"I'm here to pick it up, Granny," he said, suddenly lowering his voice when he saw me. "Is he a visitor?" he asked.

"He's Kiyoshi's father. He's promised not to see anything he sees here, so don't worry."

"Pleased to meet you," said the young man, entering the room, removing the cloth bag he had tied to his waist. The old woman slid open a closet door, revealing a large wooden box.

"Okay, count carefully," the young man said, as he dipped a square wooden one-*sho* measure into the box.

"One... two... three..." said the old woman. "Your ringworm seems to have gotten much better."

"Thanks to you."

"But just because it's showing signs of improvement, you mustn't stop the treatment. You still have the medicine, right?"

"Thanks to the Rice Relief Club. With the profits from this business, I can afford to buy pricey medicine."

"...Nine... ten... eleven... Who are you working for today?"

"Kamesei Restaurant. Lately, big-shot Japanese have started inviting Americans out for fancy dinners. Kamesei says they'll take all the rice I can supply."

"You mustn't tell them where you're getting it."

"I'm not crazy. If they bought directly from you, I'd be out of business."

"Yes, that's right... eighteen... nineteen... all right, that's twenty." The old woman returned to the hibachi and turned to me staring at the proceedings. "You remember that you didn't see what you saw, right?" she chuckled, as she prepared a pot of tea.

Holding the bulging sack, the young man sat down by the hibachi and slurped his cup of tea and turned to me with a smile. "Can you ask Kiyoshi something for me? Who's braver—MacArthur or Sanzo Nosaka?"

"Who?" asked the old woman.

"Sanzo Nosaka."

"Who's that?"

"The big boss of the Communist Party who fled Japan and lived overseas for fifteen years. He returned in triumph at ten o'clock three nights ago. At Tokyo Station. From 9 to 10 P.M. they sold 1,500 station entrance tickets to people who wanted to greet him when he got off the train. In the pushing and shoving, fifty or sixty actually fell off the platform. Don't you read the newspapers, Granny? Half the paper the last several days have been filled with articles about Sanzo Nosaka."

The old woman wasn't listening. She was intensely focused on counting the bills she'd received from the young man.

Picking up the slack, I asked, "Why would you want to compare him to MacArthur?"

"I made a bet with a friend. My friend said that MacArthur is braver. On August 30 last year, MacArthur landed at Atsugi Air Base with just 4,200 soldiers. There were still 3 million soldiers in the imperial army in Japan, of which 30,000 were, by anyone's estimation, crack units. He says MacArthur is brave because he dared to land in such a place with so few troops. But I say that Sanzo Nosaka, who just came home to enemy territory all by himself, is even braver."

The lattice door opened with a rattle again, and in stepped Kiyoshi. As soon as he saw me, he turned on his heels and fled.

"Both of them are fearless. They're a lot alike in that way," I said, leaving that non-answer behind as I flew out the door after Kiyoshi. I chased after him for two *cho* before losing sight of him in front of Yanagibashi. Why did he run?

I *know* why.

January 17

The hastily scribbled words, "Numerous Occurrences of Theft by Youth Gangs" caught my eye and suddenly woke me up. I carefully read the interoffice memo that I was about to make a stencil of. The notice said:

A youth gang of seven boys, some of them from good families, was apprehended by the First Police Investigative Unit and the

Nogata Police Station on January 12. The gang consisted of elementary and middle school students led by former military police captain Akira Kume (33). Taking advantage of a lack of parental supervision, the children began by stealing nine bicycles and selling them for approximately 1,200 yen. Under the influence of prevailing conditions, their vice gradually escalated, and, acquiring Japanese swords and knives, they broke into the home of company employee Kenkichi Igarashi (40), at Nishi Ogikubo 607, Suginami Ward, and, announcing that they were members of the Tengu Gang, demanded money, threatening Mr. Igarashi and his wife. The Igarashis realized the children were not pros, and the matter ended without incident. Next, at 10 P.M. on January 10, from the front of the home of Hikojuro Teshigawara (64), of Mukaicho-1-102, Suginami Ward, they called out: "Telegram, telegram!" luring the family out and then threatening them with Japanese swords. The family raised an uproar and the boys escaped again. Incidents of this sort involving youth gangs are becoming quite frequent in Tokyo and other cities. The authorities are called upon to pay close attention to them.

When Kiyoshi saw me the other day at the house where he lives now, he turned tail and ran. That is testament enough that he's degenerated into an apprentice thief. And he's not engaged in anything as innocent as standing outside someone's house and luring them out with cries of "Telegram, telegram!" either. I don't know who the leader of his gang is, but it's clear that Kiyoshi was an accomplice in a heist of very valuable musical instruments from the Japan Broadcasting Corporation. My two daughters are the mistresses of officers of the Occupation Forces, and my son, who is still a second-year middle school student, has become a runner for a gang of thieves. Who has put this curse on my family?

Pushing my stylus, which felt heavier than a pestle, I slowly finished the stencil. There was one more interoffice memo today, announcing that residents of the Aoyama Minami 3-chome neighborhood association have begun producing charcoal.

Frustrated by the lack of fuel rations since the autumn of the previous year, the Aoyama Minami 3-chome Neighborhood Association, at the suggestion of Neighborhood Association Leader Sudo, has begun to produce charcoal from the half-charred dead trees in Aoyama Cemetery. They've built two large kilns in the plaza at the entrance to the cemetery and, inviting a professional charcoal maker from Fukui Prefecture, are producing thirty bags of charcoal a day. At that rate, they've been able to distribute charcoal to each of the three hundred households in the neighborhood by mid-January, and by March every family will have five or six bags of charcoal. Moreover, the price is significantly lower than official price for charcoal, and will be no more than 2 or 3 yen per bag. Both the Aoyama Police Station and the Akasaka Ward Office tried to put a halt to the charcoal manufacture, but they were met with demands from the citizens for fuel rations in return. They have decided to allow the residents to continue, on an exceptional basis. Numerous residents of Kanda Ward and Kojimachi Ward, hearing of this, have felled the trees in a triangular area demarcated by the three points of Tayasumon and Inuimon of the palace grounds and Takebashi, and are also planning to make charcoal from it. It is inexcusable for the trees of the sacred precincts of the Imperial palace grounds to be destroyed and converted into fuel for the common people. On the honor of the Police Department, a stop must be put to this. We hereby instruct the appropriate officials, in coordination with the two ward offices in question and the police stations in Kanda and Kojimachi, to post guards at Tayasumon and Takebashi, and if the residents appear to be presenting resistance, to fire warning shots from the pistols that the GHQ has approved for police officers' use as of yesterday.

After I'd finished printing two hundred copies of these memos and delivered them to the Documentation Section, I headed over to the Tokyo Broadcasting Hall. Perhaps because the notice I'd just printed was still fresh in my mind, it seemed that the trees in Hibiya Park stood rather thinner than usual.

"Shinsuke, come here." The moment I entered the Language Section the resonant voice of Navy Lieutenant Commander Robert King Hall, Language Simplification Unit Officer and Language Sub-Section Chief, hit me in the face like a stone.

"I'm on my way," I said, feeling a wave of disgust. Miss Kurita has told me that calling a person by their first name is a sign of friendliness in America, but every time I hear this crude familiarity, my heart involuntarily shakes with anger. And—though of course only in an unconfirmed sort of way—aren't I Hall's father-in-law? Calling your father-in-law by his first name is completely inappropriate. I tried to stall as long as possible in front of my desk. Finally I asked Miss Kurita in a quiet voice, "Did something good happen? Did his aunt die and leave him a lot of money, or was he promoted to commander? He seems to be very happy about something. Maybe his hemorrhoids are cured."

"Hemorrhoids?"

"My daughter says he has them. They give him a lot of trouble."

"It's the first I've heard of it."

"When he works too hard, they swell up, she says."

"Who would have guessed… that someone with a face as dreamy as Robert Taylor's would have such a nasty thing going on… back there," said Miss Kurita, scrunching her nose and opening her lips, resembling two pieces of cod roe, and giving me a most unwelcome view of white chewing gum wrapped around her pink tongue.

"Anyway, what's up?"

"His proposal for converting the written Japanese language to *romaji* is finished."

"He's still planning to force us to write Japanese in *romaji*?"

"Looks like it."

"I can't believe he's still insisting on that in spite of how thoroughly I've explained to him that there are a hundred disadvantages and not a single advantage to the idea. He just doesn't know when to quit."

"Shinsuke, what's taking you so long?" This time a little sharpness had entered his voice. "I'm known as the busiest officer in the entire Allied Forces, you know."

You're busy because you spend your time giving people unasked for advice about their language; if you minded your own business, you'd have plenty of free time, I thought but did not say, as I headed into the depths of the room and took my place seated opposite the thirty-four-year-old blue-eyed blond man who had studied at four universities, earned two PhDs, and had one large hemorrhoid. He was leaning back in his chair with his large feet on the edge of the table.

"Shinsuke, have a smoke." He tossed a pack of Lucky Strikes, with their design of a big red dot, my way. "You can have the whole pack."

Americans are always throwing cigarettes at us Japanese, almost as a kind of greeting. I think they really look down on us. We're not all beggars. I shook my head vigorously several times in refusal. Then the lieutenant commander opened his drawer and took out a pouch of shredded tobacco and a Japanese pipe.

"Maybe you'd prefer this, Shinsuke." It was a style of Japanese pipe that you often saw at antique stores in Nezu before the war. From the bowl to the mouthpiece, the body was iron. The long stem split in two halfway along its length.

"Ah, a husband-and-wife pipe."

"So you know what it is."

"Do I know what it is? I'm from Nezu after all." (At the beginning of the Meiji era, most of Nezu was a pleasure district. At its peak, in 1885, 943 prostitutes resided there, visited by a half-million customers annually, making it more popular than the Yoshiwara red-light district. Seki Kato, who later became Shoyo Tsubouchi's wife, was a prostitute by the name of Hanamurasaki at the biggest brothel in Nezu, Oyawata House. She charged 1 yen a night for her company, the top price in those days. That's what it said in the guide to the prostitutes of Tokyo published in 1885 that was packed away somewhere in the back of our storehouse, anyway.) "The prostitutes in the Nezu pleasure quarters used to share these pipes with their clients. I'm sure you could find them everywhere throughout Japan, but it's a fine example of using an ordinary pipe as a tool of the trade."

"I've never seen that in any scholarly work. Thank you for adding to my knowledge," the Lieutenant Commander said, nodding and jotting down the information in a notebook with his Parker pen.

"In those days, the only Imperial university in Japan was located right adjacent to Nezu."

"Yes, that's correct. Kyoto Imperial University, the second imperial university, wasn't founded until 1897, so in the first two decades of the Meiji era, the only imperial university was the one in Hongo, in Tokyo."

He already knew that. That was what was so intimidating about this fellow who had graduated from so many universities. Still, I went on, "And then the First Higher School moved here close to Nezu…"

"The First Higher School moved to Mukogaoka, Hongo, in 1889, and then to Komaba in Meguro Ward in 1935."

"At any rate, it wouldn't do for two of the top educational institutions of our country to be right next to the pleasure quarters of Nezu," I said in a loud voice, trying to put a stop to his endless pedantry, which kept the conversation from proceeding. "In June 1888, the pleasure quarters of Nezu were moved lock, stock and barrel to Suzaki in Fukagawa. But the prostitutes left their husband-and-wife pipes behind in Nezu."

"Why?"

"I guess they realized that smoking with their clients was a waste of precious time. Why sit around smoking with someone who's already finished and paid, when you can move on to the next client? Anyway, before the war there were a lot of those husband-and-wife pipes in the antique stores of Nezu. Then we had to hand in all our iron, and the pipes were melted down and made into bullets. Maybe some of the bullets that came flying your way started out as husband-and-wife pipes."

"I was never on the battlefield. I was in the States working as a Japanese language instructor at different Civil Affairs Training Schools."

"Civil Affairs Training Schools?"

"Schools that taught what kind of civil government we should carry out in occupied countries. Talented young university graduates were enrolled, and they learned Japanese, how to preserve public peace and safety in Japan, food policy, how to get industry up and running again, how to rebuild the country, how to reorganize transportation and communications, and so forth. The Army's Civil Affairs Training Schools were already up and running in 1942."

"You were certainly prepared."

"We knew we'd win the war."

I hate to admit it, but I have nothing to say on that score. The gap in the strength between our two nations at the start of the war is becoming more and more evident each day. Newspapers are now carrying articles saying "Statistics from the start of the war show that the United States had eight times the iron production of Japan, eight hundred times the automobile production, and the total national income was eighteen times that of Japan. When these facts are considered, it was an incredibly foolhardy decision to go to war." But I don't need the lieutenant commander rubbing it in. And the newspapers have a lot of nerve, too, reporting figures like that now. Why didn't they tell us that before we went to war?

"The Japanese, on the other hand, were completely irresponsible when it came to occupying other countries. They didn't try to train a single individual to do it properly, and yet they occupied all of Asia. Who did Japan send to administer the countries it occupied? Teachers from Youth Schools and retired elementary school teachers who had never even heard the words 'civil affairs,' or ambitious opportunists looking for fame and profit overseas. They had no training, no methods. And that's why all they could do is try to force their twisted ideology that the emperor is a god and Japan is a divine nation on their occupied countries. Our Occupation policies are based on international law and supported by the theories of civil administration. We have done things very differently from the Japanese, who had no method or theory. Would you like to have this pipe, Shinsuke?"

"No, I wouldn't."

"All right then, Shinsuke, take a good look at this husband-and-wide pipe and the pack of Lucky Strikes." The lieutenant commander removed his feet from the desk and sat up straight in his chair with the armrests. "Let's call the husband-and-wife pipe 'culture' and the Lucky Strike 'civilization.' Do you follow me?"

"Not in the least."

"You can smoke a Lucky Strike in Japan, in the South Pacific, in Siberia, or anywhere. Everyone would recognize this as a cigarette, and everyone, if they had a match, could enjoy a smoke. In other words, it has universality. That's civilization. But what about this husband-and-wife pipe? It's true that the pipe is beautifully decorated, with all this lovely chasing on the iron stem, but you can't smoke it unless you have shredded tobacco, and you'd also need a bit of an explanation how to use it. In other words, it can only be used in Japan. Its area of application is limited. This is culture."

"What's your point?"

"*Romaji* are civilization and *kanji* are culture," he said, bringing the conversation around to where he wanted it. If it were Japanese chess, I'd say I felt like I'd been delivered a cowardly blow by a lurking rook. "*Romaji*, or the Latin alphabet. In English we use twenty-six. Roman letters are the most universal alphabet, employed throughout the world. They have the same universality as a pack of Lucky Strikes."

"I don't think it's fair to compare the written Japanese language to a husband-and-wife pipe."

"Nothing would please me more than to make my argument without having to employ comparisons. But when your audience doesn't understand logical reasoning, the only way to explain things is through comparisons and similes."

"Doesn't understand logical reasoning?"

"Yes. When you have to deal with people who don't understand logical reasoning, you have to employ parables, as Christ or Shakyamuni did. That's what I'm doing."

Now he was comparing himself to Christ and the Buddha. I was getting a little frightened.

"Shinsuke, this is my proposal for reforming the Japanese language. I prepared two versions, one in English and one in Japanese." He took two documents out of his desk drawer. One was typed in English, and the other was written on manuscript paper from Maruzen, filled with *kanji* and *kana*. Each was about five or six pages long. "The content is the same. Which one would you like to read?"

He didn't have to be so sarcastic. He knew perfectly well I don't understand English.

"I regard you as the average Japanese. That's why I hired you as an employee of the Language Section. You're passionately against shifting Japanese writing to *romaji*."

"Of course I am."

"Which means that the majority of Japanese will be similarly opposed to it. That was my thought. As a result, I concluded that a transitional period is necessary to make the conversion to *romaji*, and I worked through the night coming up with this proposal. I hope you'll read it with an open and unbiased mind."

The proposal was written in precise and well-formed block script.

A Shortcut for the Conversion of Japanese Orthography to Roman Letters

A Proposal for a Two-Step Process for Language Reform

Civilian Information and Education Section
Language Subsection Chief
Language Simplification Officer
U.S. Navy Lieutenant Commander
Robert King Hall

Since an immediate conversion of the orthography of the Japanese language to Roman letters would be met with opposition by the majority of Japanese, this is not a viable plan. In response, I have devised a two-step proposal, of shifting from *katakana* to Roman letters, which I hereby present to the Supreme Commander of the Allied Forces in Japan. I request that this plan be presented to the educational mission that will, at your orders, be arriving in Japan in March to observe the Japanese educational system and be advising the Japanese government on necessary reforms.

First, in Occupied Japan, the use of any materials written in characters should be outlawed and all writing should henceforth be in *katakana*.

The first reason for this is that outlawing characters will be an extremely effective means of abolishing pollution by militaristic thought and government propaganda from before and during the war. In the past, all important documents in Japan were written in characters, but in just ten or twelve years after the implementation of a policy of *katakana* orthography, the majority of the people will no longer be able to read characters, and the Japanese people will naturally forget their self-aggrandizing imperialist thought.

Second, to write in *katakana*, people will have to learn to leave spaces between words, a skill that will be absolutely necessary for the final conversion into writing with Roman letters, so writing in *katakana* will serve as a form of preparatory training for writing in Roman letters.

Third, writing sentences without characters, in other words, solely in *katakana*, will force Japanese writing itself to become simpler. In other words, one cannot write in *katakana* without abandoning characters and adopting the spoken language as the written language. The educated classes of this country have long valued the elegant over the practical, the ceremonial over the concrete, an artificial literary language over the actual spoken language. As a result, the gap between the educated classes and the rest of the populace is despairingly wide. But when *katakana* are adopted as the writing system, writing clearly will come to be accepted as correct, and this problem will be quite simply resolved. To digress slightly, perhaps, movements to unify the written and spoken languages have occurred within Japan at regular intervals. Their aim was to reduce the gap between the spoken and written languages, and many leading Japanese scholars have made great efforts to effect this kind of unification. The use of *katakana* orthography would relieve such scholars of their burden. Furthermore, clear writing is also a necessity when writing in Roman letters, which means that once again, writing in *katakana* would be training for the eventual adoption of Roman letters.

Fourth, through the exclusive use of *katakana*, the greatest logjam of Occupation labors, the backup of the work of censoring information, would immediately be resolved. Effectively censoring information produced in Japanese requires the highest level of knowledge of characters, and very few possess this. To digress again, as is well known, the spoken Japanese language is almost unbelievably simple. It has only about 114 syllables; of all known languages, only Hawaiian, with eighty, has fewer. As a natural result, its phonologic makeup is simple and regular (as proof of this, one can offer its regular and beautiful syllabary), and anyone with a university-level education can learn to speak Japanese in a matter of months. As a rule, each syllable corresponds to one *katakana*, and nothing could be easier than to memorize this set of 114 letters. But when the written language is employed, the same number of *hiragana* and the characters that strike fear in the hearts of linguists around the world as "the inventions of the devil" come into play, and to vanquish these devils, a full three years at the very least is required. But, to repeat, if there were neither characters nor *hiragana*, if, in other words, all writing were in *katakana*, Japanese would be a very easy language to master. Large numbers of censors could be educated in just a few months. As a result, the work of censorship would proceed with great smoothness.

Fifth, the use of *katakana* would contribute enormously to the learning ability of children. Up to now, almost all of elementary education is devoted to the mastery of characters. If *katakana* were employed instead, the time now spent acquiring a mastery of characters would immediately be freed up and could be used to study other subjects. Children would become productive members of society at an earlier age and could contribute to the Japanese labor force without sacrificing educational levels. Moreover, because of the time now spent mastering characters, graduates of Japanese elementary schools have not had the opportunity to acquire the language skills and practical knowledge needed to function as citizens of a democracy. As proof of this, the number of Japanese who can actually read newspaper articles and other writings concerning current events and ideas is actually unexpectedly low. By adopting *katakana* as the means of writing, in a short time a populace that is truly literate and equipped for democratic government could be produced.

Sixth, the use of *katakana* will simplify communication with other countries, because it will enable non-Japanese to master

Japanese easily. The war has acted as a stimulus for many non-Japanese to seek to learn more about Japan and its culture. When these new developments are considered, now is the ideal moment to adopt of policy of writing Japanese in *katakana*. In addition, the adoption of *katakana* will also increase the efficiency of Japanese business, because it will enable the use of linotype presses and typewriters. Simply by replacing the Roman letters on the Western typewriter with *katakana*, the realms of Japanese government, education and business will all undergo an exponential increase in efficiency.

Seventh, *katakana* is one of the rare uniquely Japanese inventions, and a very fine one at that. As such, it is a means of restoring to the Japanese people, now prostrated in defeat, a sense of well-deserved pride and accomplishment.

Eighth, from the past, the Japanese have been quite accomplished at carrying out major transformations on a national scale. The Westernization that Japan undertaken during the Meiji Restoration is a prime example, during which the Japanese industrialized their nation faster than any other country in history. This is due to the extreme centralization of power in Japan, which has also fostered subservience to authority as a characteristic of the Japanese people. This characteristic can be exploited in achieving with minimum resistance widespread acceptance of the exclusive use of *katakana*. In prewar and wartime Japan, the imperial edict was the key; now it is the orders issued by the GHQ. One simple order from the GHQ can lead to the implementation of *katakana* as the national writing system.

Ninth, it is important to note that the ideas of adopting *katakana* or Roman letters as the sole writing system are both familiar to the Japanese already. Since the Meiji Restoration, starting with the proposal by Hisoka Maejima to abolish characters, numerous figures have spoken out for reform of the Japanese language, including Yoshikazu Nanbu, who urged the adoption of the Roman alphabet, and Fumihiko Otsuki and others, who have argued for the reform of *kana* and other language reforms. In other words, the ideas of abolishing characters and adopting *katakana* or Roman letters as the Japanese writing system have already appeared naturally from within the country, and are not something that the author seeks to force on the Japanese people from outside. This is the moment when the Japanese should indeed heed the voices of their wise forebears.

In conclusion, while it is true that characters do have an inherent aesthetic value that cannot be communicated by alphabet systems such as *katakana* or Roman letters, they should be completely abolished in the near future as the general writing system and an alphabetic system, in other words, initially *katakana*, and eventually Roman letters, should be adopted. It is worth adding that for the sake of the growth of the Japanese as a democratic society, and for their reentrance into international society, the use of Roman letters is far preferable to *katakana*. Incidentally, the author regards a ten-year period as appropriate for this shift from *katakana* to Roman letters.

While suitably impressed that a non-Japanese could write the Japanese language so well, I was at the same time overcome with anger at the content of this proposal and, not knowing what or how to say it, I just sat there making inarticulate growling noises as the lieutenant commander took the document from my hands and said, "So, Shinsuke, tell me what you think."

"Is this going to be put into effect?"

"Brigadier General Dyke, the chief of CIE, agrees with me. I explained this to him this morning, and he nodded in agreement with each point. And I think the State Department in Washington will also agree. Assistant Secretary of State Benton has always expressed his respect for my opinions. All that's needed is the Supreme Commander's signature. And this will become the official opinion of the educational mission coming here."

"So it will be put into effect."

"What I want to know is, how will the Japanese people react? That's why I want to know your opinion, Shinsuke. That's why I've shown you these classified documents."

"My opinion? It's ridiculous. That's my opinion!"

"You don't approve?"

"Ha!" I sputtered for a moment, searching for something to say, then blurted out: "The acme of not approving!"

"The acme of not approving? That's an interesting way of putting it. I'll have to make a note of that."

"Just don't take your eyes off of me when you do. You say that *kanji* and imperialistic ideology are the same thing. But imperialism didn't grow out of *kanji*. As proof, there are countless people who used *kanji* when they denounced imperialist ideology in writing—though most of them were thrown in jail as result. And it's just as wrong to say that an alphabet makes a society democratic."

"Really?"

"Come on! What about Germany? What about Italy? According to you, they're both anti-democratic, fascist nations, but they both use Roman letters, they both use the alphabet."

"There are always exceptions."

"I'm not finished. I was saving this for last, but your theory has a fatal flaw."

"No, it hasn't."

"Ah, but it has. You've overlooked the existence of *furigana*."

"I have not. As far as *furigana* are concerned, the great Japanese writer Yuzo Yamamoto's call for their abolishment in 1937 settled the matter. He argued that the custom of writing *furigana* next to *kanji* encourages the use of overly difficult *kanji*, is unattractive, and makes printing much less efficient. The newspapers and magazines agreed with him and…"

"Just because he fills sheets of paper with his scribbling doesn't mean a writer is always right about the national language. If you ask me, Mr. Yuzo Yamamoto was wrong. He's a fool and a fraud. *Furigana* are an alphabet. Since they've been outlawed, it's much harder to read *kanji*."

"I see. You can go back to your desk."

"I have one more thing to say. You say you wrote that in a single night, Mr. Hall?"

"Yes, I was up all night."

"That's what's so ridiculous about it—you think in a single night you can overturn something that millions of Japanese have spent thousands of years creating. That's not just arrogance, that's the acme of arrogance."

"All right. That's enough. Just pretend you never saw this document."

"I most certainly will not. My neighbor is a newspaper reporter. He's been my instructor on this subject of reforming the Japanese language. I'm going to ask his opinion about it."

"You must not do that. You cannot talk about this to anyone."

"I hereby submit my resignation from the Language Section. I can't bear to waste any more of my time or energy on this outrageous absurdity you're cooking up."

I left the room and took the subway from Shinbashi to Asakusa, where I saw a play by Kidoshin and his theater company at the Shochiku New Theater.

January 18

Though I'm happy-go-lucky by nature and not the sort to drag yesterday's problems over into today, the feeling of intense aggravation from my argument with Language Simplification Officer Lieutenant Commander Hall yesterday afternoon would not leave my mind, and I still felt agitated this morning. Even sitting down to what these days is a very luxurious breakfast of wakame seaweed soup, salted salmon and white rice failed to cheer me up. Still, it was good food, so when I held out my bowl with a grumpy expression for my third bowl of rice, my wife handed it back with a generous dollop of sarcasm.

"Here you are enjoying this fine breakfast, so why the glum face? You should show a little gratitude for this food that your two hard-working daughters have brought home for you."

"Is Fumiko still the kept woman of that idiot?"

"What?"

"I'm asking if she's still sleeping with that Navy Lieutenant Commander Hall."

"I don't think you have any right to talk about your own daughter that way," replied my wife angrily, putting down the rice bowl. "I won't let anyone, even their father, call those girls things like that." Then she took the bamboo chopsticks in her hands and broke them in half. I've been living with her for twenty-five years, but I never knew she was that strong. Cowed, I put the salmon skin over my rice, poured tea over it, and went back to eating silently. My wife stopped eating and, after gazing absent-mindedly at the headlines in the paper lying beyond the rice chest—"A New System of Food Policy," "Coeducation Making No Headway," "Government's Constitutional Revision Plan to Be Announced before General Elections"—slowly lifted her head and looked directly at me.

"Those girls have their own reasons for keeping company with American military men, so I'll have to ask you to be very careful about the way you speak. For example, Fumiko and Mr. Hall may actually be thinking of getting married."

"That won't be possible any longer."

"Because of your argument with Mr. Hall?"

"Oh, you know about it?"

"When Fumiko came back from the Imperial Hotel earlier, she was complaining that you had acted like a child and blown your top. You just don't have any self-control, do you?"

"You may say that, but did you know that that American Hall, who makes such a big show of his pitiful bit of learning, is planning to take *kanji* and *kana* away from us? And after he does that, he's plotting to force us to use *romaji*. You expect me to let him get away with that? Any Japanese man would have let him have it. Even you, what would you do if that newspaper over there was written in *romaji* from top to bottom? You couldn't read a word if it."

"I'll deal with that when it comes to that. I can learn *romaji*—or anything else—if I need to. I'm not worried about it."

"I'm not talking about you. The whole legacy of Japanese culture may be about to be broken off, right here and now in 1946. Japanese culture is under the axe."

"I've had it up to here with big talk about Japanese this and Japanese that," my wife said, putting our dishes on a tray and vigorously wiping down the low table we'd been eating at. "It's all a bunch of hot air. 'Manchuria and Mongolia Are the Empire's Lifeline,' 'The Showa Reformation,' 'The Advanced State of National Defense,' 'The Severity of Times of Crisis,' 'The Spiritual Mobilization of the Entire Nation,' 'A United Nation Rallies,' 'Staunch Fortitude and Persevering Endurance,' 'The Age of Substitutes'..." She was rattling off the slogans as if goading me. "...'The New Order of Greater East

Asia,' '2,600 Years of Imperial Rule,' 'Monday-Monday-Tuesday-Wednesday-Thursday-Friday-Friday,' 'One Hundred Million United in Spirit,' 'Imperial Rule Assistance Association,' 'The Whole World under One Roof,' 'Death over Dishonor'—all this high-sounding words written in your nice, shiny calligraphy, with those fancy *kanji* you men used to talk about 'the destiny of the nation'… what kind of nation are we left with now? Anything near as nice and fancy as your big *kanji*? I can answer that for you—you men and your precious *kanji* turned Japan into a ruined wreck. That's what you did."

"And what about you? Don't you remember what you were doing?" As I pounded on the table in retaliation, I felt a burning smell at the back of my nose. I always feel that when we're about to have an argument. "Wearing your Great Japan Women's Association band and shouting, 'Advance a billion strong, balls of fire!' and marching cheerfully around Shinobazu Pond. Was that you or me?"

"We were idiots, too."

"Who put up a banner in Ueno Hirokoji that said 'Extravagance is the Foe!' and cut off the long kimono sleeves of young girls' formal kimonos?"

"I regret that."

"Who chopped off the permed hair of women with Western hairdos?"

"But in spite of that, we women are much less to blame than you."

"What are you saying? Men and women were both at fault."

"You show me even a single woman in the government, the army or the navy." She balled up the washcloth and threw it at me. "You show me a single female representative in the Imperial Diet. I can't think of a single case when a woman brandished those *kanji* you say you love so much to declaim about 'the state of the empire.' In fact, we were forbidden to do so. We women don't bear one ten-thousandth of the responsibility for Japan ending up in this mess that you men do."

Her words took me by surprise, and I had no reply. I was reduced to silently opening and closing my mouth, like a fish. It may well be true that women bore no responsibility for our war with the outside world in the last two decades.

"That's why I think I understand Mr. Hall's belief that a new Japan will never start unless we throw out *kanji* and replace them with *romaji*. Lord, how I hated those *kanji* 'Death over Dishonor.' Whose death? Whose dishonor? I'll tell you whose dishonor—the old men who sent our boys off to throw away their lives while *they* sat back on their fat haunches spouting fancy phrases. It's disgusting."

"You've become quite a soapbox orator," I said, giving up arguing. I'd have my say no matter what the result. "I just have no use for Hall, I don't care what you say. I don't care if he asks to marry Fumiko. It will never happen while I'm alive."

"You have nothing to say about it."

"Who do you think is the head of this household?" I shouted, throwing the dishrag back at her.

"Fumiko and Takeko, obviously. We're living off of what they earn, after all."

In my rage I tried to flip the table over, but strangely, it didn't budge. My wife was holding it down firmly with both hands and it wouldn't move. Instead, I kicked the legs at hard as I could. But I had no idea my wife was so strong. I don't know when she got that way, but I'll have to watch myself from now on.

It took me twice as long as usual to get to the Metropolitan Police Office. When I kicked the leg of the table, I hurt my right foot and I'm having trouble walking. When I finally made it into the Documentation Section Annex, I removed my sock and discovered that I'd torn my right toenail. As I was wrapping a thread that I got from the former proprietor of the Hongo Bar around it, trying to secure the nail back in place, Umetani from the Documentation Section stopped by and handed me a piece of paper, saying, "This is it for today. When you finish this, go to the CIE. The Documentation Section has received the request from them."

"I quit my job there yesterday."

"Yes, apparently something did happen yesterday, but you can't fight the Americans. And we don't want to get involved."

"This involves every Japanese, which is why I'm fighting the Language Section chief. Mr. Umetani, Chief Hall is trying to ban—"

"I don't want to hear about it," he said, stopping me in mid-sentence, with both hands raised and backing away from me. "I don't want to have anything to do with the Occupation's policies."

"But this is really important."

"Chief Hall called me on the phone. 'Has Mr. Yamanaka told you anything about our argument yesterday?' he asked. I said you hadn't, and he said, 'Make sure you don't hear anything about it in the future, either.' You seem to be treading on dangerous ground, Mr. Yamanaka."

"Dangerous ground?"

"You haven't by any chance had access to any classified information, have you? You'd better be careful." Listening to the sound of his footsteps as he trotted back to the Documentation Section Office, I regretted having come straight here. In my anger following my fight with my wife, I forgot to stop by Mr. Takahashi's house. The first thing I should have done is tell Mr. Takahashi about Chief Hall's plan. I know he'd appreciate the threat inherent in Hall's proposal. "I have to make sure to see Mr. Takahashi today," I said to myself as I picked up my stylus—only to drop it again in surprise when I saw the content of the memo.

As a rule, all letters from Japanese citizens to General MacArthur are shared with the Japanese here at Police Department, but we have discovered that a certain category of letters are not being forwarded to us—letters relating to the imperial system. For example, a letter sent to General MacArthur in September of last year by a certain Hiromichi Kumazawa (56), a variety store owner of Chikusa Ward, Nagoya City. In his letter, Kumazawa declared, 'I am the true and legitimate emperor of Japan, and I have many articles to prove my claim. I call on you, General MacArthur, to issue an order restoring me to the imperial throne.' The GHQ revealed this letter to an American newspaper reporter last December, and reporters from *Time*, *Life*, *New York Herald Tribune*, *Stars and Stripes*, and other magazines and papers came knocking on Kumazawa's door. Suspicious, officers of the Chikusa Police Station, working secretly with Clerk Kobayashi sent from headquarters, were able to gather the above information. According to Kobayashi's report, in addition to this "Emperor Kumazawa," there have been claims by an "Emperor Tonomura" and "Emperor

Miura" in Aichi Prefecture, an "Emperor Yokokura" in Kochi Prefecture, "Emperor Nagahama" in Kagoshima Prefecture, "Emperor Sakamoto" in Okayama Prefecture, and "Emperor Sado" in Niigata Prefecture. All of them have written to the general calling upon him to restore them to the throne.

It is believed that the GHQ is waiting for the right moment to make these letters public, which is why they have not released them to the police. They plan to release them all at once in an attempt to shake confidence in the imperial house and observe the reaction of the Japanese people. If the people react by angrily denouncing these self-proclaimed emperors, the GHQ will interpret this as a sign of continued support for the imperial system; if the public welcomes and ridicules these many claimants to the throne, the GHQ will interpret this as an indication that the people no longer feel the need for the imperial system. This is regarded as the Occupation's strategy.

According to information we've been able to gather, an article about Emperor Kumazawa will appear in *Life* and *Stars and Stripes* in the near future. This will probably lead to demonstrations calling for the abolition of the imperial system, for which we should be prepared.

Furthermore, in addition to these individuals in outlying areas, there are no doubt some in Tokyo proclaiming themselves emperors, so it is advised that the authorities be on the alert.

At last the riddle of Kobayashi's disappearance at the end of last year was solved. Though I hated him, as a detective of the Special High Police, for putting me, Shinsuke Yamanaka, an ordinary citizen who had committed no crime, into prison at Yokaichiba for nearly four months, still, for some perverse reason, I suppose, I missed him when he suddenly disappeared. Knowing where he was picked my spirits up a bit, and I was able to make today's stencil in beautiful Qing-dynasty-style lettering that was quite something if I do say so myself.

After delivering the printed copies to the Documentation Section, I was dragging my aching foot through Hibiya Park toward the Tokyo Broadcasting Hall and, just as I'd arrived at the Hibiya Public Hall, I noticed a man in black who seemed to have been following me.

Whenever I stopped to rest my foot, he stopped. Glancing casually over at him, I saw he was a small man of about forty, wearing a large, loose, but high-quality black wool overcoat and a black wool ski hat pulled low over his forehead. More than half of his face was covered by a black beard, and he was wearing black boots. He was black all over. I walked over to the public hall, leaned on a pillar, and took off my right shoe, looking at my aching toe without removing my sock. Perhaps because I had little experience in being followed, and he had little experience in following people, our eyes met.

"Pardon me," said the man, flashing white teeth from the area between his beard and mustache, and then suddenly making an expression of concern. "What's wrong with your foot?"

"You've never seen anyone drag their foot before?" I replied sarcastically to Mr. White Teeth. "You seem to have taken an interest in it from back there at the Supreme Court Building." I took a Lucky Strike out of a pack and slowly struck a match. "I'm not stupid, you know."

"Actually, I've been following you since you left your home in Nezu."

Startled, I expelled a puff of air and unintentionally extinguished my match. The man with the beard took a Zippo lighter out of his pocket and approached me. "I was waiting in front of your house this morning. And then for another two and one-half hours at the employees' entrance to the police station…"

"Have we ever met before?"

"No, this is the first time."

"Then why do you know my name? And why follow me all the way from Nezu? Have I done something illegal? Who are you? A Special Higher Police officer?"

"Don't be silly. There are none of those any more."

"Then what are you?

"Please, stay calm." He extended the flame of the Zippo lighter, which he held in both hands, toward me. The tip of my Lucky Strike was trembling, so he had a hard time lighting it. "I run a company called America, Inc., in Komagome Katamachi. To tell the truth, I'm a black marketer."

"Ah, a black marketer." I inhaled deeply on my Lucky Strike,

finally lit, and exhaled vigorously in the direction of Black Beard.
"What is it you want with me?"

"I've heard that you have friends in the Police Department
and among the Americans. I've been following you this morning
because I wanted to ask you if you couldn't help me out." There
was something about the way he spoke that made me think he was
a former military officer.

"Then why didn't you just say something? You gave me the
creeps."

"When it came to it, I just couldn't bring myself to speak up. I really
should have just waited for an introduction from Mr. Aoyama."

"By Aoyama you mean the Aoyama who's the head of the Nezu
Neighborhood Association?"

"Yes, Kiichiro Aoyama is my wife's older brother. Allow me to
introduce myself. I am Saburo Himeda." He gave me a business card
printed by mimeograph on rough yellow card stock.

America, Inc.
Saburo Himeda, President
Hongo Ward, Komagome Katamachi 30
Air Raid Shelter #3

As I looked at the printing I felt a wave of nostalgia wash over
me. It had the special characteristics of the mimeograph ink I knew
only too well. There as just a trace of white ink blended in with the
black, offsetting the usual heavy gloss of mimeograph printing ink
and rendering it a much more subdued and elegant shade.

"You have a very fine business card. Was it printed at Daiichi
Tokosha on Suzuran Street in Kanda? Or Daini Tokosha at
Kanefusacho, Shinbashi?"

"At Daini Toko," said Black Beard, his eyes wide with surprise.
"How did you know?"

"It's quite simple, really. First, Tokosha is the only company that
uses ink this way. And in all Japan today, the only place that has white
ink is Tokosha. In autumn of the year before last, the president of
Tokosha in Suzuran Street hid away fourteen or fifteen pickle pots of
white ink in the mountains of Fukushima. That's how I knew." Mr.

Himeda seemed fascinated by my lecture on ink. "Third, I learned how to cut stencils at Tokosha in Kanda. The company president was my teacher. And that's why I know his secret of blending white ink in with black."

"I see."

"If we keep standing out here in the cold we'll both end up as human icicles before long. Let's go over there," I said, motioning Mr. Himeda over to a place under the eaves by the entrance to Hibiya Public Hall. I somehow felt I could trust a fellow who had a business card printed with Tokosha's famous blended ink. "Now what is it you want me to do?"

"It's a long story, but don't you have to get to the CIE?

"No, no, if I'm there in time for lunch, that's plenty of time."

"But…" He suddenly stood at attention, as rigid as if he'd swallowed a stick. "At noon on August 15th, I heard the Emperor's radio broadcast at the 252nd Naval Air Squadron Base in Mobara, Chiba."

Since I couldn't exactly take pride in the fact that on the same day I was in a prison in Yokaichiba, not far from Mobara, I didn't say anything.

"There were thirty-eight Zero Type 52 fighter planes stationed at the base for the final battle of the home front."

"You were a pilot?"

"No, I was a member of the base's garrison. After the Imperial broadcast, as I was standing there in a mental fog, my company leader tapped me on the shoulder and said there was something he wanted to discuss with me. That something turned out to be dividing up the three months' worth of food and the clothing stored on the base. Now that we've surrendered the company would be disbanded, he said, but after we allow every company member to drag home as much as he can carry, there will still be a lot left over. 'What are you going to do about that?' he asked."

"And how did you answer?"

"With the company disbanded, we had no way of earning a living, so I suggested we become black marketers with the rest of the stores."

"That was a pretty bold reply."

"So seven volunteers, from the company leader on down, took

fifty bales of rice, twenty bales of wheat, ten bags of flour, thirty tubs each of miso and soy sauce, seven bags each of sugar and salt, one hundred wool blankets and thirty pairs of military boots and started out in the black market. That's what America, Inc., is."

"It doesn't sound like you have any problem to me." I was getting bored. "That must be enough to keep you sitting pretty for a long time."

"But you're bound to reach the end of the road eventually if the only way you're getting by is selling off your belongings. Now's the time for us to dump these goods, put together some cash, and build two movie theaters, we decided." He dug around in his pocket and came out with two more business cards.

Theater Komagome
Saburo Himeda, General Manager
Hongo Ward, Komagome Katamachi 30
Air Raid Shelter #3

Central Komagome
Saburo Himeda, Vice-Manager
Hongo Ward, Komagome Katamachi 30
Air Raid Shelter #3

Both of these were also printed with Tokosha's special blended ink, too. This guy really likes business cards, I thought.

"Movie theaters, even if they're just a screen in a barn, are always full to overflowing these days. With the movie theaters, the seven of us, and our fifty or so dependents, can get by. If they're a success, we can even build another one or two."

"So again, what's your problem?"

"I'm getting to the meat of it now," said Mr. Himeda, bringing his bearded face right up to mine. "We'd worked things out with a moving company in Shinjuku, and we had them rent five big charcoal trucks. We managed to get thirty sacks of charcoal for fuel, we loaded up the trucks with the thirty bales of rice, thirteen bales of wheat, fifty wool blankets and the rest of our supplies, and departed from Komagome. That was yesterday, before dawn."

"Where had you been hiding all that stuff?"

"We were using air raid shelters as our warehouse. Shelter #1 was for food and Shelter #2 was for clothing."

"And where were you taking it?"

"Aichi. A lumber dealer in Kariya had promised to exchange the supplies for lumber. But just a short while after we set out, at the banks of the Tama River at Rokugo, we were stopped by the police."

"You didn't just keep on driving?"

"The police have recently received permission from the GHQ to start carrying firearms."

"Oh, that's right."

"They threatened us with their guns, and took everything, trucks and all, and impounded them at Shinagawa Police Station. They're saying it's a violation of the Economic Stabilization Law. That's undoubtedly true, but unless we can do something about it, our dream of movie theaters goes up in smoke. Worse, the members of seven families will be hung out to dry. Here is an inventory of all the goods that were confiscated," Himeda said, carefully taking out a sheet of paper from his coat, as if it were very precious. "I came up with a plan on the spot, and said to the police officer, 'I'm just a hireling. If I go back to my boss like this, I'll be in big trouble. I need something that proves that these goods were confiscated by the police.' I held my ground and just kept shouting that over and over until finally they gave in and wrote this out for me. When he handed it to me he said, 'Tell your boss he's got to make an appearance here. With this much stuff, it doesn't end with just having it confiscated. He's got to come and take his punishment like a man.'"

"And you care about your former troop leader too much to allow him to take that scolding." It all became clear to me. "So you want me to pretend I'm him. Don't be ridiculous. Who'd be willing to do that?"

"Don't get ahead of me and start inventing things."

"But you said you had a favor to ask me."

"Please listen just a little longer. As a matter of fact, I've figured out a way to get the confiscated goods back."

"Ah…"

"What do people fear the most in the world?"

"Up to August 15th, I guess it was, first, the military. Next, the Special Higher Police. Third, the regular police. Then earthquakes, lightning, fires and fathers, in that order."

"And after August 15th?"

"The Americans, of course. Emperor Moatside would be at the top of the list, then the military police, the MPs..."

"That's it, Mr. Yamanaka. I'd like you to introduce me to an MP."

"I'm afraid I don't understand what you're saying."

"If an MP drives up to the Shinagawa Police Station in a Jeep and says to the police chief there, 'The goods you've confiscated have been requisitioned by the U.S. Army. How dare you confiscate them?' what do you think would happen?"

"Everyone at the station from the chief on down would bow and scrape like chickens in the yard, and hand the stuff over without a peep."

"Wouldn't they? We'll be glad to pay you an introduction fee. Can find us a cooperative MP? We'll pay him a lot, too. My first preference would be a second-generation Japanese MP who needed the money, but—"

"Do you really think such an MP even exists?"

"If you could just see your way to—"

"I can see my way all I want, but unless an MP sees his way, it's pointless."

"I'd owe my life to you. I implore you." Himeda dropped to his knees on the cold cement, kneeling formally and pressing his palms together.

"All I can say is I can't do the impossible. I'm going to pretend you never asked me this." I turned and left him there.

When I arrived at the office on the fifth floor of the Tokyo Broadcasting Hall, Miss Kurita said to me: "The boss left a message for you. He has something he needs to talk to you about today, so he wants you to stay here and wait for him."

It's 8 P.M. Lieutenant Commander Hall, who said he needed to talk to me, still hasn't shown up. Through the curtain of falling snow, I can see Himeda leaning up against the wall of the Hikokan Building across from the window. He's been there since the afternoon in the same position. Still, it's very strange. How did he know that the

Language Section is on the fifth floor, and that this window faces the
Hikokan Building?

January 19

This Saturday is very sunny.

It seems that the wind blows colder these days than it used to,
with nothing to block its path. This morning, however, for the first
time in several days, there was no cold wind. On a nice day like this
it would be pleasant to just pass the time sitting on the veranda in
the sun, but after the biggest fight I've ever had with my wife in the
twenty-five years we've been married yesterday, a cone of silence has
fallen over the house. And on Saturdays and Sundays my daughters,
the "companions" of officers of the occupying American army, are
likely to be at home. When all the women are here together, I'm
sure they'll start up with their usual chorus these days of "Why are
men so useless?" so I'd much prefer to sit and chat with the former
proprietor of the Hongo Bar at the Metropolitan Police Office
Documentation Section Annex.

On my way out I stopped at my neighbor Mr. Takahashi's house.
I wanted to find out what he'd say about the plan being hatched
by Language Simplification Unit Officer Hall. If MacArthur signed
the plan and the education commission visiting Japan in March
accepted it as their public statement, it would be awful. *Kanji*
and *kana* would disappear. The Japanese language would stop
being Japanese. Who would want to write a diary if it had to be
done in *romaji*? We'd had enough of that silliness with Takuboku
Ishikawa. Though I might be denounced for just parroting ideas I'd
stolen wholesale from someone else, I was determined to use Mr.
Takahashi's opinion as my weapon to beat Lieutenant Commander
Hall's logic into submission.

"My husband has gone to Nagano," said Mrs. Takahashi at the
back door. She seemed to be in the middle of breakfast. I could see
the table out of the corner of my eye. Whatever was in her rice bowl
was a kind of greenish yellow, so she must have been eating rice
gruel with sweet potatoes in it.

"Did he go to Nagano to buy food?"

"No, he was sent off on a business trip. He was ordered to

accompany an American reporter who wants to investigate how rural reform is proceeding. It was suddenly decided the evening of the day before yesterday, so he had to make his preparations in a rush. From Nagano he's going on to Akita."

"When will he be back?"

"He said about a week or ten days."

This was no good. If I didn't act quickly, Lieutenant Commander Hall would submit his plan to his superiors.

"Are you here about... Shoichi?" Seeing my reaction of disappointment, she seemed to have concluded that I was there to talk about her son. "What has he done now?"

I'm pretty certain that Shoichi is, together with Kiyoshi, an underling in a gang of professional thieves, but apparently Mrs. Takahashi hadn't caught wind of that development yet. I didn't want to worry her unnecessarily, so I smiled and said: "I saw Kiyoshi the day before yesterday. He and Shoichi are studying at the headquarters of their Tokyo Rice Relief Club in Asakusabashi. There's an elderly woman there who does all the cooking and laundry, so they're living a life of luxury. They have everything they could possibly want. The university students living with them there are teaching them English, too." "But they still go to Akita and Yamagata to buy black-market rice, don't they? I can't believe my son is a mule." She touched the corner of her apron to her eye. "He's just a first-year middle school student. I didn't raise my son to be a black marketer."

"You shouldn't look down on black marketers. If we left it up to the authorities, the entire population of Tokyo would starve to death in less than three days. Everybody knows that, even kids of three or four. It's the intrepid and fearless efforts of the black marketers to get food into Tokyo that make it possible for us to get by here, one way or another, by hook or by crook. My eldest daughter Kinuko's father-in-law used to say that black marketers are courageous deliverymen. The authorities, on the other hand, are mindless idiots. They can't do a thing to solve the food shortage, but they try to punish the only people who are really contributing to our survival." About halfway through this it occurred to me that I was actually trying to persuade myself even more than I was attempting to convince Mrs. Takahashi. "You feel bad because you think that your son ran away from home to become an apprentice black marketer, but if you take the attitude that he courageously decided to become independent and started up his own delivery business while still attending school, things look a lot brighter. That's the way I want to look at it, I can tell you."

"We shouldn't have let him spend so much time with the likes of Kiyoshi." She lowered the apron that she'd been holding to her eyes just enough to shoot me a look of piercing accusation. We've been neighbors for twelve years, close enough to run over and borrow some soy sauce or rice. This was the first time she's ever looked at me with those eyes or said the words "the likes of Kiyoshi." Little shivers of fear raced through me, quickly changing into anger.

"That's a little unfair, don't you think? It's not like you. Anyway, from the time they were little, Kiyoshi has always been the follower and Shoichi the pack leader. It could well have been Shoichi who got Kiyoshi involved in this, not the other way around."

"There was no reason for my son to leave home. But for Kiyoshi, after all, his sisters…"

So it had come down to that. I guess everyone looks askance at a family that's served up its daughters on the half shell to U.S. military officers. My anger suddenly subsided, and I felt a kind of sadness, and as if a stick I'd been leaning on had snapped. "Does your husband feel the same way?"

"He doesn't talk much these days. I don't know what he thinks."

For some time, the man in black had been standing at the entrance to the alleyway, sending vigorous puffs from his cigarette into the sunny spot between us. Himeda, the man who approached me the other day, was waiting for my answer. I said goodbye to Mrs. Takahashi and walked off in the direction opposite from where he was standing.

Following the sun, I found myself walking down a broad street to the south. A mountain range of dark brown debris extended down the middle of the street, blocking my view of the cars on the other side. When I looked in that direction, all I could see were the tops of people's heads as they walked north and south. The sun reflecting off the forehead of the tall Mr. Himeda occasionally flashed over to my side of the street.

Because I, Shinsuke Yamanaka, through my two daughters, am

acquainted with U.S. military officers, and because, though I've already handed in my resignation, I was employed at the Language Section of the Civilian Information and Education section of the GHQ, and finally, because my original workplace is the Metropolitan Police Department Documentation Section Annex, which also happens to house the Provost Marshal's Office, Metropolitan Tokyo Area, Himeda has asked me to help him recover five trucks of black-market goods that have been confiscated by the Shinagawa Police Station by finding him an MP who would drive to the station in a Jeep and demand the return of the confiscated merchandise. It's ridiculous. No MP anywhere would get involved in such risky business. But how am I going to persuade him to accept my refusal? As I was walking along thinking about this, I noticed three vehicles that looked like tanks driving with a roaring sound around on top of the pile of debris.

As I got closer, I saw that they were modified Type 97 Chi-Ha tanks of the former Imperial Army. Their gun turrets had been removed and the driver's seat was completely exposed. Men wearing military uniforms and with sweatbands tied around their foreheads were gripping the steering wheels. A large piece of metal about the size of a tatami mat had been attached to the front of each tank, and the drivers were slowly pushing the rubble with it.

"They want to get this cleaned up as quickly as they can. After all, it's right next to the Ginza that the Americans are so fond of." I looked over and saw Himeda standing by the street posts at the intersection. Raising my gaze, I noted that "10th Street" was painted in black on the white sign for the street running north and south, and "Z Avenue" on the sign for the street running east and west. That meant that I was at the Miharabashi intersection of Showa Avenue and the road leading from Hibiya to Tsukijima. Following the sun had led me considerably out of my way.

"But these construction companies sure are quick off the block," said Himeda, pointing to the side of one of the tanks. A construction company's name was written on it in white paint. "They buy these tanks cheap from the government, and then they use them to do government work. They must be making so much money it's killing them. Not like us, who have to rely on our own resources to take care of ourselves."

"The thing you talked to me about yesterday—let's just say I never heard it," I said, walking off briskly down Z Avenue at a pace that would have done a competitive athlete proud.

"There must be twenty or thirty MPs in the Police Department Annex," said Himeda, who waited for me to pass Hibiya Crossing, where the number of people thinned out considerably, before running up to me to continue pressing me. "Surely one of them is desperate for some extra money."

"You don't give up, do you? The MPs are all honest, upstanding young men. After all, Provost Marshal Captain Rupkey is right there in the former fire chief's office on the first floor of the Metropolitan Police Department, on the side by the Justice Ministry. The MPs are like his loyal guardian-attendants. They're strictly on the up-and-up."

"Then how about the MPs stationed at the former Naval Accounting School in Tsukiji?"

"Camp Burness?"

"Yes, there's a huge battalion of MPs there. They must be coming and going all the time at the Police Department Annex, and you must know one of them. When they need money, it's the Japanese they come to."

"I don't know any MPs."

"I don't mean to insult you, but if it's a matter of money, I'm prepared to offer you a finder's fee. I can get 5,000 yen to you within the day."

"Let's just say that I never heard any of this, and that I never met you, either. Understand?"

"There's a dance hall called Tenka Club in Karasumori, Shinbashi. It's our hangout. I'll be waiting for good news from you there. Please, Mr. Yamanaka, you've got to help us. After all, the livelihoods of seven men and their fifty family members are at stake." He seemed about to prostrate himself on the ground to implore me once again, but I paid him no mind, turned on my heel, and scurried into the Police Department.

The former proprietor of the Hongo Bar was sitting outside, soaking up some sun as he was peeling onions. When I said hello, he pointed his knife toward the interior of the annex and said, "You've got company." Then he walked up to me and whispered, "I see you have a beautiful lady friend."

Looking through the window, I saw Tomoe, in profile, seated in a slightly hunched posture on a wood chair and twisting a handkerchief she held in her lap. In the light coming in from the window, her neck was very white and stood out as if it were sculpted.

"I guess you've still got the magic. Who is she?"

"She's just my tenant. I'm her landlord, she's my tenant. You know Toride on the Mito Highway?

"The town where it crosses the Toné River."

"She's the widow of a saké brewer there. Her father-in-law went funny in the head when a bomb dropped too close to him, and she has two children who are staying with relatives in Fukushima. She has to provide for all three of them." I couldn't very well tell him that she was someone I have secret feelings for or that she makes her living by selling her body to an American officer at the Imperial Hotel, or that she's second-in-command of the famous band of seven women called Tokyo Seven Rose. "She rents a room from us, and works at the Japan Water Company."

"They say a beauty never lives long."

"That's her story. Can I wrangle a cup of coffee for her out of you?"

"I've already given her one."

I opened the door and was met with a delightful fragrance. Tomoe stood up.

"I just missed you back at Nezu. I know it must be a bother, but I decided to come here and wait until you'd arrived."

"Yes, I took a little detour this morning. They've started cleaning up Showa Avenue."

"Have they," she said, reseating herself in the chair. As she did, her two braids swayed slightly over her slender shoulders. Her bangs were pulled up, making her forehead appear wider than usual. It was white and cool looking.

"Your color isn't good," I said, moving the mimeograph board over to a shelf. I get uncomfortable when I'm alone with her if I don't keep moving. "Aren't you working too hard?" This time I placed the stylus inside the desk drawer.

"Do you know anyone who might be interested in buying this?" she asked, taking something wrapped in paper out of the pocket of the checked blouse she wore beneath her dark brown cardigan. "You know so many people that I decided to ask for your help." Her carefully manicured hands trembled slightly as she opened the paper. It held a ring sporting a large pear-shaped black pearl that glowed like dew in the night.

"What a fine pearl."

"It came down to me when my mother-in-law passed away. It's the great treasure of the Yamamoto family."

"Why are you selling something so precious?" She couldn't need money. From her work, she had access to cigarettes, whiskey, chocolate and everything else American. If she sold them on the black market, she'd have enough to build a small house.

"Someone I know has acquired a big debt playing poker. He owes it to the Matsuda gang in Shiba Kotohiracho."

"The Matsuda gang—the ones who run the market in front of Shinbashi Station?"

She nodded sadly. "You know that Senbikiya on Ginza Avenue is a cabaret for the Occupation soldiers. The Matsuda gang has a secret gambling den next door to it, and my friend fell into their trap. He picked the wrong people to play cards with. They're threatening that if he can't pay up they'll go to his commanding officer to collect. If it were discovered that he'd even played poker for money with Japanese, he'd be thrown in the brig. Now he owes them 30,000 yen. He's doing everything he can to get the money, but so far he's only come up with less than half. That's why…"

"And is this friend an American military officer?"

"No." Tomoe lightly waved her handkerchief back and forth in denial, sending the fragrance of her toilet water uncoiling in my direction like a conjurer's rope. "He's Australian. He's the third son of a family with a ranch outside Sydney. He's an MP with the British forces at Camp Ebisu. You know, the Naval University that used to be in Meguro. He's stationed there."

Suddenly the face of Himeda, who had been so persistently tailing me since yesterday, flashed into my mind. An MP is an MP, even if he's an English MP.

"British soldiers were frequenting the Matsuda gang gambling den, and he went there to arrest them, but he ended up getting sucked into it himself."

I'd heard that the British soldiers are hot-tempered. They seem to be quick with their fists and are constantly getting into brawls with the soldiers of the American engineering battalion in Shinjuku. There are regular reports of these scuffles in the interoffice memos of the Police Department. They probably like to gamble as much as they like to fight.

"And this MP from Camp Ebisu—what is he to you?"

"David says he wants to take me back with him to Sydney. Oh, yes, his name is David Badham."

"Then he's more than just a lover."

Tomoe blushed slightly. I blanched.

"I see."

"But when he goes back, we'll part ways. I'm twelve years older than he is, and I have to think of my children and my father-in-law While he's in Japan, though, I'd like to spend as much time with him as I can."

As long as I thought that Tomoe was seeing a number of unidentified men, it doesn't bother me. And of course I have a wife, and I've always lived by the rule that any other woman is as far out of my reach as a blossom on a mountain peak, or the crescent moon reflected in the water, so I'm sure Tomoe doesn't know my feelings. But it's odd that my heart should flutter like this as soon as I learn that she's in love with a specific individual.

"What's wrong?" Tomoe asked. When I came to my senses, I saw that the desk was shaking, and it was my trembling hands that were the cause.

"If you can't sell the pearl, or if you can only get a few thousand yen for it, what will you do?"

"Perhaps we should commit suicide?" she said with a deprecatory laugh.

"You shouldn't say things like that, even as a joke. Think how sad your children and your father-in-law would be."

"I know that."

"Anyway, there's no reason to do anything rash. I think I may have a way out of this." I decided to go and meet Himeda again. I'd solve the problem that was troubling my Juliet. That's the mark of a truly noble passion. "There is, however, a small degree of risk involved."

"Risk?" Tomoe's eyes blazed up and she brought her face closer to mine, over the desk. I could see myself in her eyes.

"But it should all be over in less than five minutes. Your lover David needs to drive to the Shinagawa Police Station in a Jeep and say to the police captain there: 'In the early morning of January 17th, at the riverbank at Rokugo, officers from this police station confiscated the contents of five trucks, but it was the Allied Forces stationed at Camp Ebisu who had engaged them to transport those goods, which must be returned at once.' There should be an interpreter at the police station, so he can say it in English."

"And someone will pay him for that?"

"About 20,000 yen, I should say." I carefully explained Himeda's situation to Tomoe. "When can you contact David?"

"We're planning to meet at noon at the Hibiya drive-in nearby."

Anyone who knew about the MPs' duties would know what she meant. They drive around the city all day in their Jeeps, resting several times a day at drive-ins for the Occupation Forces located throughout the city. The Hibiya drive-in was finished ten days ago, and is just a five-minute walk from the police department.

"Then tell David to go to a dance hall in Karasumori, Shinbashi, called the Tenka Club. If you can make it, why don't you go, too. I'll go there after lunch."

"Couldn't you have this made into a necktie pin?" asked Tomoe, pushing the ring toward me. "I want to express my thanks."

"I'm just an old fan maker. I'm a craftsman. Do craftsmen wear neckties?" I pushed the ring back. "Give it to your children some day."

"But I don't feel right about this."

"If my wife found out, I'd be in a mess of trouble, anyway."

"I'll tell her about it myself."

"That'll just cause unnecessary fuss." And as we were pushing the ring back and forth, Tomoe's finger touched mine. Time seemed to stand still and a shock ran through my body.

"All right. I'll knit you a sweater," said Tomoe, standing up energetically. "I promise."

"I don't need anything," I said to Tomoe's back as she left the building carrying her coat. I don't know if she heard me or not. I sat there in a daze for a while, until it occurred to me that I should record the shock that ran through my body in my diary, and I quickly unwrapped the cloth I was carrying it in and took it out. I had two hours to write until noon.

(an interruption)

If you ask anyone in Tokyo today what the liveliest spot in the city is, a hundred out of a hundred will answer, "Shinbashi." And then if you ask them why Shinbashi is so bustling, ten out of ten will reply, "The market there has everything you could want, and Shinbashi is a safe place." But no matter who you ask *why* Shinbashi is so safe, you'll find them stumped for an answer. But since I'm always printing the Police Department Documentation Section's interoffice memos, which are a kind of daily police gazette, I can answer that with confidence: "It's safe because the Kanto Matsuda yakuza clan controls the territory from Shinbashi Station to Toranomon."

The Kanto Matsuda gang appears regularly in the Police Department's interoffice memos. Their headquarters are in a burned building in Shiba Kotohira-cho. Light machine guns formerly belonging to the army are attached to the roof of the building, and young yakuza who look like former Special Attack Forces pilots, wearing their old air force uniforms, are always on the roof glaring in the direction of Shibuya, so the police have to keep close tabs on their activities. Naturally they can't allow the yakuza to possess anything as dangerous as light machine guns, so the police regularly raid the place, but each time they do, quite mysteriously there're no guns to be found on the roof and the yakuza are just lazing around smoking Lucky Strikes. The reason the machine guns are aimed at Shibuya is because of the battle going on between the Matsuda gang and the Taiwanese yakuza gang that controls Shibuya. When members of the two gangs happen to encounter each other in Akasaka, the border between the two turfs, you can practically see the sparks flying. You could almost light a cigarette with them, it's that obvious.

It all started in the fall of last year when a Taiwanese set up a stand at the Shinbashi market. As one of the Shinbashi gang members kicked the stand to pieces, he shouted, "Lately you Taiwanese are getting too big for your britches. You brag that since August 15th, you've been liberated, you're no longer Japanese subjects, and in fact, you belong to one of the victor countries. We're not about to let any foreigners set up stalls in our market. Go back to Shibuya where you belong—or better yet, go back to Taiwan."

Three days later the corpse of that particular gang member was found floating in a roadside canal in Sukiyabashi. This incident immediately put both gangs on hair-trigger alert. The head of the Shinjuku yakuza, Kinosuke Ozu, tried to mediate to prevent a full-scale war. When the head of the Kanto Matsuda gang arrived at the inn in Kamakura that had been selected for the ceremony sealing the truce, both the Shibuya gang and the head of the Shinjuku gang almost fell over backwards. The boss of the Shinbashi gang was a woman in her late thirties. She was a real beauty, with an oval face, her hair pulled up in back and overpowering sex appeal. Intoxicated by the smell of her makeup and powder, the Shibuya gang agreed to the clearly disadvantageous condition that from now on the Taiwanese would restrict themselves to the Shibuya area and keep out of Shinbashi. I have to admit, I understand the Shibuya gang's surrender. A heavy odor of urine, pickles and the acrid smell of smoke hangs over the city these days; anyone suddenly finding himself face to face with the alluring fragrance of a woman's powder would lose his senses. In our times, the scent of a beautiful woman is more powerful than even pistols and machine guns.

In a recent Police Department interoffice memo the chief of police observed:

Though there may be a few minor disputes, for the most part both Shinbashi and Shibuya are quiet at present. The Kanto Matsuda gang and the Taiwanese mafia have their respective territories firmly under control. Considering the shortage of police officers in Tokyo at present, for the time being, it seems wise to entrust the preservation of the peace in Shinbashi and Shibuya to these two gangs. As for the future, when the police department is better prepared, we can ignite a spark between the two sides, poised as they are in an extremely tense stand-off, and allow their mutual animosity to explode into a full-blown conflict. Then, with the support of the military police of the Occupation Forces, under the guise of quelling riots and restoring peace, we can bring both areas under our control, disperse the black markets and rebuild the areas.

Reading this, you can't help but conclude that the power of the police trumps even a woman's face powder.

I found the Tenka Club that Himeda had told me to meet him at on Karasumori Street, which the barracks headquarters of the female boss of the Mastuda gang looked down over. More than twenty singed Tokyo Municipal buses converted into temporary housing line the street except for one section, where recently built barracks stand. The Tenka Club sat between a place serving stew and coffee on old wood barrels for tables and a pharmacy with a sign reading, "De-worming Medicine in Stock."

I opened the sliding door with solid wood panels at the bottom and oilpaper at the top and was hit with the sound of a foxtrot playing on the phonograph and the overpowering odor of wood. It might be just a barracks, but it was new, which is why you could still smell the wood. The record seemed very worn out, and the scratching noise of the needle in the grooves was almost louder than the music.

The room was about the size of two elementary school classrooms, and the thin wood floors undulated in waves under the weight of customers. Three couples were dancing in the middle of the room, all wearing wooden sandals. It was a third-rate dance hall at best. From the dark counter on the right came a voice: "Welcome!" I walked in that direction and a young man with a dark expression, wearing an army shirt with a stiff collar, handed me a glass of water.

"Unfortunately, at noon time the dancers are out eating lunch. What would you like to drink?"

"What do you have?"

"Coffee, beer and potato vodka. But we only serve the beer and potato vodka after five."

So all they had was coffee. He was a strange bartender. I cocked my head, and the eyes of the young man flashed.

"You got something to say?" he asked.

"No, nothing."

"You can't fool me. I saw that look in your eyes. Isn't that right, mister?"

"All right, since you insist. Wouldn't it have been better if you had just said from the start, 'During the day we only serve coffee. Would you like some?'"

"So you don't like the way I do things, is that it? Who do you think you are?" He threw the towel he had in his hand at me and leaped over the counter. Before I knew what was happening, he had grabbed me by my suit lapel and was lifting me off the floor. My peaceful day up to that moment was suddenly just a memory fading into the distance, and I felt like I was being dragged into a frightening, distorted time where there was anything but peace and safety, or, to put it simply, for the first time in a long time I smelled a charred odor and was inundated by the silent terror that used to wash over me whenever I heard an air-raid alert.

"You need to be taught a lesson. Come with me."

He started dragging toward the back. As two thoughts were spinning in my head—one, that I was going to get the crap beaten out of me and, two, how had this happened—suddenly a voice said: "He's with me, Ken." It was Himeda. "Give him a cup of coffee with plenty of real sugar."

"He's with you, chief?"

"That's right."

"Well, excuse me," said the young man Himeda called Ken, walking back through the swinging door to the space behind the counter. The woman who'd been dancing with Himeda leaned up against a pillar and watched us, lighting up a Lucky Strike.

"It's quieter over here," said Himeda, leading me to a table near the windows, across the dance floor from the counter.

"What was that about?"

"It's part of his job. He goads a customer into making a complaint, then picks a fight, steals his wallet, and chases him off."

" But… but that's a yakuza trick."

"And he's a yakuza. This place is operated by Fumi Matsuda. Surely you've heard of her."

"The boss of the Kanto Matsuda gang."

"Yes. They run it this way to keep outsiders out."

"One visit would certainly be enough."

"In other words, this is only for, well, 'family.' And as a result, you know that anything said here will never leak out. I guess you could say it's a kind of Matsuda gang combined conference room/ entertainment center."

Things were starting to add up: Himeda's business cards; the platoon leader of a garrison of the 252nd Naval Air Force Squadron in Mobara when the Emperor announces Japan's surrender; a sharp-witted demobilized soldier who starts America, Inc., selling goods lifted from the base's stores; the plan to build two movie theaters...

"Some of my men had pretty much given up on things and couldn't see returning to regular civilian life. They were going on and on how, after all they'd been through, they wanted to enjoy life and go out with a bang, so I sent them over to the Matsuda gang. In exchange, they let me use this as my office," Himeda explained, as if he had read my mind. As I listened, I took a sip of the coffee the hair-triggered bartender had brought me. It was every bit as good as that made by the former proprietor of the Hongo Bar. "So, Mr. Yamanaka, about what we were talking about, did you find me an MP?"

"There's an MP who's gotten involved with gambling and dug himself into a hole. His lover is a Japanese woman I know well. According to her, he has racked up a debt of tens of thousands of yen at a gambling joint in the Ginza. He's an MP with the British Armed Forces stationed at Camp Ebisu."

"All I need for my plan is someone with an MP armband to drive over to the Shinagawa Police Station. It doesn't matter what kind of MP he is. I don't care about the nationality. Though I suppose a black MP probably wouldn't be as effective."

"He's an Australian by the name of Badham. His family runs a ranch outside Sydney. He's a British MP, so he wears one of those red berets, as I'm sure you know. He probably has a moustache, too. But I'm certain he's white."

"That's good," Himeda said, "good." Then he asked the bartender for a beer. "Let's celebrate. Now, he's going to be driving an MP Jeep, right?"

"He'll be here in a minute. You can ask him yourself."

"Thank you, Mr. Yamanaka. I owe you one." He poured the beer into my cup and with his other hand reached into his suit and pulled out a fat envelope. "There is 20,000 yen inside."

"No, no, I don't need it. I didn't introduce you to Badham for money. The Japanese woman, well, I feel sorry for her. That's why I played the role of go-between."

The short-fused bartender grabbed the envelope from Himeda and stuck it in my face like a knife. "Don't insult the platoon leader."

"All right, all right, I'll take it. But it's a strange coincidence, isn't it? The gambling den where Sergeant Badham lost the money in the first place is run by the Matsuda gang."

From the absence of any reaction, apparently this didn't strike Himeda as the least bit ironic. He continued pouring the beer down his throat.

"In other words," I continued, hoping to make my point, "to pay back money he owes to the Matsuda gang, he's doing a job for you, who has connections to the Matsuda gang. Don't you think that's an interesting coincidence?"

"All I can say is, it's a small world. By the way, Mr. Yamanaka, working at Police Department as you do, have you seen the MPs going out on their patrols in the morning? Can you describe the setup for me?"

"Well, they never go out on patrol alone. There are always two of them."

As I wrote at some earlier point in this diary, I work on the first floor of the Metropolitan Police Department Documentation Section Annex, behind the main building, and the second and third floors of the annex are the barracks for U.S. military police. So of course I'm almost as familiar with their daily routine as I am with my own. I'm sure the British MPs follow pretty much the same procedures.

"The Jeep always stops in front of the main entrance of the Metropolitan Police Department. Top-flight Japanese police officers selected from all the police stations around the city are stationed at the front gate, and one of them gets in the Jeep and rides in the back seat. They go out on patrol of their assigned area in this three-man team."

"That's a strange arrangement." He suddenly slapped his knee with his hand. "Why, it's just the same with the yakuza!"

"What?"

"They always go around in pairs, so that they can each keep an eye on the other. And the two MPs keep an eye on the Japanese cop, while the Japanese cop watches the MPs. That's what it's about."

"I see."

"And how about the patrol routine?"

"Tokyo is under the authority of the Occupation Forces. Their duty is to keep the peace in Tokyo. They go around to each police station and ask officers who speak English or interpreters there, 'Any problems? Anything out of the ordinary?' Usually, the Japanese police answer, 'Nothing worth mentioning.' In other words, short of some major event, the police just say nothing happened."

"Why?"

"Because they don't want the MPs to get involved in their business. It would just complicate matters. Then the MPs sign the police log and head to the next police station."

"It's more of a pleasure drive than a patrol, then."

"But not entirely. The MPs are also looking for soldiers who've gone AWOL. And when Allied troops are on the move, the MPs ride in the vanguard. They also guard the trucks carrying bank notes from the central bank to other banks around the city. And they recover weather balloons that have come down... What's the matter?" Halfway through my explanation, Himeda had stopped listening and was looking up at the ceiling, as if lost in thought.

"We're going to need another MP. And a Japanese cop, too."

"I'm afraid that's beyond my abilities."

"You're involved this far. How about it—why can't you be the second MP?"

"You must be kidding!" I said, leaping out of my seat. "Have you forgotten I'm Japanese?"

"You could always pretend to be a second-generation immigrant."

"Do you think there are any Japanese-English MPs my age? Anyway, I'm not an actor. Why don't you do it?"

"I've already been to the Shinagawa Police Station two or three times. They know what I look like. If you don't want to be the MP, you can be the Japanese cop. I'll take care of the uniform and everything else."

"Absolutely not."

The fist-happy bartender looked over our way, his eyes reduced to slits as sharp as razors. Go ahead, beat me up, I decided, and I placed the envelope with the money slowly down on the tabletop. "This isn't what we'd agreed on. I'm out, Mr. Himeda."

"No, but… You…" Himeda's white teeth emerged from his black beard, and he flashed a grin as he looked toward the entrance. Turning around, I saw a huge man the size of a sumo wrestler with a red beret on top of a head of sparkling golden hair being led our way by Tomoe. He had a golden mustache and an MP band around his bicep.

"Shinsuke, this is my… Sergeant Badham from Camp Ebisu."

The giant said something in English and embraced me. The odor of coffee, butter and milk rose from his skin. I saw Tomoe's face from under his arm. Tears were falling from her large eyes, and (in my imagination) splashing noisily on the floor.

"There's no reason to cry, Tomoe. For your sake, I'll masquerade as a Japanese-American or a police officer or anything you want."

"I'm sorry, Shinsuke."

"There's no need to apologize. I do it gladly. Let's drink a toast to it. Hey! A beer!" I shouted to the bartender behind the counter.

"Ken," Himeda called out right after me, "order us some sushi!"

March 16

This morning I left the Monkey House—what they call the jail of the Provost Marshal's Office of the Metropolitan Tokyo Area—located at the Teikoku Seimei Building that faces Hibiya Park across A Avenue, which leads from Kanda Ogawamachi through Hibiya Crossing, Shinagawa, Rokugobashi Bridge, and on to Yokohama—in other words Keihin Highway One—and walked home to my house in Nezu Miyanaga-cho for the first time in two months. That bastard Hall, officer of the CIE Language Section… But it's no good. I just don't have the energy to push this glass-tipped pen across the paper any more today.

March 17

"So tell me, what was it, what crime did you commit this time?" my wife asked, carrying the rice container out from the kitchen as I was breaking apart a piece of dried horse-mackerel with my chopsticks. "Of course I heard the general story from Fumiko and Takeko, but I'd like to hear the official story from your own lips." As she spoke softly, she placed before me a large bowl of rice mixed with crushed soybeans. "After all, you were away from home for fifty-six days."

"I was arrested on suspicion of obstructing the aims of the Occupation." There was wakame seaweed in the soup. "This is magnificent. I must be the only person in Japan enjoying such a splendid breakfast." As I sipped the broth and poked at the newspaper, memories of our honeymoon in Izu came back to me. Actually, the fact that they served us wakame seaweed broth at each meal was rather annoying at the time. "According to this survey in the newspaper, only fourteen percent of Tokyo residents eat rice three times a day. Seventy-one percent have it once a day, and fifteen percent don't have any rice to eat at all... This horse-mackerel is really meaty."

"It's from Sagami Bay, Odawara. The horse-mackerel, the wakame and the rice are all from Fumiko and Takeko. When they dropped it off they said they knew you must be tired of Western food after living on bread and soup for so long. And so what exactly what was it that you were suspected of doing to obstruct the aims of the Occupation?"

"I guess they just didn't like what I did."

"That's what I'm asking. What *was* it you did?"

I couldn't very well confess that I'd impersonated a police officer for Tomoe. "I'll tell you later. Can I have seconds?" I held out my soup bowl.

The daily patrols of the MPs around town are one of the most highly visible signs that Tokyo is under the rule of the Occupation Forces. Two MPs ride in a Jeep, with a Japanese police officer in the back seat, visiting the local police stations. The MPs ask the police stations chief or his representative, "Has anything out of the ordinary happened here? Any problems?" Not wanting to get the Occupation Forces involved with their business, unless something really extraordinary has taken place, the standard reply of the Japanese police is, "*Zearu izu noo toraburu, saa*" (There is no trouble, sir). Then the MPs write "nothing" on their form, sign it and move on to the next police station.

Nothing out of the ordinary, perhaps, but the kinds of events that found their way into the stencils I printed as the daily interoffice memos of the Metropolitan Police Department probably qualify as something out of the ordinary. For example, a "huge man with 13 *mon* shoes, smelling of liquor" persistently harassing a Japanese girl; or "a giant black man" breaking into a Japanese family's house and demanding money; or a group of residents mobbing the local ward office, demanding that goods that have been hidden away by the government, or by former military officers, or by military supply factories be equally distributed among the people; or a roving gang shaking down farmers in the metropolitan area for the rice quota that they would normally sell to the government. In cases like that, the police chief says, "*Zearu izu a biggu toraburu, saa*" (There is a big trouble, sir) to the patrolling MPs and calls for the Tokyo Metropolitan Area Military Police to rush to the rescue.

Having written this, I just remembered something. On January 8th of this year, the Meguro Police Station appealed to the MPs with *a biggu toraburu, saa.* "About two thousand young women have gathered at a school that survived the bombings and are shouting and making a lot of noise. The situation appears to be out of control, so we would like to request the MPs."

When the MPs came driving up in their Jeeps, what they found was not a group of housewives demanding rice or female students holding a rally for democratizing the schools, but a huge gathering of young women in front of the Sugino School of Western Dressmaking. According to the school authorities, they'd decided to try to restart the school with a small class using a room in the school principal's house that had survived the air raids. They attempted to cut off registration at thirty students, but the young women who had flocked there to apply for the classes started rioting in protest. They shouted their demands to the Japanese police who followed meekly after the MPs.

"We didn't have anything to wear during the war. I'd like to be able to at least make clothes for myself and my family. Please let me into the school."

"If I knew how to sew Western clothes, even while I was evacuated from Tokyo, I could have done part-time work at home to buy food and daily necessities. As long as we have to rely on the black market for survival, I'm going to need to learn how to sew Western clothes just to get by. You've got to let me in."

"I learned during the war that you can't work in Japanese clothes. We'll be wearing Western-style clothes from now on, so I have to get admitted."

"I'm a war widow, and this person next to me missed her chance to get married because of the war. We're all alone in the world and need to find a way to support ourselves. Sewing Western clothes is the best way to do that, so please accept both of us."

With the MPs as mediators, the school had promised to build a temporary classroom within six months and, even if they had to hold classes stacked three or four in a row, to allow all who had come that day to enroll. This event is in itself a clear example of the kind of power the MPs exercise.

That's why Himeda, the former platoon leader of a garrison stationed at the 252nd Naval Air Force Squadron base in Mobara, decided he needed an MP. Luring Sergeant David Badham, an MP of the British forces stationed at Camp Ebisu with promises of money to pay off his gambling debts to the yakuza, Himeda came up with a plan to send Badham to the Shinagawa Police Station to retrieve the thirty sacks of rice, thirteen bales of wheat, fifty wool blankets, and the rest of his goods that the police had confiscated from him. Himeda was going to barter those goods for lumber to build two movie theaters, thus supporting him and his six partners and their combined fifty family members. I sympathized with his concern for his military comrades, which is why I decided to help him out.

… No, I can't lie to my diary. I agreed to this risky plan solely because Sergeant Badham is the lover of Tomoe. I wanted to make Tomoe happy by helping Badham back to the straight and narrow. A puppet of my heartstrings, I was perfectly happy to spend fifty-six days in jail if I could please Tomoe by doing it.

"It looks like your year has about seven hundred days," said my wife when she noticed I'd finished eating, pouring some tea into my bowl. It was real roasted green tea. "Or maybe even eight hundred."

"What are you talking about? Three hundred sixty-five days a year is all anyone gets. Don't spoil this delicious tea."

"What I mean is, you were hardly home last year, and yet you're as unconcerned as if your year had eight hundred days in it. How many days *were* you here last year, anyway? First, there was the prison in Yokaichiba, right?"

"Yes, that was about three months."

"Actually, it was one hundred twelve days. Next there was the solitary cell in the basement of the Metropolitan Police Department."

"I was there for two full months."

"Sixty-seven days. And then this time fifty-six days in the jail of the Provost Marshal's Office. That's a total of two hundred thirty-five days. You were away from home two-thirds of the year. I hope you'll put an end to all this foolishness and try to stay put from now on."

"I know. But you seem to have a very precise accounting of my absences."

"While you were away, I used your diary to make my calculations, so I'm sure I'm right."

"My diary? How dare you read my diary!" I slammed my bowl down, splashing tea on the table. "Reading someone's diary is worse than stealing!"

"I know how precious your diary is to you. I just wanted to make sure nothing happened to it, so I kept it right beside my pillow. Eventually, I guess I just succumbed to temptation. I found it very entertaining."

"I didn't write it to entertain you. I can't believe what I'm hearing. I'm stunned."

"And by the way, about Tomoe…"

That's the real reason I was so upset. "I think I'll take a stroll to Nezu Gongen Shrine to walk off that breakfast. I'm a parishioner, after all. I should report to the god that I'm home safe again." I got up energetically. At times like this, escape is always the wisest policy. "And maybe I'll circumambulate the precincts a hundred times as a prayer that my wife doesn't read my diary again."

"You're wasting your time pining after Tomoe."

"How long are you going to sit there spouting nonsense?" I stepped down into the entryway and started to slip on a new pair of wood sandals. "Tomoe might be important to me, but so are Tokiko Furusawa and Kumiko Kurokawa and Kayoko Makiguchi. They're all women that we've taken under our wing. You're imagining things if you think it's anything else. Maybe I'll walk from the shrine to the black market in Ueno and buy some eye medicine for you—if they have anything that would work on you." The navy blue socks I was wearing were also new, and they stuck to the straps of the new sandals. As I stood there trying to stuff my feet into them, my wife, who was cleaning up the breakfast table, said casually, as if it had just occurred to her: "I don't mind if you go out for a walk, but try not to be away too long. We're going to be using your room for a wedding on April 1st, and I'd like you to put away your books and newspapers. I'll take care of the rest."

"What did you say about a wedding?"

"Yes. Tomoe is getting married."

"What?" I spun around with such momentum that one of the sandals flew off my foot and landed in the corner of the entryway. "Tomoe is getting married?"

"That's why I said it's useless to go on pining for her."

"By any chance, is she marrying a foreigner?"

"A Japanese. And someone you know very well..."

"Who?"

"He's forty-four, never been married..."

"His name—that's what I'm asking."

"Gentaro, the tailor."

I was so astonished that I just stood there, frozen. If what Kazue was saying was true, Tomoe was intimately involved with two men. It was hard to imagine from her modest mien—which is I guess is what they mean when they say you can't judge a woman by appearances.

I was even more surprised to learn that she would be marrying Gen. He lived just three houses away, and had inherited the tailor business from his father. When he was ten years old, he was playing on the main street and got run over by a horse cart, which crushed his right leg, and since then he'd devoted his life to his work, pedaling away at his Singer sewing machine with his left foot—to the point where you could say that sewing machine was the closest thing he'd ever had to a wife. He had been in love with my oldest daughter,

Kinuko, who was killed by an incendiary bomb in an air raid last May 24th; once he made her a beautiful overcoat. Since there was a difference of more than twenty years in their ages, I turned down his request for Kinuko's hand, but he had never talked about being love again after that, and was a very serious, extremely reserved middle-aged man, whom no one would characterize as a catch. I tried to imagine the expression on his face when he proposed to Tomoe. I guess this just goes to show that you can't judge a man by his appearance, either.

"Gen's right where I was a little while ago." At last I'd succeeded in putting on the sandal. "I feel sorry for him."

"What's there to feel sorry about?"

"Are you thick-headed? Gen must still believe that Tomoe is working in the accounts department of the Japan Water Company, when in fact..." and I just whispered the rest to myself, because it was too painful to say out loud:("she's dancing away the nights in the bed of an American military officer at the Imperial Hotel." If Gen knew the truth, he'd go berserk. He'd break it off in an instant."

"He knew everything when he proposed. He knows she has had to support her two children and her father-in-law in the mental hospital, and that as a woman, she doesn't have a lot of choices. That's what he said to her. Isn't that gallant?"

"You're not a professional storyteller, so don't repeat things you didn't see and hear with your own eyes and ears."

"Gen proposed to her right here in this room. I saw the whole thing, as I was pouring their tea."

"And what did Tomoe say?"

"She said: 'My work will be finished in March. I'd like to go back to living a peaceful, normal life starting in April. I think it would wonderful to sit quietly by your side and help you with your work.'"

"It sounds like a scene from a novel."

"Yes, it was like watching a movie starring Kinuyo Tanaka and Ken Uehara."

"I think Tomoe's more like Keiko Sonoi. And Gen is more like Sadao Maruyama than Ken Uehara. I can see Gen wearing a navy blue apron and pulling a jinrikisha. He's a ringer for Sadao Maruyama as Muhomatsu in *The Story of Matsugoro Tomishima*."

Slender threads of rain were falling on the other side of the glass of the door. There are thin strips of paper were still pasted on the glass in a lattice pattern. We don't have to worry about the aftershock blasts from the bombs blowing out our glass anymore. It would be a shame to go out in the rain and catch a cold, I thought. Maybe I'd spend the day scraping the paper strips off the glass instead.

"Gen says it was love at first sight. And Tomoe had noticed him for some time, too. So when he proposed, the whole thing just fell neatly into place.

"What time is 'for some time'?"

"About the beginning of March, when Tomoe's brother brought her children down to Tokyo from Onahama and they were staying here—for about five days, I think. From the day after they arrived, they started going over to Gen's place to play. They became very fond of him."

"Hobble the horse to bring down the general, I guess. He probably bribed them with candy." I began to peel the paper off the glass in the door with my fingernails. "The oldest trick in the book."

"The morning they returned to Onahama, Gen brought over two new school uniforms he'd sewn for them and said to Tomoe, 'I found this nice serge cloth, so I made these for the kids. Let's take the old ones apart for cleaning rags.'"

"How transparent."

"To show her appreciation, Tomoe gave him some American canned goods and cigarettes in return, and cooked for him."

"Absolutely predictable. How boring."

"As you know, Tomoe's an accomplished seamstress. From then on I would see her sitting in front of the sewing table with Gen. They looked like they'd been married ten or twenty years."

"How long are you going to keep up your jabbering?" I removed the glass door from its track. "I'm going to take off these paper strips. Bring me a bucket of water."

"Hmm. It seems a bit early in the year for thunder, doesn't it?"

"And don't forget the scrub brush."

"And oh, I almost forgot. Gen wants us to act as the official go-betweens at the wedding."

"Let them get together on their own. They're both adults." I didn't want to think about anything today. I spent the rest of the day washing all the glass doors in the house.

March 18

I was thrown into a cell in the "Monkey House," the jail of the Provost Marshal's Office, Metropolitan Tokyo Area, a partially underground area at the back of the first floor of the Teikoku Seimei Building on the southeast corner of Hibiya Crossing. I didn't receive a single visitor the entire time I was there. People these days are very cold.

Actions obstructing the aims of the Occupation are usually tried by a U.S. military court set up in Conference Room No. 1 of the Metropolitan Police Department, and I was looking forward to being able to enjoy a breath of fresh air as I was led from Hibiya to Sakuradamon for my hearing, but in the end I was only taken up to the Criminal Investigation Unit on the second floor of the building I was in, and only on one single occasion, where I was questioned for about three hours. That was the sole time I was out of my cell, and I spent the rest of my fifty-six days glaring at the concrete walls boxing me in. Toward the end, I couldn't tell where I stopped and the walls started. I have to say that I gained a new respect for Bodhidharma, who stared at the wall for nine years.

When I was released from my cell, there was no one waiting for me, either. I had no idea if I still had my part-time job cutting mimeograph stencils for the Metropolitan Police Department or if I was still a full-time employee of the Civilian Information and Education Language Section

It's Monday. To find out just what my status is, I left my house in Nezu Miyanaga-cho at seven this morning. When I closed the glass door in the entryway—sparkling clean as a result of my hard work yesterday—it occurred to me to go see how the fortunate Gen was doing and, though it was a bit out of my way to go to the main street, I turned left. Gen's house was three houses down on the left.

"Hey, it's been a long time." It was my next door neighbor Mr. Takahashi coming out of his front door, raising his national civilian uniform cap to me in greeting. He seemed to be on his way to work at the newspaper, and we walked along together.

"Your wife told me you went on a business trip," I said, picking up from two months ago as if it were yesterday.

"Yes, I was, but…"

"As a matter of fact, there was something I had wanted to ask you, which was why I stopped by."

"Yes, my wife told me. I went to your house as soon as I got back, but by then you were… away. It was a very strange business trip they sent me on. To tell the truth, I wished I'd refused and spent my time talking with you. But it was at the command of the Occupation Forces, so I couldn't say no."

"At the command of the Occupation Forces?"

"Yes. An American newspaper asked specifically for me to accompany an American journalist to farming villages in Nagano and Akita. That was fine, but they only told me that evening, and they wanted me to leave the same night."

"How unreasonable."

"We traveled by special Occupation Forces trains and Jeeps and stayed at first-rate inns, eating only the best food.…"

"It sounds great. The emperor's also traveling around the country a lot these days, but it sounds like you outdid him."

"Yes, that's what was so unsettling about it. And the American journalist didn't have the slightest interest in agricultural reform. He only made the most perfunctory inspections, conducted the most lackadaisical interviews, and asked the most uninspired questions, and then after a half-day I realized he wasn't a real journalist at all. I'm a reporter, so I have a nose for whether someone is the genuine article or not."

"Is that so?"

"Yes. Another strange thing about it was, it seemed that his real job was to keep tabs on me. For example, when I used the inn's phone to report back to the office in Tokyo, he'd always be standing nearby. When I went to the toilet, I'd see him back in the room looking my way, as if he didn't believe I was really going to the toilet."

We were passing Gen's house, so I glanced inside the shop. He was sitting at his machine busily sewing away, smiling about once every two seconds as if enjoying a pleasant memory. The lucky bastard, I said to myself, returning my attention to what Mr. Takahashi was saying.

"...and this was the conclusion I arrived at. Maybe I wasn't being sent to the countryside as his guide, but he'd actually been assigned to get me away from Tokyo. Considering the rush in which we were forced to leave, it appears somebody felt the need to remove me from Tokyo in a hurry."

"And who would that somebody be?"

"The Occupation Forces?"

"What problem are you for them?

"I still don't know the answer to that question. After all, I'm just an ordinary newspaper reporter. I'm not important enough to attract the attention of the Occupation Forces, so maybe I'm mistaken. Oops. I got so carried away with my story that I've gone too far."

The main street was crowded with people hurrying to Ueno Station. There was nothing to be done about the crowds, since Nezu, one of the few places remaining undestroyed by the carpetbombing, now had five times the population it had before the war.

"And what was it that you wanted to talk to me about when you came by to see me in January?"

"Nothing short of the scoop of the century."

"Aha!" Mr. Takahashi stopped suddenly in his tracks. The middle-aged man with a thin mustache walking right behind him swerved to avoid him, and his felt hat flew off with the momentum. "Idiot," barked the mustachioed man, picking up his hat. "You shouldn't stop suddenly like that."

Mr. Takahashi and I apologized and decided to walk on the edge of the street, out of the crowd.

"That felt hat doesn't fool me—that's the voice of a former military man. From the tone, I'd say an army major or lieutenant colonel."

"Mr. Yamanaka, could you tell me more about that scoop of the century?"

"A plan to change Japanese writing to *romaji*. Put together by the CIE Language Section."

"But you've already told me about that several times."

"Yes, but now the proposal is about to be adopted as official SCAP

Occupation policy. An educational mission from America will be coming to Japan soon to completely redo the Japanese educational system. And as part of that…"

"Wait a moment. The educational mission is already here."

"What? Really?"

"There are thirty members. They arrived in two contingents by plane in Tokyo on March 5th and 6th. Right now they're spread out across Japan observing Japanese educational institutions."

Staring at a wall for fifty-six days, I was like Rip Van Winkle.

"The mission is supposed to stay for a month, observing and studying Japanese education, and before they leave present their report to SCAP, I believe," Mr. Takahashi continued. "Japan's new educational system is supposed to be based on their report."

"The American educational mission's report is like the old Imperial rescripts. In other words, it's absolute."

"Yes, just as you say."

"What I'm trying to tell you is that the CIE Language Section's proposal for replacing the Japanese writing system with *romaji* is going to be part of that report."

"That's impossible."

"That's what I wanted to tell you in January. I was hoping you could write an article about it in the paper."

"That wouldn't be easy, with the Occupation Forces censorship apparatus in place, but if what you're saying is true, this is terrible."

"I'm not making it up. After all, I'm an employee of the Language Section."

"Mr. Yamanaka, I have a favor to ask you." Mr. Takahashi stopped again, and a young woman who almost bumped into him as a result glared at his pale face out of the corner of her eye as she passed us. "Can you stay home today? After I've checked out some things, I'll come over to your house." Unsettled by the gravity of his tone as he said this, I did as he asked.

It's 10:30 P.M. now, and Mr. Takahashi still hasn't returned home.

March 19

This is the fourth day since I was released from the Monkey House, but I still find myself unable to record what was done to me (well, technically, what *I* did) two months ago on January 20th at the Shinagawa Police Station. I don't want to lie in my diary, and I've taken up my pen several times and said to myself, "This is the day," but each time something inside me shouts, "I can't. Just remembering it is unpleasant enough." So I've held out until today without writing a word about it. Nevertheless, I think I need to get it down in writing while I still remember it clearly. I'm pretty certain that my morning job as a temporary employee cutting stencils for the Metropolitan Police Department as well as my afternoon job as a full-time employee of the CIE Language Section are both down the toilet (since I was arrested for obstructing the aims of the Occupation, it's only natural that they'd fire me), so I have a lot of time on my hands right now.

And on top of that, sitting here on the veranda, where I've pulled my desk, the sun warming my back, I feel very good. Maybe today I can write about it.

On January 19th, during our discussions at the Tenka Club dance hall in Karasumori, Shinbashi, I said: "It looks like I have to pretend to be either a second-generation Japanese-immigrant MP or a police officer from the Meguro Police Station, but I just can't see myself as an MP, no matter how hard I try. You've got to see that." Eventually they did. We decided that MP Sergeant David Badham would find another British MP from Camp Ebisu who was in need of some quick cash.

Then I said, "I agree to pretend to be a police officer, but I need some time to prepare. Fortunately, I'm a temporary employee at the Metropolitan Police Department, so I can probably get the necessary information about the Meguro Police Station to play my part, but I need a few days."

Tomoe brushed aside my plea. "Tomorrow is an auspicious day. If we do it then, everything is certain to go smoothly."

Himeda wanted to get the goods confiscated by the Shinagawa Police Station (thirty sacks of rice, thirteen bales of wheat, fifty wool blankets, etc., etc.) returned to him as soon as possible. Sergeant Badham would do exactly as Tomoe told him to, from first to last, so it was agreed that we'd carry out our caper the following day, January 20th.

It was a Sunday.

We met again at the Tenka Club, and I changed into the police uniform that Himeda had procured, with its raised collar and the white epaulets against the black fabric. When, standing in front of the mirror on the dance floor, I put the black cap on my head and the armband with the words "Meguro Police Station" on my left arm, I did in fact look like a reasonable facsimile of a police officer. As they say, clothes make the man, I guess.

The British MPS also drive Jeeps. Sergeant Attenborough, another young MP in need of money, whom Sergeant Badham managed to recruit at Camp Ebisu, drove. He owed approximately half his earnings to the Matsuda gang for gambling losses incurred in the same gambling den in Ginza. Sergeant Badham sat in the passenger seat, and I sat in the back.

We drove under balmy spring skies for about ten minutes, arriving at the Shinagawa Police Station in Minami Banba, Shinagawajuku, at 10:30 in the morning. A police officer guarding the entrance shot out toward us like a bullet from a pistol, and addressed me: "Thank you for your hard work patrolling the city." Speaking to Sergeant Badham, who lumbered out of the Jeep, he said in a high, tense voice: "*Zearu izu noo toraburu, saa.*" Then he looked toward me again and said, "Ah, that's right, the MP has to sign the log. Wait a moment, please. I'll go get it." He headed back toward the entrance. My time to act had come.

"We're not on patrol."

"Then what is it?" he asked, turning back to us. "Is there some kind of *toraburu*?"

"Yes, your station has sown the seeds of some trouble, I'm afraid, and we need to nip it in the bud, before it grows into a big mess." Badham said something behind me in English.

"What did the MP just say?"

"He asked if there was an officer who spoke English here."

"Not on Sundays," he said, again looking at me.

"The Shinagawa Station is big. There must be an interpreter in a police station of this size."

"We just got a Keio graduate from a company to work here for us, and he's very good at English, but he's off on Sundays."

"All right. I'll interpret. Ah, let me introduce myself," I said. "I am Yamada of the Meguro Police Station."

"I am Kobayashi," said the officer. "I'm in charge of economic offenses at the Shinagawa Police Station."

"An economic offenses police officer on security duty?"

"Yes. The first postwar elections are coming up, and candidates are starting their campaign activities. The majority of our officers are out watching over them, and so we're a bit short-handed."

(MacArthur is pretty serious about the upcoming general election. One of the police department interoffice memos recently contained this warning from the GHQ authorities: "The Japanese police should strictly enforce any violations of the new election law and be on the alert for attempts at vote-buying or other transgressions.")

"Women will be voting for the first time, so there are a lot of problems."

"So what's the *toraburu?*"

"Three days ago, before dawn on January 17th, officers of the Shinagawa Police Station intercepted five trucks filled with goods on the banks of the Rokugo River that feeds into Tama River and confiscated the contents. The trucks were heading for Kariyamachi in Aichi Prefecture. The cargo was thirty sacks of rice, thirteen bales of wheat, fifty wool blankets…"

"Yes, I know about that. I'm one of those in charge of that incident."

"Ah, I see. That's right, you're in the economics offenses department."

"It was a clear violation of the Economic Stabilization Law. The man driving the last truck said that these weren't their goods and they were just delivering them for someone else, but when I asked him to tell me who had engaged him to drive the trucks, he clammed up. It was crystal clear—they were decommissioned soldiers who had pilfered these supplies in the confusion at the end of the war and were trying to make off with them."

"No, that's not the case."

"But the man's face, his way of talking—he was definitely a former army man."

"No. Those are strategic military supplies of the British forces. And quite special supplies at that." I turned around and looked at Sergeant Badham. "Why don't you show him the orders?" I said in some approximation of English, drawing on what I'd managed to learn in business class way back when I was enrolled in the professional department of Meiji University. It sounded convincing enough to me. You never know when your studies will come in handy.

Sergeant Badham waved the typed forms back and forth in the air like a little flag. He'd sneaked into the office of Camp Ebisu last night and forged them, so they had the look of the real thing, right down to the official paper.

"These are the forms for the return of the goods," I said, taking them from Sergeant Badham and giving them to the Shinagawa Police Station economic offenses officer. "Where are the trucks? In the back?"

Himeda would be recognized by the officers, so he was laying low, having left from Shinbashi with five truck drivers an hour ago and waiting now on the opposite shore of the Meguro River, which flowed along the north side of the police station.

"The drivers we've engaged should be here any minute. Shall we take the trucks? We don't want to make this any bigger than it is already. That's a promise. To tell the truth, these goods are being exchanged in Aichi for lumber to build movie theaters."

"Movie theaters?"

"Yes, the lady friend of the commander of the British forces..." and I lifted my little finger in the gesture for a paramour, "I won't say who it is, but she's an actress at the Toei Studios. One night, she wheedled a movie theater out of the commander, it seems, which is why we've given up our Sunday to get these materials back. But I like to look on the bright side. I suppose it's worth it if it means Tokyo will have another movie theater."

The economic offenses officer accepted my explanation and showed us to the trucks. I waved in the direction of Meguro River. We were finished—or that's what I thought. But from that moment on the script took a turn in an entirely different direction. The economics offenses department officer said: "Can you wait a moment? I need to confer with the police chief."

"The chief?"

"I know it's presumptuous for an ordinary officer to say something like this, but our chief is a very industrious fellow, and since August

15th last year he gives up every single Sunday to work here at the station. When we tell him not to overdo it, he says, 'Every day I stay home is one more day on the streets for the low-life scum of the Shinagawa precinct.'"

As he said this, the economics offenses officer jumped to attention like he'd just been zapped by an electric jolt. He must really respect his chief. Our plans had encountered an unexpected obstacle. I stood there frozen, unable to think of what to do next. Behind me, Sergeant Badham seemed to be asking what was going on, but I could only wave my hand back at him to be patient. We mustn't panic.

"And the chief lives on his salary alone. Here in Shinagawa, he's known as the reincarnation of Confucius, he's so honest. Oh, yes— he can speak a little English, too, so he'll be able to pay the MP there a compliment or two. He only started learning English since the defeat, staying up all night studying, and in just five months he's made astonishing progress. Isn't that remarkable? Let me show you to the reception room. We call it the reception room, but it took a direct hit in the air raids, and it's a real mess, but at least we can offer you a cup of tea."

The prospect of a cup of tea with the police station chief was about as welcome as a fly in my soup, but if we gave up now I had no hope of rescuing Tomoe, my damsel in distress. I decided to leap courageously into the tiger's den. Sergeant Badham seemed upset that things weren't going according to plan, and even though I knew he wouldn't understand me, I whispered to him in Japanese, "This is all your fault anyway. If you hadn't been hanging around a yakuza gambling den, we wouldn't be in this mess in the first place. Now it's time to reap what you've sown. I'll do my best to get you out of this." Then in a loud voice I said, in my best pseudo-English, something like: "He wants to invite us to a Japanese tea party. He's going to introduce us to the station chief. Come with me." And so I walked behind the economics offenses officer through the police station, which had rough boards and singed tin nailed here and there to cover up damage from the air raids. I revised the script in my head to include an extra scene of a five-minute meeting with the station chief, collecting all the necessary documents, and still successfully pulling it off.

I sat down on the uncomfortable wood stool in the reception room and said to Sergeant Badham: "I'll talk to the station chief, so don't worry. Just sit there looking big and intimidating." After I'd repeated that several times, the tea arrived, brought in by a man of about fifty with a pencil mustache. His plump body was stuffed uncomfortably into his black uniform with a standing collar. The five buttons on his coat, polished to a sparkle, seemed about to pop off from the pressure of the jacket's contents.

"Good day. I'm Okochi, the police station chief." He placed two teacups with chipped edges on the table. His fingers were as plump as sausages. By his appearance, it seemed impossible that he was living on his salary alone. Extending his pudgy hand to Sergeant Badham, he said: "It's very *naisu* to meet you. *Uerukamu*," in a mix of Japanese and English, the English pronounced in pure Japanese fashion. Obviously he wasn't the master of the language that his economics offenses officer thought he was. "And you're Yamada, I hear." He drew the papers we'd brought out of his breast pocket. "These forms are in perfect order. We will immediately return the trucks and their contents to you."

"Thank you for your quick action on this matter."

"There is, however, one condition."

"And what would that be?"

"Who's the girlfriend?" He moved his face close to mine. "You said that the commander of the British forces had been wheedled into building a movie theater by an actress at the Toei Studios. That's what I heard from Komori over there."

"She's a top star at Toei, so I can't say who she is."

"Then I won't return the confiscated goods," he said emphatically, his eyes flashing.

"But…"

"I'm just kidding. Mostly. So please, tell me."

"You have to promise not to let anyone else know." I knew we had to get out of here in a hurry, so I told him it was Isuzu Yamada—my favorite movie star, along with Michiyo Kogure.

"Hmmm. The British commander has surprisingly Japanese tastes," said the station chief, seemingly impressed. "But I would have chosen Hideko Takamine, hands down."

This was our chance, as the station chief was lost in his dreaming. I stood up. "Excuse us," I said in a low voice, making my exit.

"Thank you," said the police chief to my back. Just as I breathed a sigh of relief, he launched his second arrow. "Ah, just a moment. That fuss about the Officers' Wives Mutual Aid Society at the Meguro Station. How did that end up?"

"Officers' Wives Mutual Aid Society?"

"You're from the Meguro Police Station and you don't know about the Officers' Wives Mutual Aid Society?"

"Of course I know about it," my mind racing as I tried to somehow control the blood pounding through my veins in rising panic. I had seen mention of the Officers' Wives Mutual Aid Society in the Metropolitan Police Department interoffice memos, so I knew, at least, that it was a mutual aid organization made up of police officers' wives. But I had no idea what kind of fuss there was about it at the Meguro Police Station. Just as I thought, I should have done some research before taking part in this scheme.

"Which side is your wife on?"

"Well, I guess the ones in favor."

"So she's a Red."

"No, not really."

"How about you?"

"I'm definitely not a Red."

"In other words, you're against it."

"Yes, I guess you could say so."

"You and your wife must fight night and day. You'll probably end up divorced, too."

At this moment, I suddenly remembered an article in the interoffice memos four days ago.

The day before yesterday, on March 14, the date of the village council elections in Kamigo Village, Ina County, Nagano Prefecture, Communists were elected to twelve of the eighteen seats. Moreover, both the first and second vote-getters in the election were Communists. This is one of the first elections following the defeat, and as such deserves careful attention as the prelude to the upcoming national elections. The overwhelming victory of the Communists is a sign that careful observation is required in the future. GHQ, SCAP has also issued a top-secret directive to the Police Department yesterday saying, "The trend manifested in Kamigo Village must not be allowed to predominate throughout the nation, particularly in Tokyo."

So that was it? The officers' wives at Meguro Police Station seem to have been poisoned by this nationwide trend. Based on what I could figure out from the police station chief's words, the women were split into two factions.

"Even if I end up getting a divorce, I'll stay true to my beliefs," I said uncertainly, groping in the dark.

"Good for you," said the chief. Stroking his moustache, he added: "No matter how hard it might be to live on our salaries, it's unheard of for police officers' wives to bully their husbands into forming a union and demanding higher wages. When women start interfering with their husbands' work, it's the end of the world."

"I agree," feeling as if I'd avoided the tiger's jaws. I glanced at Sergeant Badham, who was observing our conversation apprehensively, signaling with his eyes, "Let's get out of here," and said to the chief, by way of covering our tracks, "Police officers forming a union and demanding a raise, even threatening to strike if they don't get it. Who could that please? Only criminals and crooks. I think the wives of the Meguro Station police officers who urged their husbands to form a union were very seriously mistaken."

"I agree. By the way, how's Kono's condition after all that?"

"Huh?"

"The station chief. *Your* station chief."

"Exercising the same brilliant leadership as always."

"The same brilliant leadership?"

"Yes. Why just this morning he told me he was counting on me to see to it that this matter of the British commander's goods was quickly resolved."

"After his divorce from his wife, Kono had a nervous breakdown, and he's on leave as we speak. He's supposed to be taking rest cure at a hot springs in his home town of Izaka in Fukushima."

"Yes, that's right, taking a rest cure. It seems to be going well. It was the vice-chief who said that to me this morning…"

"By vice chief, you mean Furuhashi."

"Yes."

"How's his wife?"

"Just fine. She was waving her little Red flag again this morning."

"Red flag?"

"Well, that's what it looked like, but maybe it wasn't."

"Of course it wasn't. Furuhashi's new wife is a student in the inaugural class of women officers studying at the police academy right now. A fledgling police officer wouldn't be a Red."

"I'm afraid I'm a little color blind… Maybe she was just waving her laundry."

"Yamada!" said the police station chief, clapping his hands loudly. "Recite the names of the officers at the Meguro Police Station in order of rank."

"Chief Kawano, Vice-chief Furuhashi…"

"Next?" His eyes, which had been crinkled in a smile up to now, suddenly widened and glared at me like an owl's. "What's the problem, Yamada? Or is Yamada just an alias?"

I was desperate. "Tadashi Wakabayashi, Hideo Fujimoto, Minoru Kasamatsu, Hideo Shimizu, Kozo Naito…"

"Wrong!"

Of course it was wrong. I was reciting the names of the pro baseball players with the top five ERAs in the last year the game was played, which was three years ago. "Toshiaki Okamura, Toshio Kurosawa, Michinori Tsubouchi, Shingyo Go, Fumio Fujimura, Kiyoharu Sakata, Den Yamada, Yasuji Hondo…" I'd switched to the top twenty batting averages as I tried to make my escape. When I reached the door, I was planning to dash down the steps. If I could just make it to Sergeant Badham's Jeep I'd be protected by the authority of the Occupation Forces. "Hideo Fujimoto, Fujio Ueda, Hiroyoshi Tsukamoto…" I had made it to the eleventh ball player when my little escape drama came to an end. Three police officers were waiting at the exit, blocking my path.

"I see you like baseball, Yamada." The economics offenses officer was standing there with a pair of handcuffs. "You can start your visit to the interrogation room by coughing up your real name. Don't expect any tea this time."

I realized now that the police chief's clapping had been a signal to these officers, but by now it was too late.

That's the main outline of the event. I was determined not to mention Tomoe's name, so the only information I gave them was my name and address. Within the same day I was transferred to the jail of the Provost Marshal's Office, Metropolitan Tokyo Area, in Hibiya, labeled as being under suspicion of activities obstructing the aims of the Occupation, and, after fifty-six days of incarceration and a single three-hour-long interrogation session, released.

But when I record the events in detail like this, several questions come to mind. When you actually write out the blow-by-blow in your diary, details that simply don't occur to you when you roll things over in your head in a vague and aimless sort of way pop up like mushrooms after a rainstorm. I'm glad I've finally done it.

This whole thing was precipitated when five trucks filled with black-market goods belonging to Himeda, former platoon leader of the 252nd Naval Air Squadron Base in Mobara, were confiscated by officers from the Shinagawa Police Station. The confiscated goods represented the future livelihood of Himeda and his pals. By hook or by crook, he had to get them back from the Shinagawa Police Station. That's when he turned to me, Shinsuke Yamanaka, an employee of the Civil Information and Education section. He implored me to introduce him to an MP who was in need of money. His scheme was that the authority of an MP would intimidate the Shinagawa Police Station into backing down. I refused, insisting that I didn't know any MPs in need of money. That's when Tomoe appeared with British MP Sergeant Badham. She explained that Sergeant Badham had incurred huge gambling debts at a Matsuda gang gambling den in Ginza, and was in serious trouble. He needed money. Now that was strange. As soon as I needed an MP who was having money troubles, the very same appeared out of nowhere, as if by magic. It was all too convenient. This was my first doubt.

Next, at that time Tomoe said that Sergeant Badham was her lover. And of course when he showed up, he treated her as if that were true. But next month that very same Tomoe was going to become the wife of Gen the tailor who lives in our neighborhood. If that were true, Tomoe had been carrying on with two men at the same time, but that was odd, too. I just couldn't imagine Tomoe having it in her to do such a thing. This was my second doubt.

Here the thread of my conjectures got tangled with something that Mr. Takahashi, my next-door neighbor, had said. Just when this whole thing was starting, Mr. Takahashi was ordered by the Allied Forces to make a sudden business trip away from Tokyo. He was supposed to be assisting an American journalist who was looking into agricultural reforms in the area from the Shinshu through the Tohoku region. But during the trip, it seemed that what the reporter was actually doing was keeping tabs on Mr. Takahashi.

"Maybe," Mr. Takahashi had said, "I wasn't being sent to the countryside as his guide, but he'd actually been assigned to get me away from Tokyo. Considering the rush in which we were forced to leave, apparently somebody felt the need to remove me from Tokyo in a hurry." Who might that someone be? That bothered me, too.

And going back even farther, to the time when Himeda first made his appearance in my life… yes, it was the day after my argument with my boss, Language Simplification Officer Robert King Hall. The cause of our argument was his arrogant statement that after his proposal for the adoption of *romaji* was adopted by the U.S. Educational Mission coming to Japan in March, before long the Japanese people would be writing their language in *romaji*. This infuriated me, and I submitted my resignation, vowing to do what I could to stop him. I tried to tell Mr. Takahashi about this nefarious plot, but he had been sent away on a sudden, strange business trip.

"It's noon," said my wife from the living room.

"I've been wondering for some time why you didn't come to visit me in jail," I asked in the direction of the living room. "And not just you. Neither Fumiko nor Takeko nor Sen-*chan* came to see me, either. That's pretty cold-hearted, isn't it? I'd think one of you'd at least want to bring me some fresh underwear. After all, we're husband and wife, father and daughters."

"I was forbidden to."

"By whom?"

"By Fumiko and Takeko."

Why would my daughters do that? Another riddle.

"Your noodles are going to get soft."

"I'll stop writing and come in a minute."

March 20

This morning I went to see the lay of the land at the Documentation Section Annex of the Metropolitan Police Department. A young woman was there cutting stencils with a pleasant sound. Clerk Umetani, who was watching her hand in motion, turned to me and said: "Well, well, our special undercover agent has returned." He held out his right hand and continued, "I'll ask you to share your tale of your heroic exploits some other time. This is Toshiko Ogawa. You now have an assistant. From today the two of you will work together on the interoffice memos. I hope you'll get along well. But I'm afraid Miss Ogawa surpasses you when it comes to cutting stencils."

She did indeed possess a refined and clear-cut Mincho-style script. It was ranks above my own Gothic-style lettering that made too heavy a use of the grating on the back of the mimeograph board.

"It would probably be better if you took care of the printing, Mr. Yamanaka."

"You mean I'm not fired? I was absent without permission for fifty-six days, so I just assumed..."

"No, we received a request of absence for you."

"Not from me you didn't."

"No, Navy Lieutenant Commander Hall, the Language Simplification Unit Officer of the Language Section of the CIE, submitted it. As I remember, it said something to the effect that Language Section employee Shinsuke Yamanaka was to be on extended special duty on Occupation business."

Now, that was odd.

I, Shinsuke Yamanaka, fifty-five years old this year, a fan maker in Nezu Miyanaga-cho, was sitting in the Monkey House on charges of suspicion of various actions obstructing the aims of the Occupation. The judge of the Occupation Forces Military Court clearly stated as much, and I myself knew that pretending to be a police officer aiding a British MP trying to steal illegal goods was wrong. But now an officer of the same Occupation Forces was saying that I was "on extended special duty on Occupation business."

One of the two was a lie.

"Since the Americans said they needed you, there was nothing we could do about it. But we couldn't stop printing the interoffice memos, which is why we had Ms. Ogawa join us. There's plenty of room for two in the annex, and the number of interoffice memos is growing."

The pleasant aroma of coffee had been floating into the room from the kitchen next door for the last few minutes.

"Shoji, could you bring me a cup?"

"Certainly!" said a heavy voice echoing from far away.

"What happened to the former proprietor of the Hongo Bar?"

"He was promoted from the cook for the fourteen or fifteen MPs upstairs to the head cook of Nigatake Camp, where he'll be feeding two thousand. All he has to do is check the food that his assistants prepare, and he'll be making five times the salary. It's quite a step up."

"Where's Nigatake?"

"Sendai. It's the biggest U.S. Military base north of Tokyo."

"When did he go to Sendai?"

At just that point, Miss Ogawa seemed to have miswritten a character, for she struck a match.

"He was asked to go there the day before last."

She gently moved the match close to the stencil and melted the wax.

"He went off in a special U.S. Army train at seven in the morning yesterday. I saw him off at Tokyo Station."

She lightly smoothed the softened wax with the back end of the stylus with an expert touch.

"He said that he'd wanted to say goodbye to you before he left."

"That's nice. But how sudden."

"He said the same thing. He was upset that they didn't even give him time to pack—'they' being the officers waiting for him at Tokyo Station."

"The Americans accompanied him?"

"Yes, it was a very intimidating scene, actually, like a convicted murderer being escorted away under armed guard."

"Another strange thing."

"But he's definitely gone up on the world," said Umetani, opening the door leading out of the annex. "What I really envy is his being able to travel by special Occupation Forces train. They're really fast, they say. They make a trip that would ordinarily take eight hours in four. And they even have soft velvet seats to sink into, like the second-class cars—an unbelievable luxury these days. You're a special undercover agent for the Occupation Forces, and the old cook is new head cook for a huge camp. The Documentation Section employees are all making names for themselves. Work hard, Miss Ogawa, and you may find yourself sitting prettier than you could ever have imagined."

An hour later, the interoffice memo was printed.

"Your work is beautiful," I said with a sigh of appreciation. "Where did you learn?"

"At the Ministry of Education."

When she was in her second year at Saint Hilda's School in Shirokane Sanko-cho, she went to work at the Ministry of Education as part of the national student-work program. Her handwriting skills were soon recognized, and she was assigned to the minister's secretarial staff. A seventy-year-old part-time employee worked there as a mimeographer. He was a master of his craft who, when he was eighteen years old, had taken part in the attack on Pyongyang in the first Sino-Japanese War as a mimeograph soldier, for which he'd been rewarded with the Seventh Class Order of the Golden Kite and a pension of 65 yen.

"The mimeograph soldiers were attached to the commanders, and they cut stencils and printed the orders that were then delivered to each unit. They didn't have telegraphs or telephones in those days, so that's how the orders were communicated."

I guess you'd expect someone who had studied under a mimeograph soldier of the Seventh Class Order of the Golden Kite to be good.

After delivering Miss Ogawa's masterpiece to the headquarters, I went to the Japan Broadcasting Corporation in Uchisaiwai-cho. No one was in the Language Section on the fifth floor. I sat in my desk, next to that of Miss Kurita, and lit a cigarette. Some kind of chart was posted on the wall in front of me. If Miss Ogawa's exemplary Mincho writing could be likened to a goldfish with gracefully flowing fins, the clumsy writing on the wall was a stubby brown minnow. It said:

Schedule for the United States Education Mission

15 (Friday)
Mission leaves for Kyoto on night train

16 (Saturday)
Morning: Sightseeing at Nishihonganji; visit Ryukoku University (lecture by Ryukoku University president, "The Significance of Buddhism in Japanese Life and Education"); visit Chion'in
Afternoon: Sightseeing at Kinkakuji temple, Ryoanji temple, Arashiyama, Katsura Detached Palace
Evening: Presentation on the treasures of Nara at Biwako Hotel; Report Draft Committee produces report outline; stay at Biwako Hotel

17 (Sunday)
Morning: Sightseeing at the Nara Imperial Museum, Nara Park
Afternoon: Visit Nara Girls Higher Normal School; Kasuga Shrine, Sangetsudo, Todaiji
Evening: Attend Japanese dance performance in Gion, Kyoto; stay at Biwako Hotel

18 (Monday)
Morning: Check in at Kyoto Hotel; general meeting; individual committees confer with Japanese educators
Afternoon: Visit Kyoto Imperial University; reception and tea ceremony sponsored by university president
Evening: Attend Noh performance, followed by Japanese dance performance in Gion

19 (Tuesday)
Morning: Individual committees visit schools in Kyoto

Committee #1: Kyoto Municipal First Girls High School, Seisho Elementary School, Kyoto Municipal First Trade School
Committee #2: Men's Higher Normal School, Momozono Elementary School, Heian Girls Academy
Committee #3: Kyoto Prefectural First Middle School, Third Higher School, Art Professional School
Committee #4: Doshisha University, Otani University, Textile Professional School
Afternoon: Sightseeing at Heian Shrine, Kyoto Gosho Palace, Nijo Castle
Evening: Return to Tokyo by night train

20 (Wednesday)
Return to Tokyo, check-in at Imperial Hotel
Morning: Individual committees discuss compilation of report; mission members Freeman and Deimer meet with Minister of Education Yoshishige Abe.
Afternoon: Sightseeing Yoshiwara
Evening: Mission Leader Stoddard and mission members Bowles and Andrews meet with General MacArthur

21 (Thursday)
Morning: Individual committees discuss the composition of final report, from 11 A.M.; Japanese Language Simplification Subcommittee attends Kabuki at the Imperial Theater (performance by Kikugoro and Kichiemon)
Afternoon: Visit to Sugamo Prison; Japanese Language Simplification Subcommittee observes the procedures for entrance to Keio University in Mita, Shiba

22 (Friday)
Morning: Individual committees prepare reports
Afternoon: Sightseeing of black markets at Shinbashi, Shibuya, Shinjuku, Ikebukuro, Ueno, Asakusa; Japanese Language Simplification Subcommittee attends modern theatrical comedy at the Yurakuza Theater from 3 (Enoken Company, with special appearance by Shizuko Kasagi)

Evening: Japanese Language Simplification Subcommittee discusses its report…

I had got this far in the schedule when the door opened with such force that I thought it had been yanked off its hinges, and a woman with hair as long as a koi banner undulating in the wind came in. She had thick lips and the bright red, moist lipstick that's popular these days, making her look as if she had just eaten someone. She stopped before me with such precision and suddenness that it seemed her feet had been nailed to the floor. Behind eyeglasses, her gaze was more piercing than an arrow. All her gestures and movements appeared strangely exaggerated, as if I were watching a play.

"Who are you?" she asked in an astonishingly thick, harsh voice, throwing the materials she was carrying down on to Miss Kurita's desk.

"I suppose I should say that I'm the secret undercover agent of the Language Section back safely from his special mission," I joked, putting out my cigarette in the ashtray on Miss Kurita's desk. The ashtray was filled with cigarette butts smudged with lipstick. "But seriously, I'm Shinsuke Yamanake. I work in the mornings in the Documentation Section of the Metropolitan Police Department and afternoons here at the Language Section."

Her flat nose, until now invisible because of her lurid lipstick, wrinkled. "Ah, so you're Mr. Yamanaka."

"It's the 20th. According to that schedule, the U.S. Education Mission is discussing the compilation of their report. I suppose Miss Kurita is serving coffee to the committee members at the Imperial Hotel."

"Kurita?" she asked, tossing the match she had just blown out into the ashtray. "Who's that?"

"Who's that? Miss Kurita is the office manager of the Language Section. You know, she has a permanent wave?"

With her cigarette hanging from her lips, the woman pulled out a black folder from the file stand on her desk and began flipping through it at an extremely leisurely pace.

"She's always chewing bubble gum, that Miss Kurita. I think she said she lived in Yanagibashi, Asakusa Ward. But hold on a minute.

Who are you? You shouldn't be pawing through Miss Kurita's files like that."

"The person you're talking about has been transferred to the Hiroshima CIE Branch Office." She held the black folder out to me. "The CIE is building a library there, and she's working on the advance preparations."

There it was, the resumé of one Teruko Kurita, inside the folder with the black cover. There was a notation on her resumé, "Transferred to Hiroshima in charge of the establishment of a library at Hiroshima Branch Office. Period of assignment: one year."

It was issued on January 21st. The date stirred something that had been lying dormant in my mind up to then. I'd been arrested at the Shinagawa Police Station on January 20th. The next day, Miss Kurita was sent to Hiroshima. As soon as I was released from jail, the former proprietor of the Hongo Bar was transferred to Sendai. Why was it that the cook and Miss Kurita, both of whom had close contact with Shinsuke Yamanaka, just happened to be transferred to new and much better positions—away from Tokyo?

Something else bothered me. It was three days before I was arrested at the Shinagawa Police Station, so it was January 17th, that I had that argument with Navy Lieutenant Commander Hall. He'd had me read his proposal with the title *A Shortcut for the Conversion of Japanese Orthography to Roman Letters*, which he would be submitting to the U.S. Education Mission, and after I'd heaped scorn on him and his ideas, I threatened to tell the newspaper reporter Mr. Takahashi about it and I resigned. I never got around to telling Takahashi about it because he'd been sent on a sudden business trip that very night.

Two phrases kept revolving in my mind: "paid off" and "shut up." Eventually they took shape as a thought: I was locked up in the Monkey House to shut me up, and I was paid off for my silence by having my job at the Police Department kept safe for me. In other words, I had stumbled upon some very important secret. To keep me from spilling it, I'd been taken out of circulation and everyone I was in close contact with had been removed from Tokyo. The secret had to be…

A Shortcut for the Conversion of Japanese Orthography to Roman Letters.

It had to be related to that. At last the wheels of my mind were beginning to turn.

"I want to see the chief."

"He's not in the office today," she said, turning the pages of the folder with her red-tipped fingers.

"I suppose I could see him if I went to the Imperial Hotel."

"Even I'm not admitted to the conference room, and I'm a staff member."

"*You're* a staff member?"

"That's why I can 'paw through' these documents, as you put it. I'm actually pretty ticked off at being transferred here from the CIE Education Section. Though I guess since both the Education Section and the Language Section are babysitting the U.S. Education Mission, it doesn't make a whole hell of a lot of difference."

"What a vulgar way to speak. Are you a second-generation Japanese immigrant?"

"Last year at this time I was bawling my eyes out because my husband had been killed in the big air raid on the old downtown district." She held up the folder to me like it was a mirror. I saw my own resumé and the comment: "Nezu Miyanaga-cho 35, Hongo Ward. Fan maker and seller. Presently unemployed because of the lack of fan-making supplies. Works in the mornings at the Metropolitan Police Department Documentation Section Annex printing interoffice memos. On January 8th, temporarily employed as a test subject to study the degree of the knowledge of *kanji* among Japanese. Arrested on January 20th at the Shinagawa Police Station for committing acts obstructing the aims of the Occupation of the Allied Forces. Employment terminated same day."

The woman slapped the folder shut as if she were trying to kill a mosquito that had settled on its pages. "You're fired. You don't have any more connection to the Language Section, so there's no reason for the chief to see you. That's the way it is. Please collect whatever's owed to you at the Office Affairs window on the second floor."

"I have a reason to see him, all right."

"Like I said, you can't."

"And why shouldn't a man see his son-in-law?"

"Don't make me laugh," she sneered, pulling an adding machine to her and cranking the handle. Apparently this newly appointed office manager hadn't yet caught wind of the relationship between Navy Lieutenant Commander Hall and Fumiko. I had no duty to tell her, so I just said: "I'll be back tomorrow. And every day after that, until I get an explanation from your chief." And with that I walked out the door and slammed it with just as much force as she had opened it earlier. I could hear her howling angrily at me from the other side.

It was becoming extremely doubtful that the events at the Shinagawa Police Station on January 20th were what they seemed. Something that had the guise of an actual incident certainly took place, and my deception was exposed in front of the Shinagawa Police Station chief, which led to my arrest. But it was all nothing but an elaborate, cleverly arranged ruse.

I got on the Yamanote Line at Shinbashi and went to Komagome to confirm my suspicions. It was Saburo Himeda who started the plot in motion by approaching me and saying that he needed to borrow the authority of an MP to get back his black-market goods. His business card, I recalled, gave his address as "Hongo Ward, Komagome Katamachi 30, Air Raid Shelter #3." It was probably phony.

The only familiar sight when I stepped out of the south entrance of Komagome Station were the trees in front of the Iwasaki Mansion; otherwise, like the rest of Tokyo, it was nothing but empty plains of scorched rubble. I got on the streetcar in front of the mansion and stepped off at the third stop, Komagome Kichijoji Temple, which was Komagome Katamachi 30. I asked at a shack selling dried foods where Air Raid Shelter #3 was, and the old woman in the shack replied there were no air raid shelters in the area. "We were supposed to take refuge in Kichijoji Temple in an emergency," she added proudly. "It has a big bomb shelter, and Komagome Hospital is right next door, so we felt pretty secure."

Chewing on the dried sweet potato I bought in appreciation for her help, I cut through the grounds of Ikubunkan, the school whose students were a source of irritation to Natsume Soseki because their baseballs kept coming flying into his garden, and arrived at the grounds of Nezu Gongen Shrine. By then my mind was clear. Walking really does help you put your thoughts in order.

From the perspective of Navy Lieutenant Commander Hall, the chief of the Language Section and the Language Simplification Unit Officer, the plan was easy to understand. Shinsuke Yamanaka had read his top-secret proposal. Miss Kurita, the office manager of the Language Section, had been present during their argument, so he assumed that she also knew about it. Shinsuke Yamanaka had said that he was going to discuss the content of the proposal with his neighbor Mr. Takahashi, a journalist, and he had probably also spoken of it to the cook at the place where he worked in the morning, since they were good friends. The proposal must not become public before the U.S. Education Mission arrived in Japan. Navy Lieutenant Commander Hall used Saburo Himeda to set a trap for Shinsuke at the Shinagawa Police Station. Then he sent everyone who had any contact with Shinsuke Yamanaka as far away as possible, gaining their silence with bribes. That must have been the plan in a nutshell.

Saburo Himeda must be a police officer. And Tomoe was lying when she had said that the MP Sergeant David Badham from Camp Ebisu was her lover. Moreover, his own daughters Fumiko and Takeko would have known better than anyone else whom he might talk to. The visage of Tokyo Seven Rose was emerging as the force behind the plot.

Suddenly I remembered something that Himeda had said that Kiichiro Aoyama was his brother-in-law, which meant the Neighborhood Association leader was also part of the intrigue.

I went to see Aoyama. His wife, as fat as ever in spite of the terrible food shortage, answered the door. "He's gone to the city hall to ask about DDT." She wrote two "D"s and one "T" on the ground by way of clarification. "It's an American pesticide. It kills rats, fleas and lice."

"So?"

"So? If we could get rid of rats, lice and fleas, we'd be able to eliminate typhus and smallpox. Do you know how many hundreds of people die of those diseases across the country every day? He's been going to the ward office and the city hall every day, urging the authorities to spread DDT here in Nezu Miyanaga-cho. He's breaking his back for the sake of Miyanaga-cho. I know it's considered unseemly to praise my own husband like that, but what he's doing is above and beyond the call of duty. Tonight he's going out drinking with city officials, and he probably won't be home until late."

"I'll come by early tomorrow then. By the way, Mrs. Aoyama, does your husband have a younger sister?

"No. There are no girls in the Aoyama family."

"That's what I thought. Well then, tomorrow morning…"

I stopped by Sen-*chan*'s house on the corner. She was away. Every member of Tokyo Seven Rose was out on the prowl. And my neighbor, Mr. Takahashi, was on another business trip, this time to Gunma Prefecture.

March 21

This morning I poured my miso soup with wakame seaweed over a bowl of rice mixed with barley and crushed soybeans and slurped it down like a bowl of noodles. My wife said acerbically, "Why don't you try actually tasting your food? These days a bowl of real rice is as rare as cherry blossoms in winter. What an unappreciative way to eat."

"I'm in a hurry. I'm off to attack the overnighters."

"Who?"

"I plan to mete out some well-deserved punishment to a group of women calling themselves by the outlandish name Tokyo Seven Rose." I threw down my chopsticks and leaped into my wood sandals. My wife was saying something, but by that time I was already on the other side of the glass door, shutting it with the hand behind my back. I have no idea what she said. More sarcasm, no doubt. There was no point in even listening.

Glaring at the door to Mr. Takahashi's house across the way, I half-dashed, like a track athlete, to the house on the corner, the headquarters of Tokyo Seven Rose. After saying he would look closely into the matter three days ago and report back, Mr. Takahashi had never shown up at my house. He must be busy with his job at the newspaper. I'd have to take care of this on my own. I couldn't count on his support.

"Good morning, Shinsuke. Thank you for agreeing to assist Tomoe and me with our wedding plans." Gen the tailor, carefully brushing away the dust in front of his house with a bamboo broom, bowed to me. "I can't believe that I'm getting married at my age. What's the world coming to?"

"You and Tomoe are quite the loving couple, I've heard. Who would have known you were Nezu's biggest playboy?"

"You're embarrassing me."

I left him sheepishly leaning on the broom and opened the door to the house on the corner.

"Sen-*chan*, is Fumiko here?"

"She's at work." She was right there before me, combing her brown locks in front of a large mirror that reflected her bright kimono, as flashy as a fisherman's banner. "What's the matter, Shin? What's so urgent?"

"Forget about me, what's wrong with your hair? It's all brown. Have you been in the sun too long?"

"I dyed it."

"You really are crazy."

"It was very expensive. I had to pay a hefty bribe to the Americans-only barbershop at the Imperial Hotel."

"You look like a monkey wearing a lion's mane."

"Who asked you, anyway? Paul likes it, and that's all that matters."

"Paul?"

"Paul Stewart. My man."

"So you have a man, too? Some of the American officers have pretty strange tastes, I guess."

"He's not an officer. He's a high official of the State Department, visiting from the United States. He's the vice-director of the U.S. Education Mission."

"I see."

"He's the one who really runs the mission. Important, huh?"

"More important than the CIE Language Section Chief, I suppose?"

"Fumi's man?"

"Yes, Navy Lieutenant Commander Hall."

"Much more important. And by the way, Hall's been promoted to the rank of Commander. Anyway, what do you want with Fumiko?"

"I was thinking of giving her a good scolding, but if she's not here that's out. Tomoe?"

"She's at work, too. Everyone's been staying over full time at the Imperial Hotel lately. I just came back to get this." She picked up a cloth wrapped around what seemed to be a rolled tube and held it to her chest.

I remembered the pattern of the cloth wrapper. "Those are the Kobayashi Kiyochika prints, aren't they?" I said in a tone as steely and hard as a three-day-old dumpling. They were my late brother's, this collection of "Famous Scenes of Tokyo" by the artist Kobayashi Kiyochika, and he had treasured them almost as much as his life. Of the prints, one of his favorites was *Nezu Shrine in Autumn*. He used to say that Kiyochika's version was much nicer than Nezu Shrine itself because someone could take a leak in a dark corner of the real shrine, but that couldn't happen to the print. "Where are you taking them?"

"Paul collects woodblock prints."

"I know that a lot of the Americans fancy themselves woodblock-print connoisseurs, strutting around like experts, just because they've bought a print or two. It's absurd. Are you planning on handing those Kiyochika prints over to the enemy?"

"I'm just showing them to him."

"No, you're not. I can see from your face that you plan to give them to him. How can you? He killed your lover."

"If you keep being such an inflexible old stick-in-the mud about everything, you're going to miss the bus and become a laughingstock, Shinsuke."

"Miss the bus?"

"You're pig-headed. You're going to find yourself left behind. Anyway, it was Fumiko and Tomoe who suggested I give these Kiyochika prints to Paul, so I won't have you saddling me with the blame."

"I have to see Fumiko."

"What are you grumbling about now?"

"And I have something I need to say to Tomoe, too."

"It seems pretty important to you." She stood there with a white Lucky Strike between her scarlet lips for a while, as if thinking about something. Then she took out a square cigarette lighter, bigger than a block of rice cake, clicked the fuse, and said: "Nothing you can say after being let out of the Monkey House makes the least bit of difference to the CIE Language Section, you know, Shinsuke." I had no idea what she meant. "Well, then, shall we go to the Imperial Hotel?"

"I thought about doing that several times. The problem is, I'd get thrown out by the MPs."

"Come with me." A Jeep was waiting for us on the main road of Miyanaga-cho. Sen-*chan* tapped the GI in the driver's seat on the shoulder as a signal to drive. We live in a strange world indeed, when a high-class prostitute of the defeated nation can order a soldier of the victor nation about with a wave of her hand.

It occurred to me I'd heard something like "you're going to find yourself left behind" before. As I was looking at Shinobazu Pond, planted with rice up to last year, the stalks bent low under the weight of their heavy heads, I remembered the slogan so popular six years ago, in 1939, "Don't miss the bus."

"Germany was really powerful at first, wasn't it?"

"What did you just say?"

"I said, in the early days of the war, Germany was really powerful. They conquered France in a flash, invaded Holland and pushed England into such a corner that defeat seemed just a matter of time."

"Ah. Yes, I suppose that did happen."

"As a result, France, England and Holland didn't have the ability to send their soldiers to protect their colonies in Asia and the South Pacific. Then suddenly war broke out between Germany and the Soviet Union. That meant that for the Japanese empire, the threat from the north was gone. That's when that slogan, "'Don't miss the bus,' became the rage. We shouldn't miss this golden opportunity, and suddenly everyone was all for the idea that we should invade French and Dutch Indochina to get a hold of the resources we needed—the Southern Offensive. Wherever you went, everyone was saying, 'Don't miss the bus.' It was when Fumimaro Konoe started his New Structure Movement."

"I remember, too. The Imperial Rule Assistance Association."

"Yes."

"I first met your brother at a party celebrating the start of the Asakusa Ward Branch of the Imperial Rule Assistance Association.

It was the night of October 13, 1940, at the Kamesei Restaurant in Yanagibashi. I was twenty-six years old, in the full bloom of youth. I was the most popular geisha in all Asakusa then." Sen-*chan* looked off into the distance. Her gaze ended at the Marunouchi Hotel, standing all alone amid the scorched rubble. The Jeep was driving through the ruins from Kandabashi Bridge to Otemachi.

"In those days, everyone belonged to the Imperial Rule Assistance Association. It was the times. The political parties and the labor unions, not wanting to be left behind, all voluntarily disbanded, because they 'didn't want to miss the bus,' and everybody rushed to join the Imperial Rule Assistance Association. And now here we are again, with the same slogan, 'don't miss the bus,' don't fall behind the times. Don't you think that's funny?"

"I don't see anything especially funny about it."

"You don't?"

"People are adaptable. If you're not adaptable, how do you expect to survive? You're the only one dragging his feet like this, Shinsuke. Though in your case, I suppose I can understand it."

"What's there to understand?"

"You've been in jail for two-thirds of the last year. In other words, you haven't spent much time in the new world."

"You may be right about that." As I was thinking of a rejoinder, the Jeep stopped directly in front of the back door of the Imperial Hotel, across from the new Ernie Pyle Theater taken over by the Occupation Forces, the former Tokyo Takarazuka Theater. Handing me the Kobayashi Kiyochika prints to hold, Sen-*chan* said to the MP on duty in a kind of phonetic Japanese-English, "*Hee izu ukiyo-e pikuchaa deeraa*" (He's a ukiyo print dealer), and walked into the service entrance and down the stairs. I chimed in, "*Iesu, ai amu ukiyo-e pikuchaa deeraa*," and dashed down after her. The MP, fooled by Sen-*chan*'s boldness, didn't move a muscle, but just stood there at attention, guarding against suspicious characters.

When we got to the bottom of the stairway there was a post office. The large clock on its wall said eight o'clock. The personnel office was next to the post office. A sizeable bronze plaque was attached to the wall, and it read:

Ten Rules of the Imperial Hotel

Consideration, politeness, promptness. These are and always have been our mottoes.

Cooperation. While every employee belongs to a particular department, he or she is also an employee of the hotel as a whole. Cooperate harmoniously to provide the best possible service.

Courtesy. Courtesy is a manifestation of the inner person and the mark of a hotel's quality. Always be courteous to guests and to each other.

Hygiene. Be hygienic in all things and strive to promote health.

Cleanliness. This is the very lifeblood of a hotel. Please keep the hotel and your own person clean.

Thrift. Never waste even a single sheet of paper. The personal use of hotel property is absolutely forbidden.

Study. Study to improve the performance of your assigned tasks and learn the preferences of our clientele.

Memory. Strive to quickly remember the names and faces of our guests.

Self-restraint. Don't whisper or laugh in front of guests, and don't stare at their clothing.

Gratitude. Never forget to say "Thank you."

Established 1925

Next to the plaque was a piece of cardboard. On it was written:

This hotel is a facility of the GHQ, SCAP. It is the billet of unmarried high-ranking officers, and all of the food for those officers is supplied by the Allied Forces Supply and Procurement Division. Accordingly, each slice of bread and pat of butter is U.S. Army property. I strictly prohibit the removal, pinching or pilfering of this food, which is reserved for the three hundred officers residing here, by employees. This is the eleventh rule of the Imperial Hotel.

When employees enter the food storage area, they are required to keep whistling the entire time they are there. This is the twelfth rule.

September 17, 1945
General Manager of the Imperial Hotel
Army First Lieutenant Joseph M. Morris

Sen-*chan* came back from the corridor to the right and pointed toward the back. "Our rest area is at the end of the corridor. What are you doing dawdling here?

"This thing about whistling..."

"He's terrified of people stealing food. Being that suspicious of us Japanese—it's terrible. That arrogant little twerp."

"What arrogant little twerp?"

"Morris is a twenty-two-year-old pipsqueak. He's the heir to a meat business in Chicago—he knows nothing about running a hotel. He has no idea what he should be doing, so he spends his days scurrying around the hotel digging through trashcans in the hope of finding stolen goods an employee has stashed there. It's the only thing he knows, that one-trick pony."

I followed Sen-*chan* down the dim corridor. Our footsteps made absolutely no sound. The floor was lined with cork! For a moment I thought I'd died and become a ghost. I tried consciously to make noise with my shoes against the floor, imitating the single-file marching for fire drills, but to no avail. "The hotel has every amenity. It's no wonder that the Allied Forces chose to take it over."

Suddenly music seemed to flow from the direction toward which Sen-*chan* and I were walking.

"Is that jazz? How cheery, so early in the morning."

"They're warming up. They'll be playing in the first-floor dining room soon."

"It can't be good for the digestion."

"It seems to suit the stomachs of the Americans fine," Sen-*chan* said, as we passed a sign on a door that read "Wine Cellar." "Did you know that one reason the GHQ took over the Imperial Hotel was its wine cellar? Word got out that the best vintages of French wine had been were kept in this very wine cellar. So of course the GHQ set its sights on that."

The corridor came to an end soon after the wine cellar, as we approached a door that had a color photograph of a rose that might have been clipped out of a magazine. "It's me," announced Sen-*chan*, as she opened the door. "Shinsuke is with me."

The room was about the size of a classroom. In the center was a large Western-style table reeking of varnish, one corner of which was charred. Ten wooden stools, each showing scorch marks, were arranged around the table. A curtain hung across the back of the room. After directing me to a chair with her gaze, Sen-*chan* spoke to someone behind the curtain. "Shinsuke is here," she said again.

"Does it smell like something's burning to you?" I asked her.

"You know the main banquet room of the south wing of the hotel burned down in the May 24th air raids. This used to be the furniture storage room in the basement of the south wing, which survived the fire."

"Now I understand the smell. What about that curtain?"

"It survived the bombing, too. In fact, the uniforms of the female staff are all made from curtains that survived the fires."

A maroon desk was pushed up against the wall. Sen-*chan* placed a small kettle on the electric hot plate on the desk. "Would you like some coffee?"

"Yes, please," I answered as I sat down at the table. "About the uniforms—I noticed that some staff wear blue uniforms and some pink. Does that mean anything?"

"The older female staff wear blue, and the younger wear pink. Some blue curtains survived the fire, and some pink curtains survived the fire. No meaning beyond that."

At that moment, to the sound of sliding metal curtain rings, the curtain in the back of the room parted, and several women in white robes, which also seemed to have once been curtains, filed out toward the large table.

"How are you, Dad?" asked Fumiko. Her hair was pulled up on top of her head.

"Your hair has gotten more gray," said Takeko in a voice gravelly with sleep, a scarf wrapped around her neck.

"Thanks for taking care of my grandfather and grandmother," said Tokiko Furusawa, blowing on her red fingernails.

"It's been a while, hasn't it?" said Kayoko Makiguchi, who had cut her hair in a bob since I last saw her.

"We talk about you every day," said Kumiko Kurokawa, who had shaved her eyebrows.

"I remember that you like these," said Tomoe, sitting directly in front of me and taking out two Lucky Strikes from the pocket of her robe. She pushed them gently toward me. "Please."

"Do you know what kind of a man Gen the tailor is?" I asked, pushing her gift back toward her and sitting up straight, after taking a sip of the coffee Sen-*chan* had served me. "He's not just some ordinary forty-year-old man sitting at his sewing machine all day. He..." I brought out one of my own black-market cigarettes out and lit it. "He runs that sewing machine with a heart that's pure and loving, cuts his cloth with his scissors in utter honesty and integrity, wields his needle with complete innocence, and irons with absolute sincerity."

"That's true, I agree."

"Because that's his nature, Gen hasn't had any luck with women. Just this morning he was sweeping his yard singing happily to himself. It was more like he was dancing than cleaning. I've known him for forty years, and that's the first time I've seen him like that. He's floating on air. This is all because you cast your spell over him, Tomoe."

"I honestly care for him. I am completely serious about Gentaro."

"How can you say that you care for him and that you're serious? You already have a lover at Camp Ebisu. Tomoe, I'm begging you to stop toying with Gen's affections. I'm afraid this will come to a very bad end. I wouldn't be surprised if Gen threw himself into Shinobazu Pond and drowned."

"Not in Shinobazu Pond, he won't," said Takeko. "It was filled in and planted with rice. The water only comes up to his knees."

"Takeko, you stay out of this. Tomoe, if you're really serious about Gen, I want you to break off your relationship with Sergeant Badham." Now, of course I suspected that Sergeant Badham was a fiction. I was just throwing this out as bait.

"Well?" I persisted.

Tomoe looked at Sen-*chan*, who had been powdering her face. Placing the puff back in her compact, Sen-*chan* announced, "Let's tell him the whole thing. To tell the truth, that's why I brought him here."

"Yes, I suppose we should," said Fumiko, who'd let down her long hair. "We can't allow him to keep wandering in the dark forever."

"In the dark?"

"Yes, in the dark."

"What do you mean by that?"

"We sketched out a master plan. You've been wandering around in it like a maze."

"What do you mean?"

"On January 17th, you had a big argument with Bob. Or technically speaking, Shinsuke Yamanaka, employee of the CIE Language Section, had a fierce run-in with his boss, Language Simplification Officer Robert King Hall. You remember that?"

"How could I forget? Your boyfriend Bob is plotting to outlaw the use of *kanji* and *kana*. He was spouting off about how the Japanese people were going to have to write in *romaji*. And he was going to use the U.S. Education Mission coming to Japan to get Emperor Moatside to sign off on this policy. If I didn't do something, the Japanese language would end up written in *romaji*. Of course, I had a run-in with him."

"Saying that you were going to talk about it to your friend, a newspaper journalist, you ran out of the office."

"I wanted our neighbor Mr. Takahashi to write an article about it in the newspaper."

"Bob panicked."

"As well he should."

"He didn't want his plan leaked before the arrival of the U.S. Education Mission. The Japanese people would make a fuss. His

226

proposal would go down in flames and end up just a pipe dream. Bob came crying to me about the whole thing."

"A whiner."

"There was really no reason to do anything. Even if a journalist found out about it, it would never have been published."

"Why not?"

"The newspapers don't have the guts to write anything about the Americans. They're happy to write praiseworthy articles about the supposed good things the Americans do, but they don't have the courage to write about secret plots and plans. And even if they did, the censors would never permit it."

Of course. Maybe at this very moment Mr. Takahashi was being scolded by his bosses, who were warning him to keep the information to himself, or else.

"Still, Bob was making quite a fuss, worried about what might happen if by some off chance things went wrong. And it's true, if word had gotten out, it would have caused a lot of trouble—for us most of all. We all talked about it here, and Tokiko came up with a brilliant plan. We would put a lid on every possible source from which the story might get out."

"I suppose you could say I'm the one who sent you to the Monkey House," said Tokiko, aligning her ruby red nails on the desk and bowing her head in a supplicating gesture. "I'm very sorry."

"First, Bob arranged for Mr. Takahashi to be sent off to the countryside as the guide for an American journalist looking into rural agricultural reform. By doing that, we separated Mr. Takahashi from you."

"The American journalist was an imposter," said Kayoko, extending her handkerchief to me. I was so caught listening that I didn't notice my cigarette ashes falling on my jacket collar. "Lieutenant Commander Hall had a member of the CIE Education Sub-Section pose as the journalist."

"What about Saburo Himeda?"

"A former Special Higher Police detective," said Kumiko, refreshing my coffee cup.

"So Miss Kurita's promotion and the transfer of the former proprietor of the Hongo Bar to Sendai were all the doing of

Lieutenant Commander Hall—or rather, Commander Hall. Or at least at his orders."

Sen-*chan* nodded. "And an American Army captain who lives on the second floor of the hotel here pretended to be Sergeant Badham. By captain I mean floor captain."

"The officers at the Shinagawa Police Station?"

"Commander Hall arranged it with them in advance."

"This is unbelievable. All of you—you were all in it together with Commander Hall."

"Up to a point," said Tomoe, taking over the narrative. "We were planning on destroying Commander Hall's proposal to change the Japanese written language to *romaji* from the inside. Having people on the outside making a senseless fuss would have spoiled our plan. That's why we had to silence you."

"Wait a minute. What do you mean by destroying the plan from the inside?"

"Commander Hall is completely in the thrall of his proposal. There was no way to put a stop to it from outside. So we came up with the idea of targeting the Language Simplification Subcommittee of the U.S. Education Mission. If we could control the subcommittee, we'd win and we could quash Commander Hall's plan. The idea would never be raised again. This was the plan that we came up with."

"It's an idiotic plan. But you're dealing with the heads of American departments of education, state departments of education, university presidents, university professors, the most eminent figures in American education. How on earth do you think you're going to infiltrate them?"

Tomoe's white teeth peeked out from between her well-formed red lips. "We've already infiltrated them plenty."

The other six laughed.

I picked up one of the Lucky Strikes lying on the table in front of Tomoe and lit up. Clearly I'd gotten involved in a plot of vast proportions and complexity. I had to stay cool. I had to think. I slowly took a drag on my cigarette, looking up. The ceiling of this room in the basement of the south wing of the Imperial Hotel, which had managed to escape destruction, was black with soot. Light from the doorway struck the ceiling, and the shadows of six women, Sen-*chan* in the lead, were exiting into the corridor.

"It's breakfast time," said Tomoe, drinking the last of her coffee. "Waking our guests is the first job of the day. Each of us is taking care of one of the members of the mission."

"Does that mean you have to take care of them at night, too? What happens if they say they'd like to join them in a little nighttime romp?" It was hard for me to ask this, but I had to confront the reality of the situation. Right now what was required of me was to find the courage and will to do just that.

"If that happens, we do as they ask," said Tomoe with surprising firmness. "That's our job. Except for Fumiko, of course. Fumiko has her exclusive partner, Commander Hall."

"And who's your partner?"

"George Stoddard."

"I think I've heard that name before."

"He's the leader of the U.S. Education Mission. He's the head of the New York State Department of Education."

"And why does the head of the New York State Department of Education need to have a Japanese woman in his bed? That's a laugh."

"He's a gentleman."

"But still, surely he must be tempted by your charms and find himself wanting to forget his problems in your embrace?" I almost added, "I certainly would," but stopped myself, blushing.

"That happened, once," said Tomoe in a low voice. "He's quite elderly, and it wasn't easy."

"You'd better not let Gen hear that."

"He knows everything. I tell him everything that happens."

"I don't care what a saint he might be, he must have been angry."

"He laughed sadly and said he understood how a man who's been waiting for the courtesan he's always loved to serve out her contract feels." Suddenly Tomoe's expression changed. Both her eyes filled with tears. "I want this to be over." She took a handkerchief out of her handbag on the table, together with a piece of paper folded in four, and while she dabbed at her eyes with the handkerchief, she passed the paper to me.

"A week ago, on March 13th and 14th, there was a meeting of all members of the education mission. This was presented at the meeting."

It was mimeographed and consisted of five pages in very small handwriting. On the cover in large characters was written: "Language Reform Proposal." Next to it in smaller characters was written: "Naval Commander Robert King Hall, GHQ Civilian Information and Education Section Language Section Chief, Language Simplification Unit Officer." Next to that was a Japanese name: "Former Taihoku Imperial University President Masatsugu Ando."

I hadn't suspected that a Japanese would be a party to this, so I was taken aback for a moment.

"Commander Hall's lecture was in English, and Professor Ando's was in Japanese. An official of the Foreign Ministry translated Commander Hall's lecture, and this is what the Ministry of Education put together based on it. It's being distributed to intellectual leaders throughout the country."

"What are you asking me to do about it?"

"Just read through it. I'll go wake Stoddard in the meantime." She left the room, stirring up a faint breeze of her perfume, and then I was alone and all was quiet. The only sounds were the jazz playing in the dining room in the distance. I laid the pages on the table and lit another cigarette.

The lecture of the Language Simplification Unit Officer to the full membership of the U.S. Education Mission began with the line, "The Japanese writing system begins with the introduction, in the fourth century, of Chinese civilization." According to Hall, Japanese "is, phonetically speaking, one of the simplest languages in the world, but when it comes to its writing system, it suddenly becomes an unfathomable language of unbelievable difficulty.

"First, it has four kinds of orthographic symbols: *kanji*, *katakana*, *hiragana* and *romaji*. Moreover, it is quite common for the briefest sentence to combine all four, creating a degree of confusion that is beyond description."

Without realizing it, I felt the same fury returning, and I found myself shouting, "What kind of crap is this?" We clearly distinguish between these sets of symbols, using *hiragana* for native Japanese words, characters for words of Chinese origin, and *katakana* for words originating in Western languages.

"In addition, Japanese has a multiplicity of stylistic forms, including vernacular style, literary style, epistolary style, and others. All Westerners who have visited Japan to date have declared it 'a language invented by the devil,' and indeed it is of devilish complexity and perversity."

Of course he didn't say that the Japanese people, able to read and write such a language, must be very intelligent as a result.

"Until they succeed in simplifying their writing system, the Japanese cannot become full-fledged members of international society

"Characters, at any rate, are more than just difficult, they are simply absurd. For example, the compound 和尚 is pronounced *kasho* in the Tendai sect of Buddhism, *kujo* in Shingon Buddhism, and *osho* in the Zen and Pure Land sects. Most ordinary Japanese cannot make these distinctions and pronounce the characters *osho*, *bosan* or *bonsan*. At the same time they have no compunction about inventing specialized and idiosyncratic terminology in their own fields of expertise. To give just one example, the Japanese word for 'constant' is *josu* in mathematics and physics, but in engineering it's *teisu*, and in chemistry it's *kosu*. What a strange people the Japanese are."

Any Japanese would recognize this for the distortion that it is. Picking just two or three exceptional examples to conclude erroneously that "therefore, the entire Japanese language is like this" is devious and manipulative. But what happens when Americans who know nothing about the Japanese language are told things like this by one of their countrymen, who asserts them with such self-confidence? By far the majority of them will rashly agree.

"To digress a bit, let's look at the fact that the Japanese have so few names for stars. All of their names for the stars and planets— *Kasei* (Mars), *Kinsei* (Venus), *Dosei* (Saturn), *Kaiosei* (Neptune) and *Hokkyokusei* (the North Star) were borrowed from Chinese. The Japanese have named only one star or planet themselves—they call the Pleiades in the constellation Taurus that is above their heads on winter evenings, *Subaru*. In fact, the Japanese are a rarity among the world's peoples, lacking the noble custom of gazing up into the starry night sky and contemplating the eternal nature of the universe.

They never take the long view. It would not be inappropriate to describe the Japanese way of thinking as near-sighted."

This is just a lie. "Are you saying that the old women of Kujukurihama Beach aren't Japanese?" I shouted, slamming the papers down on the desk.

When I was incarcerated at the prison in Yokaichiba, near the ocean, I worked with old women from a nearby fishing village to make fish sausage out of ground sardines. They were always talking about the stars, in their local dialect. How can fishermen even navigate the seas if they don't look up at the stars? All this amounts to is that there aren't universal names for the stars that are the same everywhere throughout the country. In fact, Ino Tadataka, who made a scale map of Japan by his astral measurements of the stars sparkling in the night sky, was also from Kujukurihama Beach. The Japanese look up the stars just like any other people.

"To digress again, the Japanese language is extremely rich in names for plants. Names for plants with long, narrow leaves are particularly numerous. *Take, sasa, shino, ashi, kaya, susuki, suge*—there are more than can be mentioned. The long leaves of these plants are used to thatch roofs and build walls, and then the Japanese shut themselves up in their grass houses and live out their days without ever looking up at the stars. The reason that so many Japanese homes were destroyed in the American air raids is that they were made of grass..."

The faces of my daughter and my brother who lost their lives in those air raids, seemed to rise up out of the mimeographed pages. That merciless bombing of civilian targets was a violation of international law. How base and cowardly to try to shift the blame to "grass houses." I was so outraged at this point that my eyes just slid insensibly over the rows of words, not focusing.

"As an example of the needless difficulty of characters, I'd like to point out the fact that each character has both a native and a Chinese-style reading. The name of the present Minister of Education, written in characters, is 安倍能成. No matter whom you ask, they'll be unable to tell you how to read the characters 能成. Some will suggest Nosei, others Yoshinari, but no one will be certain. Astonishingly, the name is read Yoshishige. As this demonstrates, the Japanese are satisfied to allow one of the most important things in the world, a person's name, to remain vague and undecided. It is widely recognized that the typical Japanese facial expression is a vague and inscrutable smile, and the vagueness and ambiguity of the readings of characters may well be regarded as one of the reasons for this. To press this point farther, when even names are deliberately vague, it is impossible to pursue a line of rational thinking with any accuracy, and the ambiguity and confusion of Japanese thinking can also be traced to this source."

I was quivering with rage as my eyes sped over the page. Before I realized it, I had actually bitten through two cigarettes.

"When writing Japanese with characters, the most common method is to employ a single character to represent a single word, as, for example, 山 for *yama* (mountain) or 川 for *kawa* (river). When there is no character for a particular word, it can be written for convenience and—and this point is important to note—quite capriciously, with characters of one's choice that happen to have the appropriate sounds in either their Chinese or Japanese pronunciation. This 'weird reading' is called *ateji*. Characters that have no semantic relation to the meaning of a Japanese word are borrowed to spell it out based on their Chinese-style pronunciation, as in cases such as 素敵 *suteki* (fine or wonderful) or 兎角 *tokaku* (anyway). The Japanese pronunciations of characters may also be borrowed to write foreign loan words such as 背広 *sebiro* (suit) or they may be used to indicate the pronunciation of a native Japanese word, as in 矢張 *yahari* (after all) or 出鱈目 *detarame* (nonsense). In fact, as is the case with 型録 *katarogu* (catalogue), these methods are often combined in a single word. The writer Natsume Soseki, so highly admired by the Japanese, was one of the most learned men of his time, a graduate of Tokyo Imperial University, the highest educational institution in the nation, and even sent by his government to study in England. Yet these weird *kanji*, conceived on the spur of the moment—for example, 馬穴 (for *baketsu*, or bucket, but here written with characters meaning 'horse hole') are quite common even in his writing. Since even a man of Soseki's accomplishments and learning commits such blunders, it is easy to imagine the result among less elevated minds. Characters have been a factor in cultivating the lamentable Japanese tendencies toward the temporary, the consciously obscure, and the inconsistent."

I removed my suit jacket and tore off my shirt. My body was on fire.

"Following the horrors of World War I, the belief in the value of peace and disarmament began to spread widely throughout international society. As is well known, the League of Nations was born with the mission of strengthening this highly desirable trend. But the Japanese Empire, defying international opinion in its treatment of the Manchurian Empire, in spite of the fact that Japan was one of the four permanent members of the League's Council, left the organization. Following in Japan's footsteps, Italy and Germany also quit the organization. That this was one of the causes leading up to World War II is a fact that cannot but remain fresh in our memories. At the time, many around the world decried this development and asked, 'What can the Japanese be thinking? They are incomprehensible!' It is the incomprehensibility of characters that has in fact fostered the incomprehensibility of the Japanese. The Japanese are bizarrely complex, idiosyncratic, weird, near-sighted and live in grass houses. The Japanese excel at ambiguity and inconsistency. It must be concluded that it is impossible to conceive of the return of the Japanese people to the international community as long as they remain mired in this singular incomprehensibility. The Japanese must take this opportunity of their defeat to abandon the use of characters, adopt Roman letters, completely reform their national character and cultivate a universality that equips them for international society."

I threw Hall's lecture on the floor and ground it into the boards with my shoes.

The lecture of former university president Masatsugu Ando remained in my hands. It was titled in both Japanese and English, the English title being, "On Problems Concerning the National Language and Its Characters."

"I'm counting on you, President Ando. Give Hall's arguments the thrashing they deserve." Mentally placing my palms together in supplication, feeling like a virgin whose chastity was being threatened by a gang of lecherous brigands, waiting anxiously for her Lohengrin to appear on his swan, brandishing his shining sword to rescue her, I began to read.

"Japanese literary style is quite complex. It can be divided into two major categories, one, employed in imperial proclamations and laws and ordinances, using a mixture of *kanji* and *katakana*, and the other, used in public and private writings, a mix of *kanji* and *hiragana*. Both of these are distinct from the vernacular, spoken language, complicating the Japanese language."

Traitor.

"In the early Meiji era, some expressed the opinion that characters should be outlawed and Japanese written in *kana* only. We also have the brilliant proposal by Aikitsu Tanakadate and many others suggesting that Japanese be written with Roman letters. In that sense, I see in Commander Hall's proposal traces of the vision articulated by pioneering thinkers of the Meiji era."

The obsequious toady.

"The sudden abolishment of characters and the enforced use of Roman letters, however, runs the risk of causing confusion among the masses of Japanese. As a provisional solution, then, it is suggested it would be more effective as an initial step to drastically restrict the number of characters in use and supplement them with *kana*."

His tone was changing.

"After passing through this transitional phase, following thorough consideration, it is desirable to decide whether *kanji* should be abolished and replaced with *kana*, or with *romaji*. In conclusion, the purpose of language reform is to ease the educational burden on Japanese children, and the full cooperation of all the Japanese people is necessary to achieve this aim."

Another case of shaking a mountain and having nothing but a mouse dash out. While I understood that he didn't feel he could go against the policies of the Occupation Forces, wasn't he supposed to be representing Japan? The least he could have said was something like, "It's thanks to the Japanese written language that we have the world's first novel, *The Tale of Genji*."

As I was picking up the papers from the floor and smoothing them out, the scent of perfume wafted into the room.

"He says he's going to stay in bed until just before they go see Kabuki at eleven. It's his age, I suppose," said Tomoe, sitting down in front of me. "What did you think of the lectures?"

"If Hall had been here, I would have thrown myself at him and beat him to a pulp... though I know that since he's younger and bigger than me, I'd probably be the one to take the beating, but I'd have tried my best anyway. I was just about to give Masatsugu Ando a good slap or two across the face, too."

"We all feel the same way."

"All?"

"Tokyo Seven Roses." As I watched, Tomoe's white neck with its single black mole slowly flushed to a pale rose color. "I lost my husband in a bombing raid by a B-29, and the bombings made my father-in-law lose his mind. Your daughters Fumiko and Takeko lost their sister Kinuko in an air raid, and Sen-*chan* lost her husband and son, Tokiko lost her parents and her brother, Kayoko Makiguchi and Kumiko Kurokawa lost their entire families. The leaders who brought us into this war are to blame, and we also bear responsibility for following them. We understand that full well, but still, we hate the Americans. And I hate myself for selling my body to the Americans. When I think about all of these things, all sorts of thoughts and feelings start churning inside me in a confused tangle and I don't know what to think any more, but anyway, taking our *kanji* and *kana*, our way of writing away from us—well, that's just too much. That's how all the members of Tokyo Seven Roses feel."

"You're right. America is going too far. We may have lost the war, but that doesn't give them the right to take our very language from us."

"I don't know how to say it, but somehow having *kanji* and *kana* taken from me are even worse than having had my husband taken from me. Maybe because it will have such an effect on my children. I can't really explain it."

"I understand."

"Now I know what a terrible thing we did to the Kims," Tomoe went on. I had no idea what this sudden change in topic meant. "I grew up in Keijo, in Korea, and I had a good friend at school named Kim. One day she suddenly stopped talking to me. When I asked her why, she replied angrily, 'You Japanese are trying to take our language away from us.' Her father was a philologist, and he'd spent many years compiling a Korean dictionary. The Japanese military government confiscated his manuscript, giving the reason that 'Koreans are required to use Japanese from now on, so there's no need for a Korean dictionary.'"

"Koreans were Japanese then, so it couldn't be helped. What did they call it then? Imperialization?"

"But the Japanese Constitution didn't apply to Koreans." Tears were starting to form in Tomoe's eyes. "If Koreans were Japanese, the Japanese Constitution should have applied equally to them. But that only became true just a few months ago, last year, in the fall of last year." Tomoe's face was suddenly white—because she had covered it with an open handkerchief. "That was just a pretense, saying that the Koreans were Japanese. Now I understand how painful it is to have your language taken from you. Now I understand how Kim felt." Her voice broke, and she stopped speaking. Why had she gone off on this tangent about the Korean Peninsula? It seemed to me that there must be some mysterious reason behind it.

"Mr. Yamanaka, have you made Tomoe cry?" asked Tokiko Furusawa, her red nails flashing in the light as she came back into the room. "What did you say to her?"

"Nothing. We were just talking about the lectures delivered by Commander Hall and Masatsugu Ando at the general meeting. Something upset her, and she suddenly started to cry."

"I'm glad to hear it's not something you said. Anyway, how much has she told you?"

"More importantly, tell me how the members of the U.S. Education Mission reacted to the two lectures."

"They applauded for a very long time."

"Which means?"

"The two speakers' ideas are going to be incorporated into the final report."

"And?"

"The report will be sent to General MacArthur. Which is only to be expected, since it was he who invited the mission to Japan. Then, at the end of the month, the mission, having completed its work, will go home."

"And after that?"

"The contents of the report will be implemented through Japanese government channels. If it's MacArthur's orders we'll have no choice but to obey."

"So it's impossible to avoid the replacement of the Japanese writing system with Roman letters."

"Yes, at this point, almost impossible."

"There is, however, one individual who can make the impossible possible," said Kayoko Makiguchi with a heart-melting smile, her bangs cut in a perfectly straight line.

"Who? Where is this person?"

"Why, it's you," she said, carefully placing the wrinkled shirt and jacket I'd thrown down on the table on my shoulders.

"I know it's asking a lot, but please do your best."

Kayoko was the daughter of a wealthy oil wholesaler in Yotsuya and was brought up as a pampered child in the lap of luxury, but a single bomb dropped on her home took everything from her. The oil her family sold was fuel for the flames, and no other member of her family survived. She was always very calm and composed, not the kind of young woman who bantered or jested. Perhaps her work of late had changed her character.

"I'm just as serious as the others about the fate of *kanji* and *kana*. Don't tease me."

"All of us in Tokyo Seven Roses chose you, Mr. Yamanaka. You're the only one who can do it. Isn't that so?"

They were all back in the room now, and they all turned toward me and smiled. Tomoe put her hand on Kayoko's shoulder.

"Thank you, Kayoko. I just couldn't bring myself to explain it to him. When he started to get too close to the truth, I had to toss him a red herring. I even cried."

But what on earth did they want me to do? What did they expect of this half-unemployed fifty-five-year-old whose only talents were making fans and cutting and printing mimeograph stencils? I was just a middle-aged man who'd lost his eldest daughter in an air raid, whose wife was giving him the cold shoulder, whose second and third daughters were now the playthings of American military officers, and whose son had left home to become a thief and black market rice dealer. What did they want me to do?

"I devised the plan," said Tokiko, bringing her chair right next to me and sitting down. "It's the old badger game." She, it seemed, was the brains of the Tokyo Seven Rose operation. It was her strategy that had landed me in the Monkey House, too. "A variation on the badger game, really."

"I don't have the slightest idea what any of you are talking about. Can you explain it to me slowly, in a way that makes sense? Then I can decide whether I'll do it or not."

"But once you hear it, you can't say no," said Sen-*chan*.

Her threatening tone gave me a bad feeling, and I rose from my chair. "If that's the case, I'll just leave right now."

Sen-*chan* and Takeko pushed me back into my seat by my shoulders. "Just listen," said Sen-*chan*.

"So I have no choice?"

"Here's a list of the members of the U.S. Education Mission." Tokiko took a piece of paper out of her handbag and placed it on the table. There were twenty-seven names on the list. The names of three of them had little red circles by them: Dr. Harold Benjamin, U.S. Department of Education; Dr. Willard E. Givens, Executive Secretary of the National Education Association; and Paul Stewart, Department of State, Mission Secretary General. I recognized the last name.

"These three have something in common," said Tokiko, lightly tapping one of her red nails on their names. "Can you guess what that might be?"

"It's no use asking me. I've never met any of them."

"Yes, that's right, you haven't. All right, their first point in common. The other members of the mission are university professors of education or the heads of state commissions of education. They're all educational specialists, but these three are high-ranking government officials. And they're all influential figures. In other words, they're powerful."

"I see. So you're going to try to somehow trick these three."

"You catch on quickly," said Tokiko, giving me a little kiss on the forehead. "A little reward."

"I'm too old to enjoy anything like that. Stop fooling around and tell me the rest."

"The second point in common. All three of them are womanizers. Givens is my partner right now, and, well, I don't know how to say it, but let's just say I never seem to get enough sleep."

"What's their third common feature?"

"All three of them write home every day. Whom do you suppose they write to?"

"How would I know?"

"To their wives. In other words, all three are terrified of their wives."

"I see. Since they're afraid of their wives, they're kicking up their heels here in the distant Far East, doing things they wouldn't dare do back home."

"Yes. And that gave me an idea. Wouldn't it be interesting to take a picture of these three men naked in bed having an orgy with some Japanese women? If they were told the photograph was going to be sent to their wives back home, they'd be terrified. They'd throw themselves at our mercy and beg us not to do it. They'd wring their hands and weep, promising to do whatever we asked."

"I see where you're going now."

"Yes, you must."

"And so tonight, I'm going to ask Mr. Givens if he wouldn't like to try something interesting. 'Just think how exciting it would be if there were three couples all doing it together?' He just loves things like that."

"And then in the middle of it, you take the photo."

"Yes."

"And then you ask him to see to it that the proposals presented by Hall and Ando aren't included in the report, or you'll send the photos to their wives. Actually, you don't ask, you threaten."

"That's it."

"That's certainly the classic badger game."

"Pretty clever, don't you think?"

"I wonder. They're not going to be eager to let you take their picture. In fact, I can't see how they'd permit it. They wouldn't do anything that would leave any proof behind."

"That's why *you're* going to take it."

"*What?*"

"Secretly, from inside the wardrobe." Tomoe took a shiny black camera out of a wooden box in the corner of the room. It had a little round silver hood on the top. "Your neighbor Mr. Takahashi lent it to us. It's a Leica from the newspaper. When you press the shutter, the bulb inside this hood flashes and makes the room as bright as day. You don't have to be a pro. All you have to do is snap the shutter, and six naked men and women will be captured on film."

Tomoe passed the camera to Sen-*chan*. "At nine tonight, come to Room 244 on the second floor of the North Wing. I'll leave the camera inside the wardrobe in the room. You used to be quite a camera buff before the war, so you should have no problem with it, but this is the shutter. Got it?" I was frozen to the spot and couldn't even move my lips. If someone took a photo of me now, they'd have a perfect shot, without the slightest blur.

"Come to this room again at eight. Kumiko will take you to Room 244, so you don't have to worry about getting lost or anything. Oh yes, that's right—I need to tell you a little about the layout of the room. It's a special room, one of only sixteen in the entire hotel, called a suite—it has a bedroom and a living room that are open to each other. It's the room of my partner, Vice-director of the U.S. Education Mission Paul Stewart."

"Wait just a minute." At last my mouth was moving again, though I still tripped over my tongue. "I have several questions."

"What's the matter? You seem to be scared to death."

"You bet I'm scared. Scared enough to wet my pants. It's all well and good to have Kumiko guide me to the room, but how am I supposed to get inside Room 244? Sen-*chan*'s partner, this Paul, the high State Department official, is going to be solidly encamped there. I'm not a ninja you know. I can't just make myself invisible."

"Mr. Yamanaka, that's easy," said Kumiko, painting crescent-shaped eyebrows over the ones she had shaved off. "Sen-*chan* has a key to the room, and there's a performance by Bob Hope at the Ernie Pyle Theater next door tonight. Every member of the mission will be there, without exception, so it'll be a cinch to get in the room. A three-year-old could do it."

"Bob Hope? What's that?"

"A really popular American comedian. He's here to entertain the GIs. Tonight the Imperial Hotel is going to be empty as a cavern from 7 to 9 P.M. He's incredibly famous."

"All right. I see how I'm getting in. I take the photo of the six men and women in their naked orgy. But then what? Your Paul, and the other two officials, Willard Givens and Harold Benjamin, are going to realize it when the flash goes off. What am I supposed to do then?"

"They'll all be naked," said Sen-*chan*, sending a puff of purple cigarette smoke from her red lips up into the air. "As they say, 'You can't go calling in your birthday suit.' Don't you think the Americans must have a similar proverb? They'll be flailing about, grabbing their pajamas or a sheet to wrap themselves in. That's when you make your escape."

"You head north down the corridor toward the Ginza," said Kayoko, beckoning. "You'll come to a door with a sign that says "Private". I'll be standing there, waiting for you to show you the way. Once you get that far you're safe. You can pass from there to the employee passageway, down to the basement, without worrying about anyone following you. When you get to the bottom, you'll end up in front of this room, whether you turn right or left. You'll recognize it because of the picture of the rose on the door. I'll be there to guide you, anyway, so you have nothing to worry about."

"That's right, nothing at all to worry about," said Sen-*chan*, lighting up another Lucky Strike. "I guarantee it."

"If that's the case, why don't you do this yourselves, without coming to me, asking an old man to take part in such a caper? What happens if I run out of breath and get caught?"

"They know our faces. We'd be caught in a flash."

Yes, that was probably true. I took the camera and put my right eye up to the viewfinder. It was like looking through the wrong end of a telescope; everything seemed very far away, and the faces of the seven women with their heavy white makeup looked like seven white roses.

"You said you borrowed this camera from my neighbor Mr. Takahashi. Does that mean he's in on your little scheme?"

"More than just in on it," said Fumiko, her face filling the viewfinder. Her long face was distorted vertically, making her look like a white horse. I lowered the camera from my eye and set it on the table. "Mr. Takahashi caught on to the subterfuge behind his so-called business trip and came to ask us what was going on, so we explained the entire thing in detail. When I came up with this plan, we went to ask him if we could borrow a camera."

"He told us to leave the development and the printing of the film up to him, and also offered to guard the negatives for us." Takeko had been drinking coffee steadily for some time. The unpleasant rasp of her voice must surely be from drinking too much coffee. "It was a perfect role for him."

"What do you mean?'

"He works at a newspaper. If the negatives are at a newspaper, even if the GHQ censors come snooping around, the fact that they're there in the first place is a silent and very powerful threat to the U.S. Education Mission."

"I see. You really covered all your bases."

"It seems that the band has stopped playing in the dining room," said Tokiko Furusawa, fingering the pearl in her ear lobe. "Do you have any more questions?"

"No. I've asked everything I wanted to."

"All right then, we need to go to work. Don't let us down."

The seven women left. Tomoe, the last, smiled slightly in my direction as she closed the door. The clock above it said nine.

I called Mr. Takahashi at work at his newspaper in Sukiyabashi from the phone at the end of the employee corridor, and with a pleasant breeze at my back, two parts cold winter and eight parts spring zephyr, I walked to Shinbashi. I ate two bowls of beef over rice at the black market there at 25 yen per bowl. In both bowls combined, there were perhaps three little scraps of something like beef, but the rice in my stomach made me feel better as I made my way to Hibiya Park.

The wind had died down and the park was filled with warmth and a pleasant aroma—though if I focused carefully on my sense of smell, I could still detect the odor of charred earth. Looking off to the Music Hall on the left, I sat down on a stone bench; in the light of the sun, the ancient stone was like a ceramic heat box. The sharp shadow of a tree was pointing to a repair on my left shoe. Five or six years ago, when spring weather arrived, it was my custom to go to the wholesalers in Asakusabashi and talk about new designs for summer fans. If I was able to successfully conclude the task that lay before me now, maybe I'd go around to Asakusabashi.

As I was sitting there thinking these things, Mr. Takahashi arrived.

"Sorry for asking you to meet me like this, when you're at work." I dug into my cloth backpack for the five Lucky Strikes Tomoe had given me when she left, offering two of them to Mr. Takahashi. It was a gesture of thanks and apology.

For a while, we both just sat there watching our cigarette smoke disappear into the soft spring light. People were sitting on all the stone benches in the park, soaking up the sun. Little first-grade elementary school students were singing in high voices, competing with the songs of the birds in the trees, as they walked down a narrow path opposite us.

"Paradise," murmured Mr. Takahashi, stubbing out his cigarette on the ground and then carefully retrieving the butt and placing it in his tobacco case. He'd smoke it later in his pipe. "Sitting in the warm spring sun and smoking a cigarette. I never thought I'd ever experience a day like this again… You know, it's such a shame."

"What is?"

"That we'd convinced ourselves that the nation and the people are the same thing, and that we published our newspaper based on that way of thinking. I can't help but think what a terrible, terrible shame that was. Don't you agree?"

"I guess I'd have to say, I don't really know what you mean by a shame."

"We used to think that if the Japanese empire disappeared, the Japanese people would vanish with it. So we had to fight to the bitter end, to the last man, until every single one of the One Hundred Million had chosen death before dishonor… That's the belief, the way of thinking that was the underpinning of our newspaper. But it wasn't true. It's true, the Japanese Empire is gone. But if you ask, did the Japanese people vanish with it, the answer is no. We're still here, everywhere, and we still have our language. The only thing that's disappeared is the old ruling class. You could even say that the substance of 'the Japanese empire,' its contents, was nothing other than the ruling class of the time. We didn't understand something as simple as that; that's what I mean when I say it's a shame."

"I see. I thought that was pretty strange myself, to tell the truth. In those days we used to say 'Fight to the last man to defend the country.' But if that last person was killed, the country would have vanished without a trace. If our real aim was to protect the country, the right thing to do would be to survive, for as many as possible to survive, I used to think."

"I can't say that there weren't moments when I didn't think the same thing. But I never tried to reflect that thought in the pages of the newspaper."

"But you couldn't have, anyway. For example—"

"For example, even the readers believed that they, the people of Japan, were identical with the nation. If I had written that the land of Japan, and the people living in that land, and the language they spoke, were distinct from the national government, the newspaper would have been closed down. But—"

"But you have to remember the military, with those stern, mustachioed faces. They had all the newspapers completely under their thumbs. There was nothing you could have done."

"You know the expression, 'There's fox hair in a writing brush.'"

"No, this is the first I've heard it."

"We should have out-foxed the military—with the power of our writing brushes. We could have written cleverly, so the military wouldn't realize what was going on, but in a way in which we could still present the truth to our readers. I think we could have done that."

"I hope you'll do that now," I said briskly striking a match to light another cigarette. "Tonight I'm going to take a photograph. You mustn't allow the negatives to fall into the Americans' hands."

"I promise," said Mr. Takahashi, placing his right hand softly on his heart.

"When the time comes, that's our weapon to put the screws to the U.S. Education Mission and the CIE Language Simplification Unit Officer."

"Steamed buns, three for 10 yen!" A woman wearing cotton trousers, with a five-year-old boy dragging behind her, walked by. Ten yellow steamed buns sat in the flat bamboo basket hanging from her neck.

"I'm hungry, Mom," said the boy, stretching his hand out toward the buns.

She slapped it briskly away. "I'll make you some when we get home."

"I'm hungry now!"

"If you keep complaining I'll leave you here."

"If you give me some, that'd be fine with me."

"Here, over here!" beckoned a young man in military uniform four or five benches away.

"Yes, sir, I'll be right there." The woman walked off smoothly to her customer. The little boy ran after her.

"Women certainly are strong," I murmured. "That woman just now, she looked like she could have been from some wealthy residential area like Kojimachi and Azabu, and yet she's out walking the streets selling homemade buns."

A wry smile spread across Mr. Takahashi's face. "From the war up to now, it's been the women who've had to deal with rationing, with traveling out to the countryside to buy food, with finding ways to feed and clothe their families, and with keeping body and soul together. That's what made them strong. Men, on the other hand, spent all their time mouthing fine-sounding slogans. On August 15th, all that bluff and bragging was exposed for the hot air it always was, and since then men are just sitting around in a daze, the wind gone from their sails. It's time to send in the replacement team. It's going to be a woman's world from now on—or to be more precise, we have no choice but to rely on their strength."

My wife had said much the same thing a while back, during an argument. Was she right? "We used to talk about 'the Divine Nation of Japan.' Now that was a very fine-sounding line. And along with that went 'the Emperor is the direct descendant of the Sun Goddess,' 'enduring for eternity, as long as heaven and earth exist,' 'never invaded, never subjugated,' 'the whole world under one roof,' 'Japan's glorious advance to the south,' 'Japan on the march,' 'defeating the foe seven times over,' 'defending the national polity,' 'the decisive battle of the mainland,' 'One Hundred Million choosing death before dishonor'… And then suddenly that 'living god' turns around and says, 'Guess, what? I'm a human being'… None of it makes any sense. I guess my wife's smarter than I gave her credit for.

"And Tokyo Seven Roses are especially strong," said Mr. Takahashi, rising from the bench and vigorously dusting off the seat of his pants. "They've engaged the Occupation Forces head on, reclaiming our language. Magnificent—that's the only way to describe them. I can't think of a single Japanese man today with that much courage. They have my unqualified respect."

"I'd say single-minded is a better description. They're determined not to forget the anger and bitterness they feel for the Americans. This is their vengeance for the loved ones they lost to the American bombs."

"When you open the wardrobe door, don't be in a rush, Mr. Yamanaka," said Mr. Takahashi, suddenly turning to face me. "Stay calm and open it wide. The enemy won't be that fast on their feet. It will take them at least two or three seconds to realize what's happening. That's when you press the shutter."

"I know… I know, but I'd feel better if a real pro like you were doing it."

"Only someone like you, who knows the layout of the hotel so well, can do it. I know you'll succeed."

"I sure hope so."

"The hard part comes later."

"Later?"

"Making sure that the language that the Seven Roses reclaimed for us isn't reduced to a hollow thing again, just empty sounds and forms with no meaning or content."

Thinking that I'll never understand intellectuals, I watched Mr. Takahashi walk off toward Hibiya Crossing.

The spring sun was high in the sky now and the shadows of the trees that had been at my feet earlier now retreated back to the brown grass across the way.

…

April
Today, April 10, 1946, is the twenty-second National Diet Election Day in accord with the new election laws. This is the first time that women have the right to vote, so we made a festive occasion of it, and I went with my wife, Sen-chan of the Mimatsuya, Tomoe, the wife of Gen the tailor, and

all the young women of the Yamanaka family—the complete staff of the Tokyo Seven Rose Clothing Recycling Company, in other words—to the Miyanaga-cho Elementary School to cast our votes.

After voting I left the group and walked toward the station along the paths leading over Ueno Hill, covered with the smiling blossoms of the cherry trees. Every little byway was strewn with their fallen petals, like a carpet of white and faint pink.

"We may have lost, but we still have the cherry blossoms."

Some of the people were already drunk, even though it was before noon.

"And we have saké, too. I'm ready for anything!"

"These are the prettiest cherry blossoms ever. There's a reason for that, you know."

"I know. Last year mountains of the dead were buried here. They've fertilized the trees."

"That's right. To the dead, these cherries must seem the color of the flames."

"Hey, that's enough of that. You're going to spoil our saké."

With that conversation echoing in my ears, I crossed the hill, arrived at the station, and took the train to Yurakucho. When I entered the room, one of the office girls said, "Chief, hurry, hurry." She was waving a thin piece of paper at me like a little flag. "You've been summoned by the Occupation Forces. At noon today." It was the visitor permission I'd been waiting for. It said, in typed English letters: "Special permission granted to newspaper photography department chief Iwao Takahashi to visit Shinsuke Yamanaka, under investigation for suspicion of activities to obstruct the aims of the Occupation. Present yourself at the third floor Criminal Investigation Unit of the Allied Forces Provost Marshal's Office, Metropolitan Tokyo Area, at Hibiya Crossing, at noon on April 10th. You have been granted permission to speak with the suspect for thirty minutes."

After slowly smoking a cigarette, I took the Japanese translation of the Report of the U.S. Education Mission and left the office. It was thirty minutes until noon. The Teikoku Seimei Building on the southeast corner of Hibiya Crossing had been taken over by the Occupation Forces as the Allied Forces Provost Marshal's Office, Metropolitan Tokyo Area. According to the city beat reporters of the newspaper, the jail on the first floor was for Allied soldiers who did things like get drunk and steal a streetcar conductor's whistle and walk around blowing it, or beat up the train driver and take the train on a joy ride, or sell U.S. butter or cigarettes on the black market, or commit more serious acts of theft or rape, but the third floor was different. Anyone who obstructed the aims of the Occupation Forces, no matter what their nationality, was sent to the third floor Criminal Investigation Unit.

Shinsuke had been held there since the evening of March 21st.

Shinsuke leaped out of the wardrobe at about ten that night, pressed the shutter of the camera, set off the flash and captured on film the naked Sen-chan and her cohorts, partnered by Harold Benjamin, Willard Givens and Paul Stewart.

But when he was rushing out of Room 224, he tripped over a seam in the carpet and fell. Though he got up immediately, he had by then lost track of which way was north or south in the corridor, and after going off to the right, turned back and went left, whereupon he found himself standing face to face with a glaring Paul Stewart. Stewart and the others managed to pull the film out of the camera, and Shinsuke was sent to the Tokyo MP Office on the first floor of the hotel, but in fact, Shinsuke was not the only one taking pictures at that time. Tomoe arranged to let me into Room 224 at eight where I waited on the veranda, and I snapped my Leica just as Shinsuke's flash popped. It's not that we didn't trust Shinsuke. Tokyo Seven Roses and I were just making sure we had a backup.

"Ah! Mr. Takahashi!" As I stepped off the elevator at the third floor and was about to head toward the reception desk, a voice came from a sofa nearby.

"Why are you here?"

"I've come to see you." A young American MP was sitting at the reception desk reading an English newspaper. He was a large man wearing a khaki shirt, a dark brown necktie and suspenders. A band with the insignia "MP" encircled his left arm. I showed him my permission form. He lifted his right hand slightly, waving me in and turned his eyes went back to his paper.

"Those being held on suspicion of obstructing the aims of the Occupation are not allowed visitors," said Shinsuke, wide-eyed. *"I'm surprised you got permission."*

"We did a little maneuvering behind the scenes. But you look well. That's what matters."

"It's my second time in the Monkey House. You get used to it."

"Can we talk here?"

"From the fact that the sergeant didn't say otherwise, I guess it should be okay. There isn't a visiting room, anyway." Shinsuke sat there uneasily for a while, then sat up in his chair.

"*I'm so sorry. I let them pull the film out of the camera. I wasn't up to it.*"
"*No, no. Actually, you did us a great service by getting caught.*"
I told him that I'd taken a picture from the veranda at the same time his flash had gone off. "*Then I sent a large blow-up of it to Language Section Chief Commander Hall. With a letter. 'If you aren't satisfied with leaving the reform of the Japanese language up to the Japanese people, this photograph will be sent to the* New York Times. *Depending on your reaction, we've also made arrangements to have the negatives sent to General MacArthur.' That sort of thing. We had Commander Hall arrange this meeting, too.*"
"*Really?*" Shinsuke exclaimed, and the MP shushed him.
"*What happened with the U.S. Education Mission?*"
"*They wrote a report and returned home on April 1st. This is a translation of the report that they submitted to General MacArthur. It was just released three days ago. Read the second chapter, 'Language Reform.'*"
I opened it to the place I had marked with an article cut out of the newspaper and handed it to Shinsuke. Having already read it myself, I knew that this is what it said:

The need for linguistic reform has long been recognized in Japan. Distinguished scholars have devoted much attention to the question, and many influential citizens, including publicists and editors, have explored various possibilities. It is reported that some twenty Japanese organizations today are concerned with the problem.

Broadly speaking, three proposals for reform of the written language are under discussion: the first calls for a reduction in the number of *kanji*; the second for the complete abandonment of *kanji* and the adoption of some form of *kana*; and the third for the complete abandonment of both *kanji* and *kana* and the adoption of some form of *romaji*. It is difficult to decide which of these proposals should be adopted, but the mission believes that the advantages of *romaji* outweigh those of *kana*.

Recognizing the many difficulties involved, sensitive to the natural feelings of hesitation on the part of many Japanese, and fully aware of the gravity of the changes proposed, we nevertheless propose:

1. That some form of Roman letters be brought into common use by all means possible.
2. That the particular form of Roman letters be decided upon by a commission of Japanese scholars, educational leaders and statesmen.
3. That the commission assumes the responsibility for coordinating the program of language reform, during the transitional stages.
4. That the commission formulates a plan and a program for introducing Roman letters into the schools and into the life of the community and the nation through newspapers, periodicals, books and other writings.
5. That the commission studies, also, the means of bringing about a more democratic form of the spoken language.
6. That in view of the study drain on the learn-time of children, the commission be formed promptly. It is hoped that a thoroughreport and a comprehensive program may be announced within a reasonable period.

Shinsuke looked at me with a bitter expression. "They're going to change our writing system to romaji!"
"Don't worry. Look at the next page," I said.

Any change in the form of a language must come from within the nation. It is proposed that a language commission made up of Japanese scholars, educational leaders and statesmen be formed promptly in order that a comprehensive program may be announced within a reasonable period.

As he looked up from the report, Shinsuke's eyes were damp. "Japanese language reform must come from the Japanese people. Music to my ears."
"In other words, they made a lot of demands, but they're leaving the conclusions up to the Japanese people."
"Heavenly music, even if it is from our enemy."
"It's the Tokyo Seven Roses who wrote that heavenly music—and that flash of your camera." Seeing his bright smile, I added. "MacArthur is carrying out his educational reforms based on this report. Which means, while

there will be major changes in many areas, we have their promise that they're going to keep their hands off the Japanese language."

"Good."

"The U.S. State Department is infuriated, however. Here's an article about a press conference given by Assistant Secretary of State William Benton, who sent the mission to Japan.

Shinsuke began to read it aloud in a low voice: "At a press conference at the White House on April 8th, Assistant Secretary of State William Benton said: 'I believe that the call for the reform of the Japanese language is more important than any other proposal. Unless the Japanese language is reformed, the other reforms cannot not realize their full effect. Personally speaking, I believe it would have been preferable if the report called more strongly for reform in that area. I wish it had included much stronger language, in order to force the Japanese to take action.' 'Personally speaking.' I see."

"You can almost see the smoke coming out of his ears."

The large MP looked over at us. He seemed suspicious at our voices rising in something like exhilaration. He looked at his watch, then at the clock on the wall, and lifted his right hand.

"From next month, the CIE Language Section is getting a new chief. Commander Hall is going back to Columbia University."

The MP's gesture seemed to signal that our time was up. I placed the report on Shinsuke's lap and rose from the couch. "The report is for you."

"Thank you. And Hall, is he being demoted?"

"It looks like it. With his knowledge and credentials, to be given an assistant professor's position... he's being made to take the heat. You just have to make it through April. Commander Hall had you thrown in here out of spite, so when he's gone, there's no longer any reason to keep you locked up."

"Then Fumiko will probably be the first one out of a job."

"Fumiko spends her days at home at her sewing machine. My guess is that she dumped Hall, not the other way around. And not just Fumiko, but all of the Tokyo Seven Roses are working away at their sewing machines from morning to night. They took all their earnings and bought seven sewing machines on the black market."

"Why on earth did they do that?"

"They started a company."

"A company?"

"Tokyo Seven Rose Clothing Recycling Company."

"That's a pretty long name for a company."

"I agree. I'm sure they'll end up shortening it. It's too long for anyone to remember, so it's going to end up Tokyo Seven Rose. It's only been ten days since they started, but they're doing very well and are flooded with orders for remaking clothes."

The elevator arrived.

"And Shoichi and Kiyoshi have come back to Nezu. Oh, yes, and one more thing—I have a message for you from Tomoe. She says she'll have that sweater she promised you finished very soon." By the time I'd gotten those last words out, the elevator door had nearly closed, and Shinsuke's face was getting narrower and narrower, cut off by the doors from left and right. From the last sliver of an opening, I caught a glimpse of a tear shining brightly in his eye.